CAIN'S VERSION

A NOVEL

CAIN'S VERSION

A NOVEL

FRANK DURHAM

Library of Congress Cataloging-in-Publication Data

Durham, Frank, 1935-
  Cain's version : a novel / Frank Durham.
    p. cm.
  Includes bibliographical references and index.
  ISBN 978-1-59652-501-6 (alk. paper)

  1. Middle-aged women--Fiction. 2. Older people--Care--Fiction. 3. Family secrets--Fiction. 4. Louisiana--Fiction. I. Title.
  PS3604.U7336C35 2008
  813'.6--dc22

                              2008033689

Iroquois Press
An Imprint of Turner Publishing Company

200 4th Avenue North
Suite 950
Nashville, Tennessee 37219
(615) 255-2665

www.iroquoispress.com

Printed in the United States of America

08 09 10 11 12 13 14 15—0 9 8 7 6 5 4 3 2 1

For Donna, and Deanne,
and for Darla always

Thus all the days Adam lived
were nine hundred and thirty years;
and he died.

Genesis 5:5

CAIN'S VERSION: PROLOGUE

I will find my mother Eve by means of philosophy. Already by reasoning I have understood the Atlantic sea and the outlines of the New World, and have crossed the one and penetrated the mongrel greenness of the other. She cannot be far away.

I am presently alongside a minor river, whose name could matter only to the simpletons who need maps, and who clog their cities and their roads with metal carts, and fly in winged houses among the clouds. The river twists on its course, while I move upstream straight toward my conclusion. Easy progress, however, was never my birthright. I was an ignorant, angry boy, short of words and barely clothed, when I abandoned the struggle my mother Eve fostered while the man Adam sat watching uselessly. I made another home at Nod, until I was again overtaken by disappointment, after which the sea offered me residence. I never again found comfort on land.

She is hereabouts.

You may object, saying, Does not the woman Eve's bitterness

for the murder of her son Abel spread from her person? And might that pain—and not any invented reasoning—be the power that draws Cain ever and again? Truly I tell you, no. Her influence on me has nothing to do with our separation. It is everything to do with dreams. I convict myself of yearning. She alone can make me whole in my heart.

What then of my method, with respect to closing the distance between me and my mother across half a world? First of all consider this: does she not treat her two women, her great-grandson's widows, as if they were her equals? After the water went down, the three of them—as I later learned—made their way to Sindhu, and from there around a foreign sea to the south of Africa, with stops along the way, and eventually back to Egypt, and so on. Their travels are always designed to distance her from me. Yet my mother's women are subject to westward tendencies.

I offer our last encounter at Juba's islands, among the westernmost dollops of what might still be assigned as the Old World. They were fully settled on Tenerife, to the point of speaking the tongues of Canaria—the two women, I mean. My mother has no use of new languages. There I happened upon them one day, to no advantage. The Spanish had arrived and were engaged in ruining the island. There on the beach amid the confusion of warriors and with boats going to and from an alien navy, I began making my case to my mother. The women would not listen; they were more concerned with the enslavement of their friends, and the odors of burning human flesh and of Plague, than with hearing my arguments. Yet I could judge a restlessness behind their grim unwelcoming faces, and could read their westward departure in my mother's silent posture.

Add their addiction to warmth, which I share, and my mother's affinity for rivers, her endless yearning for Eden and its four fugitive streams. Allow also for their contradictory aversion to the sea, which is to say, to floods. Never mind that I saved them from the first one; I alone lifted them from debris and floating bodies and, in time, handed them safely back to the vile ground. They are not so fearful of the sea, nor that I live on it, that they will not take passage. But they shun the shore, and do not stay overlong in one place. In my search I have taken full account of these elements, of their several removals since Tenerife and of the various durations which they must vaguely sense, no matter how they flee from time and from me.

This minor river that I track is a tributary, a pale copy of the one that drew the women across the wide Atlantic. I heard tell of two great rivers, both of them lying beyond the western ocean, one bisecting the northern continent, the other the southern. It was evident to me that the weak-willed women would guide my mother toward one of the two watersheds. The immense river that crosses almost the breadth of the vast southern land mass? According to the truth I filtered from a thousand exaggerations, that river's rank excess of life would be too much for the women's slack ways. That left me to seek the northern land mass and its north-to-south river, which issues through a temperate climate and whose basin provides ample variety for a plain living.

A river reveals itself by its effluvium. After crossing the ocean, I sailed into the bay between the two continents. I kept the coast below the northern horizon, and soon enough I was tacking into the scent of the river's mud. East of the river's mouth I made landfall, and bade good-bye at the beach to my boat, my one friend.

Unskilled at thinking, you will say that any number of rivers may be false clues, and that the pattern of an interior river is no pattern. Will you deny that truth may be composed from elements, no one of which shows the way? Reason accumulates and it winnows, as a stronger man in the end will delete the weaker one.

The rest has been convergence by ranging. Once on shore I

moved through and found shelter within two dozen minor cities. In due course I arrived at the continent-draining river. Several days of searching along its high artificial wall convinced me that even this river did not stop them. There are bridges, for one thing, which they are meek enough to have used. They crossed the great river, and I did the same.

Earlier today I came upon the confluence between the brown river I am following and a tannic stream that entered from my right. By appearances the clear-running river was the better choice to explore, but I had recognized in this muddy stream the leavings of agriculture, and so chose to continue along it—but not before I used the other one. Though I garner strength by concentrating salt within my body, I drank a rare long drink while swimming the clear river. At the shallows I washed the garments borrowed from a refuse pile when I came ashore. With my knife I scraped away my accumulated beard, and grabbed and cropped the coarse hair that afflicts my head like tares. I am clean after my fashion, and rid of body waste. I am as prepared as can be, for what is to come.

A full season has passed and most of another, while I dissected this geography. The future corrects the present: the sun is baking my clothes dry, but I sense a coolness to come. I have stood within reach of a thousand of them, these so-called men. I joined their queues and endured their animal stares. Silently I lingered while I puzzled out their silly exchanges. Now I am able to accost them in their own language. Tomorrow I will begin to ask them, *Have you seen three such unlikely women as I seek?*

CHAPTER 1

Behold, I have given you every herb bearing seed
and every tree with seed in its fruit;
to you it shall be for meat.

Genesis 1:29

Lindy Caton was keeping Adhah company while she picked tomatoes. They were at the new garden, Lindy's garden, behind
the weathered house that Adhah and the other two old women
shared, four miles out from Acheron, Louisiana.

Adhah, short and round, and covered head to ankle against
the broiling sun, worked delicately among the vines. Lindy, six
feet tall, slightly stooped and dressed in foundation-director
style—linen jacket, T-top, and silk slacks—wished Adhah would
hurry up. Lindy had left her office in Acheron at midday and
driven her pick-up along the river road, in order to accept the
day's pickings. No lunch for Lindy. The tomatoes made her do
this several times a week, ever since they had begun to ripen. The
other summer vegetables joined in, by turns. She would distribute
the produce to her unenthusiastic customers, most of whom were
members of the board of directors of the Moulton Foundation,
the people she worked for. Lindy had set up the garden to provide
pocket money for the three isolated old women. She had collected

going on two hundred dollars, which the old women so far had refused to accept.

Lindy's patch, that's what Adhah and Seelah called it, ran in two rows almost from woods to woods. It was like a green fence, except for a section on the left where the cornstalks stood spent and brown, and another to the far right where yellow vines snaked lifelessly across the ground, as if that end of the fence had fallen.

Lindy was responsible for the garden's form and content. The idea came to her soon after she saw how the women were living. She had located an obliging man from their neighborhood, who brought his plow mule, possibly the only one left in Courant Parish. Never having planted a garden, Lindy waved casually, indicating back and forth. The man, shaking his head and talking to the mule, threw open a dark furrow the width of the property, and another one coming back. Without stopping, he tilted down the plow handles and followed the mule away. The vegetables were Lindy's choices, in consultation with the nursery's expert on heirloom varieties. The old women amiably saw to the planting, and now they were executing the harvest. They would not eat anything that grew in Lindy's garden. They had their own garden—if you could call it that.

Adhah stepped through an opening between the bean bushes and the tree-branch tomato stakes. A bucket of greenish-pink tomatoes hung from each of her fleshy hands. Her face was lined, and more gray than brown under the shadow of her bonnet. Her body filled the shapelessness of her faded overdress. Her feet were bare. "That makes enough of them things," she said. She moved competently for one so old and so heavy. "Your boxes are about full already. We picked the beans and pulled the carrots early, right after night left."

"Those are the ripest ones, I hope," Lindy said. She knew they weren't. Adhah and Seelah let more ripe tomatoes fall to the ground than they picked. They were less concerned with details than anyone Lindy had ever met. Picked tomatoes will ripen, won't they? But Lindy's customers were busy people, important people whose attentions could wander in the time it took a tomato to turn red.

"Anybody besides me want a dipper of water?" Seelah called. She was returning from down by the swampy lake, from the thicket which was the old women's own garden. Seelah was narrow shouldered and wide-hipped, and tall, if only by comparison with Adhah. Below her long outer smock her ankles were thick and her grimy bare feet were swollen-looking.

When Seelah reached them, Lindy got a look at what her basket held—a flat, seed-filled blue flower that partly covered weedy greens and herbs; two fist-sized bulbs, their roots crusted with dirt and their stems hanging down like open wings; several round items as green as emerald baseballs; a half-dozen fuzzy bean pods a foot long; a sprinkling of brown plumlike fruits. The basket, piled with wilting greenness, bore witness that the women's scrubby grove was productive. But it was a garden and orchard without apparent order. Overgrowth mingled with the foliage of some of the trees. Vines wrapped the dead limbs of others. Unharvested blue blossoms stood as big as faces above a dense diversity that ranged downward to herbs that might almost have been grass.

Adhah had taken off her bonnet. Her wispy hair was cut as short as a man's. "I'll help you load Lindy's wagon, honey," Seelah said to Adhah, who reached up and gave her a perfunctory kiss. All three of the old women were affectionate—including Uhwa, who seemed never to come outside the house. Uhwa was practically an invalid; she was certainly older than the other two.

Lindy took a stem from Seelah's basket and rubbed it between her fingers. The smell was at the far edge of oregano, a smell that often came from their kitchen. So many exotic aromas. She rubbed the rough surface of one of Seelah's long bean pods. For every one that got this far, there were bound to be fifty that grew out of reach. "I hope youall don't think my garden is simply superfluous," she said.

"Excess?" Adhah said, indicating with her head Lindy's garden. "Well." She looked at Lindy and smiled. "It's not excess if you can find somebody'll eat it."

"I feel like we've been feeding the multitude," Lindy said. "Like the miracle of the loaves and fishes." The older women looked blank. "At the Sea of Galilee," Lindy added. "Jesus and the apostles."

"I can't say I know those folks," Adhah said. She looked squarely at Seelah. "Lindy's little garden puts me in mind of us growing extra at Barhbel-ah, after the water went down. For the boatbuilder's children."

"His grandchildren, you mean," Seelah said. "Three dozen if there was a one of them. That's how it goes after something bad happens. Babies come."

Adhah chuckled. "A little patch of Lindy's red fruits wouldn't have fed them. Oh my, Uhwa could make things grow in those days. The children used to take the extra kernels home, and before long the boatbuilder's people made their own stand. But they were arguing about how to build the tower higher."

"Those bad bricks wouldn't hold up the timbers," Seelah said. "How many times did they start over before it got high enough to suit them?"

"Well, to suit some of them," Adhah said. "You'd call it a tower, right enough, but they were proud. They took to yelling about whether to make another one, and who that first one belonged to. It was like they stopped hearing each other. Before long the whole bunch had packed up and left."

Lindy couldn't pronounce the word quite as Adhah did, but

the place name had sounded like "Babel." "I can't say it right. Bah-bel-ah. You don't mean the Tower of Babel?"

"Babel," Seelah said with a lifting "ah" at the end. "Babel"—again, this time pronouncing it exactly as Lindy had. "That's a good enough version. We lived outside of there, but close enough to see how the ones from the big boat made a mess of building it. Gracious, child! You with no head cover."

Seelah swiped at her own sweaty hair and lumbered toward the back porch and the stone well. Adhah and Lindy followed. Adhah ceremoniously drew the water, and at their insistence Lindy drank first from the dipper that rested in the wooden bucket. The other two women drank deeply also. The shade of the porch was a relief.

"Youall saw the Tower of Babel fall?"

Seelah, nodding acknowledgment of Lindy's question, emptied the bucket into a pan and laid the herbs in it. She snorted. "The place where Uhwa's son let us out after the water went down, that was a good place. The others got there a long stretch afterwards. They took to stealing from the river bank, scooping out squares of mud. Whole fields of them, dried them in the sun. Built"—she swung her hand upward—"twice too high. A big rain came and melted the whole lot. They had to start all over. Happened more than once."

"Where was this, exactly?" How little she knew about these women. How rude she felt to be asking, after all the weeks of try-ing to help, without prying about relationships and ages—or last names.

"The boatbuilder's sons got all worked up," Adhah chimed in, as if the story were a recipe in which every ingredient counted. "Before the thing was ever finished the whole bunch moved off. Now, the one that showed up after another long lag—he was Uh-wa's kin, too. Him and his men, they found out how to get the job done. You bake the mud first." She picked up a stray tomato and tossed it into a stoneware crock that smelled of garbage.

"Was this around here?" Lindy asked. "Were you living in this house?" She had seen historic pictures of this part of Louisiana inundated, from the time before the levees were complete.

"Oh, no," Seelah said, "two oceans away from here."

Babel, after the water went down? The thought of all that confusion jogged free a singular childhood image, of an illustration: a primitive city—a tower being raised—and a beefy man in charge.

"Didn't Nimrod have something to do with the Tower of Babel? In the Bible story?" She realized that the way she pronounced Bible sounded a lot like Babel. The old women's puzzled expressions confirmed that they hadn't understood. But then who did, concerning Nimrod? Nimrod, the mighty contractor? She wasn't going to be able to keep up with this Old Testament talk, if that's what it proved to be.

"I just love the way you say a name," Adhah said. "Nimrod." She reproduced Lindy's Southern diphthong, then pronounced an altogether more exotic word.

"Smartest young fellow you'd ever want to meet," Seelah said. "That's who I was talking about, he was the one that came back and set it right. Spread a town all up the way. There was a boy could build. But then he had the advantage over the boatbuilder. He wasn't the one left half his kinfolks to drown."

Adhah, who had been nodding strong agreement, frowned at this. She picked up the pan of herbs. "I'll take these inside," she said sourly. "The other business was terrible. But that was everlasting generations ago. I'd as soon not hear it talked about. I'd rather think about the sweet children." The ragged screen door scraped and Adhah was gone.

"Generations?" Lindy asked. There must be some way to shed

light on this mutual delusion. "How many years ago are we talking about?"

"Oh years," Seelah said. "We stopped using years. But I'd say myriads, since Nimrod's troupe crowded us out. We've always wanted a little more room."

CHAPTER 2

In the bedroom after her shower, Lindy finished toweling her hair and wrapped the towel around herself, and worried about the old women. Adhah and Seelah had seemed to drift into some other kind of reality, and they made Uhwa a part of it. Senility must come in a thousand varieties.

She found the phone in the clutter on the bed and rang her father's number in South Alabama. He didn't do voice mail. The number of rings before he answered would tell her how his day had been. Her own mailbox had accumulated several numbers, none she recognized—certainly not Harold Rutledge's number. That deal was over and dead, for going on a week. His choice, not hers, and she didn't care. No more having to tiptoe around old family money. Harold owed her $24.20, going back six deliveries, the seersucker-wearing deadbeat. Maybe his sister would pay his tab, if Lindy showed up again at their mansion. The sister Lindy had not met, who had appeared not once at the leaded-glass door, but sent a maid to deal with Lindy.

She shouldn't have gotten involved with a member of her board, she knew that. Blame it on the vagueness that was Acheron. It began with the town's name. Acheron, pronounced as Ash Run. Harold said that properly it should sound like Akron, as in Ohio, and sometimes he said it that way. Everyone else softened the *ch*. Lindy had never seen Ash Run written down; but everybody called it Ash half the time, and that implied two separate words. She had asked several people, but none of them would volunteer an alternate spelling. Phonetic, like Adhah, and Seelah, and Uhwa. No spellings for them; the old women were illiterate. Ash Run had no such excuse. In such an ambiguous place, how could she not have slipped a little?

Her dad had not picked up, but he would. She called every night before ten. She had told him about the old women, and kept him posted about the cash garden. Why pester him, sick as he was, with the news that they were half-crazy, living inside the Bible? Why would outsiders poke at the pathology of three such sweet old women when nothing could be done about it? Here he was; his voice was weak but firm.

"Hello, Daddy. Hope I didn't wake you. I went back to the office after I delivered today's vegetables."

"You work too hard."

Lindy switched the conversation away from her work and onto his routine: grocery shopping; his slow march through another volume of military history; loneliness or rather his denial of it; the medications that weren't helping. She steered him to talking about arrogant internists, and away from rehashing his symptoms. She didn't want to think about his lesions, their advance, and all that meant.

Three months since the last infusion. The doctors had stopped treatment in late April, just after she turned in the renewal for her biggest state grant, and the same week her friend Eshana drove her out and showed her where the old women lived. Eshana hadn't introduced her to them. She only stopped in sight of the house and said if Lindy thought she could reason with them, now she knew the way. Eshana despised the old women, for what she called "endangering my little boy." Those gypsies, she called them, among other things. Lindy had volunteered to negotiate. That's how the old women came into her life.

Three months without treatment. At least, she thought, cancer gives you time. Lindy believed in the hope interval. You take the time since something has changed, and hope for that much more time before things fall apart. Hope, at least, for half that much time.

"Now we know how I'm doing," her dad said. His tone made it clear he was aware of her strategy, to keep him talking. "How are *you* doing, sweet baby?"

"I'm coming to see you next Friday, that's how I'm doing. My birthday, we're driving into town for dinner."

"Another red-letter day," her dad said. "Forty-one."

It was forty-two. He had done the subtraction without adding in his last birthday. Forty-two, not a prime number. Lindy dropped the towel to the floor and walked to the closet mirror to see how she was doing at forty-two minus. In the mirror, while her dad talked about the drought and she told him about brown midsummer grass, she saw that she wasn't doing badly. Legs not as smooth as in college, but beginning—a model's half-pirouette, her free hand on her hip—to get less muscular. Her breasts were back, better than ever, and her butt, too, to some degree. Roundness returning. Nice to confirm that runner's body was a reversible condition. Like smoking, it was never too late to quit. Her face, she noticed, was out of sight above the top of the mirror.

"I don't know how Adhah and Seelah keep the vegetable garden alive," she said. "They don't water anything."

"The old ladies. It's your tomato vines that are so green?"

"Well, the sweet corn is through, it's dead." The water table. That's what it was. They were right beside the lake. "I'm holding about a hundred and ninety dollars for them, Daddy. They're surely going to need it next winter."

"What did they do for money last winter?"

"If a dollar bill has moved through that house since Reagan was President, I haven't seen it. You can't live entirely without money. What if the old man who brings their firewood—donates it to them—what if something happened to him? And what if the Central Louisiana Electric Company finds out about how I got that other man to hook up their electricity? They wanted eighty dollars a month, minimum." For a bare bulb hanging down in each room. And the old TV she gave them, that was always on, in Uhwa's room.

"Makes a person glad he's not a farmer," her dad said. "Do you need to be taking time off, going out there in ninety-five degrees?"

"Did I tell you they keep a fire in the fireplace in Uhwa's room?" Uhwa, thin and frail, and wrapped in worn-out quilts in that stifling room. And the television on.

"I've seen that kind of thing," her dad said, "way back in the country. Sometimes when you get old enough, you just can't get warm."

"Making up the time is no problem. That's one good thing about the Moulton Foundation. It's small enough that I can set my own schedule. I wish I'd scheduled dinner tonight. I'm starving."

While her dad spoke mildly about regular eating habits, Lindy started toward the refrigerator. Remembering the facing kitchens across the courtyard of the apartment complex, she retraced her path and slipped her robe on.

"I'm not going to make them plant my stuff again next year," she said at the open refrigerator door.

"Are you joining in the picking? You used to help me in my garden." His tone softened. "And you were just a little thing."

"Mm," Lindy said. "Mm mm." Which meant, my mouth is full but, no, I'm not working in their garden. She put the foam box on the counter, and raked another two-finger load of cold garlic mashed potatoes from Harold Rutledge's last supper, four nights earlier. She began to lick the congealed apricot sauce off the leftover duck leg.

Their affair had been an anomaly for two cautious professionals, especially for the one of them who was as rigid as a girder. Not much communication, a high proportion of grappling. It had played out like a high-schoolers' fling. That was fine with Lindy. She and Harold had dined out a few times the previous winter, without so much as a kiss. One night they chose an Asian restaurant, in a mall so brand new that the three spaces Harold required for parking his Escalade diagonally were easy to find. Harold hated dents. After dinner his hand touched her breast as he opened the door for her, and suddenly they were in the back and going at it on the icy leather. Quick, fumbling sex, but actual, intense sex, the first sex since she had left Little Rock. Thank God for tinted windows.

"You're right, I shouldn't have done it," she said to her dad. "The garden." She had wiped out the last of the lemon filling from the soggy tart, and now reached into the open refrigerator for the carton of calcium-fortified grapefruit juice.

"Sometimes people can do for themselves better than you recognize, Lindy. I don't mean me, sweet. Your Gran—I was thinking of how long she was able to carry on."

It was true about his mother. As a girl Lindy had marveled at how Gran kept living alone, even after she needed to hold onto furniture to get across the room. Long after Mrs. Caton couldn't match a name to a living person, she had dressed herself after a fashion and scratched out tiny, unbalanced meals. Lindy loved her dad for not pushing Gran into the nursing home. He had held his mother's happiness more important than a safe and orderly life.

"You two understood each other," Lindy said. "I promise not to do one single thing for you when I get there Friday. Except I'll buy our dinner at the Captain's Table. You can do for me, you can tell me about Sunshine."

Lindy had begun to bring up the subject of Sunshine about a month ago. She figured, if she didn't learn about her mother now, then when? Sunshine Caton had run off toward Wyoming with a neighbor man. Lindy knew that much. Leaving Bob and the three little girls—Lindy, the youngest, not yet in school. Not a Sunshine syllable from her dad, all those years. In a way, not being ready to talk about Sunshine meant he wasn't close to his deathbed.

Having downed the juice, Lindy turned her attention to the ripest tomato from the kitchen counter. She rubbed it against her robe, and felt in the drawer for a paring knife. Her sister Lubie, who lived in Mobile, would be at the birthday dinner. No way Lubie could be cut out of it. Bible-thumping Lubie, with her hatred of Sunshine—those dissonant, oldest daughter's memories. Lindy, growing up, caught nothing but hell until she gave up her own memories of Sunshine. On this birthday Lubie and her endless, invidious quotations would have to step aside.

"Next Friday," Lindy said. "I'll leave early." She dangled a heavily salted slice of German Johnson tomato above the phone.

"You give some thought to those poor ladies you've got sharecropping for you."

Through with eating, Lindy started back to her bedroom. "The garden's running down. In a couple of weeks it'll be okra and pink eggplants. I can't peddle eggplants, and *nobody* can peddle okra."

"Another one of your projects," her dad said. "Three old women and a garden."

"Keeping Joeab away from there was supposed to be the project."

"The little afflicted boy?" Her dad used that old-fashioned word. Joeab had so much wrong with him—all of it traceable to his extreme premature birth—and there was so much right with him.

She was stalling. It was like the nights when as a child she couldn't stop talking to her dad, when she made him repeat the bedtime story over, with variations, and still she couldn't stand for him to leave her.

"What do you know about Babel?" Lindy had no intention of outing the women's craziness, but a reference would help.

"Nothing to know, a few verses," her dad said patiently. "They tried to make it reach to heaven. The Lord supposedly punished man's pride by confusing the languages. A Sunday school tale, but true in a way."

"I was there—Sunday school. I mean the details, who built it, who tore it down? I swear Adhah and Seelah were telling me today, that Uhwa's relatives built it—tried to build it."

"Maybe it's some family lore of theirs." He was sounding truly tired now. How had she kept him talking so long? "People used biblical names for plantations. And the slaves built them."

"Plantation memories. Huh." Industry City was part of a former plantation. Industry City itself, where Eshana and Joeab lived, was cheap subdivisions, organized but desolate. The old women lived beyond, at the far edge of a collection of improvised houses that might have been, if you thought about it, a high-water mark, the ring of debris left after a flood subsided.

"Why do you say slaves?"

"You said they have dark skin," he said, his voice forbearing. "I remember that."

"They do, but dark can come on a person for a lot of reasons," she said. "Their features—their people could be from anywhere, except for those leathery folds around their eyes."

"Hard work will thicken your features."

"Eshana could say, better than I could. She calls them everything but Black. That's because she despises them. Assyrians, Red Bones, it can't mean anything—Oh, what I'd give for skin the like of Eshana's."

"You've got nice skin, if you don't ruin it running a truck farm."

"Thanks for always listening." That was enough about skin tone. Her dad had worked outdoors all his life. Now no amount of sun would have kept the cancer's copper pallor from showing through.

"Good night, Linderella," he said. "Eat you some bacon and eggs in the morning."

"Daddy, do you remember what Gran used to call me?" She knew he did. But he had put down the receiver.

For the last years of her grandmother's life it had been "Agnes." Not Linderella—nor Lindy, she would never be Lindy to anyone in her family. Agnes was the name of a playmate from her grandmother's childhood. Lindy had enjoyed being her grandmother's peer in that way. There was a dignity about it, Lindy always thought, dignity as much for the little girl as for the faltering old woman. No harm done. No more than Adhah's and Seelah's confusion put anyone at risk.

CHAPTER 3

I will greatly multiply your sorrow and your conception;
in sorrow will you bring forth children.

Genesis 3:16

The boy Joeab placed the purple on top of the orange. The two piles were complete again, six flat wooden blocks, the three secondary colors stacked beside the three primary colors. Joeab carefully pushed the stacks over and, using the backs of his clasped hands, scattered them on the grass between his outstretched legs. Instead of beginning the game again, he got up from the ground and went to the door of the brick bungalow. The house sat unadorned on its large lot, without trees or shrubs or foundation plantings, in a row of similar houses. Across the street vacant lots gapped like missing teeth. Slipping inside the screen door, Joeab managed to turn the knob, chest-high on the front door—it took both hands to open it.

"'Dah, 'Lah," he said. His voice was a stage whisper. "'Dah, 'Lah. 'Wuh, Mom." Then he turned away from the open door and skipped toward the street. His legs bent slightly at the knee and he walked on his toes. His weight, sixty pounds on his thin beige frame, bounced forward on his untied sneakers.

Soon he was crossing the graveled parking lot to the body shop, not on the way to the women's house, but a regular stop. He studied his slight image in the coating of the plate-glass door, then he was out of the sunlight and into the dingy waiting room. He paused and smiled generally. Behind the rough gray counter the manager glanced up. Joeab tiptoed to the object of his visit, a high bulky beverage machine whose glow was the brightest light in the room. He stopped, teetering, a few inches from the red and blue plastic.

"It takes money. Three quarters," the counter man said. The boy turned his face upward and put his hands on the surface as if to touch the cold inside. "Three quarters, I told you," the man said.

Joeab crossed the room, his hands still raised, and stopped at the gumball machine, the glass globe at child's height. The boy, forever on tiptoe, smiled as his hands curved around the space outside the glass ball. He turned to face the counter. His smile was wide, and in a clear enough voice he said, "I love you." Then he was through the door and out into the unfiltered heat of the morning.

"You see that?" The employee spoke to the one customer, another white man who had sat reading during the boy's performance. "You ever see a crack baby? Way up here? Hell of a note."

Joeab found the lane with the yellow sign at its beginning and started toward the place where the women lived. The grass in the never-paved street had been sheared recently. In places the ground was scraped bare. Low volunteer trees crowded together behind what would have been curbs along the mowed lane. Joeab moved in his efficient hopping way. He was not frowning against the sun, but there was no need to smile either. Nearing the corridor that came out at the road to the women's house, he lost a shoe. Retrieving it, he sat down and pulled the shoe up past the dusty sock that had slipped below his scarred, deformed heel.

Closer to the women's place, the boy skipped past small frame houses bordered by tall crimson coleus or blue and pink hydrangeas. Tall flowers were a brilliant declaration that the fertile earth would never go back to the men whose decades-long inattention had allowed the settlement to develop. Plywood and tarpaper constructions sprouted behind or between some of the existing houses. These would be, or already were, more unnumbered, unmapped homes. Immediately beside every house was a well-tended vegetable plot. The wire fences around the vegetables were the only fences anywhere.

The old women's property lay at the dead end of a transverse street. Like the named roads, the transverse was paved, but its asphalt was rough, as if thrown down by hand, coal-black, and unmarred by traffic. The old women's place would not have stood out, apart from its position at the end of a lane—an aid to Joeab's navigation—and the greater age of the house. Its front yard was large and shaded by elderly oak trees. Designs of swirls and circles had recently been brush-broomed in the bare dirt. Garden rows extended left and right behind the house, as far as the scrub woods. Altogether the effect was to make this seem to be the beginning of a wilderness, rather than the edge of a good-sized town. The lake added to this impression. Its edge crept in past flooded cypresses— though fishing camps and boathouses stood on the far shore, out of sight beyond the trees.

Joeab entered the house silently. An angled frame of light from the open back lit up the center hall. He pushed open the door of a bedroom so dark inside that the television's glow danced on its walls. Uhwa was sitting in a rocking chair, between the bed and the chest of drawers on which the television perched. In spite of the room's intense heat, a shawl covered her shoulders. Another, darker shawl tented her head, and a ragged quilt wrapped her lower body.

The boy moved to her side and stood watching while the head in the box continued to speak, the sound soft enough to be negligible. Joeab chanced to touch Uhwa's chair, and the old woman disengaged a trembling hand from its wraps long enough to pat his shoulder. After another interval the boy stepped around in front of the rocking chair and stood facing Uhwa so that his sweat-beaded face was close to hers and she was in his shadow. At this the old woman managed to take Joeab's head between her two hands. His body shook slightly with her tremor. Then she released him, and he tiptoed out of the room to the back of the house and down the worn steps into the yard.

Adhah, bending and raising among bean plants in Lindy's garden, called out to the boy.

"Hey, honey pie. Hey, Joeab. You can come on and help me now."

Joeab stopped where he was. Soon Adhah was finished and came toward him, yellow crookneck squash showing at the top of her galvanized bucket. She held up the front of one skirt, which sagged with more produce.

"You want your satchel? It's on the bench. Go and get it."

Joeab ducked under her arm to nestle against her body.

"I can't hug you yet, dumpling. You run get it." She lifted the bucket, a gesture. The boy replied, two quick, unintelligible phrases.

"No, Joeab, we have to know what each other means. Slow down and tell me again."

"Get the help bag," he said carefully, and repeated the phrase while he went toward the house.

"Wonderful, baby."

In a little while Joeab returned, struggling to loop the tangled fabric over his head.

"Here, let me see." Adhah set the bucket down and, without spilling the contents of her skirt, shook the bag with her free hand and slipped its strap over the boy's shoulder. "You're too late to pick today. But carry some of Lindy's snap beans for me. They're too many."

23

He reached into the mass of beans she cradled before her and thrust a few between his curved hands into his pouch. Most of them fell to the ground. Adhah's hand with its swollen knuckles and dirty fingernails hovered near Joeab's.

"Good. That's it. Take another bunch. Now another one. Come on, we'll get us a dipper of water. Seelah's bringing this morning's bounty from the garden."

She and her assistant climbed the steps. The two of them piled the bean pods on the porch table, Adhah's load and Joeab's half dozen that had made it.

"Your mama? How's Eshana doing today?" Adhah asked. The boy nodded and smiled. "She knows you're here?" Joeab was still nodding.

"Fine. We got to keep you on the straight and narrow, sweet child."

Adhah, Joeab following, went to the well at the far end of the porch. He stood back, respectful of the coiled rope, while she dropped the bucket into the well and drew up the water. She helped him drink from the long-handled metal dipper, finished what he hadn't taken, and drank another herself. Then she ceremoniously poured a dipperful over Joeab's head, and two over her own head.

Seelah arrived from the back garden. Joeab hopped down the steps to greet her.

"'Lah, 'Lah, story,'" he said, the words running together. "Mine story, 'Lah." As he reached Seelah, she shifted her basket to one arm and swung him up to her hip.

"We three have got too much to do, Joeab," she said, looking down at him. "No story right now. You and me and Adhah are working. Lindy'll be here for her yield. And there's dinner to get."

She continued up the steps, still carrying Joeab. He leaned far out and looked straight up. His smile took in the sky.

Seelah placed the tumbler of water on the mantel in Uhwa's room and paused in the gloom. Ignoring the complaints of the worn floorboards, she rearranged and smoothed the older woman's covers. She touched Uhwa delicately on her rounded back and shoulders and her shrouded hands. Then she helped Uhwa to drink. Uhwa grabbed swallows from the tilting glass into her toothless mouth. Her drinking noises mixed with the constant syllables from the television. Neither woman said anything during this ritual. Seelah took a small square of cloth from within her smock, folded it, and wiped Uhwa's mouth. Refolding the cloth, she patted Uhwa's cheeks. Using the last drops of water from the tumbler, she wet the cloth and carefully touched Uhwa's eyes. Supporting herself by one hand on the sooty mantel, Seelah retrieved a wedge of white oak from the pile beside the hearth and laid it in the fireplace. A lick of blue-yellow flame, freed from the disturbed ashes, wrapped itself around the new wood. Then Seelah was gone from the room and the door was closed.

Uhwa, after a time, lifted one hand so that her outermost covering slipped off her knees. She rubbed at her left eye and, more awkwardly because she was using her left hand, swiped at her right eye. She blinked several times, slow, extended blinks, as if her eyes were indifferent to open and closed.

Voices came through the door from the direction of the kitchen, in counterpoint to the murmur from the lighted box. The chorus rose and fell with mixed rhythms: Adhah's steady talk, Seelah's antiphonal responses, and Joeab's high-pitched brief percussions—the boy's interruptions brought the altered tone of patient answers—all on a ground of shuffling and clinking, the women's labor. And always, the tepid wash of sound from the object in front of Uhwa. Uhwa raised her upper body and turned her head for a long moment as if looking for someone, as if seeking the boy who had been in the room. One of the women's voices erupted, a laugh and an exclamation like a question.

Inside the room, from the chair that, together with her narrow bed and the chamber pot under it, defines her world, Uhwa's dream memory answers. Not memory, not dream—she has no word for either—it is rather the world beyond here and beside now. It is the fellowship of what has been and therefore is. It is every sight she has seen or wished to see, and every savor and every voice and each touch. It is the company of all who have lived and therefore continue to live.

"Abel," she says, "come around where I can reach you."

Abel stands before her, full-grown but slight, here on the ground she and the man Adam have cleared. Light swims past them, the shadows are sharp. Abel's face glows. The soles of Uhwa's feet shape the crusty soil, and her shoulder relishes the pull of the heavy sack. Always when Abel is with her, her arms are strong and her back is straight. She is breathing easily. She knows what she must do.

Abel's features are pure and unlined, his eyes as searching as ever. Shy even with his mother, he leans in without speaking. He bows to her and his garment shifts to uncover his slender ribs and his hairless chest. This is his way, to approach without speaking. From the first his words were few, and those simple. His absences while he cared for the flock made his silences deeper, more studied, though the man Adam never valued the silences. Now Abel's gaze speaks of regions Uhwa knows, but has not seen. She depends on his mobility. It is power to her. Once again she must set him the journey.

Abel nods, showing her that he already understands what she will say. But there can be no missteps, no omissions. Though she can offer only the names, it is by the names that she sings the outcome.

"Go, then," she says to Abel. "Bring me Death, and this thing shall be corrected at last. Follow my words to the snow mountain Yields Nothing. Carry my song once more, the song I will sing with a mother's

need, and we will make Death know." This time Death will not hang back. He will at last see the wrong of accepting as natural what he learned from Cain. "He cannot refuse us," she tells Abel. "The task is done in the telling. It remains for you to complete it."

Already she can picture him after Death has relented. She sees Abel made one again with Abel who was—the horror undone, Abel restored to wholeness with his body. Heal the first division, and all the others will be healed. Not only Abel made whole again, but all the young who have fallen, at one with their lost bodies.

And peace for Cain who struck his brother and does not himself know how to fall.

Abel her messenger is out of sight. Their journey has begun. Already Uhwa has guided him beyond the garden Eden that was given to her and to the man, where now only she may gather. Far away Abel moves through the tall grass toward the uppermost plain, where Prefers To Jump squats six-legged and invites him to clattering flight. Soon Abel will reach the tumbling water of the vast river Swallows Boats. There he will grow feathers and a beak and join Walks Under Streams to bob along the bottoms of the rapids. Abel's is to roam, hers, the pain. The journey is succeeding because again she has garnered the names that make the pathway. She has never been closer to her goal, of giving birth to Abel again. As with the separation that birth entails, the fruit of pain will be union.

Uhwa crosses the clean-swept clearing and enters the hut. This is the hardest part. She is weeping at the thought of it, and panting. As each birthing ever is, the thing is impossible but necessary, dangerous but imperative. The outcome—made certain by her vision of the child that again will be—is confirmed by each spasm. She will complete it, and correctly this time.

Inside the shelter and away from the brightness he reposes, Abel who was, prostrate on the platform. The flesh of his thighs is slack. His right arm is crooked upward, its bone exposed by his brother's blow.

27

His sunken eyes produce no gaze. Together they carried him from where his brother left him, Adam and she. Adam, who held him while she cleared her workplace and spread a cloth—Adam who told her that it was over, that Cain had made an end to his brother. Adam, who no more visits her.

She takes water from the urn and bathes him, as she bathed every son she made within her body. His skin is stiff beneath her hands. Uhwa works to smooth it, but it will not respond. Its folds are hardening. But she is singing Abel up through the canyon Opens To Sky. She washes the blood from his shoulders and from his chest. She wipes the streaked dirt from his legs, and sings Abel around the gleaming surface of the icy lake No Bodies Rise. Each caressing of her hands, each tearful wringing of the cloth over the basin propels Abel through another of the valleys that separate him from where Death stands, crusted with snow. Her song eases the toil of Abel's clambering over the boulders that are the feet of the mountain. Here at the cliffs the shadows of his own sheep join their particular strength to hers. They ensure that he will not separate from his shadow but will climb without falling. He is rising up the steeps, while she pours sweet oil onto his brow and wipes it away with her hair. She arranges the sheaves of Cain's edible grasses, and places the fruits she has fetched for him from the garden, while everywhere Earth trades russet for malachite, and trees dream a green no eye can foresee.

And at the mountain—she can see it clearly—Abel, joyful, grasps Death with two good arms. Death shakes off frost, and the lethargy that is habit. Because they have not wavered, she and Abel, already Abel is leading Death past the caves Where Lost Breath Gathers. Abel is dancing toward her. Uhwa weeps as she sings.

Her ablutions are finished. But there will be no need to claw the soft earth near the garden, no need for an opening as deep as her knees, and wider than those they opened for the smallest ones who were not meant to be men. There will be no call to arrange fresh flowers for a bed and lay her son down onto them, nor to stand aside while Night plants pitch-darkness at the place where he lies covered.

Outside the hut, in the clearing that opens toward the garden, Uhwa waits for Abel's return. From behind her she hears his hands clapping. He is behind her and within the forest. This is not the path she sent him out along, this is not the return she has determined. Yet here he is. He has returned, but not safely. She recounts to herself each step, each motion, each incantation verse by verse. What might she have omitted, what might she have added so that what has become, will not be?

Abel has paused beside the outcropping, the same bench of rocks. He is gesturing happily toward Uhwa. He reaches down and helps Cain stand from behind the rocks. See?, his smile says.

"Find him, I find Cain." Abel laughs and cries out. "Brother! My brother!"

"My sons," she calls. "My sons, come here to me."

But they will not.

Her feet are as if rooted. What could turn it aside? For Abel has returned not with Death, but with his brother Cain, who invokes Death.

This Cain is young, though older than his brother. His body is an argument, rough and muscled. But could it matter which of the Cains it should be, from among their multiple meetings? All her pleadings have been as silence to this man who justifies himself. And anyway the strength of his reasoning strangles truth. If he would speak, he might say to her, "Do I belong to Death? I do not. I am alive, I am whole. Why then have you sent your favorite for me? I am here, and who can explain it unless you brought me? Between you and him, you humiliate and shame me, I who am real." This is how he talks. "I speak rightly in this, you know me—and, Mother, have him for once engage me, make him let me explain about the other. Else how can I be free of you?"

Her one wish is to close her eyes. Her fate is to watch.

Cain is speaking, but not to her. His voice grows strident against

Abel. If she could arrest the sound, if she were able to run to them and embrace them both, and draw Cain's rage and swallow it along with her own anger—why can he never see it? Abel does not speak to win.

Now Cain shouts and flails his arms. He flings off his gathering-bag, grain and chaff flying. Abel throws down his staff and jumps forward to join in this game of quick movements. His delight shows in his wide eyes and round mouth, and when his brother takes hold of him and lifts him, he cries out again, "Cain! My brother!"

Cain answers, "My brother." And throws him down, and bends and lifts him high and turns with him, and casts Abel face-up across his raised knee as he would break a bundle of sticks for kindling, and lets him fall to the ground.

Uhwa chokes on Abel's laughter, she gags on Cain's words. She wills her eyes shut, so that though the torrent of his arguing does not abate, the image she makes is that of Cain helping Abel to his feet, and wiping the dust from his brother's body, and of Abel rubbing himself and patting Cain, imitating his brother's motions as he has always done. And—still the air is filled with curses—the two of them are walking together. They are sitting on the bluff above the brook Murmurs Peace. Apricots are piled between them, and as they share, they toss the seeds down into the water.

She opens her eyes to Cain standing over his brother. Now he kicks at Abel's neck, and kicks with all his strength Abel's cowering arms, all this with his left foot. He stands back, clinching and opening his fists. His case is made. Abel's arm jerks away from his face. The bright sharp bone shows through the muscle. "Brother," he pleads, looking up at Cain. Cain jumps high—his peroration—and lands with both feet on his brother's torso. He stumbles away, favoring his one leg. His eyes are directed at Uhwa as if to say, "Look for me."

Abel's one arm is twisted, seeking his mother's touch, and his face is a mask of blood. Now she can move. She runs, and kneels and takes the hem of her skirt and wipes blood from his face. Abel's chest is jerking sharply. Now it stops. Now the blood ceases adding to itself. Sky is taking back its light from his eyes, and now the borrowed light is gone. She touches his eyelids, but they are bruised and will not close.

After a while the door to the dark fevered bedroom opened part way, and Adhah looked in. "I've brought your dinner," she said. "Some of those blossoms, too, that you like. We fixed them with plums." Around the women the old house sweltered under the noon sun.

CHAPTER 4

Acheron had never thrived by twentieth-century standards. The two merely eight-story office buildings near the river, and one tall hotel, spoke to this fact. Half a mile away stood the courthouse, which a century earlier had been the hub of a prospering town. The bricks of the streets around the courthouse were formed of wine-red Pennsylvanian sand that some ancient deluge had liberated from distant mountains. Now, grain by grain, the rock was completing its escape to the sea. The courthouse district consisted mostly of graveled open lots where once were small businesses. A few such buildings remained, including the one that housed the Moulton Foundation.

Inside the Moulton building Lindy was sorting through a stack of mail on the corner of Mollie's right-angled desk. Mollie faced the world from within sandbag-sized stacks of folders. She, and the barricade of folders, had been in place when Lindy took over. Mollie was a relic, a secretary in a universe of self-sufficient word processors, and if Lindy were able to look at her without thinking of the outsourcing of America, Mollie would already be gone.

"Some colored woman was in here looking for you," Mollie was saying.

"Jesus, Mollie, every woman is some color."

"Is that supposed to be profound?"

"Was her name Eshana? She's a friend of mine. Did she say what she wanted?"

"She wanted to prance around like a red Indian." Mollie was studying her computer screen and massaging her mouse. "Mostly she wanted me to stop staring at her, according to her I was staring at her. Some Gypsies, messing with somebody named Job in a boat. That's what she said, Gypsies."

"Joeab. Not Job, Joeab with an *e*," Lindy said, picking the first-class mail out of the day's litter. "It's her little boy. He's birth-damaged." Surely the old women didn't have a boat.

Mollie motioned with her head, toward Lindy.

"Mollie, please. I'll be out of your way in a minute."

Mollie motioned more decisively. Lindy followed her eyes to a six-foot-tall statue—Moroccan? of wood and hair?—painted with what might be camel dung. It stood against the wall under the big cross-cut saw.

"When did Bea get back?"

"That ghost-looking creation was here when I came in this morning. I got a call yesterday." This was extreme disclosure for Mollie, in the Bea Moulton department.

Lindy took the keeper mail to her office. On the way she gave Bea's office door, opposite hers on the hall, a perfunctory knock. No response. Bea Moulton wasn't supposed to be back in Acheron for another week. With neither title nor duties, she didn't have to keep Lindy informed. Mollie acted as Bea's travel agent, so Mollie certainly knew.

33

Bea is not in town expressly to torment me, Lindy thought. She lives here. Just the same, here comes Bea Moulton back from Africa—Africa?—with still another suspect antiquity. Bea's collectibles completely filled her office and the big storage closet across from the board room. Until today she had never left one of her finds in public view.

Bea had been the director of the Moulton Foundation for its first twenty-three years, without having accomplished much of anything. Then—pillow talk from Harold Rutledge—the board decided to get serious about the foundation's charter. Bea's father had not made it a family foundation; the board had full control. In Bea's mind, however, interest equaled proprietorship. Which to her meant that, no matter how numerous the other heirs, the Moulton Land Company with its timber and natural gas and a single huge salt mine, as well as banks that had become chips in a Charlotte outfit's growing pile, were Bea's province. The other principal Moultons, by now of whatever name, resided far from Louisiana. Bea owned no apartment in Paris nor adobe near Ghost Ranch. She occupied an original Moulton house for about four days in forty. Wasn't she therefore the one to worry about everything ever associated with the Moulton name, even if she had no authority, nor any inclination to know what was going on? Bea, in her mind, owned the Moulton Foundation as surely as she owned those banks and that salt mine that lay under the plantation pines. The board had considered and rejected the title of Director Emeritus.

Lindy didn't wonder that Bea rarely stayed home. From the way Bea clogged her borrowed space here with exotica, Lindy could only imagine what the inside of Bea's house must look like. When had the Object been brought in? Standing under the mounted twelve-foot cross-cut saw, it had looked ready to be butchered into two-by-fours. The huge saw and the two stuffed ivory-billed woodpeckers above Mollie's desk were the only three-dimensional Moulton souvenirs in the building. All the other timberland mementos, and the other thirty-two stuffed ivory-bills, were over at the Central Louisiana Wood Products Museum, a padlocked Moulton enterprise that nominally fell under Lindy's charge. Historic photographs, though, were everywhere on the dark-paneled walls. Lindy's office was lined with them. The sepia photographs were of men with trees—the salt mine had been acquired later. Some of the men wore suits and straw hats or fedoras, and were lined up formally beside locomotives whose log-loaded cars curved away beyond sight. Others, such as the men who stood, one foot on each of the two enormous logs that filled a flatcar, were as rough-looking as any specimens Lindy had ever seen. All of the trees, felled or waiting to be felled, surpassed anything now standing in the state of Louisiana. Every man in every photograph was long since dead. The Object would fit right in.

Lindy had studied the photographs during her job interview. She had decided from the costumes that the rape of central Louisiana must have happened around 1915. Lindy Caton, accessory after the fact to rape—if she weren't careful, if she settled in. She didn't intend for that to happen.

Her dad's illness had been an obvious reason to leave Little Rock. The thick envelope with the no-fault divorce papers inside hadn't been the trigger, and wasn't even a particular surprise, since Stone Prather had been gone for nearly three years. Little Rock was not a dull city. It was just the right size. You'd end up knowing interesting people and most of the leading figures—knowing an ex-President of the United States, chances were. She was happy enough directing the Fabor Center, a collection of group homes for runaway and throwaway teenagers. But she could leave Acheron after work on Friday and reach her dad's house before his bedtime. Nonprofits were odd: members of one board seemed to know lots of members of other boards. Yet none of Lindy's board friends she had confided her intentions to could point her to any jobs nearer Mobile. She found the ad in the on-line *Chronicle of Philanthropy*.

The interview process was routine. They put her up for one night at the once-elegant Royce Hotel down by the river. Harold, as board chair, presided over her meeting with the members of the executive committee, in the little brick building with the photographs and the woodpeckers. They all served up soft pitches that Lindy swatted out of sight. Bea was there but said nothing. Everyone reconvened for dinner at the home of a grand-nephew of Bea's grandfather's partner. After the interview Bea had approached Lindy briefly. She wouldn't be at the dinner, travel plans already made. The average tenure for a director was four years, Bea had explained, her tone condemning the willfulness of any non-Moulton who would claim authority for so long. Only later did Lindy understand that Bea included herself in the total—none of the outsiders hired after Bea stepped down had stayed as much as two years, and one had quit after a few weeks. But the first director to succeed Bea had managed to set the Foundation's course toward interracial community service, a retro-liberal menu which was satisfying to Lindy. This involved core grants for arts enrichment, mostly to the abysmal-and-getting-worse public schools of Acheron, and locating and negotiating visiting artists. Also hundreds of requests for money, most of them from distant academics who begged blind. And constant scrambling for supplementary state funds, which really meant federal funds.

There was a sense of the foundation's losing ground in recent years. This wasn't surprising, given the turnover in directors and the political climate in the state and in Washington. Lindy's immediate rapport with head of the state arts council was helping. Michelle, the new young assistant for grants management, was competent and cheerful, and she worked well with Mollie. Lindy hoped that she was giving the foundation a chance to hold on, and perhaps eventually to prosper. At the interview she hadn't seen why, given the community's needs and its history and the number of old-money residents and expatriates, Acheron couldn't be a model of pay-back philanthropy. Bea Moulton turned out to be one reason. When she returned from her tour, which—Lindy had squeezed it from Mollie—involved an examination of every remote, art-laden oceanic island where a World-Bank-looking American wouldn't be attacked on sight, Bea made it a point to warn Lindy. Don't talk money, their money, with the board members or with anyone else who might have serious net worth. Lindy by then had already sounded out Harold. Harold, in his stiff way, had been pleasant, but he made it sound as if knowledge of old money was a matter of national security.

Lindy was putting the annual report in the CD slot when she heard Bea's voice in the front office, followed by Bea's heels clicking on the heart pine floor. And here was Bea's short body, augmented and tucked and collagened, Bea opening her office door without glancing into Lindy's office. She was dressed in shoulder-to-floor silk, green and black and a shade of cerise that matched her hair. A white beaded headband, too, desert drag.

Lindy's printer spun out the annual report. She opened the next envelope, another batch of clippings from the biology teacher who wanted her to provide a library of creation science for every school in the region, and kept an eye on Bea. A narrow path through the jumble of antiquities led to Bea's Louis XVI desk. Bea was tapping the largest of the Chinese, or Korean, vases that stood on the sandstone capital of an Ionian column—crude, worn, stolen-looking. She turned her attention to a painted papier-maché Moses in a New York Yankee uniform, not quite life size and leaning sharply toward the wall, due to the who knew how many layers of Navajo and Chinese and Afghan rugs in the pathway to the desk. Moses in a Yankees uniform was a theme for Domson Grenier. Grenier's granddaughter had intended it as a love offering to the foundation, after Lindy gave her the grant to chase down his work and photograph it. Bea had no right to Moses.

"Jet lag," Bea said, still with her back to Lindy's office. "I should never have let the cab driver unwrap it."

Lindy joined Bea in the hall. In spite of herself she was staring at Bea's Colonial period armoire—or was it a linen press? It had shelves—which stood open near the desk. It held Kachina dolls stacked like ears of corn, and assorted carved Earth goddesses, and shapeless glass bottles and jars and jugs of iridescent green and blue. The goddesses and the glass pieces looked dug up after a long burial in a strange place, which Lindy assumed they had been. From this distance a couple of the smaller vessels looked to be from the same batch as a bottle she had seen in Adhah and Seelah's backyard.

"Have you got a dolly?" Bea said.

"You want to move it? Let's look at it." Lindy led the way to the Object.

Mollie always ordered Bea two first-class tickets, one for whatever principal artifact she snared on one of her trips. Outbound, she presumably put her purse in the second seat. At least the flight attendants hadn't had to look at the protruding, boxy eye-holes and the down-turned mouth inset with what looked like crocodile teeth. The wood at the top of its neck was less weathered, as if the head had nearly been separated from the body. The taxi driver must have held it under the chin—was chin the word for that hairy shape?—through the wrappings. Uncovered, the neck was the place to grab it. Touch it anywhere else and you'd risk kuru or some similar dire disease.

"Mollie, you hold the head, and Lindy will get it around the ankles," Bea said. Mollie was fixedly studying her screen.

"I might could find a dolly somewhere," Lindy said, and dodged as Eshana opened the door and came in.

"Have you seen a boat out there?" Eshana asked.

"Here's some help," Bea said. "She looks strong, she can take the feet. Lindy, you take the head."

"There aren't any feet to that thing," Eshana said. "Let's go to your office."

"Sure." Lindy didn't see any of the agitation that Mollie had described in Eshana.

"Are you kin to Groanie Johnson?" Bea's question was obviously directed at Eshana. "She worked for us when I was a little girl, you know. You look like you could be her daughter. She would have been about a hundred by now."

"Why isn't this thing in a museum? Groanie Mac was my cousin's great-aunt." And, rolling her eyes, "Daughter."

Lindy always remembered a Josephine Baker poster for some Parisian club, that she had seen in a cafe in New Orleans. If I could somehow manage to get my hair to look like Eshana's, she wondered, bronze hair and that perfect head shape, would large dark men pester me night and day?

"I need a cup of coffee anyway," she said. "We can talk at Camp Three."

Lindy lowered the windows of the truck and started the air conditioner while Eshana waited beside the passenger door. Midsummer etiquette in downtown Acheron.

"That is some throw-back woman," Eshana said when they were moving.

"Do you know who the Moultons are—were?"

"I know who Jefferson Davis was."

"Poor thing, she believes she's carrying the load for all the ones who can't stand to live in Ash. She hauls their past around the world, but she's the one it keeps dragging back. She's harmless enough."

"You think so? Looks like she's grabbed up some of my past."

"What boat?" Lindy asked.

"Those women are taking Joeab out in a rotten leaky boat. The biggest one wants Joeab to learn how to fish."

Lindy knew that fishing could be important to old women. It had been to her grandmother Caton. And scummy Lake St. Denis sat right behind the old women's garden. Nobody should eat anything that came out of there. No telling how full of fertilizer run-off it was. Gran hadn't cared about such trifles. Women of that generation didn't worry about location or the heat of the day. Fishing was what you did when you finished your morning chores. After the other old women in south Alabama long since switched to spinning tackle, Gran had used one of those long cane poles with the bent tip. Almost touching the water, the last thin segments could have looked to the fish like the foreleg of a great spider. The jawbreaker-sized cork would sit high in the algae, and every now and then it would bounce and she would jerk up a little bream of some kind, yellowish green, or that neon orange and blue kind that never got over five inches long. The fish went into a bucket of water. Lindy had never cared for the fishing part when she was a little girl. She would watch the captive school circle in the bucket until her dad came to take "the ladies" home.

Lindy had not seen any evidence of fishing at the old women's place. No stash of fishing poles with wrapped or tangled lines, no fish-cleaning spot inches deep in tiny scales, no smell of fish grease. For sure Joeab, if he should ever fish, wouldn't do it sitting there on the bank. The pole, if he could hold one at all, would be about three feet long, and no fish worth catching would come that close in. She hadn't seen any boat. If there was one, it must have drifted in. And why a boat, anyway? Fishers like her grandmother wouldn't go searching for better fishing. You picked your berries from the bushes you could reach. Lindy had a sudden vision of Joeab and the old women in a sparkly silver-and-blue, high-seated bass boat, the three of them poised together at the starting line of one of those million dollar tournaments.

Uh-oh, another daydream. What had Eshana been saying? Had she noticed?

She had. "My baby can't swim," she said, looking hard at Lindy. "You tired, child?"

"One of those four-berry scones will restore my youthful alertness." A technicolor scone as big as a cow patty. And enough dark roast to wash it down.

CHAPTER 5

Lindy was putting distance between them and the business district, past prosperous housing, what passed for it in the historic part of Acheron. The Camp Three coffee shop had taken over the downstairs of an almost mansion. She and Eshana had met in line—you could learn someone's life story in the time it took the help to steam-inject a six-way order. After a chance second meeting, Lindy found herself asking a social worker friend of hers what Eshana could do about her little boy who wouldn't stay home. The friend had asked Lindy, "What can *you* do?" Lindy had asked to have Eshana show her where the old women lived. But when they got there, Eshana had not been willing to get out of the car, she was so pissed at them for encouraging Joeab.

"What kind of boat?" Lindy asked once they were at a table. "Eshana, I've never known them to eat meat. They don't keep one chicken, much less a rooster."

"You weren't listening. A black boat."

"You talked to them?"

"You think I'm going out there again? Joeab's been saying black boat and fish, and Lah-de-dah—that's how he says their names."

If you're getting your facts from Joeab, Lindy thought, you've got a keener ear than I do. Of course you do, you're his mother.

"There may be two boats," Eshana said. "I don't care what they've got docked behind their house, it's wrong, the way they keep him out there."

"Has he ever gotten lost? He's mature, don't you think, in that way? I'll talk to Seelah and Adhah about the boat. They're not unreasonable."

"You think you can reach those oddities?"

Now they began talking about Eshana's failing transmission that had to be replaced—a thousand dollars, almost—which was why she hadn't been at Camp Three recently, and why she was working double shifts at a fried chicken restaurant, and had to leave Joeab for long hours in day care, which accounted for his getting to the old women's house so often. The transmission was the reason Eshana hadn't already moved them to Atlanta, to her sister Cloteile's. She was spooning a medium granita, and Lindy was sipping from her foam-sided mug with its wide safety base. Eshana talked, mostly, and Lindy swallowed piece after piece of her massive scone and thought about the ways their two lives were similar. Lindy had settled for a job in Ash to be nearer her dad. Eshana had moved back home from Detroit to be with her mother during her last long illness; this had been before they met. Eshana's mother had gone down hard, diabetes and congestive heart failure. Both the younger women, too, were divorced. And each of them had one parent who had gone missing early in their lives.

"Nothing wrong with IC," Eshana was saying. "Strong extended families, church people. If you can stand that scene. I couldn't."

IC was Industry City. It had been designated an industrial park, but no industry heavier than slaughterhouses and concrete contractors arrived. Acheron annexed it, and the modest subdivisions went in. Eshana had talked before about how she resented growing up practically at the edge of the cane fields, and had headed for Detroit and college as soon as she finished high school. Adhah and Seelah and Uhwa lived maybe a mile beyond IC, a considerable hike for little Joeab. Whether the old women's house was within the city limits would be hard to tell. No city services, in any event. With their own well they didn't need municipal water. Bathing, on the evidence, was not a priority, and the outhouse was not plumbed. You dealt with your own trash out there; but since the old women bought nothing they generated only a little garbage, and that went into their compost heap back by the garden. Lindy had decided the old women ought to have lights at least. There had been service at some past time—two skinny wires ran into a single-circuit fuse box through a cobwebby meter. The Cleco people had promised to send out a lineman to meet her and to reconnect, or throw some switch, but he hadn't showed up. And when Lindy made a little scene in the power company office, and they upped the deposit to three hundred dollars and told her there would be a fixed monthly fee as well, she balked at the cruelty of it. Lindy asked at the houses down the road until she found an older man who knew what to do.

"How's your dad?" Eshana asked. "When did you see him last?"

"I'm going down there next week. His hair is coming back, wiry, and he's almost holding his weight. Losing that round cortisone face."

"You know what, Momma didn't get gaunt. She got beautiful. She wasted down to her young self."

"That's sweet. We two are so much alike, our lives. How much do you remember about your dad, did your mother talk about him at the end? My dad, I don't know, was so hurt when my mother left. When my New Mexico sister ran across that obituary in the Denver paper, it was like, 'She's dead.' With everybody but me. I haven't said this to him. I believe Sunshine's still alive."

"Sunshine," Eshana said. "Sunshine when she's gone."

"Alice Williams Caton, but nobody ever called her anything but Sunshine."

"Momma would never say anything bad about our daddy," Eshana said. "I remember plenty, not so good. James Davis—where would you go looking for the one true James Davis?"

"I've been chasing Sunshine on the internet. You're right, it's a big country. But see? That's another parallel, like us both being divorced. What about your ex? I know exactly where Stone Prather is, he keeps in touch with my Alabama sister. He's preaching again, he never really stopped. He has a divine gift for locating rich little churches, this one's in Mississippi. He left two voice messages this week, but I didn't open them. He wants something. God help him if he gets my cell number and starts texting me. Or emails me at work."

"Larenzo's weak. Aside from that he's as good a man as you're likely to find. He sends more money than he's supposed to, for Joeab. I despise preachers."

"Who doesn't? I should never have been able to live with the preacher part of Stone. I wouldn't have been tempted, if his churches weren't way on the liberal fringe." Odd, self-sufficient churches, totally left behind by the denomination. Lindy had vowed never again to say which denomination out loud. "That part I appreciated. I basically never went to hear him preach, that helped a great deal." They had agreed about so much: politics, cooking, good wine, abundant sex, constant sex at least until well after they were married. She had been his secret life, in a way, until it turned out that a post-religious wife was only the public part of his secret life. Everybody in Little Rock—after the fact, the hypocrites—talked about how he had been sleeping with the other preacher. Bisexuality—in which direction do you come out from that?

Eshana looked at her watch. "The mechanic said he'd have my car ready by eleven. Could you drop me? It's between here and your office. I'll pick up Joeab from Mrs. Thomason and take him for a hamburger and a shake." Mrs. Thomason was the neighbor who did informal day care, the one who could no more keep Joeab from wandering than anybody could.

"I'll wait and take you on home if your car's not ready," Lindy said.

"I've got another plumber coming this afternoon. The first one wants three thousand dollars to straighten out the front bathroom."

"The house looks pretty good to me. Couldn't you put it on the market like it is? I mean, you don't have to be down here to sell it."

"It's my brothers," Eshana said. "Jody, especially, can't bear not to have a place down here. Momma's funeral was the second time he's been back from Phoenix since he left."

"I know of families in the country, where they walked away." Her cousin Stevie, for one. Too much trouble to fix it up, or they couldn't stand to negotiate after the mother was dealt off to the nursing home. Usually it was the mother. Men died abruptly. Houses just sitting there, children living in some suburb and dreaming of home. Did Adhah and Seelah have children in Chicago or somewhere? Or was it the other—somebody gave up and the women just moved in?

"Can I buy you a refill?" Eshana asked. "Get you hopped up enough to face that boss of yours, and her claptrap."

"Sure. Thank God, I don't work for Bea. Listen, when is the plumber coming? What if I pick up you and Joeab later, and we go out to the women's place? If you talk to them one more time, it might solve the whole thing. Joeab can show us this flotilla they've got out there."

"I want to say this carefully." Eshana looked to be about to cry. "You just made a joke about it. I can understand how you and the preacher decided not to have any kids—oh shit, that's mean. Okay. Joeab's all I've got. They're careless. They put him in danger, and they don't care, and they don't care what I think about it. And they don't care what you think."

"Don't you think Mrs. Thomason could do better? It's her house he's leaving." Lindy thought of Joeab with Eshana at Camp Three, how he liked to share Lindy's pastry but ignored his bagel, and how he went from table to table smiling and patting everybody's arms, until he would be out the door, nobody the wiser for a while.

"They attract him," Eshana said. "They need him there. There's treachery around that place."

CAIN'S VERSION: ABEL

Ihurt him, the weakling, but how am I supposed to find out how bad? I may have crippled him, *I don't know.* Six days since he went down, and they've gone, and they took him. That means he could walk, at least. I went back, but I couldn't keep waiting around there for them to do the right thing and come back. None of the three of them have *ever done the right thing* by me. Abel is the fool, but Mama and Adam—I long since stopped calling him Daddy— have played the fool this time, leaving without waiting for me to come back and straighten it out. Abel's arm, that got twisted? That arm won't ever be sound. His fault. Their fault. It didn't have to come to that.

But I wanted to know how bad it was. So I didn't go far, the first time. I slept out two nights and I *went back.* I searched all around the hut and the clearing, I yelled loud, I whistled Abel's silly whistle. Was he well enough to be away tending his dumb animals? Not likely. I hung around until the end of the day, when they'd all have to be back inside, *supposed to be.* They get scared, they confuse simple night for darkness. Nobody came, so I looked inside the old garden for Mama. I poked around the shadows, among the ratty vines and the trees and the low smells of wasted fruit. No wonder I *never once went in there* with her. Now I'm gone for good, myself. Serve them right if they eventually starve, without me to plan. That was hurtful, them leaving without saying where they were going.

Mama claims not to prefer Abel, but whenever I put the question to her, she won't look at me. They only ever take what sprouts on its own, she never wants me to tell what it's like to *force* a thing to grow. That made me fight inside myself, under all of it. When you're the one with the whole heavy load, and the load slips, it's hard to right yourself. So yes, there was contention. They had their stone fruits and their everlasting shade beans, I gave myself the job of what can grow in full sun. New parts for old plants, that's how it's always felt to me. And *the ground* my enemy, from the first day. Mama and her garden, she went in and brought out. She put together enough for us to eat—I'll eat some of theirs, they won't eat any of mine. But not enough to make them strong. And for sure not enough to make us happy. Look how sad we were. Except for Abel, of course, the fool. She and the man, they pined. Especially *Adam.* Something had broken inside him, and I don't know what or why, and now I don't care.

Gathering is the first step, but I set myself higher than gathering. Listen. Every degree of the past *stays in my head.* The amount of days; the different suns, high and low and fractions in between; and knowing to watch for a sun to slice up from the lowest notch in the hills, so I can afford to offer the seeds. The crazy tribe of moons, I know them by shapes and colors and by heights. I've learned the night how it turns, its lights and clusters and its sky-long streak. Nobody ever looked at the night yet, but me. Clouds are nothing, but remember the rain and the scheming no-rain—between the two of them they take your every other crop. I carved two buckets, but *water is not to be trusted.* Enough water to eat, that's about it. The rest feeds the gluttonous ground, or else it will run away like the river that flees the old garden and keeps it from spreading.

Both times I left, I struck out away from the dying sun, and away from the river. I wonder, did they follow the river? They're *out there* somewhere, *lost.* And why wouldn't I be angry? I have fought, against the bugs that swarm in from nowhere, and the worms that the ground *sends up* to pierce the heart of your best seed grass. The green stems heed the ground—and me left with dry pith. It always amounts to the dirt taking what's mine. I handled every bit of that. What I managed was better than berries. But they shunned it all. Why wouldn't I roar?

Six days, going on seven, and I'm wondering if I ought to drop it. Was that day any different, except that he was pestering me worse than usual? Yes, there was the matter of the long-bearded grass, we had a running feud, that high-yielding field and me. But it was Abel, his imbecile *sweetness.* Which goes with having it easy at home—went with, *they* won't find that degree of ease again. His flock straggled along when the others ran off, don't you suppose? You can't live on milk. Abel was jumping around, I was trying to calm him down. He will never learn how *a man* is supposed to stand. He'll dance with those blank-eyed sheep. They quick-step away, all of them together, and he's up and ahead of them and ca-pering and grinning, and he's crouching and cupping his hands and what he calls singing, to the lead stray, and they every one toddle around without slowing down, and come on back. The main male stands on the far hill as if his complete job was holding up those circle horns, no more *about to care for his family* than Adam was for us. And I worked from sun-up.

It's quiet out here in this strange country. Mama claimed that I put pressure on him. Pressure on him? That supposes *he and I have something* in common. I admit my head was noisy. I gave up offering her any of the rich nourishing grasses I create. She grudged what little milk it takes to soften them up, and then she'd say the hulls were uncomfortable on her teeth. She'll be twisting and winding together the hair Abel's animals scraped off on branches, and the old man will be weaving, he could do that little bit, and it took them forever to garner enough for one set of sleeping covers. But I could have fixed that. There was a young male I picked out, the hair around his front quarters was more of a mane, and curly. He was the only one with that look; all it needed was to drive off the other males, if I'm right about lambs. Abel valued the short-haired ram. Abel can't hold onto two steps of thinking, and Mama *forever backs him* against me. They took the covers with them. Good, I won't be sleeping under oily hair.

This loam I'm passing over, would it partner better with the rain? I won't pause for a while yet. You throw down the seeds, but that effort, nor scratching them under with your stick, doesn't oblige the land to cough up anything. The ground eats the seeds and it waits—that's fine by me, I know it's mulling the choices, and a lot of what it sends up is nothing I ever offered. I enjoy that, because one of the tares if I pet it, might take to me. Otherwise I rip everything out and throw it away. That part feels good, too, when I throw all of it on a *rocky place*. That day, Abel had taken his animals up the hill to where the young cedar was moist, because there was no rain, nothing left around home except my own grass, and that as tall as a man's shoulder, they knew not to crop it. The last thing I needed that particular day was Abel in my face. I had hauled water to that main field for full two moons worth, and every one of the flowers had made fat kernels. I went out *that morning* and met an odor like the earth's choked-up gut. Every head I touched went to grime. Add this: there went my offering of saved seeds, and where *are* any seeds to match those? I stomped the sick grass, and the sorry soil that did it. That's when I should have left, right then. When

Abel went down, I couldn't believe it. *They didn't warn me* of what could happen, just from *us being brothers*. It was my arms all on their own, it was my wayward feet, and my legs getting even with the ground. Yes, there was blood. He kept smiling, didn't he? I see me standing over him, and I have to say he wasn't damaged all that badly. In spite of his arm, which made it serious, which made it terrible. Mama was watching, way off to one side. Who did she call out to? Not to me, and I went away looking at her.

Along here, underneath the weeds, the ground is almost black, before night came I made that out. I'm treading on grasses nobody ever saw before. This thing has freed me to roam, to look for who I can be, but I can't stop, I can't take a chance that this ground is kin to the other that blighted me. I'm not going back, that much I'm glad of. Mama leaving me? No. I can't forgive that.

CHAPTER 6

It might be, Lindy was alertly aware, the Ethiopia Something at Camp Three, that had her lying awake. Kenyan, Ghanan, Zimbabwean, Africa's weak revenge on this minor delta. All those life-shortening millions of extra heartbeats, almost all of them privileged heartbeats, almost all of them thump-thumping against the red underside of white skin. Hearts drumming penance for sugar cane and for cotton, and for those rows of slave shacks between the highways and the cultivated rows that extended out of sight for two hundred years now—the unpainted square cabins still lived in, as worn as the old women's house but without trees or a lake to distance them from the past. What was going to happen to Joeab? What about her dad, all alone? By extension, what about Sunshine? It might be the coffee, but it was definitely the worry.

Time to use the railway car sleep inducer. She turned over onto her stomach and pulled the pillow over her head, and there it was, waiting at the end of the tracks to take her away into the night. This would address one problem right away—jangledness. Food was what was needed, and she always stocked her private car's walk-in refrigerator and the stainless steel pantry with amazing edibility. She left the choice of wines to the chef, a new dreamboat each time, brilliant and cheerful, who would be up front already simmering the stocks.

There on the table was the first bottle, a California sparkling wine too self-assured to call itself champagne, some label that until tonight had never been east of the Sierra Nevada. And a silver Williamsburg bowl of whipped cream, not ultrapasteurized but entirely fresh, tinged with some ambrosial liqueur and waiting to be dipped into by the huge perfect strawberries. A happy, out-of-sequence dessert there on the linen-covered table just inside the art deco rear windows.

The chef would have heard her tasting. He would appear—yes, definitely—offering the sautéed foie gras, not the paté, but sliced straight from the bird. Meanwhile, where would she head tonight? Western Canada again? India was so hard to manage. Not west to Sedona, that always stranded her in Dallas. Who would be coming along with her, who would join her in the royalty-sized bed under the largest of Cezanne's canvases, the life-sized *Bathers,* never seen outside Lindy's imaginary sleeper? She reached back to rub the bad place inside her right shoulder blade. That young guy with the nice smile and the high-topped sneakers and the red-rimmed writer's eyes, who was always sitting on one end of the only sofa at the coffee shop. If she waited beside the massive steel barrier at the end of the tracks, the arrester, whatever it was called, would he find her there? Never mind, the kid had his own dreams.

Instead images came of Adhah and Seelah awake at midnight in one bed, and Uhwa awake in the other. It would be relaxing to take the women for an outing until daylight. They could tell Bible stories. It would be like sleeping through one of Stone's sermons. She pictured Seelah or Adhah helping Uhwa onto the little stepstool that on a real train the conductor would pick up and carry inside with him. The other two pushing Uhwa, with Lindy on the rear platform, pulling. Up Uhwa came, wrapped in half a dozen shawls, and—Lindy realized she had never seen Uhwa stand up, had never seen Uhwa's feet. She'd be barefoot, too, why not? Uhwa's gnarled toes, her flinty toenails, her dusty feet on the imaginary cast-iron steps. Now Uhwa was settled inside and Adhah and Seelah were leaning comfortably on the railing of the observation porch. They had found the strawberries and were ready for the all-aboard.

She would let Uhwa choose their destination. Lindy had never heard her speak, apart from some singing, faint and unrecognizable through her bedroom door. Let Uhwa say where Babel was, and they'd go there—unless it was nearby, this side of some place with a name like Florien. In that case they would whistle through the little town and keep rolling in the same direction forever. Had the old women taken a train before? They must know everything about actual passenger trains, from when they were young. Acheron sat in the middle of the state, east-west north-south, which had to mean real schedules, every day in all kinds of directions. The former station still said Acheron, but it had become two or three so-called art galleries and an ice cream parlor. How would the old women ever find the sleep train? Just imagine a spur out to their house, that would do it. Take the train to the women—a poetic move, since the undeveloped streets beyond Industry City were laid out like a child's sketch of a railroad line.

The old women never went anywhere, as far as Lindy knew. They never ventured onto the street that dead-ended, apparently by accident, at their property. Help seemed to come to them. They hadn't touched the staples Lindy had taken them, including the box of salt—and what about salt? Do you or don't you die without salt?

This was too much work. Eshana would probably run up about

now anyway. Eshana would be claiming Joeab was with the women. Well, he might be. Hello, sweet little boy, she thought, addressing Joeab, who was cupping a fat strawberry in both his hands. Come on, Eshana, there's room on this train for everybody. The women are strange, but Joeab is safe here.

The lights behind her eyes began mercifully to flare, to form into tall-stemmed flowers that moved closer. One apricot popcorn cluster resolved into shapes. One of the shapes sharpened implausibly and became a human figure. Not her dad, he slept so soundly these nights. Gran?—would Lindy hear the soft voice call her "Agnes"? No, it was Sunshine, on the observation deck. Sunshine, much younger than Lindy, not dead after all. Blonde Sunshine, without a face you could focus on, and looming taller than little Linderella. Hi, Momma, you going to tuck me in?

Oh hell no, here was Stone Prather, in memory looking like his stocky overdressed self, an intrusive memory to drag her to stark wakefulness and probably into thinking about the divorce. So good-bye, vanished Sunshine. Every soul on the dream train was instantly gone, the old women and Joeab and Eshana—and the chef, and the engineer and fireman way up front in the locomotive she hadn't gotten around to creating. Shoo, Stone-memory, she told herself, I don't care what part of our history you want to revise. She had worked with men and slept with plenty of them, and been married to one. All of them acted as if women collect experiences so that men will have puzzles to work out. Perhaps the muscle in her upper back, now in spasm, had summoned Stone. Or was it his voice mails that she had canceled without listening to? The sleep car was still there, if barely, so she might as well think herself into the most comfortable bed in the world, and remember how Stone used to massage her tired muscles. Rubbing her back and talking the whole time, that was one thing he had been good for.

The bed that came to her was in an altogether other bedroom.

The door was opened by the total stranger, the small watery man who had been wearing nothing but an unbuttoned tuxedo shirt. This was the scene at Leontine House, there in New Orleans, where Stone had been for a week; the scene where she learned that Stone was breaking up, not only with her but with Grayson, his former associate pastor. How many times had she rewound this sequence? Stone, she thought, I am not a homophobe, and I don't believe I was one back then. But let's work on it.

There was the man in the tux shirt who stood staring through her, outside the door to Stone's hotel room. The man's sexual apparatus was outsized. She remembered thinking "apparatus," and that the word was one reason his organ looked clownish. His upper lip was bloody and his eyes were blazing with some train of thought that wasn't going to involve her. As always she lifted her suitcase and swung it at him, awkwardly, ineffectually every time: the bag's thin bar was not made for lifting. The man tottered past her toward the patio where gigantic banana leaves were clapping hands. The sharp odor of nutmeg and ether, had that been the man's cologne, or did it point to whatever had gotten his eyes into that state? Inside the room, in the wrong bed, here was Stone as always, covers pulled to his neck. His hair needed washing and one eye was bruised. The room was a rectangular sienna cave, with no priceless Cezanne, only dusty brocade drapes over window frames that were nailed to the wall.

"Didn't I tell you?" Stone said. He had, of course, told her to stay away, when she called from Little Rock. "You don't know your own mind, I'm coming down there," she had told him. Or something that silly—she was no longer sure. His greeting under such circumstances, yes, exactly; you don't forget opening sentences. But even when it mattered that much, most of it was long since transformed. Our best memories amount to created nonfiction.

The biggest change was not in the replaying, it was in the meaning that came from knowing what happened afterward. Nothing much had happened, except that they divorced. Stone had not become a denizen of the French Quarter. He had not given up his vocation, nor become a gay activist. Nobody found out about the scene at the hotel, least of all his pious mother. The two of them moved on. It had been necessary ritual for Stone. Lindy viewed it through that lens. The street sex, the cutting off of any communication between them, even the sacrilege, the abuse of the book of Matthew. All of it a bridge to a new state of mind for Livingstone Prather, minister of the gospel. God bless the little son of a bitch, he couldn't help himself. Lindy had come around to that degree of forgiveness. Which didn't help much with the memory.

"At least you're not running the streets with your clothes off," she had said, approximately, while Stone lay silent and covered with bedclothes. She unzipped her suitcase on the corner of the king-size bed, yards from Stone's feet, and grabbed out an armful of clothes and began to stuff them into the nearest drawer. Her body was cold, all sensation drawn down, her substance concentrated on making this make sense. Her eyes were watering now like Stone's—tears that had not been fear, nor anger. Tears from frustration, and the nutmeg-ether chemical.

Hadn't I told you? Stone had repeated. He spoke reasonably, as if she were a chambermaid who had just stashed unnecessary towels. Keeping the covers around his shoulders, he pushed himself to a sitting position. Hadn't he said she didn't belong down there? He had. The two questions she had brought with her had never gotten asked. Did Stone love her? And did he love Grayson, the other preacher he had come to New Orleans with? The other preacher—it hadn't taken her long to determine that the other preacher no longer mattered. Stone had already dropped the other preacher—she was not going to think "Grayson"—before she got to New Orleans. The word love never came up. Sitting on the corner of that bed, she got the picture and there was no love in it. Besides, he only used the word from the pulpit, and then always with attribution: St. Paul's charity, or some stilted phrase from Frederick Buechner. The meeting of two minds, a soul understanding, was what she remembered him saying, right before he admitted that his and Grayson's affair began the first month that the two of them were in seminary. He fed her all this in the too-sober intonation she had heard develop during their early years together, the tone he used even when he ordered fries with his burger. She had accepted the pulpit gravity. It had been one of those things you lived with, like a smoker's cough if your partner couldn't kick the habit.

The next thing she had asked him was where his bisexuality fell along the line between straight and gay. I know you're bisexual, she had said, because you weren't faking it with me. Answer that and we might survive this as friends. Embarrassing to think that's how impoverished her thinking was; but the stress then had been overpowering. It's not a spectrum, Stone had said, certainly had said. It's a three-dimensional continuum, he said. No one of us is a single point sexually. We splatter, we evolve, we breathe. God gives us agency.

Right. God, agency. There aren't that many rules, she said, you could have played by them. Or you could have told me you weren't able to play by our few little rules.

You fucked around, too. No, he wouldn't have said fucked. You fool around.

Wrong, Stone, but watch me from here on out.

Sex with a woman is good, he said, but sex with a man is better. Wait, that hadn't been Stone, he was too discreet to admit such a thing. That had been Ian Broward, a gay friend from college. At the time Lindy had agreed with Ian, as far as her experience went.

You wanted me, she said.

You haven't lost that vitality, not completely, he said.

Your mother, she said. She didn't suspect, if I didn't? Your eerie mother—had she said that, invoking his mother's cold piety?

A person takes care to be born in a small town so he can plan to move away. You did the same thing, he said.

We have here a preacher man in bed with a street person, Lindy thought from her own bed, and the preacher's wife moving to the greasy couch in a third-rate hotel room in the city where they met and fell in love. Bearable only at a distance of years.

You claim to be called to preach the gospel, she said. And since you've been drunk every time I heard you say it, you mean it. Mothers produce preachers. Which leaves open the question. Is preaching a life-style choice, or is it genetic determinism?

That's cute.

You got born and right away your mother felt the Call.

That's not cute.

Like the Annunciation in reverse. I've talked to her, Stone. She told me you saved her life.

Stone's mother, he liked to tell his intimates, including the other preacher, would weep over her miserable life while six-year-old Livingstone sat at the kitchen table and vowed to make the world a happy place for women. It hadn't entirely worked out.

Everybody has a mother, he said. Well, you didn't have one.

I want to understand this, she had said, and told him that she believed he didn't have a choice for either of them, preaching or who he screwed. What did he believe? But that question, also, never got answered. Didn't she stand guilty of homophobia, by means of the way she kept bringing up the entire scene?

"Are you down here cheating on the other preacher?" she had asked, not knowing. Or was this some kind of fling, was this supposed to purge the wildness out of your system? Who was he expecting to go to North Carolina with, Lindy or the other preacher? Or that naked guy out there? Stone had taken a job at a hospital in North Carolina, that was another thing he had told her on the phone. No use to come down, because he wasn't coming back to Little Rock. All these questions were long since answered in unexciting ways, but that didn't keep them from coming back late at night, any more than Lindy could keep the tears away, nor her fists from clenching as they had done then.

"The other preacher has to think about his congregation." Stone had used the man's name, Grayson. His inflection was one he might use to state the second of three points in a sermon. "Arkansas is not California. Later, when he's got some age on him—the other preacher's hands are tied."

He hadn't known what those particular people would do. She had told him that. They put up with her coming to church once a year, didn't they? How different could it be, having him partnered with Grayson? Stone had the skill set to be a preacher's wife.

This was where Stone's gaze turned away, toward the snap-hiss from the direction of the door. The man with no pants was back inside the room, with a soda. He tilted the can to his lips while he fiddled with the buttons at the bottom of his open shirt.

"You want some?" the street person said past the can, to Stone. The brown liquid dripped from his chin onto his skinny chest.

"Who is this creature?"

"This is—" Stone said. But he didn't say the name; he coughed up something and swallowed whatever it was. "My sinuses. He was a stranger, and I took him in."

"You want me to get you a Pepsi?" the man said. "This one's about gone." He had removed his shirt. It was twisted around one hand.

"I was athirst," Stone said, "and you couldn't chase down a Coca-Cola?" The man was rubbing his stomach with the damp shirt.

Let's skip this next part, Stone, she thought. None of it was ever an option. You're a preacher, you were born to be a preacher. Go to South America and feed the poor by letting them wait on you? Never. But she couldn't skip it. Let the scene roll, she decided. She couldn't stop it anyway.

"A man used to have options, now all of them are gone except taking a church." Stone resumed his tutorial. "There was teaching at the seminary, but the seminaries are gone. There was always the mission field. If nothing else worked out, you could always go to South America."

"There's six of them," the man said. "Hungry, thirsty, a stranger, naked." He pronounced it neck-ed. "I was hungry and you gave me meat. That's number one." He winked broadly at Stone.

"What about your mother?" she said, only now and not earlier. This was how the dialogue had in fact gone down. A few more passes, and the smarter version would be true. "Stone, I'm never going to tell you what to do with your life, but your mother did. And she hasn't died during the last week. I bet you've called her from right where you're sitting."

"That's a low blow," Stone said. "I can take care of Mother."

"What are you going to tell her? Do you expect that I'm going to explain all this to her? She still expects you to be bigger than Billy Graham."

"You're not helping me, man," the man said. "Hungry, and thirsty, and a stranger, and naked, and took me in. That's five out of six, or is it three of them? Sick and in prison—I know that's two different ones."

"You must have been dying inside, all this time," she said. The ache in her neck was moving up. No, it wasn't, there had been no neck ache, only tonight's back muscle. "Why didn't you at least give me a chance? Stone, if I couldn't see you were in that prison, how could I visit you where you were?"

"When saw I you thirsty, S-boy?" the scrawny man asked

through a last gurgling swallow of cola. "When clothed I thee? That one's not in my job description."

"Thee, you—it's all translations," Stone said. "You've got it close enough. We'll start the beatitudes tomorrow. After Lindy is back in Little Rock." He stood up on the bed and took a couple of tentative steps. Above and below his everyday white briefs his body glistened with something like Vaseline, but shinier.

The man flung the can across the room and was airborne toward the bed. He tackled Stone around the ankles, the bed's recoil throwing Lindy's suitcase to the floor. Lindy stood up, had stood up, involuntarily.

"When you minister to the least of these my members," the man said, "you minister unto me." He had Stone's legs and was pulling him down. He maneuvered their bodies, for her benefit, so she could see the way he was holding Stone's penis in both his hands.

"Members, yes that's used sometimes." Stone's voice almost boomed from the bed. "But brethren is better. It's brothers in the Greek."

And so it ended, their marriage. Lindy packed her clothes and left New Orleans, and drove to Alabama where her dad was not judgmental when she told him a highly edited version of the hotel scene. Divorce happens, he had said. Back to her sleepless self, Lindy thought, Who wouldn't have been pissed off? There almost certainly went her marriage. Who wouldn't have been shocked, her own husband, even if it was his perfect right? If she could have talked him into taking her seriously, if she could have made him less dodgy, even today, wherever he was. That afternoon had been the last chance. Yet the separation had not been so long ago, only three years plus. The few times she had been around Stone afterward she could tell that he looked at her and saw the hotel room, the end of their arrangement. She, even now, remembered when they met, remembered the questioning grin that broke across Stone's face at the Maple Street Book Shop when he looked around and caught her studying him. Was that another stereotype, a woman's way of thinking about marriage—the start of it, the bliss? While men focused on the bitter end?

CAIN'S VERSION: FROM NOD

My life is shapeless at the first telling. No act of mine assumes a pleasing contour at first recollection. Meaning emerges slowly, no matter that I am quick, and though I am never mistaken. I make my case, it may be, after the one who needs to understand has gone. What is less true for being argued at length? Yet in the end, because my voice lacks music, my truth is not persuasive.

Nevertheless I try. Living here on the sea, at last I am gaining control of my past. Memories must be managed, or else a life vanishes. I turn the past over as you would stir a porridge of mixed grains, and in time I am pleased with it. Aloud—in hearing myself I find the form of memory. Even so, a proper memory calls out for a second listener. I had such a one, or thought I did. My wife.

I should never have ended my journey so soon after Abel was hurt, after we all fled. The whole thing is, I did settle in. First of all, I had no idea that a life without grubbing was possible. Then the ground at Nod misled me; it was different in its look and timbre, but not in its essence. And too, I found the one good wife, who seemed to heed me. What happened with her is too raw yet to make sense of, even safely here at sea. I know this much: she gave me a son, and she seemed to listen, and her rejection uprooted me from the ground.

My wife gets no blame for waiting so long to let me know. No, all along it was my disposition for carrying around clashing thoughts. After my wife lay down, after she called my talk the floor of her discontent—after she would not get up, and my heaped-up words did not persuade her—then I knew my misshapen self had trailed me the whole way and deformed the new one. Discipline. When she made me understand how I was and I believed her, it needed a drastic move for me to become the person I always was, or meant to be. Once I could not count on her, I had to walk away. Which meant another journey, and then another long journey.

Her lying down released me. I took none of Nod, no seeds to eat or to sow, nor stick nor blade. I packed the memories of the best days with my good wife, and of my son when he was small and beautiful. Left behind was his growth into a hairy man whose words overwhelmed and silenced even me. Crossed out was the day he threw down his scythe, and what he said concerning me, and how long his mother wept. What I carried instead was the well-formed memories of Mama and Abel that I had polished for my good young wife and for the child my son was. Of the pleasant, cool grove where I grew up and lived easily, and the beauty of the trees and the bounty of their fruits—no use to name them, I do not expect to see them again—and of Mama's forbearance, and how cheerful Abel always was and how competent a shepherd, and how the three of them moved to I was sure a better place, without intending to leave me, while I ranged and grew wise.

The way Abel is simple—my son grew up smart, he is more like me than I am—and how Abel got knocked down? No, these things

I dropped somewhere along that first path. They will not live on the sea.

How can I hold the land accountable, in spite of its scorning me, now that I have found the sea? Land itself is nothing. Loss inhabits the ground, out here that is obvious. At Nod I was too busy wringing out newness, whipping the ground. At Nod every field will whip you back. We would go at it, the ground and me, I raking and pulling, the dirt rising to cloud my eyes and drink my sweat, and laughing when I spit his filthy breath back onto him. I should have noticed that it wasn't making any kind of melody. I did well—so I thought—to leave the racket outside when I came into the house. My wife's confession confirmed what I knew and had forgotten. Hard work unfits a man for living.

It began with a vision—the conclusion did. The vision ushered me to the hut outside the glade where I first knew life. We were long scattered, them one way and me the other. In the vision everything in the hut was as it had been when we lived there, except for the strong smell of Abel's animals. Somehow his sheep were living inside there, three or four of them were nosing around me. They were searching for Abel, I understood that. Abel was somewhere around—so their presence seemed to indicate. In the way you bring knowledge to a vision, I knew better. This much I also brought, no matter that I was sleeping: a vision is a dream. It is not experience, nor a source of good or bad. If visions were real, every crop of mine would have been flawless and every harvest a bounty, and my wife would be the supple and beautiful girl I found long ago. If visions were within the world and not adjacent to it, no backs would ache and all families would be together, talking and listening. This much I knew while the sheep came and went through the door of the hut.

The vision continued. Men arrived and mixed among the sheep, while I puzzled. Why was I presented these sights and not others?

One of the strangers had brought a skull, or perhaps I had watched him discover it on the floor, among the sheep who occupied my former life. My thought was, What can be learned from a sheep's skull? Of what value are the bones of any animal? They are a residue merely of their lifeless movements, and lacking a shred of the utility that justifies their presence. The man silently studied the skull, and I saw that it was no animal I recognized. The snout was missing, yet a semi-circle of teeth remained, and above the teeth, square downturned eye sockets. Behind the eye holes the skull bone was swollen gourdlike. Another of the strangers held up a jawbone with teeth that matched those of the skull. None of the men had noticed me. At the edge of the dream I touched my nose, felt its softness. I ran my tongue over my teeth and touched my brow with my hand. Impossible—the skull was not my skull.

At that moment I was overcome with a low and hopeless emotion, the feeling that my life was foreclosed—not at all the productive fury that framed my days with the ground, but confused and debilitating and altogether new. My need to escape from the sense of loss was itself a form of hopelessness. The strangers began to pose strong questions I could not decipher—the questions were for me, but why, and from whom?—which made the feeling stronger, almost overwhelming. I begged myself for release from the questions, and for escape from the dream.

And now a woman was standing beside me—my wife, who had been there all along, though she looked nothing like my wife. She no more knew the men than I did, but she held the power to address the yearning the men's threats created in me. These things were clear to me, and I turned to her for the relief I could not grant myself. The wish to be enfolded by this woman whose life had been my responsibility was as unfamiliar as my despair. She could—might she not?—dismiss the others and restore me to myself. Could she not shelter me as a child (though, awake, I know I never had or wanted such protection from anyone)? These were not questions, but were a part of the longing I felt.

I woke, still washed by unworthiness. Perhaps because I had never spoken of a dream, I went outside without waking my wife. The dark mood stayed with me through an ordinary workday during which I did not stop to eat, only grabbing handfuls of tender clusters. The grains were ripening, so my meals often were taken in the fields. The two of us had no reason to speak during this season. When I returned at the end of the day, I described for my wife the affirmation I required. To bring up the dream itself would only have confused her. To her thinking, visions were ordinary happenings.

–I have been good to you, I said to her after I spoke my statement of need.

She lay on her pallet, not answering. She had not done her duty by the house, and I realized that she had hardly risen for some days.

–No, she said after a long while.

I repeated my explanation, this time admitting how I yearned for her help against this base feeling.

She gestured for water, and I fetched it for her. Her right arm, I noticed, was swollen to twice its size, though her other arm, like the rest of her body, had wasted to thinness. She held the cup, wavering, in her better hand.

–I have brought stability in my dealings with you, I said. –This is a matter of certainty. You perhaps do not know of my struggles when I am out of sight.

–You are deep inside yourself, she replied. –You describe that royal place. You care only for it, and make of this one a wasteland.

I believed her, that I had not brought myself the whole distance from home. I must have seemed to her like Mama and Daddy did to me, looking back at a better time: no hope in a foreign land. Striving for the new had made me appear to be old.

More than a few sentences was not her habit. Each of our brief exchanges had moved us measurably along the twilight boundary, and through it, until she lay silent—unwilling I knew to speak into darkness. For my part I dreaded bearing the weight of her withdrawal until the distant morning.

I lighted a torch and brought it inside. I asked her if she had eaten. Night was her master, never mine. I stood by her, trying to find words to express my submissiveness, which threatened to consume me like the burning resin of the torch. I spoke my need fully, and was not surprised by her silence.

—I chose you in order to do better, I said at length.

—My life has been empty, and now pain is all. Her voice was weak.

—Do you care for me? I asked.

—No power could make you pleasant.

From under her pallet the earth spoke to me. What have I been telling you?, it said.

I held the flame nearer to her face. Her eyes gleamed, but not from anger. There was a difference in her skin, its texture was that of a fallen leaf. Was the bruised look due only to the flickering light? Certainly there was a transparency I had not noticed. Her skin strained to cover her cheekbones and the sharp edge of her jaw, so that her teeth showed. Though mine—I ran a forefinger across my mouth—were a judicious number, her teeth were as numerous, I realized, as those of the skull in my dream of shame. At that moment a shudder ran through her body, and a foul odor spread through the room. Her robe was stained brown, the brown of earth. She was joining league with the earth, and she did not care for me. There was no reason to linger.

What a voice the land can muster when you reach its edge, where it is possessed by the penetrating sea. Soil bleached white and deep, and textured as fine and even as millet seed. Step by step it sang to me as sweet as full-dried honey. It spilled up dry, over my feet, without trying to swallow me. When I climbed the last rise and saw, far away, the edge of the sky, and in between the long surface of the sea curving smooth and green and jostling with life, then every dry place shriveled to a handful of chaff.

I have since met boatmen and their diverse boats, but I alone fashioned mine. I watched. Fishes, seabirds. Not just any fish—not the floaters with dangling poisonous vines, nor yet the small flat rapid ones that I grab by the dozen and swallow wriggling; but the great surface fishes that blow out of their backs and push with a tail like a man's arms. Trace in your mind their outline. Trace within your eyes the hollow under a floating bird, then turn it around and think it into motion. A right boat is as hard to shape as a past is. I floated shells, and before long I could float myself, a useful skill. Out of sight of land, my thoughts clarified. The first smooth vessel freed me from the land. I will never return to the dirt.

This life therefore is open to few. It is one shape, always the same clean shape within the swells.

I have wondered if my wife would have been able to turn against me, if she had such fare as I find. Water is the only food that could torment, and even then one plan is enough: capture what falls. The other, that looks like water, is the body of the sea and the pulse of the world. It supports me uniformly. No matter the day or night, the sea does not begrudge its riches, but shares without rancor. I give little attention to preparation of the creatures I consume. Whether swallowed, or stripped and dried, or ripped and bitten and returned swimming to its host, its clean salt variety I find good. Sometimes I will drift in sight of the boundary of the sea for the variety, the succulent shelled animals that lie underneath on the almost earth, and their brothers that walk with many purposeful fingers. I dodge to the edge deliberately, in order to remind myself where I left meanness and confusion. When urgent need forces me to stand on the ground—wood for a repair, a meal of water, new fiber (rarely, since I conserve my garment by rolling it up and stowing it)—wrongness begins trying to worm up into my body. I despise the sight of hills lumped up. I grab the wind that blows from what lies behind them, and ride its reek until I reach the company of sea breezes. Dry land is the world's excrement.

CHAPTER 7

Everything was ready for the meeting. Lindy surveyed the board room table, its varnished top quarter-sawed and pieced from a single huge pine, and forming a surface large enough for twenty lumbermen to get their high-laced boots under. At each place were agendas, annual reports, financial statements, yellow legal pads, historic ballpoints with the logo of the extinct Moulton State Bank. One stack in front of Lindy's too-large leather chair, another for Mollie to ignore while she took the minutes, and seven more for the board members who had indicated they would make the meeting. The tenth pile was for Bea in case she decided to drop in—Mollie, as usual, had done this on her own. Like setting a place for Elijah, Lindy always thought. She finished charging the coffee maker at the marble-topped table in the corner, and crossed toward her office.

There was just enough time to check whether Seelah and Adhah's Babel story to any degree matched Genesis. But then, she had not seen a single print item at their house. It had to be some kind of distorted oral tradition, as her dad had suggested.

The Bible, the vestigial Bible that her Gran gave her to com-memorate some childhood achievement, was in one of the card-board boxes she hadn't gotten around to unpacking. Lindy had never used it. The book was altogether too fine, leather-bound and heavy, the pages so thin that you might worry that they would dis-solve between your thumb and forefinger. The workaday Bibles that she had carried to church were cheap and portable. The last of those had stayed home when she moved to the dormitory at Tuscaloosa. She had, in effect, graduated from church into college, though during her first year at the university she would drift to the appropriate campus religious center, in that semi-conscious way college freshmen have of trying to bring home along with them. She even met a neat boy there, and spent some delicious experimental evenings at an antique drive-in movie they located. Years later, mar-ried to Stone Prather, she had been perhaps the only minister's wife in history who didn't show up at the women's Bible study circle. A Bible-free life.

She lifted aside one box labeled Framed Pictures, and another, Misc.—Never Mind, and found the one labeled Arkansas Books / Useless / Do Not Open. The big black book was halfway down, be-low the dregs of her last job, the tomes on adolescent behaviors and on managing time, but above the lowest literary sediment, a dozen novels whose plots she had forgotten and didn't want to recall. She lifted the Bible with both hands and saw for the first time that the cover was not leather but pebbled paper. The gilt edging was in good shape, although some accident had wadded a sheaf of the elegant pages inward. She opened the book to repair the disrespect to Gran, and was looking at the Index to Biblical Place Names. Thebez, Ur, Zanoah—no need to look up Babel; it was middle Genesis, before Abraham, and after the water went down, as Adhah and Seelah would say.

At her desk, Lindy opened the Bible at the beginning. The

inscription in her grandmother's vigorous cursive hand read, "To Linderella Caton as she enters the Girl's Auxiliary of the Women's Missionary Union, Much Love, Gran." So it had been third grade, Gran's last year of clarity. Turning a pinch of tissue-thin pages brought up "The Most High and Mighty Prince James by the Grace of God King of Great Britain, France and Ireland Defender of the Faith, &c," followed by a long preamble. She fingered past a cluster of pages and came, not to Genesis but to a long dictionary. Aman Amana . . . Chaldea . . . Er Esau . . . Jesimiel . . . Praetorium Prophet . . . Saul. . . . Nobody could have been intended to locate a specific passage in this thing. It was a symbol, a decoration for Godly coffee tables. People like her grandmother had known every name and every incident they cared about. They didn't need a reference book. Not that they didn't read the Bible all the time. They just hadn't seemed to see most of what was there.

Another thin bunch of pages, and Genesis appeared, chapter 4. Halfway down the column, "And Abel, he also brought of the firstlings of his flock and of the fat thereof. And the Lord had respect unto Abel and to his offering: but unto Cain and to his offering he had not respect. And Cain was very wroth, and his countenance fell." Poor Cain, she thought, no respect. And poor Abel. But she needed Babel, not Abel. After thirty years together the pages were loath to part. They yielded at the middle of chapter 34. The heading read "The Shechemites slain." In spite of herself she glanced through the story of the slain Shechemites. It was about Jacob— well, his sons. The sons couldn't go along with whatever it was, apparently to give their sister away to Shechem. Unless Shechem agreed to be circumcised. "Don't do it, Shechem," she whispered to herself, "they're going to kill you, it says so right at the top." She read down the column: all sorts of negotiations, Shechem and his dad persuading the others that "these men are peaceable with us; therefore let them dwell in the land, and trade therein," leading to "every male was circumcised." And on the third day, "when they were sore," Jacob's sons came in and killed every one of them, and looted their city.

She was sure she had never heard this story, though it had sat in Genesis chapter 34 the whole time. A childhood and adolescence spent listening to sermons should have delivered the entire Bible into her juvenile brain, during the months of Sundays she sat on those hardwood pews. The preachers kept to their favorite texts, but what would it have mattered if they had preached Genesis to Revelation and started in again at Genesis? Already in these few seconds she had forgotten the names of Jacob's sons. Impossible, once it stared you in the face, not to read some of it. Even so, she had done well to retain the broad strokes, such as how much pleasure the whole scriptural enterprise took from describing murder.

The pages refused to separate rationally. "So Abram departed, as the Lord had spoken unto him." Chapter 12, Abram—Abraham. That bracketed Babel, so she went back. "And Joktan begat Almodad, and Sheleph"—all those names, it went on and on, nobody on earth could care about most of what was in there. But, yes, "And the whole earth was of one language, and of one speech." That was it. She had found Babel, at last. Why not simply have turned to the concordance? Because she ought to have known where Babel was. And why flip back and forth fruitlessly, when page by page would have worked five times faster? Because flipping was the technique they taught you for sword drill. Her sister Lubie had been captain of a state champion sword drill team, which had been enough to set off Lubie's obsessive memorizing of Bible passages, even now a barrier to civil conversation. Lindy, when her turn came, had been the worst sword driller at Temple Church—the worst girl, none of the boys tried to win. A sudden vivid memory of standing with a row of other children; Sunday evening assembly, the plain basement room, its windows half-papered with pastel-robed, Hollywood-looking characters. The usual aura of kid sweat. The five of them—one boy and four girls, grim-faced, each with an illicit thumb between Psalms and Proverbs, and she knowing she had never been the first one to step forward with the chapter and verse. A temporarily elect cadre, they stood rigidly at attention while a dozen other kids sat scraping their chairs on the vinyl floor and snickering. Imagine if she had been holding Gran's massive volume. Surely she would have lost her grip on it as soon as the teacher called out "Daniel six, five" or whatever. She would be grabbing frantically as it slipped to one side and turned over and escaped to the floor, and the sound of the page ripping out—the wrong page—and all the boys pointing at outsized, slumping Lindy. She made a note of it to tell her dad about how she saved Gran's Bible from desecration by never opening it.

She read on, silently. "And the whole earth was of one language, and of one speech. And it came to pass, as they journeyed from the east, that they found a plain in the land of Shinar"—Noah's family, on the march with muddy feet—"and they dwelt there. And they said one to another, Go to, let us make brick, and burn them thoroughly. And they had brick for stone, and slime had they for morter." Mortar? Nothing about making inferior bricks. What did Seelah say, it all crumbled into a pile? "And they said, Go to, let us build us a city and a tower, whose top may reach unto heaven; and let us make us a name, lest we be scattered abroad upon the face of the whole earth. And the Lord came down to see the city and the tower, which the children of men builded." Just the two verses, and not even the name. There had to be more. God was fixing to knock it down. "And the Lord said, Behold, the people is one, and they have all one language; and this they begin to do: and now nothing will be restrained from them, which they have imagined to do." She was reading aloud. "Go to, let us go down, and there confound their language"—confound indeed; if King James's scholars had

God sounding like an Englishman, how much of it had they translated right?—"that they may not understand one another's speech. So the Lord scattered them abroad." Her eye was already on it: "Therefore is the name of it called Babel; because the Lord did there confound the language of all the earth: and from thence did the Lord scatter them abroad upon the face of all the earth." The genealogy started back in, with the tower still standing. That was all, they were chased off and went about inventing new languages. Apparently God, like a genteel neutron bomb, had depopulated Babel and left the buildings standing.

But wait a minute, where was Nimrod? Nimrod offered her a chance to fumble another assignment under the pressure of time. A different Sunday school drill, the regurgitation of standard verses and the identification of exotic names from the list the kids were supposed to have studied all week. She could never retain enough, while the other girls mastered them as easily as spelling words— which made her no better than a boy. Who would have guessed that a couple of those boys would end up being preachers? But the assignment would have been "Who is Nimrod?" which was easy, not "Find Nimrod" without chapter or verse, which, Bible re-opened to Genesis, she had not so far accomplished. Certainly he came after the Flood. At the end of chapter 11 she glanced at "And Terah lived seventy years, and begat Abram, Nahor, and Haran." Abram, soon to be Abraham, her signpost to go back. By now the other children would be working on the next command from the teacher. Here it was. "And Cush begat Nimrod: he began to be a mighty one in the earth." Cush was the son of Ham, it said. So Nimrod was Noah's great-grandson. "A mighty hunter before the Lord"; and another "mighty hunter." Nimrod was redundant before the Lord. "And the beginning of his kingdom was Babel, and Erech, and Accad" and so forth. Not a word about these cities getting built. And the timing was oddly careless, with Nimrod owning a list of cities including

Babel, a whole chapter before anybody got to Babel. Yet how scrupulous did they have to be about time, when five hundred years amounted to half a lifetime for their characters? Nimrod at Babel, she had been right in that much. The old women had made Nimrod out to be the boatbuilder's kin. But people who would call a plantation Babel might be carrying names like Noah and Nimrod. And mighty hunting would have been easy, with the pine forests right across the river.

Voices in the front office. The Brendels, Alan and Naomi—always on time, always the first board members to arrive. Old-line social activists, ultimate do-gooders, they were the ones who had finally maneuvered Bea out of office and started the Foundation doing what it had been chartered to do. The Brendels never quibbled about produce. They smiled at everything Lindy brought, and claimed to prefer the woody Zapotec Pleateds, the most primitive tomato in the world. Better hurry. She closed the black book—her grandmother's book, after all, and not hers. A few sparse verses on the tower of Babel, yet in her mind she saw what ought to be in Genesis but was not. The massive tower rose in the background, teams of slaves everywhere, rough wooden-wheeled wagons drawn by oxen, overseers in Egyptian-style headdresses. Then the great tower falling, rocks flying, the crowd fleeing open-mouthed—which brought up the sick, uncanny drop of the south World Trade tower, the most vivid sequence in her entire memory bank. She repressed its obscenity, as always. Her Babel was no column of horrifically vacant smoke and spinning paper. The scene of destruction was fainter, faded shades on a brownish background. And in the next panel, a bearded and scowling God, hanging above the destruction with his arms folded. The next panel? Her Babel came from one of Lubie's old Classics Comics.

The meeting was winding down, all the necessary business out of the way. The annual report had put everyone in a good mood; and the poems the current visiting writer had sent from Zora Neale Hurston School brought laughter and almost-tears. Bea's chair was empty, always a pleasure. As board chair, Harold Rutledge preferred not to be involved in the agenda. But he had showed up, and had sat through the meeting without altering his superior near-smile. Lindy kept all her meetings under an hour; it made for better attendance. Even so she liked to allow an interval for free discussion. Everyone understood that if they had an appointment, the end of new business was the time to check out. The Brendels never did. They must have rear ends of iron, Lindy thought, as many meetings as they sit through. Today even elderly Dr. Albert Lafayette Burford stayed, who was snap beans only, and who sometimes headed out the door after ten minutes, as if the board room were a bus and he had reached his stop.

Jane Helmes, the art history professor, had her hand raised eagerly. Jane cooked Cajun; she accepted okra. "Go," Lindy said. Jane was so sincere.

"You know the Donatello sculpture, *St. George?* Early fifteenth century? It's revolutionary, because it's not Gothic-static. St. George looks like he's fixing to jump out of his niche and axe that dragon. I was showing my big survey class a slide of the panel below St. George. It's equally revolutionary, right?"

Lindy studied the dark pine paneling and the Moulton logging photographs, while Professor Jane went on about the knight and the maiden and the dragon, and how the carved background—an Italian word for flattened—was so subtle, and Donatello invented it. Lindy, from the corner of her eye, examined Harold Rutledge, and thought of Stone Prather. Harold and Stone, apart from their shared air of self-importance, might be different subspecies. Why didn't the memories of ex-husbands flatten like clouds carved on Italian tombs?

Professor Jane was getting around to her point: the flat earth was alive and well in the college classroom. "Now here's the joke," she had said sometime back. "I said to the class, 'But then who needed perspective,' I said, 'when the earth was still flat in 1417?'"

Mild laughter or dutiful smiles from the board.

"The students didn't move their eyes," Jane said. "I hit the switch to raise the shades, and the students were reaching for their backpacks."

Mollie, unaware, plopped her purse on the table and dug for a lipstick.

"And then this kid at the back of the room, he was looking out the window, I guess at the world. 'It's round,' he said. 'I'm willing to go that far.' Evolution and continents drifting? Needing the degree was the only reason he wrote them on the tests. On an impulse I asked for a show of hands. Maybe ten voted that science is true. Most of them wouldn't say."

"These old women I'm seeing about," Lindy said. "The tomato ladies?—you're helping them out more than you know. They're no more in touch with reality than the average college student is. It takes all my self-control not to try to straighten them out. They believe they personally helped build a plantation called the Tower of Babel. Thanks for a good meeting."

"Truth is in the human touch." Old Dr. Burford had roused himself. The board members politely stopped where they were. The last person to say "no" to him must have been his wife, and she was long dead. The doctor lifted his liver-spotted hands and considered them with satisfaction.

Lindy checked herself. Who knew whether the Moulton Foundation was in the old man's will?

"They spend their days in sloughs of test results. If they simply

were willing to touch the patient. Blame it on Galen of Pergamum."
The doctor's snapping-turtle lips formed a smile. "The disease process—hah! Life is not theory, it is flesh and blood. Follow me while
I enter the room of a dying young mother, as I did this morning,
and you will not make a billion years any part of your philosophy."
The old man stood and hitched himself toward the door as if he
were trailing residents.

"Thank you all for a productive hour," Lindy said to their
backs. An hour and three minutes, even with redoubled weirdness.
"Same time next month. E-mail me if you have anything at all."
She would be calling each of them, even Harold.

The Bible was still on her desk. Might as well look up Noah
and the Flood, and be done with the whole project. Chapter 6,
quickly enough. It did seem to go faster if she read aloud. "And the
Lord said, I will destroy man whom I have created." Your turn now,
Jehovah, she said to herself. Step up and show us how it's done.
Kill us all, why don't you. "Both man, and beast, and the creeping
thing, and the fowls of the air; for it repenteth me that I have made
them." Adhah and Seelah hadn't invoked any version of God. That
was maybe stranger than their talking Babel. Every woman of their
generation that Lindy had ever met was pious. Seelah and Adhah
didn't seem to know who Jesus was. Was that what finally happened
when you lived all alone at the end of the road, and you hadn't ever
been able to read? She was scanning the tops of the pages. "In the
six hundredth year of Noah's life, in the second month, the seven-
teenth day of the month, the same day were all the fountains of the
great deep broken up—." Here was the Flood itself.

"What was the name of that plantation? Not Tara, I hope?"
Harold was standing just outside the door. Harold's power-forward
frame, six foot seven, and his shock of graying hair, and his amused
eyes behind the horn rims. He seemed always to be mildly enter-
tained by the smallness of anything he didn't already know.

Lindy advanced, carrying the open Bible in both hands. "I said tower, tower of Babel. Because they talked about Babel and a tower. That was careless of me. I don't know for sure there *was* a plantation. You must know the name of every one there ever was, around here."

"Not so many worthy of the designation—this side of the river flooded often, before they leveed it." Harold extracted a small notepad from his suit pocket. He fancied himself an oral historian, but as far as Lindy knew, he had never published anything.

"Yes, I've seen those photographs in the old Fisher hardware store," she said. Harold's wingtips were at the exact outside of the threshold to her office. Notebook out, and pen poised.

"The planters switched to sugar cane around 1840," he said. "And that meant they missed out on the cotton boom of the '50s. Once upon a time I thought I would look into the 1837 slave uprising, but General Banks torched the record of the trial, in 1864. General Banks is why I concentrate on my Bourbon project—first families, quality. The landowners suffered terribly at the hands of the Reconstructionists, until the Bourbons took control of the state in 1900. That's my period, 1866 to the present."

"Fascinating." She considered the extraordinary hardships associated with being a former slave-owner. "So you never heard of any place named Babel?"

"These elderly ladies who pick your vegetables, what exactly is their connection with Old Ash Run? Or do they trace from Oakville?" Oakville, just across the river, that was settled before Acheron. How had she ever let herself get involved with such a boor?

"Adhah, Seelah, Uhwa, yes, they're old. They live out beyond Industry City, in a dogtrot house old as creation. They have this wilderness garden. Seems like they've hardly talked to a soul in ages—except to Eshana, once. Eshana, she's a friend of mine, that's

83

how I got started with them. Her little boy—Joeab, he's the most angelic child—keeps going over there and she worries that he's too young, in his mind, to be wandering that far. Babel, and Nimrod. Aren't country people fascinating, the stories they tell?"

"What is the family name? They *are* African?" Harold put his notebook and pen back into his coat pocket.

"I've been looking for a way to describe them and all I can come up with is that they look like the salt of the earth. I don't quite know their last names." Their last names were no business of Harold's.

"As you know, Lindy," he said. She knew. "I have interviewed a host of people over the years, the great majority of them from the best families. Not by any means all of them well-off. Good blood surmounts the most diminished circumstances; my research confirms this quite thoroughly. The families who are careless about such matters as asserting the family name, who lack the intelligence to retain the thread of history? Co-mingled bloodlines. It is not rare. Melrose Plantation at Chopin is only one example. Thus my questions."

"I wish you would drive out there and ask Uhwa that one. Ask her about bloodlines. Write down her answer in your little spiral book. Then go talk to Joeab about surmounting diminished circumstances. How could I ever have shared a bed with a creature like you?"

"Is that a Bible you're holding there? Not the New Oxford Annotated?"

"No, Harold, this is the goddamn King James."

CHAPTER 8

But a mist came up from the earth
. . . the breath of life.

Genesis 2:6-7

Adhah was seated at the front of the skiff, so that she faced the lake and the trees that grew from its shallow bottom. Seelah stood beside the boat, on a grooved log that lay transverse to the shore. Joeab teetered beside her expectantly. Seelah reached down and lifted him into the boat.

"Go to Adhah," she said.

Adhah guided Joeab onto her lap.

"Don't ever stand up in a boat," she told him.

The outer end of the boat settled sharply as Seelah stepped down. Still standing, feet wide apart, she reached down for the smooth barkless pole and pushed hard. The boat didn't move. She extracted the pole and tried again, the muddy end against the log. This time they were under way. Now they were moving through the shade, under cypresses that stood as wide-based and stable as Seelah. Adhah gave Joeab another hug and helped him to the middle seat. He swung his bare feet in the muddy water at the bottom of the boat, and admired the stirring they made. Behind them, where the boat had rested, several water snakes, unsettled by the light, rolled their ivory-segmented bellies and sank out of sight.

Adhah held a woven palmetto-leaf fan. Occasionally she gestured with it: Tree. And Seelah—without looking around—easily changed direction.

"That feels something like a breeze," Adhah said, waving the fan. "Joeab, can you say breeze?"

"Bee," Joeab said, reaching for the fan.

"Fan," Adhah said, and handed it to him. "Fan."

"Fen," Joeab said. He held it by one edge rather than the handle, steered it carefully back and forth; made no fuss when Adhah took it back. She began to fan generally, laving herself and Joeab. Holding the fan horizontally, she sent air in Seelah's general direction.

Seelah continued with her poling, the boat gliding slowly backward in the shallow water. She made no effort to reverse the boat.

"There's a patch," Adhah said.

Under the trees the surface of the water was a meadow of yellow-green algae and plants that floated or grew up from the bottom. None of the plants interested the women, except the clusters with blossoms like tiny white bugles. Seelah leaned on the pole while Adhah harvested the dripping, rootless plants and dropped them into the slatted wooden box on the seat beside her. Breaking off a few of the narrow dark leaves, she rolled them in her fingers and held them toward Joeab, who leaned forward and took them into his mouth.

"Tastes good, don't it." She began to chew some of it herself. "Like salsifer, kind of. Don't know what they call it. Water salad."

The search went on slowly under the cypresses. Out where the water was deeper, Seelah used the pole against the trunks and the cypress knees that thumbed above the water. Joeab, chewing, smiled greenly.

"Here, Joeab honey," Adhah said when they had not seen any

of the water salad for a while. "Your turn, to fish." She took two pieces of coarse bread from a pocket and held out one of them. The boy received it and, leaning cautiously, propelled it from his cupped hands down toward the water.

"Fish," he said, making the word two careful syllables. Adhah handed him the other chunk of bread and he began to gnaw at it.

"Fishes," Seelah said. She had sat down and was holding the boat against a small tree. "Here they come." The swirls now were on all sides of the soaked bread, which began to jump about under the force of the tiny attackers. Adhah, eyes closed, was humming softly, a tune not in any songbook. Joeab watched the spectacle intently. He sang along wordlessly, approximating Adhah's melody.

After the bread was gone from the water—sunk, destroyed—Seelah reached for Joeab with one arm, and, ignoring his dripping feet, set him on her lap. The boy offered her the last of his bread. She took it and ate, chewing with a sideways motion of her jaw. Now the boat had turned and was drifting slowly forward, so that Seelah and Joeab faced the outer limit of the trees toward the open lake that lay beyond, too bright to comprehend in the glare of the sun. Far across, in front of the matching perimeter cypress grove, was another boat that might be like theirs. One of the two tiny figures in the distant boat moved an arm. Then the other did the same: fishers, casting.

"Boat, boat." Joeab said the word plainly. He was leaning against Seelah's cradling grip, to see around Adhah. Now he twisted up to see Seelah's face. "Boat?" he repeated—a question now. "Back boat," a statement.

"All right, son," Seelah said. "I'll tell you the black boat."

They had reached the margin of the trees. Any farther and they would join the lake's wide center. Adhah, humming, grabbed a handful of feathery cypress leaves so that the boat swung around to a stop. On the ridged bark of the tree a gray wolf spider, slender fore-and-aft legs as long as human fingers, napped in the shade. The boat rocked on the subliminal waves that came to them in their haven—signals from an outer world, faster than heartbeats, lapping musically underneath the little classroom.

"Two boats." Seelah held two fingers in front of Joeab. His attempt to match her gesture went nowhere until Seelah helped him, gently pressing down his thumb and outer fingers and helping the index and second fingers toward straightness.

"Two," Joeab said.

"Floating." Seelah indicated with flattened hands the lake around them. She grasped the sides of the boat and rocked it. Joeab giggled and leaned from side to side on her lap.

Then she held out her two hands, one an upward palm and the other with thumb measuring the first joint of a forefinger. "A big, big boat and a little tiny boat. The only two boats. One of them hardly no bigger than this here one. And the other boat, too big, too square, too dark." Her hand gestures matched the words. For "too dark" she put her hands over Joeab's eyes and removed them. He dissolved in laughter, holding onto her hands, trying to pull them back over his eyes.

"Big water. Two boats on the big water." Another sweeping gesture, her eyes looking heavenward through the cypress tops. "So much water the trees went down, and the hills hid."

Here Adhah, whose eyes were closed and who still grasped the limb, used what leverage she had to pull the boat forward, and they began to drift in the direction of the next trees and toward the shore.

"We were in the little boat," Seelah said.

CHAPTER 9

And every living substance was destroyed
that was on the face of the ground.

Genesis 7:23

"Adhah? Seelah?" No one answered Lindy's hail at the front steps. Her first non-vegetable visit in a while. Early afternoon, she had given herself the day off. Plenty of time to get the facts about Joeab and the alleged boat, which was the purpose of this trip, and perhaps to draw them out about Babel now that she knew what was not in Genesis.

She was in the front-to-back hall that divided the four rooms two by two. Shuffling sounds were coming from the kitchen, and cooking aromas, and other banging sounds from out back. The old women tended the front yard with bundles of tied-together sticks, swept it clean of leaves and dressed it with the brush brooms until the ground was a Van Gogh *Starry Night* in dirt. If they had a broom for inside, Lindy hadn't spotted it. The floor of the hall sagged to the middle, a shallow bowl of never-painted pine and unswept lint. Overhead, the roof was pure corrugated rust. The whole thing was bound to go down, and hiding back here away from town should not have saved it. But beneath the aromas from the kitchen the resident smells of the center hall announced, this house is dry. Dry as dust—dry as last year's unshelled beans and the boldly colored gourds and the stone jars of who knew what, that lined the hall. After a dozen visits to the house, if she ever waked up blindfolded in any one of the rooms, she would be able to name that room by its emanations. Adhah and Seelah's room, front left, on her right, would be easy. It was filled with those two—direct, without any of the old-woman perfume or talcum Lindy would have expected. Maybe that was what Eshana had picked up on, the earthier smell. Was that it, more than the heavy clothes and the sun-darkened skin and the strong features, that made Eshana say they were foreigners? Lindy had not seen the inside of the room opposite the two women's bedroom, the room they hadn't opened for her. Even so, she would be able to identify it in the dark. It would smell like abandonment. Had Uhwa ever lived in a cave? The absurd thought came unbidden at the sight of Uhwa's closed bedroom door opposite the kitchen. Uhwa's den—talk about identifiable smells. No hurry, going in to speak to Uhwa could wait a few minutes.

The old women didn't know she was in the house, so Lindy took this chance to examine the two large, framed photographs that faced each other across the center hall. They were hung directly on the planed boards, no wallpaper on any wall. Oval frames and oval prints, a young woman and no doubt her young husband, in their finest clothes. The two might have been twins, with their thin faces and straight dark hair, the woman's pulled back tightly above her ears, his combed across. High stiff collars, blue eyes touched in by the same hand that had pinked-up the lean cheeks. The artist's rosy overlay did not hide the lines on their brows and at the corners of their eyes—the first warnings of the stern life ahead for nineteenth-century farmers, if that's what they were.

These were no kin of the old women. The young couple may have built the house; or perhaps they came here, alive or preserved in ovals, as part of the family that raised the house here. The house was holding these pictures up, saving the couple from burial in a tomb of fallen boards. Houses have their reasons to carry on after you write them off, Lindy thought. It was people who would disappear before you released them to go. The old women weren't of a mind to drop away. But they seemed to be too deeply caught up in the past to bother with the house as house. They used it, that was all, like riding a strong horse very slowly into the ground.

At the kitchen door Lindy didn't speak to Adhah but stood watching her stir one and another of the pots steaming on the wood stove. Adhah caught sight of her and pointed her wooden spoon. "Well, young lady." She took in a ponderous breath and straightened up without gaining any height. "Lindy!" she called. Seelah answered from the back porch, an echo of affirmation. Adhah gestured to the two cane-bottom chairs at the simple table. "Have a seat." She opened the stove and thrust in a piece of wood from the pile beside it.

"I love being out here," Lindy said. "Can we talk about Joeab and the boat?" She decided she would stay in the hall. The kitchen was full enough with just Adhah in it.

Adhah continued with her preparations. On the table the bags of flour and sugar and the blue can of Crisco sat unopened, where Lindy had set them months before. A few smoothed-down bills and several quarters lay beside the staples—the first proceeds of the vegetables and the only money the women had not refused. The more recent bag of coffee was there, too, that Lindy had brought out after the time she tried their herbal tea. A quarter-pound down after they boiled a saucepanful for her, the coffee would be a permanent staple before Lindy took another sludgy cup. It completed a tableau of cultural irrelevance worthy of Bea Moulton.

"You will take dinner?" Adhah asked. "I'm waiting on the bread."

"Thanks, no. I'll say hello to Uhwa and then I'll go." Bad timing.

The blast of heat when she opened the door to Uhwa's room was not so much overwhelming as it was implausible. The wood smell always sorted into today's burning, the more aromatic one, and the bitter, years-old component. Uhwa sat bent toward the television. As if she could have straightened up her rigid thin self, Lindy thought.

"Dear Uhwa. I'm not in a rush today, so tell me what you know. Tell me every single thing you've ever found out." She was rubbing Uhwa's shrouded, bony back, the every-visit routine.

Uhwa's "Um-um" was almost answer enough. Uhwa's silence was not deafness, that was the tendency Lindy had to fight. Uhwa spent so much time by herself, the habit of conversation was bound to have suffered. Not getting answers from Uhwa was an entirely different feeling, compared with not getting answers from Gran. Uhwa was in there, Uhwa projected full intelligence disengaged— Lindy's fault also, she felt, for posing questions that were yes-no, or impossibly broad. Someday, though, someday.

The other chair in the room was piled with bedclothes; Uhwa was set for winter when it should come. But that meant no place for Lindy to sit down, except the bed, and the bed somehow wouldn't do. Nor would it do to be closer to the fireplace. Lindy knelt beside Uhwa and took her hand. Uhwa, as she often did, began to hum softly.

"Now we're talking. Let me try some names on you. Squeeze my hand if they remind you of anything. Babel? Babel-ah? Nimrod? Shem? Ham?" Uhwa was in fact squeezing Lindy's hand, but rhythmically, comfortably.

The television, with its rabbit ears that had been so hard to find, sat on the oak chest of drawers in front of them. The same Channel 55 was on, TV church around the clock. The sound was the barely audible level Adhah had prescribed on the day Lindy brought it out.

"What are you so pleased about, stuck in that plastic box?" Lindy said to the image in its bishop-looking robe. He was wide and brown, and held a Bible high in one large hand while he pointed with the other. "At least you're not mad at us personally," she said. "You don't care if any of us out here are listening, do you?" Behind the preacher the deacons in dark suits nodded, That's right. "You're happy speaking your own language, and we can have ours. Uhwa and I took the wrong road out of Babel as far as you're concerned." Lindy was relishing this exchange, and to judge from the level of her droning, Uhwa was too. "Bah-bel-ah-umm? Babble at me, preacher man." The camera closed in on a woman in the congregation. Her head was going Yes, yes. A photograph, a slide, interrupted the action. It showed a prefab corrugated building overlaid with a logo: Dominion and Glory Tabernacle Tannehill Louisiana. It was a local video, not some celebrity Los Angeles healer.

Uhwa, rocking beside Lindy in the gloomy heat, was mixing syllables with her humming. That's not Louisiana talking, Lindy decided. Take away most of my teeth and leave me in here a couple of days, I'd be speaking in tongues, too.

Back at the kitchen Adhah had three places set, each with a deep plate and a tarnished tablespoon and a cup, before the two chairs. From the stove she was serving another plate, almost a bowl, presumably for Uhwa. How many total motions did it take to make such a meal?

"I really don't need anything," Lindy volunteered from the hall. Especially not to make them eat in shifts.

Joeab ducked past Lindy into the kitchen. Adhah murmured to him and pointed to the plate between the chairs. Joeab, a member of the household, apparently. And neither of the women had said a word about him being present. He was inspecting a pan of what might be cornbread, if cornbread could be that grassy shade of green, and he was, in Lindy's judgment, too close to the hot stove. She retrieved him into the hall.

"There we are," she said. He leaned easily against her.

"Do you know about Mrs. Thomason, who takes care of Joeab?" she asked Adhah. "Every time he comes out here, he basically has to run away from home. You're driving his mother kind of wild." Joeab smiled up, yes to all of that. How hard could she push these sweet, maybe not so sweet women? They certainly might have mentioned that Joeab was here.

"One for each," Adhah said, holding out two offerings she had assembled. A split square of bread for Lindy, half that for Joeab, both dripping with a dark filling. Lindy was reminded of her grandmother Caton's vintage fig preserves, so outstanding they could never be opened. Whatever the filling was, it tasted like those preserves. Not like figs, like ten years old. She ate hers and helped Joeab not to spill his. Delicious for all that.

Seelah had been commenting from the back porch, short declarative sentences between spells of pounding and grinding. Dinner smelled good; this was a good batch; could they hear the kingfisher? Two old women, always working, forever together, and still something to talk about.

"Send Joeab on out here," Seelah called. "I've found him a toy."

Lindy guided the boy out. A wooden tray and a pestle—Seelah was reducing a heap of desiccated green and white root to coarse flour. She turned, beaming, to Joeab. "Listen, baby." Seelah shook two saber-curved okra pods next to Joeab's ear and held them out for him to grasp. He took one in each hand. "Mine thing," he said, and shook them tentatively. "Thank a 'Lah." Seelah bent back to her task.

Looking past the two gardens in the direction of the lake, Lindy wanted to say Fishing, and Boat, and Joeab Must Not Go Out In That Boat; and I'm Not Supposed To Be the One That Has To Fuss.

"Eshana says Joeab talks all the time about a black boat."

"Oh, the black boat, yes. It's one of his favorites."

"He prefers going out in the black boat?" One of?

Seelah laughed. "Not in the black boat. Weren't many invited in the black boat. Not us, for certain."

"No black boat? It's just another story?"

Seelah shook her head, no.

"Joeab, honey, you want to go with me to the lake?"

Seelah glanced up from her pounding. "Why would you go down there? You'll mess up your boots."

"I go with me," Joeab said. He jumped down the steps and continued to Lindy's garden, where he compared his toys with the baby pods on the okra plants until Lindy arrived and directed him past it.

"Keep an eye on him," Seelah said to their backs.

There it was when they got there, a flat-bottom aluminum skiff dragged to shore alongside a long log. Not black, but peeling green paint. Inches of water in it, no oar, only the tag end of a rope. Somebody's third-string boat that drifted in from some distant shore.

"This is not the black boat?" As if he could make something up.

"Fish boat," Joeab said. "Here." He handed her his okras, and with surprising balance jumped onto the log and out along it. He stood teetering on the log and rubbing his sticky hands together, dislodging the remaining crumbs of his bread down into the water. The project was helped by his being barefoot.

"Joeab! Get back here!" But he was already climbing into the boat. "We fish," he said when he was seated.

She retrieved the boy, a process that required her to balance on the log and gesture to him to slide toward her on the boat seat and lift him up; and that because it was carried out in silence except for his giggles and her sighs, made Joeab happier and Lindy more frustrated. To her it felt like wrestling, even though Joeab's resistance entailed only wanting Lindy to pay attention to the dimpled shallow water, and pulling an arm free to point toward the open water, and generally holding back—Lindy guiding him, at times tucking him under her arm, until they were on their way back to the house. Easy to wish a boat scuttled, not so easy to make it disappear back to wherever it drifted in from. Necessary, for once, to wish a boy could mature.

"I need both of you to hear this," Lindy said to Adhah, once again at the kitchen, with mud-spattered Joeab consigned to the back porch.

"Seelah is giving Uhwa her dinner," Adhah said from the stove. Seelah had not been on the porch, and indeed two voices were coming from Uhwa's room.

"You listen, then. How do you account for that boat down there?"

"It's a skiff, of metal," Adhah said. "We use it. Won't you eat?"

"Sometimes even I—careless old women!—I'm taking Joeab home."

But he was no longer on the porch, and neither was he at the lake. Surely there had not been time for him to drown, no, clearly not. Lindy ran back to the house one more time. Seelah and Adhah were eating, seated at the table, the third plate removed.

"Did he come through here?" Lindy was panting. Joeab's okras were in her hand.

"He's gone home," Adhah said. Seelah studied Adhah's expression, and turned the careful look toward Lindy. "Of course he has," she said.

But it didn't take long to spy him up ahead on the road through the squatters community with its rife insistent plantings and its propped-up mailboxes. Old people in their gardens looked on with interest. "He's going home," one of them said as Lindy passed.

Joeab looked around impishly when Lindy caught up with him. He was carrying his shoes; his socks showed in his pockets.

"You know how much you scared me? Here's your toy." What exactly had he done, though, that any small boy wouldn't want to do? And who had taken him to the lake, just now? "You can't come back along here as long as there's that boat."

"Okay, Windy." Perfect lisping clarity. "No boat."

No boat. That was it. Lindy could move the boat herself. She had handled skiffs, she knew how to paddle, and paddles were for sale all over Acheron.

"Let me call your momma." The cell was in her pocket.

Eshana was immediately on speaker phone, a three-way discussion, greetings between mother and son, puzzlement solved. Eshana was in control, telling Lindy to take Joeab back to Mrs. Thomason's house, Lindy happy to relinquish the role of mother. Sure, she would walk with him, they could visit better that way. Joeab talking toward the telephone, a bigger voice than usual. Maybe he was growing up, a little.

"You know the boat?" Lindy said to Eshana early in the exchange. "Trust me, I'll take care of the boat."

Lindy occupied one of the two ladder-backed chairs on the old women's front porch. She was back at the house after moving the boat and hiding it. And why not, given that she had ended up a bare hundred yards away from their property? She was satisfied with her work, if scratched and bug-bitten from her emergence from the woods by the shoreline.

The softening light eased the harshness of the plain yard and the dead-end asphalt street, and spoke to Lindy's mood of relief and of guilt. Seelah, who was taking up half the bench against the wall, concentrated on her knitting. There were no stops to her needles, Lindy noticed, only two thin metal dowels. If you whittled away the wood from a couple of eraserless pencils, you'd be left with something like that.

True to her promise to Eshana, Lindy had moved the boat. After the long hike back from Industry City, she had retrieved her truck from the women's place without going inside again. She had selected a classy, long-handled paddle at the hardware store, after she went to her apartment and changed into jeans—time out first to call her dad, who reported no new symptoms, and had been feeling well enough to run some of his favorite errands. She had left the paddle. A brand-new paddle might make the derelict skiff more appealing to whoever ran across it—certainly would make it easier for a claimant to take it away. But maneuvering among the cypresses and the water weeds had been not so easy, more of pushing against trunks than straight paddling, which in any event she had forgotten how to do. A hundred yards had been an achievement, and landing the boat among the cypress knees without having to wade, a slow process.

Lindy had described to Seelah the safe return of Joeab to his day care, and the satisfaction of having talked to Eshana about how things would be better, and how Eshana was feeling better, up to a point. She had not mentioned the removal of the boat, and had not quoted Eshana: no "those gray-skinned creatures."

"Don't you worry, though, about little boys and deep water?" she asked now. "He's, you know, fragile." A safe enough topic, with her mission accomplished.

Seelah's repair job, rebuilding one side of an old skirt, didn't require her to look down, except occasionally to select a new thread of yarn from the pile that lay on the bench next to her. She kept her eyes on Lindy, but as usual when Eshana was the subject, she was hardly answering. Which was beginning to be all right. Sitting in the twilight was restful enough that solving problems seemed pointless.

"We make him sit still," Seelah said, pulling a thread. "The mother. We understand Joeab's worth."

"So do I," Lindy said. "That's why I came back by, to apologize for how I spoke. You and Adhah are good for Joeab." Especially now that I stole your boat.

"Joeab's gift, he brings goodness. To us, to Uhwa." Seelah held her work up and inspected it in the gloom, and started in again to knit. "Another blessing—his purity will never abandon him."

Lindy formed a picture of a painting, Joeab on a donkey with Eshana walking alongside and elevated expressways in the background: *The Flight to Atlanta.*

"I'll be right back," she said. Her lower legs were burning— these porch mosquitoes were more experienced than lake mosquitoes. She dashed to the truck and retrieved the skin lotion that was useless except as bug repellent, that unlike the chemical spray didn't hurt her skin more than the mosquitoes would.

"It's so pleasant, when the day turns down to simmer," she said when she returned. Her shoes were off and she was slathering her feet and ankles. From somewhere in the black-green shadows beyond the yard, a sweet night-blooming fragrance ventured out early and began to compete with the dimestore smell of the lotion.

"Rest, the beginning of the day," Seelah said. "Good thing your wagon has lanterns on it."

Lindy watched the miniature needles waggle between Seelah's slow thick fingers, fingers that hardly moved as they paid out the thin thread, invisible now in the gloom. That kind of handwork, done in that patient way—so relaxing to be out here just now. Her bites were hardly stinging. Peace, even on the Joeab front.

Seelah's calm confusion about the time of day, and her calling the truck a station wagon, put Lindy in mind of the conversations Stone recounted to her from his internship during the last year of their marriage—his exchanges with mental patients, about nothing much, passing time without a sense of time passing. That would have to be the main benefit of being crazy. Not that Seelah was talking crazy, that ugly, imprecise word. Stone's career swerve had been to resign his pastorate in Little Rock and sign on as a clinical pastoral intern at the state mental hospital. The chaplain trainees were not allowed to get close to the patients who were roaring, and the silent ones were useless for training chaplains on. Stone and the other interns were steered to the patients who, despite the illness and the drugs, wanted to work on their spiritual lives. The thing was, he couldn't abide hearing anyone but himself discuss Jesus in any form. So she pictured Stone, the nascent chaplain, constantly changing the subject away from religion. Every evening he would recount hospital conversations about nothing at all, laying them at her feet like a cat bringing his mistress a whole series of plastic mice. It fit with their catatonic marriage situation. And all the while Stone was roaring inside himself. Look what I use my down time for, Lindy thought. Like the old song, Precious memories, how they linger.

Adhah emerged carrying a shallow bowl and a cup with no handle, and offered them to Lindy. "Just a few leftovers. A person has to eat or their strength will drip away."

Lindy accepted the cup and the bowl and leaned up slightly for the cheek-to-cheek greeting that came with them, another chance at reconciliation. The liquid in the cup was lukewarm and bitter, either soup or tea. She sipped a few swallows and set the cup on the floor. In the dusky light the overlapping mounds in the bowl were colorless; they had been various shades of neutral in full sunlight. She ferried the flavors up to her mouth one after another, the wooden spoon like the beak of a parent bird.

All were variations on boiled vegetable, but she couldn't quite identify them.

"Water salad. We got a nice mess," Seelah said, gesturing toward Lindy's food.

"We sometimes don't boil it," Adhah said. "It's fine either way." She had taken possession of the other half of the bench and was awkwardly kneading Seelah's shoulders with both hands.

"This is all good," Lindy said. "Didn't you catch anything today? Joeab was talking—"

"You wouldn't say catch," Seelah said.

"Pull," Adhah said, and chuckled. "That's all it takes. Greens don't generally run away."

"You don't chase fish. I knew that." Too bad about the end of the old women's hunting for water salad.

"Do you?" Adhah asked. "Swallow every breathing object?"

Lindy had had this discussion before, with any number of people. The best public list of prey for a carnivore was no list. The monotone supper was crying out for a piece of Gran's fried chicken, a juicy thigh, a greasy back, a chewy gizzard.

"A bad habit, but I haven't been trying to quit. I used to have a theory, but never mind." The theory, though she wasn't going to describe it, had been that predator behavior required real protein for its execution. Predator behavior was not all about running down prey. Predatory included aggressive acts such as appropriating somebody else's boat, acts leading maybe to saving a boy's life. On further consideration that was nonsense, wasn't it, as far as fuel was concerned. Just the same, she wanted more chicken, for a start. Fricasseed for the perfect gravy, or roasted with rosemary, or barbecue sauced. Seafood sauteed, broiled, poached—mix and match—shrimp, crabs, squid, fish; oysters and scallops and mussels, anything that sank or swam—no, not the mammals, no manatees. An obvious inconsistency within the quadrupeds, too: no house pets. Game? Hungry or not, she felt the list dissipating. How about songbirds?—remembering the time she shared a breakfast of toasted grackles and scorched potatoes some boys from her neighborhood cooked up over their backyard campfire. Flaming marshmallows for dessert. She poked with the spoon at the runny residue of Adhah's vegetables and thought of food unwashed, of food sitting in the old house for months and years. Cutworms, beetles, weevils, silverfish—another list, of animals with no partisans.

"I judge you were born without the habit," Seelah was saying.

"That they were cooped up with the animals amounted to an excuse," Adhah said through the gloom. "No question about it."

"Not even if they were beside themselves inside the boat," Seelah said, "because the dry land was bound to come back." She folded and refolded the fabric in her lap, pushed the needles farther in. "They might easily have stopped."

"Boat or no, it was the same as before, once the water went home," Adhah put in. "Only they never thought so."

"It wouldn't much grow. Enough, though, even right at first." Seelah was telling this directly to Lindy. The porch was in near-darkness. No light came from the house, the TV's glow was stoppered in the room where Uhwa must be sleeping. The nearest mercury lamp formed a bluish dot way up the road.

Lindy's spoon, amazingly, had delivered a salty bite. She had thought they didn't use it. "Salt," she said.

"Saltberries," Adhah said. "We like to mash them up separate."

"No, I mean the salt. Not much grows in salty dirt."

Both of them were nodding. Let me in, she thought. Or at least show me how you do it. "So it just started to rain?" she asked.

Adhah laughed softly through her nose, two or three airy sniffs. "No. Seelah tells it best," she said. "I don't know why I'm laughing, it wasn't anything funny about it." Seelah began to gather herself to stand, but Adhah put out her hand. "I know it's getting on, and we're all tired. Tell her about the boats. The part you say to Joeab, at least."

"If you can," Lindy said. "It's early." Did that sound as perverted to the women as eating meat did?

"The water was salty, all right," Seelah began cheerfully.

"Quietly, dearest. Night is here." Adhah's voice was soft. "And not the water right away, you need to start with the black barn. Don't dwell on the bad parts."

"You tell it," Seelah said. She didn't sound irritated.

Adhah whispered hoarsely, "This is the story of how we came to be travelers." She cleared her throat. "It starts with that, I almost forgot."

"It starts," Seelah said, "any way a person wants it to start."

Lindy held her breath, but Seelah went on. "'This is how we came to be travelers' is Uhwa's version. It's as good a way as any."

Lindy's eyes were adjusted to the light. She could see faces again. Seelah's look was mischievous. She leaned toward Lindy and spoke in a stage whisper, "Uhwa's version is Uhwa's version. It's not my version. At the time I blamed our husband's son. Well, who else would you blame, him hogging the great huge boat? Uhwa blames her oldest son, always will. For the whole thing, and a lot more to boot. Which we never could understand at all. It's caused no end of trouble, if you ask me."

"Why not hog it," Adhah sighed, "since none of us seen it was a boat. Go ahead and tell it—make over Uhwa's start to it." She sighed again, less softly. "Blame."

"Joeab likes to hear about the big boat," Seelah said to Lindy. "I give him bits and pieces, us in the water, and how we pulled through. He loves to hear those parts."

Lindy realized her eyes were closed. Had she dozed? Was it one of the vegetables, something they routinely ate in order to be able to sleep at sundown? Speech was an effort, but she was determined to hear the story.

"Pretend I'm Joeab."

"I'm fixing to go on inside." Adhah was already up. "Here I got us started palavering, and I'm heading to bed. I got less stomach for hearing it again, than I thought I did."

"Wait, never mind," Lindy said. "I can go." But she didn't feel like standing. The straight chair, at that moment, was the most secure place in the world.

"You don't move, young lady," Adhah said. "You're counting on hearing it. You want to get a good story. You and Joeab are just the same."

"I could tell it like it was me seeing it, but Uhwa saying it." Seelah raised her voice toward Adhah, who had made her way to the door and continued inside without answering. Seelah waited a moment, then leaned forward toward Lindy conspiratorially. "But Uhwa's way leaves out what she doesn't like to hear, and puts in half the people that never lived. I'd rather my way, which I believe won't take us the whole time till the sun gets up.

"It was full black, all right. And full square—to this day Adhah doesn't believe it was supposed to be a boat." In spite of her attention to speaking quietly, Seelah's voice changed as she began to tell the story, its pitch rising and its timbre becoming more musical.

Lindy woke to Seelah's altered voice. She realized she had dropped off—Adhah was gone and Seelah was into the story. But surely the lost interval, between "counting on hearing it" and "supposed to be a boat," hadn't been more than a second or two. She struggled to concentrate. Seelah's composed speech soothed her like the public radio news that waked her before dawn and, after she reached to turn down the volume, sent her drifting down for a last nap—not the anxious content, but the stream of practiced syllables, a comforting flow that drowned her worries.

It was full black all right. And full square—to this day Adhah don't believe it was supposed to be a boat. Black, because—much as we call him that—he was no boatmaker. I'm talking about our husband's son—had him by the next wife, that followed on us. Anybody could see the boatbuilder didn't trust his men's work either. Who would of, they weaving it together out of reeds and branches, working quick as they could, piling up that great huge thing. Give them credit, they dressed wood for the insides and the top. And when they came up with tar, and coated the outside—and, people said, smeared the insides the same black? Well. Even painted the bottom—which might have tipped us off, the way they built it on top of those stacks of logs. It bulked there, dark and ugly and wide in every direction. The river wouldn't have held it.

If you'd have met him, he wasn't one to carry off such a grand scheme. Except by then he was rich. After his granddaddy died—that was our husband's daddy, he like to never died—he got the land, and money in plenty. And, oh gracious, servants. Every last one of them set up to perish. The boatbuilder started them in on erecting what he was the only one knew was a boat, and he sent his overseer out with another bunch, and they began to wander back with different strange four-legged animals. When the contraption was ready, he took to keeping his livestock inside. It made a good enough barn, but absolute dark, bound to been. I wouldn't have lit a torch in there.

Wasn't he proud, though? His own house was plenty nice, but you would have thought the black monstrosity was a palace. Folks took the situation as comical—not us, because he didn't see to Uhwa. Did he care that she was his many-times grandma? No dealing with him, not to mention his main wife being an Erechite. Which meant the wife was kin to those men our husband had stabbed—a sad affair, all of them drinking together, and our husband the one left standing. By the way, that business was why our husband didn't inherit. Not that we would have been in on it. So the old man's property went to his grandson the boatbuilder, so-called. Made him worse to drink; he surpassed his daddy, even. And the tarred pile standing next to the river.

All of that sounds like we were studying those people, but we didn't. Nor talk to our husband either, him having divorced us long before for some reason or other—all the same we hated it that he never came out of the water. We lived our lives. Uhwa was still in her strength. And me and Adhah, we've always had each other.

Well, it was the sea that brought the water. The winds weren't a party to it—not a regular sea storm, more like the ocean had a belly-ache. We were the only ones awake to see it, and we didn't see much, not at first. About exactly as dark as it is right now, when the sea swelled up and came our way before first light. The three of us had sneaked down to the river early—against the rules, but which no doubt saved us. We were standing in the water, washing our clothes. Everybody else was inside asleep. And here it came under the moon. The first thing we knew the marsh grass was slick gone, the river running the wrong way, the sea lifting in a trice, and us under it.

The new water was as warm as a person. You couldn't feel if you had arms and legs. Inviting us to a long sleep, but we declined—we found the top and got together. It was Uhwa who thought of untying our skirts from around our waists and using them like bladders. Of course she needed holding up more than we did, we've always been generous for size. And when it got light she's the one that grabbed hold of—I recollect it as a bench, about the size of this one I'm sitting on. Oh, property was swirling around us, people and animals floating up. The water had wrestled with all of them and won.

Then didn't it rain? The air was up and down green, the ocean trying to cement with the sky. We glimpsed the black thing not far off, sitting low in the water. Now then it was getting to act like a boat. The boatbuilder and that one wife and her brood, they had taken to spending nights in there, sleeping with the filthy stock. Her children, and only her children—now there's the kind of talk Adhah wants left out. Afterwards, the same children counted on us. So we knew when it buoyed up they were all in there. And we were alone in the water.

We smelled the other boat before we ever noticed it—fish. From under the side edge of it you could see the craftsman's skill, no tar necessary. Thin boards, curved around—sleek is the word. Joeab loves to hear how pretty that boat looked to us, and about how it had a skinny round timber in the middle, and about the old man in the boat grabbing down the sail and hauling us over the side. Once we were in, I almost preferred the water, the reek was that bad of killed fish.

As soon as we saw his face we knew he was Uhwa's people. And this old man was Uhwa's first son, Uhwa's son that killed his brother and ran off. Uhwa had told us the story many a time, of how he threw his brother down and stomped all the life out of him. And taking no notice that their mama was standing there watching. Neither one of them barely more than a boy.

You'd have thought this son would have been buried long since, all of that having happened before Adhah or me were born. And us— huh!—not young. But here he was with his boat. How come?, you might ask. All I can say is, Uhwa. There's much passes between those two. Now Uhwa's husband was long since laid away. And Uhwa's other sons and this son's sons, all of them no doubt about it, gone. Our husband who disappeared in the water—that they didn't invite on the boat; never mind us women, how could he let his own daddy die?—our husband was the umpteenth-grandson of him that plucked us out of the water. I believe that's right. Or it may be Uhwa's son is only our husband's uncle, way back. Uhwa won't talk about it, and Uhwa's son doesn't have no way to know, does he? We never saw any of our own children again.

You're wondering why I keep not saying his name. Well, we have no idea of his name. Uhwa's mum on the matter. She gave it to him, she took it back. Everybody knows her husband's name, but we go along with her and call him the man. The son has no interest in his offspring, that's for certain. His concern is to torment his mama. But now I'm way ahead of myself.

There in the boat, Uhwa and her son went at it, disputing till their voices were ragged. It was sad to watch. He pulled her out of the water, I'll always believe that's what attracted him. And he saved us too. We welcomed this man as our husband's kinsman. But not Uhwa, she wanted to go on about how this oldest son was still alive—still in his body, she'd say—and her second son, had to leave his—body, I mean— and if he hadn't, she said, maybe nobody would have ever had to die. And how the second son was the spotless, the best one. No doubt he was, we tell Joeab about him. Yet and still, life is for the living. Uhwa doesn't see it, she doesn't draw a fine line between the living and the dead.

They contended about all of that, and more. He gave as good as he got—better, there's never been stronger a one to argue than Uhwa's oldest son. But then, who did he get that from?

Uhwa stopped debating—she about clammed up. Except for whispering advice to the other son. That's right, he was with us, so she declared as soon as we were out of the water. Said he was the one made his brother bring the boat around—she didn't give the oldest son the least credit. For his part, that one wasn't denying that the younger son was in Uhwa's head, only that Uhwa was wasting everybody's patience by talking about it. I'm all for family, but you can get too much of it. I never yet met the second son.

Us three women kept close together, up in front of the sailcloth but turned backwards away from the rain. When misery is that steady you all but get used to it. We could see the old son the whole time. He would study his mama, him sitting at the back by the tiller. He'd sail most of the daylight, taking his clues from the winds, which I don't imagine the winds had their bearings either. Nights we'd drift. Light would arrive and prize our eyes open, and he's staring at her, and he'd start in again. First-born this and full-appreciation that—as if the world was made for anybody to lord over. Uhwa would make a face sometimes at his version, and she'd grind her teeth, but she kept still, she never took the bait he trolled.

Between rounds of making his case, he gradually told us his life. No hurry, was there? He told how his wife died and he took to the sea, where all he'd been and how many scrapes he'd come through all unscathed—according to him, nothing can touch him. How he learned to make a boat as big as you like before he settled on this kind he could handle by himself. No sticks nor branches. And how he got to be a peril not just to brothers but to fish.

One thing leads to another. When it was over the ones that rescued themselves kept on murdering the stock they had in their charge. That's when they began to sacrifice varieties of animals to their appetites.

Right about here, Adhah would say they no more saved themselves from the water than the rest of them died on purpose. They were every one of them inside, she says, and one of the houses just happened to float. According to her there's no blame in the black boat, that's how she worked it out. I say look at how he treated Uhwa beforehand, and look how they did the animals that were their passengers.

And we're no better. Eating was not a problem at first, so much on top of the water and we gathered enough of it with his net, a pretty sorry net but I wasn't going to mend it for him. Round fruits and berries still bright, and leaves—but soggy, we gave most of it back. Later on it was nothing for us but seaweeds. The main thing, he had his urns; we kept quite some of the rain. Toward the end—Adhah, when we talk together, won't let me tell this—we'd take the green matter the old son found inside the fish he dragged in. And we ate that. We figured we'd never see land again, but that doesn't excuse it.

This one day—it hadn't stopped raining, so this was early on—we drifted towards a piece of ground the sea had not consumed. A sight to freeze your blood. There was a great crowd of people on that little bit of hill. I say drifted, it may be the fisherman brought us there, him and the ocean being business partners. Adhah and me asked him to move us

*in, but he wouldn't do it, he stood off. He said the water wasn't finished
and it would take this peak shortly.*

*Everybody was facing toward the water. It seemed like they couldn't
see us. And the rain was coming down hard. Sure enough, the whole
place was sinking. Before he took us away, we watched them, we couldn't
help it. The ones at the top, they had their boxes and their bundles. The
closest ones, the water was starting to wrap around their legs. They
didn't step back, none of them. Not a one of them registered the boat; I
reckon they had already seen enough. Because of the rain you couldn't
make out their faces. Just the same I feel like I saw their eyes. And us
both begging the fisherman to ride in closer—there were bound to been
babies in there. And him already turning the boat.*

*After the sinking hilltop our voices left us—the rest of us I mean,
Uhwa had shut down awhile back. The old son ran out of stories,
which tells it all, bad as he is to repeat himself. Finally Adhah and I
couldn't find a word worth sharing. Just sitting. The rain tied off and
lifted away, and we didn't see another living being. Apart from fish, of
course.*

*Well, no. A strange thing, I forgot. There was a bird. Now and
again it would come into sight, with its long wide wings and that heavy
body. We'd spy it shaving over the water, and we'd watch it get small, a
dark dot, and nobody saying a word. It wasn't like any sea bird I ever
saw.*

*And twice more, the tarred boat. Once toward the end of the
rain—this was soon after the standing people—we practically hit it.
Woke us up, we could feel it squatting like a hole in the night. Uhwa's
son straightaway arranged his sail and we left. If the hill quieted us
down, after that nobody spoke a word. Oh, Uhwa would weep, now
and again. The other time was a long span later. You could make it out,
far off at the bottom of the sky. We never did ask the ones who crouched
inside the black boat what they saw.*

The days went by. I won't say how many—we had no use for count-

*ing once we stayed on the fisherman's boat. We all slept, Uhwa slept
most. And she was older when those days were finished that we sat on
top of the sea.*

*Did the fisherman know where he was going to put us down?—he
was the one who found it. While he was helping us get to ground he
never spoke a word, but his eyes were pleading with his mama. If her
heart had wanted to soften, that would have been the place to do it. Because he's begged her plenty since then. Uhwa only closed her face, even
while he took her up and lifted her across to my arms. And she moaned
and cried out for her son. The fisherman rounded the boat away. Farther out he begin to declaiming again. We could hear him, making his
case to his mama. Then he was gone.*

*We skip all that for Joeab, quite naturally. We just say Uhwa's son let
us out at a good place. And he did. We stood on the dry land, and with
Uhwa we walked on the living earth. The ground had been drowned
silent. Now it got back a voice, by way of the fruits and greens and roots
that were given in plenty for Uhwa and the man.*

"We skip all that for Joeab, quite naturally," Seelah said. She
was speaking in the same musical way, although her gesture seemed
to mean that the tale was completed. "We just say Uhwa's son let
us out at a good place. And he did. We stood on the dry land,
and with Uhwa we walked on the living earth. The ground had
been drowned silent. Now it got back a voice, by way of the fruits
and greens and roots that were given in plenty for Uhwa and the
man."

Seelah's voice regained its normal cheerful timbre. "That's it,"
she said. "You listen mighty quiet for a body that wanders the roads
at night."

CAIN'S VERSION: THE FLOOD

How did I know the sea was burgeoning, you ask, since all I could do was ride on top of it? That would be a good question if, when the surge came up, I hadn't been taken along, if I hadn't been shown the land being disposed of as quick and neat as throwing a cloth over a table. Nobody ever crafted a better boat than this present one of mine: sleek, responsive, kindly. It registers the least sea change, so I can sleep unsurprised. The first stirring woke me under an oval moon. By dawn the last of the shore was gone and I was steering among logs, some of them whole trees with their leaves still alert, and doors and furniture and pots bobbing among the mats of roofing thatch. And because of the season, flower petals were everywhere, yellow and blue and white, some of them clinging to the bodies of animals and of men and women and children. What a sight.

The effort that day required the whole of the ocean. My home sea, where I spend my days, could not have managed it. The first time I dared to wade in above my waist, and long before I started to explore it, I knew that the whole of the ocean is to the dregs—which is to say, to all the dry land—as the entire sky is to the lonely full moon. This must be the proportion, otherwise the foulness of the land would be the principal fact of the world. In my judgment the land does not float. I haven't unraveled the moon, and you are welcome to disagree about whether either one of them floats. No matter, the land is dung, and the ocean is the great hump-backed beast that stalks where it will. Yet this beast remembers its residents, even when it rages—no, not rage: when it reared up against the dry ground there was no fury, only a calm reaching, a verdict as necessary as when you crush a spider in your fist and toss it away.

Which when it did, was the gladdest morning of my life. What a privilege that was, to witness the ocean swat the land.

I don't take any credit for the flood, though I yearned for it. Consider the ocean's flows and its moods. Who can gauge its depths, or canvass its storehouses? Who can trace the breadth of its curvature—curving beyond sight, as a sailor knows from the different suns it generates, suns more various than any dirt farmer sees, who lives and dies in one place? It was not my wishing. It was more a matter of the ocean being patient.

There they were, three figures among many caught in the flood—my family, or so I thought. I don't know how I could tell from such a distance that one of them was Mama. People change their looks, but certain elements hang on, the line of the brow, the shape of her hair, wet as it was. I was already glad for the land going down, and now this gift. I felt rescued. But why would Daddy and Abel have their heads covered? That was backwards.

Then I saw that the other two were women. Two ponderous women floating easily, hardly needing to hold on to the narrow upside-down table, and Mama with her arms around one table leg as calmly as if she was expecting me.

–Where is Abel? I asked.

They were grabbing hold of the boat.

The big women, Seelah and Adhah are their names, looked at each other in the water and they stared at me with their pleasant round faces. I got them over the side, Mama first and easiest, she's always been thin. The other two, it was a job. They all three settled on the bottom of the boat, at the front, and were wringing out their skirts and not seeming to worry about Abel.

–Was he with you? I asked.

I set the sail and began moving us through the rubbish.

–Where's Daddy? I asked.

–You've forgotten what you did to your brother, Mama said.

–He was all right when I left him. Where did you three run off to? That was unnecessary.

–They have abandoned their bodies.

–Dead? You can't claim that. Surely they have found something to cling to, among all of this.

I wasn't going to say that Daddy might give up and let himself sink. Abel? His energy would save him, no matter how crooked his bad arm might be. I squinted around for the disturbance he would make. Those three hadn't moved from the keel—they didn't raise up and help me look. I scanned. Something was splashing a good way off, but it was only a man and woman that had tied themselves together, and they soon went under. The only other commotion, the whole day, would be a sea eagle beating on the surface, lifting off with a meal of fresh carrion.

–You broke Abel's body through and through, and he relinquished it, Mama was saying. –We took him to the place beside the garden, and laid what remained into the ground, alongside the almost-children. The man's husk I buried myself, in a quiet place I picked out.

—Buried? You threw dirt in Abel's eyes and into his mouth? Was he watching while you did it?

—And yet he is with me. The man keeps to himself, as he always did.

Abel dead. There was no way I could deny it. Long since I had prepared a speech, a greeting for Abel, an explanation and a new beginning. And now Abel was destroyed. The realization brought him back to my mind's eye. He was cowering on the ground, and the ground was lusting for him—had him close to itself. I watched the toes of my left foot curl back for protection against the blow that was coming. I felt the ground reaching up through me, and my leg draw back and lash out, and the ball of my foot connect with the side of his head, and the blood gush from his ear. I saw his smile freeze into a vacant gape. The ground wanted him more than we did.

—I annihilated him, I said.

But I never understood how until that moment.

—Annihilate? Mama said. —Is he a mosquito that you could erase him from the world? Is he a clump of grass, so shallow-rooted your hand could rip him away? Your eyes are yet Cain's eyes, the shape of your tongue is his tongue. Your body caused your brother's body to suffer, and me to grieve. Yourself, you slaughtered on that day. Why do you disturb us? If Death be present, he sails with you. Cain, though his body has pursued me and stands upright before me—Cain it is who is dead.

My mind was overflowing. Abel gone, Abel lost to reconciliation. Mama making no sense—had she refused my help, had she refused my hands around her waist, had she begged not to be lifted to life? How many days could they have lasted without me? What after all separates us—any of us—from annihilation? Not strength, not competence, not will, not acceptance, nor companions, nor robust living. Long life is postponement, not ratification.

115

The hated dependency once again washed over me, the longing, the incompleteness that had driven me to leave my wife at Nod. In my aching I almost wished I had perished with her. Mama dreamed of Abel. So what? So did I, of some other Abel than hers, of some other Abel than Abel had been. Clouds of false Abels, meaningless as vapor. I realized I was shouting all these things. I realized I was proclaiming death and denying dreams.

–You may scream at me, she said, as you did at your father. –But why on this occasion insult your brother? Is this how you treat him when he visits you?

–Abel visits? Look around you. Where is he?

–I need not look in order to see, she said from below the gunwales. –Your friend the sea is a murderer. You are a team, the two of you. The sea takes bodies. You would remove all else but the body.

I had gone too far, I knew that. I tried to say that I exaggerated, that Abel came in many guises to my dreams, just as I must into her dreams. I told her that I was not responsible for my own dreams, and still less for hers. She said I would never be through with abusing my brother, that my conversation was a wolf gnawing at its own intestines.

Far along the sea's downcurve an odd structure floated, that the sea's force had been insufficient to contain. I had watched it earlier, when it was nearer—a large built object, a squat blob formed of reeds and sealed over with pitch. A black turd expelled by the ground, it rocked listlessly on the swell.

I am at ease far from land, and only far from land. But this was too much of a good thing. Three women depending on me and no room for comfort, nor prospect of release, it grated. Adhah and Seelah, especially. Accommodating as they were, I could have done without two over-sized women, one tall and one short. One day I found us a prominence—not much of it was left showing—that might promise a place for settling the two women. Mama also, it would have been, since she was too peeved at me to be any kind of company. And besides, the three of them were bonded close, though the two wives were closest. As we approached, this hill too was sinking. The great crowd of people who had reached it were going under, row by row and without the least resistance. So the three women stayed with me.

Somewhere on the far side of vastness there was bound to be a dry place, some great tower, some mountain higher than any I had looked on. But which heading to search? The wind was as puzzled as I was; neither of us could get our bearings. He took us here and there, while I waited for my sadness to subside.

It didn't help that they were finicky eaters. For a while they gleaned what floated up from the recent fields. They would eat seaweed, and I found them sixteen varieties. But who can live on seaweed? With my throw net I could manage the occasional gull. The first one I nabbed caused us such a row, when I slit through the feathers and fingered for and offered them the half-formed eggs—an egg is not meat—that I quit casting for birds.

That was the last argument we had. An argument about meat—about flesh, and the meaning of flesh. They assume our actions can save us, but we are no better than a grab of sardines. Why then would the women shun animals and stray toward starvation? That was my point, and they didn't refute it. Adhah and Seelah wouldn't even take up the thread. Mama contended about the right way to eat, then she shifted back to Abel, and then to me. Nurture your flesh, she said. Swallow all the meat you can, she said. Batten your empty body, she said, and hasten from my sight.

After that nobody said anything for a great long while. By the manner of their silence, I judged that the other two did not disallow my views about Abel and dreams. I read that in their open faces.

I waited for a headland to set the women on. What arrived, after a long interval, was slimy low ground. I was forced to wonder about

117

the flood that rushed in to swallow the ground—had this side been lent by the far half of the ocean? Was it a great, slow sloshing, and would it come back on us? That was one possibility. To me it felt like a simple swelling, the ocean bowing its shoulders. A comforting dilemma. Either way, this had been only the first such deluge.

The women did not have to tell me what they wanted. I found an inlet and gave them over to their mud.

I needed one more exchange with Mama—until the next time—but she managed to look everywhere besides at me. Her mouth was moving, she was talking silently. I beached the boat and stepped over the side, and they handed Mama to me and I carried her to the edge of the sea. Even in my arms she was in conversation with Abel—Abel, who is dead. I helped her to stand, and still she could not see me whose muscle and resolve had preserved her. The other two joined her, and they thanked me. I do not doubt that they will thrive in their way. They are capable women, strong and competent. The years have not touched them. Mama is undiminished—a little diminished—but from that moment she depended on Adhah and Seelah. I believe that.

I pushed off and hopped in, and there I sat in the stillness, not ten lengths out. No purpose in raising the sail, it was as helpless as I. The women punched a triple trail of holes in the new muck and trudged out of sight.

Out of sight, the beach? Suppose it was the same land under the new soil. Suppose that the sea had done no more than to hold it under. Then it was drowned land. Images now came to me that I had not sent for. I'll admit I had pictured my wife's bones—the earth, her ally, releasing her bones into the first wave that washed over our house. But I had not pondered the garden, Mama's garden, being submerged. I had not considered that Abel might have been released from the ground, might be joined with the sea.

I rested, and considered whether the sea was disciplining the wind and me. I came close to picking up the oars, but that would have been to admit that the sea had deeded me back to the land. Then a breeze arrived, not apologetically but fresh and steady. The wind and I moved off, reassured, proud to have our strength back. Mama and the others hadn't turned around a single time, but I couldn't help looking over my shoulder. I saw soaked dirt, unrelieved except for their steady tracks, from the shoreline right up to the brow of the hills. Why would anyone choose mud?

As soon as I turned from the shore my dark mood lightened. The feeling of need began to dissipate. Abel was gone, I had to get that straight in my mind. I left him hurt. He could not recover. He died. His body—what little was left of it—had declined the sea's invitation and lay where they placed it, under the sodden ground and within sight of the slack vines and dripping limbs of the dead garden. I tacked across the breeze. The sail, as it crossed the hull, began to slap against the mast—applause for the sudden pod of porpoises that had arrived with their habitual rolling dance. Abel is not among them, I told myself. Abel will not surface and shake the spray from his hair and beckon me to join him for a swim. Only the wind is laughing. I formed the proposition: Abel is not swimming beneath my boat. I began the work of believing that.

CHAPTER 10

By the sweat of your face will you eat bread,
till you return to the ground;
for out of it you were taken.

Genesis 3:19

On the way from her office to lunch at O'Malley's restaurant across town, Lindy might have missed them, it was raining that hard. Seelah and Adhah, walking comfortably, emerging into the warm rain from under the marquee of a long-closed dry goods shop. She splashed a U-turn, pulled up at the brick sidewalk, and got out pushing open her striped golf umbrella. Soon they were all three crowded into the truck, not an inch to spare.

"How in the world did you end up here? I would have guessed that you never came to town."

"We were on our way back," Seelah said. Lindy could feel the wet of Adhah's shoulder against her.

"And the rain caught you. You walked all the way to town?" The truck bounced heavily through submerged potholes.

"No, a man invited us to ride," Seelah said. Neither of the women was looking at Lindy.

"A man in a car?"

"You'd say a car," Adhah said.

"He offered to take us home," Seelah said. "Put both of us on the back bench, and went the wrong way from where we needed to go. Then he got loud about the money. And made us get out, you saw us."

"Money can be a good thing, sometimes," Lindy said. "And he brought you to a bad part of town, because he was mad. I'll carry you home. Was anything painted on the car?" Lindy glanced at the women's profiles for any sign of distress.

"He said he had to find some paying work," Adhah said. "And he told us to get out. It's nice you were there."

No hint of worry about finding their house. Did they navigate by the earth's magnetic field? She had known country people who could not get lost. From years of walking around in the woods, she supposed. Her stomach, which had forced her away from the keyboard, was in the driver's seat. She had made the turn toward O'Malley's, the lunch place. The two women seemed content, packed together with the windows rolled up against the rain. Something got them into that taxi. Where had they been that a taxi could even approach them?

"You weren't far from your house? You were just being nice, to accept a ride."

"Not far, at first," Adhah said. "We know some of the people along Joeab's road."

"Restless," Seelah said. "And we kept walking a good long way. We need to see how things are changing. So the man and his car were a gift. You are too." She was shifting, tugging at a few of her skirts. The effort forced Adhah closer against Lindy.

"You were worried, all of a sudden this morning? Yesterday and last night, you were okay."

"Neither one of us could sleep," Adhah said. "That befalls us sometimes—" "When a thing clamps onto our hearts," Seelah continued.

I threatened you with taking away Joeab forever, Lindy said to herself. I did take away your boat, your one entertainment. I messed up your sleep, and I got a nap while you practically acted out the flood story. I got you all worked up. At least I can buy your lunch.

"At the verge, we've been there before," Seelah said. "It's been the nights for a while now."

"Don't fret in the least about us," Adhah said. "And dear one, don't you fret her about us. She has her own concerns."

"Isn't it awful chill in here?" Seelah asked. Lindy slid the air conditioner tab to off, and the windows immediately began to fog.

"Was it anything about the boat? I don't mean the black story boat. Did you know your boat is gone?"

"We saw it's not there. Everything begins to signify," Seelah said. "I dreamed about a boat."

Adhah cleared her throat, apparently to close the subject, since neither of them spoke for a while.

Lindy changed her mind. Lunch would have to be someplace that treated vegetarians better than O'Malley's did. At O'Malley's salad involved fried oysters. She would take them to Norris's cafeteria, where they did vegetables the old-fashioned way. Then she would take them home. The cafeteria was only a few miles, out on the new bypass. Liver and onions for her, or the everyday turkey and dressing—some dish she never ate anymore. Rubbing the inside of the windshield, she wondered how long Uhwa could stay by herself.

"You need some dinner, after all your traveling around. Uhwa's okay? She can manage?"

"Uhwa don't always plan to eat dinner," Adhah said. "She'll most probably doze. She can get herself in the bed if she gets cold."

"We built up the fire, and we left her a cup of water where she knows to reach it," Seelah said. She leaned around toward Lindy and winked. "And your picture box for company."

"Last night you said 'Uhwa's way of telling.' Where do the stories come from, that they're so vivid? Your people are not from the mountains?"

"Not exactly," Adhah said. "Look at all these bridges, right over the fields."

"Because Appalachian people are great storytellers," Lindy said. "My people don't embroider much, when it comes to anything about the past."

"Uhwa knows stories that nobody will ever hear again," Seelah said. "But be careful what you tell yourself." Perhaps in protest Adhah began to sing one of her melismatic tunes, a repeating three-tone figure.

"Sometimes you tell your story like it was made up, and it costs you," Seelah repeated. She was looking from Lindy to Adhah. "We have to keep alive how strong Uhwa was."

At the cafeteria parking lot the last of the noon crowd, toothpicks like antennas at the corners of their mouths, were emerging into the early afternoon humidity. Lindy led the way after helping the women heavily down to the pavement. She held open the glass door while they approached. Adhah stopped short, rolled her eyes, and mouthed, "My." Seelah, a dozen feet back, appeared to be wilting.

"What is it, Adhah?" Lindy asked. "Is Seelah all right?"

"You can't tell those flavors?"

To Lindy what came from inside the cafeteria was a bouquet of important Southern aromas. That bouquet—Lindy had not planned on Seelah and Adhah paying attention to the mangled animals. She only expected them to walk into the effluvium and push trays past the carnage, and sit beside Lindy while she washed down her favorite body parts with unsweetened tea. The vegetables too were in complicity—that's what she had forgotten, the real gaffe—lying in stainless steel pans and lapping the juice of corpses. A slaughterhouse conveyor slid through Lindy's mind, red forequarters with sawed-through ribs, scalded hairless heads and hacked hooves, and her own meal tray riding along surrounded by the gore. Her stomach tightened, but it was hunger, stronger at this moment than any virtual disgust.

"I know another place." Ruth Keyser's house, back to town, only a few blocks from the coffeehouse. Lindy more or less reversed their course. Everybody sat recovering from the cafeteria.

"The couple in the hall," Lindy said as they came down from the elevated north-south interstate. "I looked at them." Had they brought elaborate stories from the Blue Ridge?

"That's Miss Johnson and her brother," Adhah said. "They took us in, back then, the three of us." Seelah picked up, "Just the two of them in that whole house. He was soon enough gone, a fever. Before he died he would take us around in his buggy like you're doing, he would show us everything."

"We ended up taking care of her," Seelah said. "The rain has wandered off, can you open this window pane?" She was pushing against the window. Lindy lowered both windows, and they breathed outside air.

"Miss Johnson left you the house?"

"We were left in the house." Adhah said. "I wish you could raise one of them windows. It seems like it's not as warm down here, as it used to be."

"It would snow back then, you know. We won't change, unless it would be to get cold." Seelah was frowning at Adhah.

The women's accents, while they remembered the Johnsons, seemed to have shifted, their mouths slightly altered. Like me, Lindy thought, when I'm at Lubie's house and her twang infects my ears. "There's always the Southwest, have you been? The desert has absolutely filled up with people."

"Oh no," Adhah said. And Seelah, "We hope we can stay."

They hoped they could stay—a whole subject that Lindy had not considered. Except for themselves, the women had no resources for their last days. She imagined that they wouldn't move Uhwa, probably wouldn't summon a doctor whatever should happen. What had driven them to go walking around this morning? Might they consider leaving after Uhwa was no longer there—if they were strong enough?

"This morning, last night?" Oh, here was Mrs. Keyser's. "Let me see if she cooked today." Lindy ran up to the porch of the three-story frame monster that had been Ruth Keyser's boardinghouse, and rang the bell and stood back to wait. In this neighborhood the sun was going strong. A finger of cloud pointed to the northern horizon, as if the sky had burned down to ashes. And here came Adhah and Seelah resolutely up the concrete steps to the yard and the wooden ones to the porch, Seelah managing with dignity, Adhah leaning forward to push, hand to thigh, step, up, step. Ruth Keyser opened the screen door.

"Remember me, Mrs. Keyser? Lindy Caton? Michelle brought me a couple of times? This"—gesturing—"is Adhah and this is Seelah, my friends, they're in town today. They live out past Industry City."

"Call me Ruth, Lindy, I told you that," the elderly woman said. "Ziller. Aider—I always call it with that long *a*. Youall come on in the house—flies. I started out here convinced you was Bobby. I'm always expecting him at dinnertime, or afterwards for a bowl of cobbler. He's my son, he's Robert Keyser Power Sports on the Marksville Road. Kawasaki."

This good woman, Lindy thought, goes around believing she's still five and a half feet tall. And she would be, provided you ran the tape measure along her bent back and almost horizontal neck, and added an allowance for arthritis-bowed legs. The front of her shirtwaist dress grazed the floor. Ruth—Lindy decided to think of her that way, rather than as Mrs. Keyser—looked at Seelah and Adhah and they looked at her. Not a bleary gaze in the crowd: six sharp, deep-brown unaided eyes. Ruth's face, translucent pinkish crepe over slender jowls, with more smooth snowy patches than scaly age spots, spoke of sun avoidance and daily lotion and elderly weight loss. If she took exception to the other two's weathered peasant features, dotted with fleshy wens, or to the strong odor of wet straw that remained from their soaking, she wasn't registering it. Boardinghouse proprietors no doubt had sat at table with odder than whatever the next customer could be.

They stopped in the wide hall that led to the sweeping stairway while Ruth Keyser narrated the architecture of the house, and her personal history. The first time Michelle brought Lindy here, Ruth had given the same speech. Widowed young, Ruth Keyser had turned her large house to good use, as many another woman had in an era before each citizen required a thousand square feet to live in. How many years had it been since the last boarder slept in one of the many bedrooms upstairs? No traveling salesmen made this their base of operations, no woodsmen nor lone bachelors, no men—men only had been the rule—with men's expectations. Ruth was free to satisfy her pure old self. She had banished flesh and bone, whether laid out or rendered for broth or stock. The son she always mentioned must indulge her bias. What remained of her recipes—blanched and steamed, or boiled and simmered for hours, the simple lost magic of salt and black pepper and onions and butter—provided enough variety to dazzle a highway crew if they should show up, if the world had not long since forgotten her existence.

"Michelle's over in Texas this week," Lindy said. She realized that might be the last word she got in. You would think a person would finally run out of talk. Ruth, to the contrary, was on track to wring a hundred cents from her life's conversation dollar.

126

"At her uncle Dub's, that's right," Ruth said. "If you're looking for something good to eat," she added, burying her hands in her dangling apron, "you've come to the wrong place. But you're welcome to the pitiful little I've got."

At this language Lindy's mouth began to water. It meant a sideboard of pitiful, perfect fruit pies, and whole cream to douse them with. She had wondered why Ruth allowed dairy. Because milking was harmless at worst? The phrase delivered her to the Fairmont New Orleans, the afternoon she taught Stone's mouth the right way to approach her breasts.

"We're not putting you out?" Adhah asked. "An adventure for us, somebody else's cooking." "I detect a number of things," Seelah said. "You're good to have us." Both women were standing with their chins tucked back attentively.

"You don't have to eat one bit of it, just because I cooked it," Ruth said, leading them past the second parlor with its four upholstered chairs and two sofas, and opening the door to a bathroom under the stairwell. "Right in there, soap, plenty of drying rags. I'll set out the plates while you wash up. Clean hands at my table. The last cold I caught, Mr. Herbert Clark Hoover was the President."

After their turns at the lavatory—Lindy went first so she could leave the water running, in case the other two didn't know what to do with a faucet, then went back in to turn it off—the three of them angled up to the long buffet under the pair of plum and alabaster stained-glass windows, and filled their plates without ceremony. Ruth had placed frayed bathtowels over the chairs at two of the three places she had set. Catching Lindy's look, she brought her hands together anxiously and wobbled out of the room. In a moment she returned with another towel. "I don't know why I bother," she said. "They'll have to pile my furniture up in the street and put kerosene to it."

The eating had begun. Lindy was feeling a lot better. Now Ruth was bringing in another dish, and a tray of lard-free dinner rolls, from the kitchen. "I can't stand cold bread," she said, "and Bobby likes his turnip roots warmed up." Lindy admired the no longer perfect display on her plate and considered *e coli*. Boardinghouse eaters had been famously inclined to consume every scrap; that's what they paid by the week for. But Ruth couldn't be making all this fresh every day. Was she alert enough to put the excess in the refrigerator every night? You have to watch and learn, Lindy supposed, what will kill you after two days and what you can eat until next week. Adhah and Seelah, who were leaning together and comparing their choices, no doubt were immune to such reservations.

"There'll be aught left for Bobby if he gets over here," Ruth said, surveying enough food for a dozen large men. "He's good to come, every week at least once. I don't keep house at all, compared to the way I used to. The stairs are about too much." She had not sat down yet. "Ninety-three years and eight months old, I can't believe it, can you? Keep moving, that's the thing. Ain't that it, girls? Cooking's all preserves me from the nursing home."

The two old women were giving full attention to their plates. Finally, Ruth eased herself down onto one side of the chair nearest the kitchen.

"These lentils," Adhah said, looking up. "Yes, indeed." Her mouth was half-full of field peas. "I've nursed folks myself," she added. "You're good at it, I imagine."

"A nurses' home," Ruth said. "That's right clever." She looked ready to jump up at any moment. "Now, I didn't get your last names. You're sisters, I take it? Sure look it."

Seelah sighed. The question, or perhaps it was the creamed corn, appeared to have stirred her deeply. Ruth shook her head sympathetically.

"I'm looking at you," she said to Seelah, "and I'm guessing that me making inquiries has got you thinking about your husbands."

Seelah kept chewing. "Keyser was killed on September 23, 1938. Not a day goes by that I don't stand in front of his picture and study it. I imagine if I ever skipped two days running, I'd clean forget what he looks like. They slip away from your mind so easy. Isn't that so?" She looked at Lindy and raised a wispy eyebrow. "They'll leave you sudden."

Lindy concentrated on buttering a third roll. She would as soon Ruth didn't get started on her again. The last time she and Michelle were here, Ruth had brought up the subject of marriage in exactly the same way. Marriage led them to the subject of divorce and, somehow, into the matter of Stone's leaving her for a world full of men. Ruth had expressed no surprise. Anything can happen in a marriage, she had said. Then she had counted with her fingers, naming male and female relatives of hers who had acknowledged they were, or who she had come to believe were, "different that way." People have been a bunch of different kinds, she had said, since the first day. They just don't get trapped into crossing the border, marrying, as much as they used to.

"I was thinking," Ruth said. "Lindy, you work for the Moultons." Lindy fit a nod of assent into the negligible pause. "I did tell you Keyser was working for Anderson Moulton when he was killed?"

She had told it, how her husband died in a collision on the highway. Anderson Moulton was Bea's grandfather.

"Anderson Moulton was the stormiest *rich* man I ever run into," Ruth continued without a pause. "This time it was three thousand acres in Concordia Parish—see, Keyser took care of the sawmill machinery, and the Moulton Land Company would break down those peckerwood mills and haul them to the town nearest where they was cutting. Kept him away all the time—fine with me, I had this house to run, that he bought. Well, Keyser was over by Larto Lake. That low, swampy country—cypress, by then all the heart pine was off propping up Yankee shingles. The woods wasn't his usual place, it was some matter he needed a Moulton to sign off on, and Ash was seventy miles away. Anderson Moulton couldn't abide sitting in an office but he loved to boss. Affected to ride a horse, even in town. I reckon it was so he could look down at the rest of us.

"This day I'm talking about—1931, this time of year—it rained all night, but it stopped. The draw cable nor the oxen was making any headway towing those big trees out of that bottom. Keyser told me he waited slap two hours hoping Anderson Moulton would ease up and come over to where Keyser was cooling his heels. When it came to speaking, Keyser was always a patient man, but law, when he got home to me, he wanted it right then that minute. Well, Anderson Moulton had that roan of his, he was jerking it left right left, in the mud and the hubbub, a lot of the hoorah being his yelling. So he never heard Keyser nor the men shouting, never saw the ninety-foot cypress that flattened him and that thousand-dollar horse flush to the ground. 'And him cussing Almighty God for a bald-headed son of a bitch with his last breath.' That's exactly what Keyser said. You'll have to pardon the language, but that's exactly what Keyser said. Cussing Almighty God for a bald-headed son of a bitch." Ruth's face was beatific.

"Lahmockah," Seelah said, putting down her spoon and looking at Adhah. That's what it sounded like to Lindy, "Lahmock," with the mandatory "uh" at the end. Seelah pronounced it from back in her throat, projected it with her forward pecking motion. "Our husband's name. And goodness, yes, he has been gone almost beyond memory."

"Your husbands' name, singular," Ruth said to Seelah, and shifted her gaze to Adhah. "I picked up on that. These ears are sharp as ever, Bobby's getting deaf, though—cut-out mufflers. You two are sisters that married brothers. Your people are not from Courant

Parish, no Lamonks around here that I know of. Close marrying, not a bit strange, in my day. Everybody lived way out. Double first cousins was ordinary as red hair. There was mighty few chances to pair off, you settled for who was there. Not that I did, I went off to Centenary and met Keyser; Keyser came from Indiana. I had an aunt married her stepfather's younger brother. She finally learned to stop calling her husband 'Uncle Bryce' about the time the first baby arrived."

"Noah?" Lindy asked. Maybe she could get them started. They never used men's names—even Miss Johnson's brother was just a brother. "Naw-aw?" she repeated, making it two syllables, making it as foreign sounding as she could. "The boatbuilder?"

Adhah snorted derisively. Seelah offered her short laugh.

"Noah who?" Ruth asked. She was still perched on her chair. Lindy wondered if Ruth had already eaten. Or was dialogue meat enough for her? "Somebody's kin was Noah something?" Ruth continued. "I never cared for the name, if you don't mind me saying so. Do you know your Bible?" She was looking at Lindy. "Probably not. No offense, they don't drill children like they used to. You're not in there, but the other three of us are, aren't we, girls? I've got a whole book named after me; it stands right against the First Samuel. But this Ruth didn't marry any Boaz. Keyser was George. And I told *my* mother-in-law, whenever Keyser died, it was time for her to goeth whither to her daughter's house on the Wabash. And she had money. You two ladies, your momma didn't fool around—started at about verse one, picking out names. A tricky habit, just as well it died out. I knew two sisters from Hall Summit, one of them named Mahalath, the other one Hoglah. Simpson. Neither one of them ever got married." She paused and looked intently at Adhah, then Seelah. "I'll get you some more tea," she said, leaning to one side as she hoisted herself up.

"Time, yes indeed. Time will run out on you," Ruth resumed.

She was shifting her shoulders as if to test her balance before trying to walk. Ruth's next out-of-nowhere paragraph—this one, Lindy knew, would draw Adhah and Seelah into the circle of women who had run out of time. She took this opportunity to study the pies that sat on the far end of the buffet. All three were double crusts, and all three had been cut, confirming their blackberry and peach and cherry identities, so that as Ruth went on about time and its limits, Lindy was able to work toward a rational decision among them.

"Use your time," Ruth was saying. "Take the word of somebody who knows. It's no small matter." Lindy, settling her mind on blackberry, nodded assent and turned back politely toward Ruth. The old woman was leaning forward over the table and staring keenly at her. "Don't let it run out on you."

CHAPTER 11

Finding Adhah and Seelah in the rain and listening to Ruth Keyser, and delivering the two old women home, and swinging by her apartment to change into something that didn't smell like moldy grass cuttings—none of it had set Lindy's workday back much. And Mollie for once had shown some initiative. Lindy was standing at Mollie's fortress desk paging through a sheaf of airline fares that Mollie had trawled out of the internet. Acheron, like small cities all over the country, had watched helplessly while a single major carrier shooed away a couple of bottom-feeder airlines and tripled prices. Mollie had spotted the sale while she was arranging Bea's departure to Vancouver for the day after tomorrow. Now Lindy would be able to add at least one visiting writer to the fall program. With Michelle on vacation, Lindy would contact the writers who were already scheduled and firm up their travel dates, then she could go back to the list and chase down another candidate.

The outer door opened and Bea came in. Lindy glanced up and went back to adding airfares in her head.

"That's not the blouse you had on," Bea said. Her posture was that of a miniature arresting officer, feet apart, hands on her waist. "You had on a blue silk boat neck." Had Bea put on this imitation uniform just to blow the whistle on her for excessive blouse use? Probably not, it was more naval than constabulary, navy-blue jacket and white pants and a soft nautical hat. Did the half dozen stripes on her sleeve denote chief petty officer? You have to work your way up to chief, Lindy thought, from plain petty.

"I got wet going to lunch," she said. "I had to go change. Isn't it surprising how much punishment silk can take. Lay it in the bathtub in a little cool water, the spots disappear."

"Don't tell me about wet," Bea said. She was sliding her fingers up and down the insides of her lapels. "You drove that truck right past me at Elliott and Chester. Spraying water like a speedboat. Hauling those—whatever they were. Large people."

"Mollie did a good thing." Mollie, who was sitting at full attention. "Wait, Bea. Did I splash your car, did I make you almost wreck?"

"You'll have to make up your own mind about what you did. Do you intend to do some work around here?" Mollie had both hands around her crystal pendant, as if signing a prayer.

"Can we take this into my office?" Lindy asked. This was the first unambiguous reference to Lindy's work that Bea had ever made. Bea followed as far as Lindy's office door, but it was obvious she wasn't coming in. Lindy leaned against the front of her desk. "Bea, I'm curious. When did you become interested in how I manage my time?"

"I never would have mentioned it myself," Bea said. "I warned the board, some of them, at the interview. But now."

Harold—would he have spilled the beans to a social peer, or to anybody? Who cared anyway, if he did?

"But now," Lindy said. "Just now, Mollie was able to find some amazing fares for this fall's in-school writers. She said you're going to Vancouver day after tomorrow. Would you care to sit down, and we can share our plans?" Vancouver implied Pacific Northwest Indian artifacts, Bea perhaps skulking at the edge of a big potlatch, Bea returning with an articulated animal mask-within-a-mask, or with some large carved something strapped to the wing of the plane.

"Mollie talks too much sometimes."

The antique intercom on Lindy's desk began to buzz. "There's a phone call for you," Mollie's low-fi voice said from the speaker. "Personal." The land line got a lot of use, because cell phone reception in the Moulton building was iffy. The only reason Lindy could assign was too many antique square nails.

"Get their number."

"I don't think so," Mollie said through the box. "It's your sister and she's pretty upset." Lindy closed the door in Bea's face. Bea didn't need to hear any more.

Lubie was whimpering. The last time Lindy had heard an older sister cry, Lubie and Loretta were in high school and Lindy was about ten. Loretta had been the wailer. "Lubie, honey, it's Lindy."

"'Yet a little while and the world seeth me no more.'"

Lindy picked up the quotation, but she was long since past rising to the scriptural bait. She waited for Lubie to recover.

"Daddy. It's Daddy." With the second "Daddy" Lubie's voice went calm.

"What about Daddy? He was fine when I talked to him yesterday. He told me he saw Brayard at the bank." Brayard was Lubie's husband.

"Lord knows where they got the number. The nurse said afterwards I walked in exactly one minute after they gave up trying to start him breathing."

Lindy grabbed the underside of the desk to keep from floating toward the ceiling.

"No matter what the doctors might say, he wasn't with God yet, I know that. Follow the radiance, I told him—you know you always see the spotlight and the tunnel."

Now Lindy was at their house, was surrounded by the high, bright light of a summer afternoon. Her dad was hugging her, his beard was scratching her baby skin; it was the first time she understood that men have to shave. She felt the rough grooved weave of his khaki work shirt and breathed in the reassuring herbal creosote smell he brought home from the utility poles he climbed. Daddy, she said to the sandpaper cheek and sunburned neck that were fading away, you promised me, by keeping on feeling good. Another week. Another four hours so I can get down there.

Lubie was going on about how he had looked twenty years older, his mouth in an "O," his lips chapped—how his eyes made her know he was still inside. How the doctors had already left, how nice the emergency room nurse was.

"How?" Lindy interrupted.

"He drove himself to town. 'Nobody was home' is the last thing he said, the nurse said. He had to be talking about the new little couple across the road from his house, I don't even know their name. They got him awake for a little while when they moved him, he could have told them my name then." Lubie sounded to Lindy as if she were rehearsing her part in a play about Bob Caton's last hour.

"Where is he?"

"He's with Mom," Lubie answered too quickly. "'I will come again and shall receive you unto myself.' John 14, 3."

With Mom? With the hated Sunshine? This kind of talk from Lubie brought Lindy back to earth. "Did you tell them to call Moncrief's?" In her mind she and Wade Moncrief of the funeral home family were in her front yard when they were both kids. He was tossing a grass-stained baseball to Lindy and she was dropping it.

"They don't do autopsies any more," Lubie said. "That's what I thought. I passed two men bringing a rolling thing."

"Lubie, go tell them no, run right now and tell them no. I'll come straight to your house. Start calling people." Too far away, too far—she should have moved straight to Mobile.

Bea's office door was open, but she was not in the building. Mollie was gone, too. Back at her desk Lindy wrote out a note to Mollie and, out of respect, a longer one to Michelle, who throughout her vacation had been forwarding work. The windows cast three blurred Lindys onto the computer screen, for each of the ways her mind was split. At one level she was flashing through an album of scenes with her dad. Two weeks ago, the last time she saw him, telling him good-bye; and the evening he tended the barbecue grill while she told him about the way Stone left her. And the scene in the hospital today as it should have been, he struggling to breathe, Lindy talking to him and moistening his lips and smoothing his hair. At another level she was running through the details of getting out of town and of preparing for the funeral—the daughters' turn to choose the casket and the flowers and to make a hundred difficult phone calls. Her dad had showed her the envelope with the cemetery plot and the hymns and readings he wanted, but she hadn't let him open it. She would have to wait until Wade was through at the funeral home before she would be able to see him. Sometimes customs were too barbaric. And at the same time she was already thinking about the house, his house, their house. Closing it and afterward, forever, strangers there.

Bea and Mollie were together at the street, at the back of a Land Rover Lindy had not seen before. They were swaddling something watermelon-sized in a quilted mover's blanket. Lindy spoke to Mollie. "I left you a note. That was my sister on the phone. My father has died." At the word, tears sprang to Lindy's eyes and her body was scalding hot, as if she had pulled open the door to a blast furnace. The other two women looked at each other and went on wrapping another mover's pad around whatever it was.

"He had liver cancer," Lindy said. "Michelle will be back on Monday. I'll be in touch with her."

"That's too bad," Mollie said.

"Thanks. We don't know when the funeral will be. My other sister—"

"Take several days," Bea said. She came toward Lindy, but kept going with her keys in her hand. Lindy started for her own truck.

"Take a few extra days to think about things." Bea was following her. Lindy kept walking, nodding yes. The schedule would depend on Loretta. Loretta's husband Alan, though he was retired, was sometimes out of pocket up in the mountains. He had that airplane.

Bea was at the truck along with Lindy, at the side of the building. Mollie had closed the gate of the Land Rover and was standing nearby. "You may decide," Bea said, more coldly, "that Ash Run is not the kind of place your behaviors are cut out for."

"I beg your pardon? Did Harold say something to you?"

"Maybe this break is for the best," Bea said. "Ash Run is not an ordinary town. It's not north Louisiana, or south Louisiana. Oh, it has its sleepy central Louisiana side, and it has its share of useless people, especially large country people. But there is history here. You may well mention Harold. The Rutledges, Harold's family, built the first Protestant church here, Anglican—that's Episcopalian. 1823. My great-great-grandfather Emerson Moulton had been to England two years before that and brought back a distinguished priest."

"Bea, do you hear what you're doing? Do you think I give a rat's ass, right now, about your great-great grandfather's priest?"

"Exactly my point, young lady. I'm suggesting that you might want to think about what brought you down here, and what exactly you want to do, and what kind of place you could best do it in. Without—tomatoes." Bea paused to compose herself. "Without demeaning yourself and the first families of Ash. Without assaulting the ears of distinguished lawyers with Bible gobbledygook."

Assaulted ears, then. Harold had told her something, but not much.

"And when might we discuss my future?" She was in the truck now. "During one of your eight-hour layovers in this town that so few people deserve to live in? Christmas Eve, after midnight mass at the Rutledge's chapel? And on what basis, Bea, you and me? You'll have a long flight, time to work all that out, while I'm burying my daddy."

CHAPTER 12

From the moment she arrived—how do you prepare? The house when she walked in, smothering her with ring upon ring of familiar smells and aching with her father's absence. Lubie's insistence on a coffin with a thousand-year warranty. The way, when Lindy was allowed to be alone with him after Wade Moncrief had dressed him in the new suit she and Loretta brought, Bob Caton had become a wax mock-up of a distant cousin to the father she loved. The release that came anyway, when she put her head on his chest and stroked his painted face and talked to him. The total screw-up baby Methodist minister who, when it came time to say Lubella Loretta Linderella in the funeral sermon, finally stammered "the daughters." The cousins who appeared consolingly from cities four hundred miles away, and ate a great deal of everything the neighbors had brought to her father's house, and who visited until sundown even though they would have to drive home through the night.

And now the bourbon, Lindy thought, staring at the bottle on the dining table in front of her—inevitable. Loretta was bound to have found it, wax-sealed and dusty behind the crackers and the flour, once all the relatives had departed and the neighbors were gone home. Unavoidable, too, that two women who might take one glass of wine in an ordinary week were keeping right up with Lindy. The three of them were two-thirds through a liter, however much a liter was. Lindy didn't blame Loretta for getting them started. An attractive nuisance, she thought, the homeowner is responsible for securing dangerous materials when children are around.

Lindy leaned forward on one elbow and picked at another of the casseroles. By repeated sculpture with the serving spoons she was managing to nibble all of them straight. Behind her Lubie sat prim as a carpenter's square on the green sofa. Loretta lay on the flowered couch. Both sisters were blonde and trim and buxom, and still wearing their best dark dresses. Occasionally one of the older sisters would come over to doctor their drinks, and would spoon a gap into the corn pudding or by now as eleven o'clock had passed, dip a finger through the middle of the artichoke spinach. More work for Lindy.

"Why, when she finds out her little preacher husband is a homo, wouldn't somebody be glad he's ran out on her? This is what I don't get," Lubie said after a while, dredging up Stone Prather's materialization at the funeral home before the service.

"Well, you're the one who called him, I made him admit it. I was talking to Coach—damn, I can't remember any of their names. I was already crying when Stone came into the room."

Stone in jeans and sockless loafers, his shirt like draped lapis. Stone bulked up and buff, twenty pounds heavier than he had ever been. They had gone outside for a few minutes to talk, but there was really nothing to say. Stone, on his way to Navarre Beach with an intellectual-looking guy who waved mildly from Stone's car. Stone had left the phone messages, that she never opened, to tell her he would be passing through Acheron. He had a publisher in Lake Charles for his new book. Stone, vanished again before it was time to go into the chapel.

She rescued a sliver of ham that had dropped onto her BayBears sleeping shirt. Part of her plan to forget Stone Prather and his new muscular look involved eliminating the line on the spiral-cut. To Lindy her sisters had never looked less like their gangly, nothing-haired younger sister and more like twins. Or more like Sunshine. They had gotten through everything for three days without any-body using the name Sunshine. Lindy wasn't going to be the first one to say it out loud.

"You kissed him on the mouth," Lubie insisted. "A woman that wanted to be divorced would have shook his hand, even a woman that was fool enough to pick that particular husband. 'Unto the married I command, let not the wife depart from her husband.' That's only Paul, dressing down those base-minded Corinthians, but he's on the money. Lindy, baby, fix me another big one of these." She was holding out her tumbler, bourbon and store-brand root beer.

Lubie drinking, Lubie plain-speaking and abusing the New Testament, could dull the edge of grief. Lindy made two drinks and handed one of them to Lubie, and kept going toward the back of the house. She closed the door of her father's bedroom to shut out Lubie's revisionist voice and went to the desk, to the second drawer. Lubie was giving St. Paul a rest when she returned with the cigar box.

"Let's talk about who wants to be the husband of one wife," she said. "And who wanted to be the wife of one husband."

She opened the lid of the cigar box above the coffee table be-tween the two women and shook its contents out. A blue wooden bracelet bounced once and sailed toward the floor. Two worn keys clattered down ahead of the few other items of costume jewelry.

A small shower of curled snapshots followed, along with a folded sheet of paper and a few sepia newspaper clippings. A worn plastic card-holder from an abandoned wallet accordioned to rest beside an oversized clip-on earring, gold plate and amethyst. The other earring and a woman's silver friendship ring tarnished to pewter gray lay a little way from the pile of photographs.

"We weren't going to look at anything of his tonight," Lubie said. She sat forward and picked up the nearest earring. Loretta opened her eyes and pushed herself up on the couch.

"Sunshine," Lubie said, turning over the earring. "I remember how tacky-huge this pair looked on her."

Lindy sat down on the floor and began to gather the photographs, making a little deck of them on the table. Most of them were black and white, obviously saved from courtship and early married days. But saved, selected, not thrown away. She shuffled the photographs until she came to one of a young woman standing beside a shiny green Pontiac sedan. It was intended as a portrait of the new car, Lindy supposed. The Pontiac had been the first car she could remember. Sunshine, with what could have been the getaway car—had anyone given the escaping lovers credit for leaving the car behind? Sunshine, kept young in the shelter of the box; Sunshine's unfaded glowing eyes and flawless oval face, bare slender arms outside the tight, straight knit outfit, her light hair pulled back and blossoming at her neck. Sunshine with her mouth confidently open, as if speaking: "I know I have all this. Go ahead, anybody out there, and look at me."

"You saw Momma wearing those earrings?" Lindy asked.

Lubie's eyes widened. "You don't remember one blessed thing," she said, "except what I tell you." At ten and nine, Lubie and Loretta had been able to remember a parent who climbed on the back of a motorcycle one afternoon before the grade school let out, and rode away for Wyoming while the baby played in the backyard sandpile.

The baby had been too young to retain much except the feeling that she had caused it. Now she tried to imagine Sunshine and Buddy Millard striking out northwest, rolling up through Mississippi—crossing at right angles the route of the Freedom Riders who had bused down from Boston and New York in search of freedom for somebody besides themselves—and continuing to the Rockies. Lindy's uneasy access to the memory of Sunshine's disappearance was Buddy Millard's motorcycle. She could summon its coughing start, its rising whine, and its fade to idle. She could invoke its cream-colored bulk and the enormous black leather seat with its chrome handbar ringing the back. She could put herself in touch with it, her tentative small hand reaching out toward the raised design, a tiny Indian face at one end of a long geometric headdress, the machine with its tubes and springs leaning dangerously toward her on its thin kickstand.

"Leave it all there," Lubie was saying. "We've got to go. What time do you have to be at the airport?"

"I don't know," Loretta said. "Two-thirty, two-fifty. Look, he kept this too." She leaned forward and took the sheet of paper, which was folded into three, letter-style.

Lindy took the earring from Lubie and dealt her a photograph from the stack. At some beach Bob stood tall and very young, bulky in his trunks, dark hair already receding. Sunshine's shirred one-piece swimsuit was modest below, with short cuffed legs, but the top was strapless. It looked like a *Life* magazine set-up: working man granted outing with starlet.

The other earring lay all alone at the center of the table. She picked it up with the same hand, as if they were a pair of dice, and put them on. They pulled at her ears, but they didn't feel as heavy as they had the other time. The other time had been the summer she was twelve, the summer she had opened every drawer and cupboard in every room of the house and edged to the back of every closet, the summer she had taken possession of the house from her sisters, had lifted and turned over and put back precisely, until nothing was secret from her except her life.

Loretta read aloud, squinting and holding the sheet at arm's length. "'Alice Caton McNite, homemaker, sixty-three'—they might have put 'Sunshine,' that's a shame in a way. 'June 18, 1997.' I cut out the top corner of the page and taped it on, because I knew I'd forget the date. The Denver paper puts headlines on their obituaries. 'Homemaker' means 'this'll be quick.' Then they start all over. 'Alice Caton McNite of Castle Peak, a homemaker, died Thursday at County Memorial Hospital. She was sixty-four.' Castle Peak. That's got to be on the Front Range. Alan and I were on the Western Slope—"

"Playing high-altitude golf," Lubie said. "Just read it."

"Now wasn't I going to be in Colorado? They don't deliver the *Post* to Albuquerque. There's not anything to this thing, even the way they pad it out." She read on, holding the page in the lamp's glow. "'No services will be held. There was cremation.' Every sentence, nearly, is a separate little paragraph, makes it look kind of airy. 'She was born in 1934 in Florida. In 1981 she married John McNite in Ft. Collins. He preceded her in death. There were no survivors. Her interests included sewing and collectibles. She was a former member of the Resurrection Ministries.' That's it, that's the whole thing." Loretta waved the obituary in the air.

"No cause of death," Lindy said, "and no Buddy Millard, and no *us*." No cause, she thought, because no death. Why couldn't she say it out loud? Because no backbone. Because a liter is a quart plus. "A newspaper either doesn't allow cause of death, or they have to have it. I never noticed how an obituary is a little ritual until I wrote Daddy's for the *Register* and then for the *Town Talk* and the Albuquerque paper."

"'There was cremation.'" Loretta said. "Not even the name of the funeral home. That's so cold. I attribute it to all those sealed-up miners they had to walk away from."

Nobody, Lindy thought, would believe that we've never talked about this before.

"And the no services part," Loretta went on. "It breaks my heart."

"It'd break mine, too," Lubie said. "Ordinarily." She raised her glass and drank down some of the dark liquid.

"I'm going to be cremated," Lindy said, "but I'd want youall to have a chance to say good-bye." Lubie made a hissing sound between her teeth. "No, I mean it, you need to see the body. If there is a body. Which there hasn't been in Sunshine's case. Sunshine—that other Alice Caton was not Sunshine."

"Jesus isn't much help with cremation," Lubie said. "You've got to reach back to Jeremiah."

"Okay, big sister," Lindy said. "Reach on back, if you can." She got up and added a spurt of whiskey to her watery glass, and took her place next to the ham.

"That Jeremiah was a ranter," Lubie said. "Always repeating himself. He's useful just the same, nothing ever changes in *this* world. How about 'They shall not be buried, but they shall be as dung upon the earth'? That's him on Sunshine, let me say chapter 16."

"So sweet," Loretta said. "So comforting."

"But here's the thing," Lindy said. "I went ahead and looked for the Alice Catons. On People Find. And when there weren't any, in Wyoming or in Colorado—"

"Of course there's not," Lubie said. "She's dead."

"I told you," Lindy said. "It was some other Alice Caton."

"No she wasn't," Loretta said. "You little devil, I ought to sit on you."

"The internet is sloppy, the virtual Real Yellow Pages. And directory assistance is worse. The operator was so stupid about Resurrection and Fellowship.

"We're drunk, child, is why you two are carrying on like this," Loretta said. She was standing near the door. "I've got to get to bed. And it's not going to be in this dying, dying house. It's going to be on one of Lubie's three-foot-thick Posturpedics."

"We better all ride together," Lubie said. "Together will keep the number of drunk driving tickets to one."

"I'll drive you to Lubie's," Lindy said, "but I want to sleep in my room tonight."

The new-paved, unmarked lanes ahead of Lindy's pick-up were so unreflective that the red taillights in front of her windshield flattened into a visual display. She maneuvered the red dots to keep the road in front of her. A few of the dots moved high into the sky and began to blink—oh, a television tower. When they got to Lubie's house—this was the arrangement—if they decided that Lindy looked like she shouldn't be driving, then one of the other two would drive her back. She started over on Sunshine, to her captive audience. "And when there weren't any Alice Catons, nor any Alice Millards, I went to Alice Williams. She could have taken back her maiden name. Alice Williams is so common."

Loretta giggled, her head bowed as if she were asleep or in prayer. "Don't make me do that," she said. "I'm about to be sick."

"Alice Williams," Lindy continued, "is a common name. I don't remember exactly, it was two or three for Colorado. Under A. Williams, though, twenty or thirty. I didn't call any of them. After all, why Colorado especially? She and Buddy went to Wyoming. There are zero Alice Williamses listed in Wyoming."

"Little sister, that's because nobody lives in Wyoming," Loretta said. "Besides, she and Buddy didn't stay there, remember?" Lindy didn't remember. "At least he didn't. Somebody at Alabama Power told Daddy that Buddy wrote him and said they were laying off roughnecks around Casper."

"Roughneck," Lubie intoned from the middle of the mourners' bench. "Mr. America was more like it."

"Do you think Sunshine felt like she was obliged to go with him?" Loretta's head was still bowed. "Was the way they looked together a package that just had to be shipped out?"

"I searched Alice Caton and Alice Williams and Alice Millard and Sunshine everything. And S. Caton, and A. Williams. Even in California, just to get the scale. There are one hundred A. Williamses in California. No Sunshines that fit any of the last names, not even in California. No Sunshine anywhere. I take it back, I found one Sunshine Millard when I searched keywords. He sells insurance in Charlotte."

"Alice Caton, *sixty-four*," Lubie said. "Born in *Florida*. You need her back alive so bad, why aren't you up there this week instead of wasting your time down here? 'And they shall wander from sea to sea, and from the north even to the east—'"

"I just might go," Lindy interrupted.

"'—and they shall run to and fro to seek the word of the Lord, and shall not find it.' Amos eight, verse something—fifteen? I'm fried." Lubie poked Lindy sharply in the side. "And you're running to and fro all over this road."

"We might all go, right now tonight." When again would they all three be heading in the same direction? Might as well make it mean something. US 98 was the one that ran northwest, the highway Sunshine and Buddy had to take. Moffat Road, it turned into 98; reach it from the west loop. There it was. Right *here*. She dodged across three lanes and entered the ramp to the cloverleaf. The others didn't appear to notice.

"She was born in South Georgia," Loretta said. "I let the 'Florida' go. She must have told that to her neighbor or her last boyfriend, whoever it was turned her in to the paper, because nobody wants to be from South Georgia. Because it was a matter of her being able to say 'Florida Sunshine,' see? Mercy, I feel punk."

"Florida," Lubie said. "Florida, Florida. They moved to Valdosta when she was little, and you know it."

"Now who remembers nothing, if you two can't agree?" Lindy resisted the urge to pound on the steering wheel. "Sunshine is out there. She's seventy years old and she has trouble catching her breath—her big old breasts sitting against her stomach don't help that any—and she looks exactly like both of you are going to look in twenty years. Only, Loretta, the reason her skin is leather is from smoking, not from UV. She's outlived the old-time religion gene—Lubie's got that still to do. Resurrection Ministries, 'former member.'" Oh, that was some other woman altogether.

The highway had narrowed to two lanes. The first black-outlined shield appeared: US 98.

"Cigarettes was what killed her," Lubie said. "But I have wondered about Buddy, I admit it. He's not still alive, is he? Both of them smoked like fiends. Kill us, too, from breathing it when we were little."

"Ashes to ashes," Loretta said.

"We'll make that 'dust to dust,' if you don't mind," Lubie said. "You're certainly aware 'ashes to ashes' is not scriptural."

Nobody would believe that we've ever talked about anything before, Lindy thought. Or ever will again.

Up ahead, in the highway or on the right shoulder, a carnival of staccato, syncopating lights. Blue, that would be the state police and probably the sheriffs, and there were a bunch of them; red, mixed with white, that meant ambulance, more than one; and down below the right of way, near the woods, the circling yellow dome light of a tow truck. The traffic was flowing over to the left lane. Lindy stayed right and slowed as they drew even with the scene, and stopped on the shoulder.

"We're going to jail, if you don't get us out of here," Lubie said. "Which one of us is in any shape to convince those deputies she wasn't driving?"

Lindy was already off the pavement and running down the embankment, down toward where she had seen the motorcycle. The machine, as she reached it, lay on its side beyond the gash cut by its fall into the coarse grass. The open earth beside it could have been an almost-filled grave, and the motorcycle a deformed headstone for whoever had been on it when it went down the slope.

No one seemed to have followed her. She could hear voices up by the enforcement vehicles, Lubie's and a man's.

The man's voice said, "Ma'am, she ought not to be down there. Some people died."

"Our daddy died, officer," Lubie was saying. "We buried him today. Or yesterday—how late is it? Naturally we're all three totally drunk. Not that we drink, the two of us. Loretta is back at the truck throwing up right now."

"It's two o'clock," the policeman said, "so it would be yesterday."

"That one down there is the baby. She don't believe Sunshine is dead too—Sunshine, that's our Momma. 'The light shines in the darkness, but the darkness comprehendeth it not.' I'd leave her right here, but she's the only one knows which way it is to Baldwin County."

"Y'all better go on to the house, ma'am. I'm sorry about your daddy, ma'am."

Lindy, on her knees in the grass beside the motorcycle, felt for the side away from the torn earth, toward the gas tank where the insigne would be. Under her fingers the whole side was scrubbed bare, gouged, no manufacturer's mark. She began yanking at the twisted handlebars. If she could only stand the machine upright, if she could only make the kickstand work, if she could only get the other Indian out of the ground and touch him again.

·

CAIN'S VERSION: TENERIFE

The natural teller of stories—does his eye for experience guide him to a shoal of shimmering incidents, over which he need only throw his net? If I could bear to remain ashore, I might stand long enough within the tale spinner's circle, and so could judge. But I cannot. Does his tongue, like a whittler's knife, reduce his larger memories to a clean sliver? It does not. This much I know, for I feel myself shaving away my remembered life. Does the born narrator, then, select a single moment and scribe it as if it were the first furrow in a section of whale rib, holding his audience by advancing and varying that incision? If I were such a one—I am not, neither teller nor scrimshander—I would not need to ask where to place my memory's scribe mark. But I do ask. Would it be my refusal to rescue the slave-boy, the one the women called Mahuri? Would it be my lack of interest in facing the miserable Spaniards for the sake of a child I never met? Or would it be that I made a joke about the boy's imbecilic qualities, qualities over which the women were grieving? Do you see? All three of these choices are the same slight event, and no better a start, nor worse, than any other moment.

Mid night. I was returning from a long excursion to the north, and the tall island loomed. Long since, no extended land mass has been able to surprise me. An island, however, may intrude. This one I believed to be one of Juba's islands; Hanno's islands as told of by the Carthaginians; Nivara—the Fortunate Isles. These surely were they, or their remnants. So many names for so few islands; no doubt many of them had slid below the surface since they were first spoken of. Tenerife it was, as I learned when I landed, and before I chanced to find Mother and the other two. The women were there—and the boy, nearly—though I came upon them only after a day ashore. Now I am gone from them, again in darkness and without an opening sufficient to make an engaging tale of it. Another's story will hold the center when I make my next repair stop.

What trifling detail might the Spaniards have made of me? Make no mistake, it is not a matter of fear—though I know them. Say "cruel" and the whole world nods; say "brutal" in any language. No matter how far at sea, they claim their territory. What they overswarm, they foolishly believe they own. Like dung beetles they push forward and aggregate their holdings. And what of the boy they so casually took—of this night, his first night below deck? And what of his future? He is less than a basket of grain to them. I have seen one of their anchor chains hurry a string of men off the deck and down through the frantic surface. Uhwa's ward with his unruliness? His final dance, his casual disposal at sea? At their hands not a story, not even a weak story. Brutality buries meaning.

I was not confused, not lost when I encountered the island. My intention was to seek the west coast of Africa and follow it southward, something I long since should have done. Tenerife is understood by the steepness of its sides. It is a mass vomited up and not yet wiped away: proof that the ocean relented too soon. What

I found there confirms this. I sailed to the lee side of the island, though that meant accepting the odor of loam and the sick reek of rank vines—and by morning, signals much worse.

I folded the sail for a pallet and settled to rest. A dark night, an absent moon. The island's bulk flattened and became a triangle cut from the undersurface of the sky. Soon I would sleep, if that is the word. Though I no longer can bring myself to lie down on dry land, my sleep at sea is less solid. I endure long periods of wakefulness. I nap so lightly that I emerge dreamless and aware of the exact interval of rest. I have cultivated an interim state of almost-sleeping that allows me to move great distances without dropping my sails. At home, where discipline was enforced by the fickle earth, and at Nod, where I strove to live as if I had not left home, the dreams were constant and vicious. No more—I have gladly traded sleep for fewer of those dreams.

I have come to favor night, a preference which, though unsought, has consequences for my relationship to the sea. Take the moon. Like its rhythms, mine are not ruled by the sun. The moon was of little use to me when I was a grower of grain. Its guises are too numerous, its many cycles too interwoven. Through countless nights and days of navigating I have learned to recognize the moon's every visage: its shapes and orientations and its brightnesses by night or day; its extremes, the extremes of its extremes; and most of all, its repetitions within repetitions. Its very variability finally allowed me to solve the riddle of position, so that now I can draw on the moon—together with the sun and stars in their stately alternations, and the two wanderers whose motions are quick enough to matter—to find myself on any part of the ocean. Odd, that I once compared the precious moon to a floating island.

Last night at Tenerife the stabilizing moon had removed itself from sight so that the darkness was palpable. No fires glowed within the island's silhouette—the fires came later, with the sun. On the open sea a calm, moonless night causes the sea to sleep so soundly that it disappears. The great inverted bowl of the heavens, released from its binding all around the horizon, begins to oscillate. I treasure such nights, when my sleeping-waking state is conjoined with the swinging, turning sky. Here, however, Tenerife's outline—aided by those of two smaller islands to the west and northwest—tethered the stars, and my thoughts.

When the wind rises sufficiently over a moonless sea—it did not last night, nor has it yet this night—the stars grasp futilely at the sea, and the sea, complaining, spits up cold green light. I am not one to be threatened by the sea's angry spells, but why would a man endure them? I have sense enough to choose. I find no difficulty in skirting mid-ocean storms, those swarming beehives of the sea's resentment. Occasionally, I feed my curiosity and seek the swells and the deep-breathing tides of the North Atlantic. It was from such an excursion that I was returning when I ran across Tenerife. The frigid northern ocean had shown me the confined turbulence where it hoards its bitter intention toward the dry land—or what remains of that intention.

Those who crawl the ground will say that they are flourishing, and will offer their traffic and their multiplying coastal cities as evidence that they begin to own the sea. I cannot restrain the question: for how long? When will the ocean again bow its back and fully rid the dry ground of its load of vermin? How much blame must be assigned, that the sea failed to dispatch the land with its earlier effort? Is the ocean growing weak? Is it no longer in full health? Has it for whatever reason become less trustworthy than when I first knew it? Is it in some sense like my wife became, unable or unwilling to maintain its housekeeping duties? I hope not. Ours in any event has become a bleak kinship, the sea's and mine.

I reclined across my folded sail and pondered the larger forces: earth, sea, sky. Of conflict there is no doubt—a slow war, with death in wait for all that is, and all that can be conceived. I rank them by pairs. Sea and earth: the sea, of course, has won and will win again. Sky and sea—ah, yes, the superior strength of the sky. This is what has troubled my allegiance to the sea. The sky's cryptic dominance is what had taken me north, to give the sea a chance to answer for its own reticence. Sky and earth: there is no contest. Is not the sky the favored source of destruction? I have seen the night sky's streaks, and have heard the booming fireballs at noon. Like all who watch from below, I have admired the tailed stars that if they would, might do the job. Danger to the sea? No, added peril for the ground. The sea will embrace the visitor, and I will welcome it though I perish in the concussion, because I cannot hope to sail the sky.

The outcome is set. That leaves the matter of the future, by which I mean the interval however brief or tedious it may be, during which the past might be healed. I told myself that I am cured of such worries. But then I slept, and dreamed of roaring skyfire—and woke to the same darkness, and to fear. Creature noises populated the darkness not far off. Noises at night, beings who at the least glimmer of light swim down to where they are comfortable. Of all men I understand the animals who prefer the dark, for I am one, nearly. I did not look in their direction, I never do. Staring into the darkness teaches nothing, any more than groundlings gain knowledge through their constant studying of their feet while they walk. The deep thuds, bespeaking large bodies, reassured me. It was not Abel rising.

Yet I cannot forget that Abel sleeps within the sea and may come to me. It is torture to think of him, and to that extent I wish the monsters would keep quiet. My illness—the feeling of worthlessness, the same debilitating waning of hope that sets in with my first step onto shore and grows in the manner of a fever that cannot be cured until its cause be addressed—is tied to my brother, his absence, and his sleeping. I knew that I would land anyway.

With my eyes open I dozed until the sea returned from its slumber and the sun had dispatched a warning to the eastern sky. The two low islands to the west were uninhabited, no doubt because their subsidence was far along. They lacked the will to resist the sea, in contrast to the tall island which rose in front of me, and which as my wakefulness increased sent out noises: dogs barking, and songs of birds I recognized as stragglers from the east. Nothing with wings or legs could be original here. Clouds shielded the peak of the sea mountain. Forest dense as mold marched down to the shore. Torrents disappeared into gashes, then sprang to safety at the sea. From pastures near the clouds came the chorus of bleating sheep, and, as my head cleared, martial shouts and repeated screams. I watched the ridge beyond the grassland while smoke plumed white and brown. It was not trees burning, nor grass. The thin share of smoke that reached me brought the unmistakable odor of burning human flesh. This Island of the Blessed.

From the numbers of Iberian vessels I had skirted on my way south, I knew their forces would be crowding the harbor. Nevertheless, I could not evade going ashore. Though my sailcloth is sound, my tunic was rags and my anchor rope was beyond mending. I slept again, almost soundly, until the moment the sun crossed its high point. Then I went over the side and ferried my barrels, one by one, to a convenient spring. Re-watered, I sailed.

At the horn of the island I passed through the shadow of the peak and met the hot smell of the desert. A large island squatted to the southwest. Locusts, riding the African wind, began falling into the boat. Several of them, along with a few scoops of new water, became my dinner.

Scratching a living from the ground is miserable, and trading in the product of others is abominable. To that extent the man who finds himself on an island is doubly miserable, whatever his role, since an island is superfluity compounded. Its every plant and animal is transported from the original earth. Its only function is to remind us that erasure is the ultimate fate of the whole. These were my thoughts as I approached the harbor at Tenerife, not knowing that my mother and her companions were on the island. They of course are exceptions to the general wretchedness of island dwellers—and all land, rightly seen, is islands—because the women know how to live without submitting their will to the ground. No doubt their presence goes unnoticed by the traders and the other so-called owners of land.

High above the harbor and the town, the obstinate peak now exposed its captive snow. The dry fumes from the distant mainland had scoured all trees from the landward side of the island. I arrived at the beach toward the end of the day. All my strength was required to slide my boat to the high-tide mark. Not that I am less fit, but because the craft, grown extremely old, has become stubborn.

As I expected, the Iberians were everywhere. Their navy lay at anchor, sleek oversized caravels—some square-rigged, most with lateen foresails—and bulbous naos whose bowsprits like male members wreck the proportion of their design. Presentable enough craftsmanship nonetheless, the work of slaves, I judged. Another pair of vessels, large awkward boxes, sat farther out. Unseaworthy and dangerous, but fit for a Spaniard, these no doubt had brought the horses that struggled across the dark sand at the urging of riders in absurd finery. Perhaps also these scows had been home to the camels that stood stoically below the mountain pass from which smoke was still rising. The floating barns would never make the return trip against the prevailing winds. They would rot here, and their livestock would remain to harass the land.

My resupply was accomplished easily. All eyes were on the long-haired invaders with their jeweled caps and their soft slippers, and on their mercenaries who could have been men of the island, except for the mercenaries' long wooden lances, and that the wary residents were clothed. I cut an excellent hempen rope from the first of a collection of crude log rafts—the natives seemed not to have considered boats. From a neighboring raft I took a like length. Having coiled the ropes together at the bow of my boat, I went in search of clothing. The nearest houses were thatched, and were clad alike in whitened dried mud. A man's body leaned against the doorway of the first of these. I stepped over his head, which looked at me without surprise from the dirt floor. I called out—those who infest houses are as apt as shipbuilders to claim a private relationship with the articles they have collected—but no one answered. The man's cloak was ruined, but I found another in the second room of the house. My new garment was of a lighter weight than the one I exchanged, so I went outside to the long rude shed, a market of some sort and abandoned in the confusion. Piled there were arrangements of oranges and other fruits—one variety indistinguishable from a staple of Mother's garden. The heaps of cooked foodstuffs were unfamiliar, other than a thousand of the bright locusts, their shells burnished by a bath in hot oil. Beside them, arrays of ornaments carved from wood and—as I had hoped—shifts and other woven goods stacked neatly on the ground. I took the heaviest of the vegetable-fiber cloaks and a curious beaded headdress (which I will not wear), and several of the one fruit, no more than I required. I would have shoved off immediately, were it not for a contradictory awareness that my mood was still good.

The women were the reason. They stood far off along the strand. I recognized them from their postures—three other women of such strong bearing do not exist. No doubt they had been there all along, though hidden by a line of men which had dissipated while I was busy. The last of them were at that moment being lifted from a longboat onto the nearest of the warships.

I have formed the habit of counting my steps on land, not because of my one leg—it pains me no more on land than at other times—but as you would be aware of each heartbeat while bathing among sharks. The number required to resupply, and to reach Mother and the other two, was 640—a total of 922 paces by the time I was back at my boat and aweigh. At the sixty-first step toward Mother an islander joined me. He had detached himself from a crowd which was engaged in building a ragged addition onto a decrepit log tower, and he was wearing nothing but a bloodied cloak of gilt cloth that bunched too small over his shoulders. The man began to speak wildly about his part in the events of the past days. As he told of the slaughter on both sides we walked past flaring pyres that proved he did not exaggerate. Small, intelligent-looking dogs were worrying the bodies that waited for their chance at the flames. I interrupted his account.

–What island is this? I used his language; his speech was something like Hamitic. The invaders called it Tenerife, he told me. He looked to be a typical Lebu, tall and fair, but he called himself an Achinach. All the while he was looking toward the tower project, such as it was, logs propped on logs in the sand; and I kept an eye on the women. They had not moved, nor had they noticed me approaching.

The man's point, it developed, was that he had seen me come to shore and hoped I would take him away from the island. Like many of the resident warriors he had gone over to the conquerors, and he assumed his neighbors would need revenge once the Iberians withdrew to their enlarged garrison.

–What does it matter who kills you? I asked him.

He turned away. I shed him at 594 paces—in total to that point, or 241 from where I first spied the women.

I hailed Mother, but neither she nor the others acknowledged me. Their eyes were riveted on the caravel. The longboat that had removed the men was being drawn over its side. I interposed myself between them and the object of their concentration, and still they ignored me. Time had taken its toll. Their faces were worn, and within their robes their shapes were indifferent. For a moment I thought illness was an element for Mother, from the way her face was drawn and her cheeks were blotched. But her eyes, though wet, were full of her same power, as I saw before she turned her back to the ship and to me.

–You have traveled a great span. Your frayed person bears that out.

This was Adhah, the shorter and wider of the two. She is not given to ceremony nor to flattery. She pointed to the Iberian vessel. –Someone is on the big boat. It will be a simple matter for you to go out, before they have settled him below, and negotiate his release to you.

–You can help us, said Seelah, the tall and burly one. –I assume you have your boat.

I nodded, watching Mother. I was unwilling to speak to her back, so I again moved around to face her—five paces, six. Her stance, almost wedged between the other two, made her the only one of us who could not watch the deck of the caravel. I feared she would keep up this child's game, of hiding by turning. But she remained staring at me fiercely through her tears, while the others spoke of their insane scheme as calmly as they would choose a menu, and without looking around at me, the subject of their plan.

–You can do it, Adhah said without turning. –Even with your crooked gait, you can accomplish it before night takes over. Do not bother the costumed men but tell the Canarians that a mistake has been made. They will believe you, now that the boy has greeted them. Tell them you have come for Mahuri. Tell him you have come from Uhwa.

I smelled plague in the smoke that swept along the beach.

–This place will be emptied, I said to Mother. –And the conquerors will take the disease with them. You will need to come with me.

I knew, of course, that true release would come from the sky. But not on this day, and in any event fever and bloody delirium is no proper exit. Did she, did they, did any woman have the judgment to deal with such a confluence?

–We have seen your skill with the sailcloth, Seelah said. She was staring at the ship. –It would be possible, and perhaps less risky, for you to overtake the slave-makers after they are comfortably away from land. But the boy will become frightened. He has never faced night alone, and purity is no defense against terror, nor against pain, as you well know.

–And we want him with us, Adhah said.

–Purity? Have you cultivated another fool?

–He is the one who dances, Seelah said. –You will hear him, even if he is not in sight. He is already singing.

–I thought so. A vegetable. Is he capable of learning a new tune? Then here is his chance.

I could not restrain a laugh.

–You speak all languages, Adhah said, and no man will harm you who sees your face.

All this time the two younger women had continued to watch the ship. Now Seelah turned toward me.

–Think of the boy as your kin, she said.

While she invoked kinship—this woman who is no kin of mine—she thrust her chin forward affirmatively, as though intention were truth.

Mother's shoulders had been shaking and her breaths rapid and deep when I went around to face her, but she had recovered. I put the question to her.

–Come with me and be saved—for a time: death and the sea now wait together. The two may do as they please; this boat is but little larger than the one you knew. Promise me, and I will fetch the idiot to shore.

–Not you, Mother said.

–The ocean is old and its promises have failed. I cannot urge you fully. And still less you—I gestured to Adhah, and to Seelah who was again looking to sea. –And yet the risk is greater here.

I had been standing too long in one place. The earth's sand had seized my ankles. I could feel the sea whispering to the soles of my feet.

–Not you, my mother said. –Not you.

CHAPTER 13

*Behold, you have driven me today from off the face
of the ground, and I will be a fugitive and a vagabond
in the earth.*

Genesis 4:14

Adhah stirred on the bare bed. In the darkness her arm fell over
Seelah's thick waist; her lips found the border of Seelah's sleeveless night garment and kissed cloth and skin. Seelah, who was already awake, brought her hand up and patted Adhah's face. The
exchange of gestures was automatic, a reflex beyond habit. Still
touching Adhah, Seelah worked her feet to the edge of the bed, slid
to the floor, and stood.

"Let me make us some tea," she said in an almost whisper. "It's
permitted, the wait will go more quickly."

"Thank you, darling," Adhah said. "I believe I'll stay here
awhile. Work comes soon enough." She turned away, reshaping the
hard pillow. "I feel it, though," she said, her voice suddenly loud.
"Warm as these days are—don't you? It burdens me, how night
starts to borrowing. The darkness *will* drive the sun low and call to
the cold wind." Seelah nodded and coughed, an affirmation and a
reminder, while her hands rifled the clothing piled on the blanket
rack.

"We were on the dog island just now," Adhah said, speaking more softly. "The hot wind was blowing, high up where we were. We were on the slope of Teide, all the way up in the cumbre where no wind was ever hot—isn't it funny how a vision does you, while you sleep? Away down below us the sea was set in rows of white. Remember, we used to work our way up there to look down at the cloud blanket. No clouds this time.

"We had climbed above the tall pines and beyond the paths through the junipers. Uhwa was leading the way—she was a young girl. My goodness, we were all three of us young and supple in our bright robes. New-made robes, redder than the sky was blue, crimson from the blood-tree sap, colors deep as the blue of the sea. We were gliding through the dry waist-high grass. We were dancing in the sweet-smelling broomgrass. You know how much like hope a dream can be. Mahuri came running up. He was there, we were all the same that way, Mahuri's age when they took him."

"A locust landed right on the top of my bonnet yesterday," Seelah said, stretching a smock onto her arms in the dark room. "Behind the garden—I was taking some table scraps to the mixture pile."

"And it made you think of Mahuri, how it was a year of locusts when the men with metal sleeves came a second time, and of the day they dragged him onto their boat."

"Joeab keeps me in mind of Mahuri, sweetness. But you're right. A great yellow locust. I couldn't see what it was, only felt something arrive on my head. When I shooed her, she fluttered away big as a bat, all the way to the top of the tallest mimosa."

"She would need all her strength and all the wind to fly the sea, to join with her kin and go looking for mischief," Adhah said. Seelah could make her out, ample, turning onto her side. The bed responded, a rustling sound.

"But life, for the bugs, is too comfortable here," Seelah said.

"They have more than they can eat." Adhah laughed in the darkness, a whispered breathy laugh no louder than their quiet words.

"Thanks to us," she said. "No, they wouldn't decide to swarm across the ocean. In the dream, I saw a dot way down on the water. It went skittering out of the sunshine. That means it's certain. He's close."

"Oh, my," Seelah said. A sailing boat running from the wind. She pictured it disappearing into the shadow of the great central mountain. "And Mahuri was dancing with us?"

"Mahuri wouldn't take my hand. He was jumping and leaping and pretending to throw things, the dance the young warriors taught him. He came so close, several times. I looked him in the eyes and I leaned toward him, his dark eyes and his round cheeks and his wise smile. By this point he had gotten younger, he was a boy. So like Joeab."

"Joeab's look is Mahuri's when he was that size," Seelah said. "The gift brings the look. Mahuri was Joeab's size when the first round of men came killing." He was twice that, she thought, when we saw him last.

"And we were all three trying to bring him in the circle," Adhah said from the bed. "I needed so bad to hug him. Finally he danced away from us—he was flapping his elbows one after the other, bobbing his head, bringing his knees up—and he bounced up a ridge, and he was gone. I would have chased him but we couldn't stop for anything. We had to keep dancing."

"That part would be about the ship," Seelah said, "and how they wouldn't take us, wouldn't let us go with him. We were dancing with Uhwa? In crimson dresses? I'll bet it was fun, just the same."

"Then a hawk soared up from below," Adhah said, "from the other direction, I believe it was—no, it was from the way Mahuri went. And he stopped right over us, he was hanging in the east wind. I could smell the desert across the sea."

"Well," Seelah said. The picture in her mind was of bodies dragged together and stacked in a long, rough row—of painted men dead, their dried blood mixed with the pigments, the careful designs sliced by erasures the gleaming swords had cut. She saw in her memory two men dressed for a festival, their short coats gilded and glittering, their legs striped in green and blue cloth, the soft caps purple. The two men were hoisting another painted one. He was smaller than most of the warriors; he was no larger than the invaders who now threw him onto the pile of his brothers. He was no bigger than Mahuri, who was resisting her efforts to bring him away. She had found Mahuri there, attracted by the spectacle. Mahuri, who now saw what the games of his friends amounted to. This latest warrior fell and bounced on the heaped bodies, and rocked and was stationary. The dead man's look was one of surprise, as if he had hoped, in the instant he rose, to fly to his holy mountain. He held one fending leg stiff before him. The other had become a white-centered stump below the knee, and his girdle of magical leaves lay inverted above his waist. She saw how Mahuri's hand reached for his own leaf waistband. The gilded men went away to fetch more of the fallen ones. Already branches and fronds were stacked, and the heavy urns of palm oil waited. The dogs of the town moved in, tentative, sniffing the ground their gathered masters had crossed. At the far end of the heap the wild teah dogs resumed their grisly work. These dogs descended from those that had prospered on the decaying bodies of the first wave of invaders, whose friends had left them unburied and fled the island. The packs of dogs had multiplied in the teah forests; they preyed on sheep and followed the warriors hopefully. When the sickness spread that came from the boats, the dogs had been ready. The brightly dressed ones had returned, in strength, and this was the result. She gathered Mahuri into her arms and covered his eyes.

"Well, yes," she said. "Joeab keeps me in mind of Mahuri. And, too, Lindy told us she would be out here that next day. That's not like her. She's all right, I know that. Something came up, probably had to do with her family. Yet and still, separation starts with the first moment you part. I've been thinking fierce thoughts."

She opened the door. The gray-brown light from the hall flowed into the bedroom and died against its walls. Walking barefoot toward the back of the house, Seelah thought, Winter is all right. At the kitchen, beginning the preparations for tea, she thought, everything has a reason to live. She was moist now, a drop slipping down the back of her neck just from this little bit of moving about. Each step she took transferred coolness to her feet from the sleeping floor. She stirred the stove's dozing ashes and sprinkled the curly shavings over them until an ember grabbed the kindling. "It's not the cold, not the sometimes cold," she said to the stove and the floor. This unrest was the old man. While the tea steeped she followed the sweet odors of wood and herb back to the beach at Nivaria, to the time when Mahuri was taken from them.

She stood with Adhah and Mother Uhwa among the anxious women beside the water. The Achinach women had retreated in hopelessness from the looks the invaders threw at their naked bodies. The three of them alone waited with the prisoners.

After the men finished with killing each other that day, the glittering ones—the leaders of the invaders, the ones who were not required to gather bodies of the dead and the living—had gone into the stockade below the town. Seelah thought they must have remembered the first coming, when they had underestimated the Achinach warriors and their stone-tipped lances. A look-out perched in the wooden nest that stood above the circled log wall. Several of the largest boats in the harbor had nests like that one, cages fastened above the cross of tree trunks that cradled the largest sails. The sails were bundled like bedclothes; the boats sat, water-logged houses. A long ribbon of crimson flapped above the cage of one boat. The sun was at the edge of the sea. Above the island it created a cone of gold from the mountain's snowy peak. For some time the small boat had been shuttling the captives away. A ragged double line of men, their hands bound and tied at the waist in pairs, waited to be ferried to the bulging, high-backed ships. The line had dwindled. Soon all would have been transported. One of the tethered men was Mahuri.

A boy, a friend of Mahuri's, had brought the news. The children of the ridgelands were accustomed to roam. In spite of what they had already seen, the boys—Mahuri as usual with them—had been unable to hang back. One of the colorful invaders had beckoned the group closer. He had handed out small discs that were cool to the touch, and had let them rub his shining breastplate. Another of them had a boxy contraption of wood and string which when he held it at his shoulder, caused a noise that threw out an arrow from within the wooden thing. All the children, and Mahuri, began trying to propel their discs by holding them to their shoulders and mimicking the powerful noise. While they were thus occupied, the men had grabbed Mahuri. The others had escaped. All this, according to the boy.

The burning of a horse dirtied the air. Some of the plain soldiers from the boats had butchered a horse they must have dragged from the killing place. They had built a fire around part of it in the sand and were burning it for eating. The plain ones came, Seelah knew, from an island that could be glimpsed from the mountain. Like the chieftains of the Achinach, these men draped their lower bodies with skins. No one among the people of the dog island had been inside a boat before this day. They understood none of the soldiers' words, nor caught the language of the leaders cowering behind their walls. Only she and Adhah did, and Uhwa in her fashion. The plain men spoke among themselves, telling that the jeweled ones had promised them riches in a distant land if they would come to Nivaria and slaughter their neighbors. Many of their brothers had died this day. These also had been gathered like cordwood in the place above the town. And indeed a hotter, fouler smell now came on the breeze to mix with the smell of horse. Seelah knew this smell, which was more than smell. She looked and saw the orange flames from the pyre, and the brown shapes that billowed and spread.

"May the air take you to the caves," she said, speaking directly to the smoke. Adhah saw, too, and she began to sing one of the oldest of the songs. But they knew the Achinach dead were not reassured. They would not find the caves of the dead.

The longboat departed again. With so few prisoners remaining, the plain men who had been guarding the captives were dispersed, except for the tallest of them, who stationed himself between the prisoners and the three women. Mahuri continually waved to Seelah and the others and called his version of their names. His joy was manifest: finally he was admitted to the company of the spear-users. Seelah was aware that none of them, not the captives nor their women nor even the skin-clad soldiers from the neighboring island, understood the intentions of the leaders—no better than Mahuri did. How could the others know what lay beyond the sea, when no one had ever returned to the islands except the carriers of death? How could they comprehend that men would bundle the bodies of men and call them trade goods?

Nevertheless, Seelah thought, we know. We have seen the processions and the ships departing other ports; we have watched the traders lock the chains. We know how this business works. We know, and this soldier here must be told.

But it was Uhwa. All during the time they had waited, it was she who wept. Once, and again at intervals, she had cried out as if from a sudden pain. Now she approached the tall guard and spoke a word of greeting in the one language, her only language. "Your name?" Uhwa asked him. His expression puzzled, he told her, a word that said "bearer of gold" in many languages. Uhwa repeated the name. "The one who smiles," she said. "That one." Mahuri began to waggle his head and to attempt his warrior's dance. His partner in the ropes kicked at him. The soldier nodded.

"He is a boy in his soul," Uhwa said, putting her hand on the soldier's arm. The man was hearing her. "Bearer of gold, you see him. His body is valueless to your masters."

"I have no master," the soldier said in his language. "I do this freely and for my family. It is for their honor that I board the *carabela latina*. Riches wait for them because of my daring to cross the sea. Lands for my sons. The *nao*—he gestured toward the harbor—will take me to *España*. Livestock for my daughters, when I return." His pride in the few alien words was evident.

"You honor your children if you release the one who dances before his captors," Uhwa said. "Mahuri is his name, he is a favored one." How were they to make this one know? Nothing, Seelah decided, would save him from his pride.

"Take me, then," Uhwa said.

"Take me also," Adhah said. At the sound of his own language the soldier flinched. "Take my sister-wife and me, and our mother-in-law. Tie our arms with ropes and bind our waists, and lay us beneath inside your floating box. Our strength will not flag." The soldier began to laugh. His eyes were terrified.

"Look at us," Seelah said. "Are we not clothed? Have we not crossed many seas? Women such as we." What could she say that would matter? "Let us go with the boy." The skin-clad soldier turned away from them. Uhwa's voice rose from low within her body, a bitter cry. Seelah moved, took a step after the man, and bumped against the kitchen table. The tea sloshed in the clay pot, but didn't spill. It would be cool enough to drink now. Outside, a fish crow called four times. "Come! Hasten! Dawn!"

Using a spoon to hold back the flower pods and aromatic leaves, she poured tea into two mugs and started toward the bedroom. Adhah met her at the kitchen doorway. "Let me take those," Adhah said, "and you see about Uhwa. Did you hear her moving around? I'll ladle her a cup, and bring it."

Seelah went in to Uhwa, who though in bed was sitting up—her shadow also, sitting, on the wall. They exchanged a greeting, and Seelah eased Uhwa out of the bed toward her rocking chair.

"Adhah and I will sit outside until breakfast time," Seelah whispered. "And one of your friends is here." A regular among the talking faces was holding forth faintly on the cube's glass front. Uhwa knows this one's cadence, Seelah thought; she'll find it restful. "They don't ever get tired, do they."

But when Seelah had her lined up with the chair, Uhwa insisted, No, and would not sit. Adhah looked around the door. Silently they supported Uhwa down the hall and onto the back porch, and positioned her into her outside rocking chair. Adhah lifted one of Uhwa's hands and waited until she had grasped the cup. They sat for a while, the two younger women side-by-side on the long bench. A trio of rhythmic sippings played against the squeak of the rocker, Uhwa earnestly taking the lead. Silence dwelt beyond the house. The songbirds too were waiting for night to say good-bye.

"The tea, it's helping," Adhah said. "You said fierce thoughts, before. You've been to the island this night. I'm sorry, dearie. I told you my vision and that made it worse."

"Long before today," Seelah said. "You know it was not your vision that started it."

"I'm going to get Uhwa and me another cup," Adhah said. She got to her feet and turned ceremoniously toward Seelah. "You ready for one?"

"I'm fine right this minute," Seelah said absently. "We might have stayed on the island," she added, truly whispering now. She raised her hand and Adhah took it. "It was he," Adhah said. She turned and went into the house.

Seelah held the cup close beneath her face and saw before her Mahuri untied from his partner by the tall soldier, and placed in the invaders' longboat; Mahuri waving as the sailors dislodged the front of the longboat from the sand, and then at last as the boat retreated, Mahuri beginning to squall; the soldier striding back to where the women stood and promising that no harm could come to the boy-man—he, who soon enough would lie in shackles beside Mahuri. She saw in her mind Mahuri's figure in the last light, far off and tiny, gesturing from below the crossed logs; heard in her mind's ear Uhwa crying out as if someone had begun to beat her.

CHAPTER 14

And why are you angry?
And why has your countenance fallen?

Genesis 4:6

Lindy had been back in her apartment long enough to clear the refrigerator of everything moldy, and to segregate the dirty clothes and start a wash of underwear. The box of photographs and letters was still on the passenger seat of the truck. They were all she had brought with her. The drop-leaf table was the only ponderable thing she had wanted, apart from the mementos. Her dad had gone looking for the walnut boards the day he brought Sunshine and brand-new Lubella home from the hospital. For displaying wedding cakes, he kept saying long after Sunshine was gone. It served that purpose for Lubie's, and within a few weeks, Loretta's; but not her own wedding—a New Orleans quickie, with plenty of drugstore champagne but no cake. The table was stashed at the back corner of Lubie's three-car garage. Everything else had been hauled away to charity or placed at the curb by Lindy, after her dad's house sold on the first day the agent got the listing. Once Lindy got around to fetching the table, there would still be the question whether to bring it to Ash or to haul it to Little Rock where the bulk of her household things were still in self-storage. She looked around—the dusty living room, the breakfast table with rain-wrinkled recent mail piled on a summer's worth of catalogs and unread magazines, in the corner the mass of folded drapes that the couple who took her Little Rock apartment hadn't wanted: what her life had come to.

Driving toward the old women's place the next morning, Lindy worried about wasted vegetables. Her absence amounted to a generation in the life of a summer garden. Young produce demanded to be harvested, clamoring like baby birds for a parent's return. Adhah and Seelah would have kept on gathering the vegetables they had no interest in. Cash for the women, but she was the needy one. Maybe she could persuade them to keep the butterbeans and field peas, no doubt promptly shelled and already too dry to peddle. They could throw them into one of the baskets in the hall with the round beans the size of pecans, that they called barah. At least the sweet corn was finished. She had let the women down, but she wasn't going to grieve about it. Everything returns to the earth anyway, doesn't it.

Lindy parked in the shade near the house. In the yard the tableau was confusing. Adhah standing there, Seelah attending to someone in a straight chair that had been brought from the porch. That's nice, Lindy thought, they've brought Uhwa out to get some sunshine. But Uhwa was as swaddled as always, and all three of the women were facing away from the sun, Adhah a few feet in front of Uhwa's chair, Seelah immediately behind it. Uhwa's posture was more erect than Lindy had seen it, as if years had been taken off her age. The women seemed not to have noticed her arrival.

"Hey, guys," Lindy said. "I'm so sorry. My dad—." Her news could wait until she got a look at the man who was standing on the far side of the yard, inside the shade of the biggest oak. That's who the three women were concentrating on.

"We'll always welcome you," Adhah said to the man. "In spite of it hasn't never worked out. She's out here purely to favor us, don't you count on a thing. Go ahead then and finish your piece." Adhah's voice was loud, and with a sharp edge.

Lindy shaded her eyes to see who Adhah was admonishing. Somebody with some old grievance, and whatever it was mattered enough for Adhah and Seelah to bring Uhwa outside. Lindy studied him, his stunted body, his weatherbeaten arms outside his sleeveless shirt, his cuffless pants pulled up nearly to his armpits so that the smooth skin of his old legs showed above his run-over brogans. His eyes shone under his bird's-nest brows. And his oddly dark hair, she would have sworn, was electrified. The rest of it—Joeab in the man's grasp, and the long knife in the old man's raised left hand, the shocking arc of the blade—Lindy had taken in immediately. These things just hadn't made enough sense to give words to. She shuddered. "Who is he, Adhah?" she asked. The women had not acknowledged her presence.

The man began to speak, unintelligibly. Joeab was struggling, not to resist but to get a better look at the curved blade above him. He reached up, and the old man casually raised the knife away from the small pale palms, all the while glaring toward the women in the stick-scrubbed yard. With increasing alarm, Lindy tried to puzzle out what the old man was saying. Then, as if a switch were turned, she began to penetrate his odd accent—that's all it was—and to make out words and phrases, and then almost everything. His declaiming matched his wild look, the words coming out in erratic bursts. He swallowed some of his words, trailed off and then resumed with sudden emphasis. The accent was not like Adhah's and Seelah's. She thought she heard hints of a West Florida twang, but there was something alien about it. He hadn't lived his whole life around Acheron, that was sure.

"You need me to spell it out?" he was asking. "This old misery that's grabbed me again? I wake debased, every day. I convict myself of yearning, I, who asked no help nor gave quarter. You don't comprehend dependency, do you? Disappointment was the trigger; it was the loss of confidence that I long since placed with the sky." He was repeating himself. "Disappointment" and "trigger" had been the first words Lindy picked up. "Every shred of this is news to you," he said. "You go to your pallet when the sun sets; how could you fish up learning? Without the promise of destruction from the sky, what possibility remains? There you have it, the sickness that sent me to sea and has reinfected me, and dogs me these hundred thousands of paces from the ocean. There's your history, and there's your cause. But what of history and what of causes? Where should I find my cure?—why, at the beginning, nowhere else but you and me. You alone, in fact. Acknowledge that I am whole, is all the cure I need. Your word is enough."

The old man's talk, like his inflection, was no one thing. Simple but peppered with formal words, it sounded rehearsed, his words begging, but his tone calm. Considering his appearance, his manner of speaking couldn't have struck her as more incongruous if he were producing an operatic aria.

"You look run down," the man went on irrelevantly. "Drudgery—am I right?" He continued without waiting for a reply. "Or is the ground extracting the last breath from you? Oh, I see your crop rows back yonder. Hard to believe you took up tilling, and in such a place." He inhaled loudly through his nose. "I smell captivity round about here. I walked beside the hovels, the rows of mansions. This flat country reeks of servitude. And an excess of green absent any shade of meaning—not crops, not shelter. And divided everywhere by water half solid with green, water infected upward from the ground to its surface. This land fumes with hatred. It exacts a cost for each stride, yet I would suffer the journey a hundred times, if I didn't feel the flood's old muddy residue sapping my reason. Let

the same mismatch, heroic feet and wrists and stunted medieval bodies.

"We go along with you in this degree," Adhah said as he wound down. "Regarding how you feel, there may not be much you can do about it. We have visions, too, more than one. But think on Uhwa. She gave up a deal more than ground, as you well know, before you was ever thought of. Hard for her to go easy, after all she's known. And you're right, it's in her hands to settle it. Which I believe she will, in the right season. I'm speaking for both of us, Seelah and me."

The old man dragged Joeab farther forward in the sun-baked dirt. He was looking hard at Uhwa. "The right season?" he said. "Listen to her. Do you remember how I came to you the day before Brother and I had the fight? I was hurting, and I told you a premonition. Something was threatening to seize my prize field. I asked you—remember?—did anything ever well up and despoil your humble-minded yield? You told me everything that could go wrong in the garden had long since gone wrong, and you were through studying trouble. You couldn't hear me that time, but, Mama, you've got to hear me now. I've been working on it ever since the sea unbowed and went home, ever since I pulled you into the boat. Every time, you can't hear my side."

"Your neediness is unseemly," Adhah said. "We don't forget what happened at the island. Now then, Seelah reports you throwed away the breakfast she brought out. Won't you come and sit down while we get dinner ready? You're Uhwa's kin, and ours too, to some degree or other. We'll not send you away unfed. I'll go on and say why not stay this approaching night. Either way, I'm going in the house. You have kept her out here until the sun is frowning on every one of us. And let the boy loose, you understand. He don't like to be penned up." As she finished speaking Adhah turned and headed away.

"Oh, she says understand," the old man said softly. His voice was suddenly plaintive. "I understand every rule that hides behind the daytime sky, how the sun pushes the planets around, how it made a haven for a scheming world. I've used my time and my own deep thinking to learn a tremendous amount. You've had the same interval. But who ever added to their knowledge, sitting complacent in one place? I understand who we are and always have been, and I understand who"—the name was too exotic for Lindy to get it—"was. I was like Brother, I used time luxuriantly. Capering and dancing, only I danced under the night sky." He was breathing fast, his lips putt-putting together absently with each shallow exhalation.

Lindy shifted her feet. Her thighs had all but stuck together in the heat. Uhwa's verbose old son, she thought.

"I don't stand here anticipating reunion," the old man said at length. "Reunited here in this place? What I want is to be released to everywhere. Reunited? Send me away healed." The index finger of his constraining hand tapped Joeab's thin chest.

"Your brother could have brought forgiveness," Seelah said in a mild tone, as if she were speaking to Joeab. Adhah was already inside the house. "Study the child, and find out how you might decide her to release you."

"This cripple?" the old man said. "Read his fool's mouth, you know it's Brother all over again. He can't make a man out of the start he's got."

Joeab by now had forgotten about the belt. Both his hands grasped the crook of the old man's knife arm, and he was moving from side to side along with the man's winded speeches. It seemed to Lindy that whatever kin the women and the old man might be, one big gene they shared was patience for talk. What difference could it make whether Uhwa's son got the benediction he craved— that in her opinion he deserved, that anyone deserved before they died? Whatever he thought of Joeab, wasn't that all the more reason to let him go?

A voice brought her out of her study of the old man. Uhwa's voice—Uhwa who had managed on her own to stand, her lap robe fallen to the dirt under her feet. Uhwa's words, surely they were words, came out cracked and dry. How long, Lindy had time to wonder, since she's spoken? Uhwa coughed, and her tone began to pick up musical rises and falls, a warbling flow of almost-song that lit up Lindy's mind.

Uhwa was saying that she hadn't wanted to speak, not outside, they could have brought him into the hut, but of course that would have honored his mother; hadn't wanted to speak, not here outside.

Lindy realized she was keeping up with Uhwa without deciphering any of her words, without spotting the sentence breaks if there were any, because there was no need to. It was nothing like the hard listening required to latch onto the old man's half-swallowed English. Her high school French teacher had warned her she would never get anywhere by memorizing the elements. What Lindy had never learned was to think in another language; but following Uhwa required no such effort. It bypassed listening and became her own words, her own thought.

Uhwa was saying that her feet recognized this place, the swept offerings in the warm soil, the sun reliving that scalded day, place of separation, place where separation-death was born, this very place.

Understanding Uhwa, Lindy was transfixed. Because Uhwa was Eve, it was as simple as that. No, Eve was Uhwa. The old man was Cain, and Abel, that's who Cain had been saying the name of. Cain, and Abel his brother that he murdered, and their mother Uhwa. So that's how truth arrived: without being sent for.

Every new cluster—Uhwa's talk wasn't made of sentences but of images—flared into a bouquet, flowers with hues everyone was born responding to, and fragrances that only settled into words and clauses because these were all Lindy could manage. Whatever Uhwa's meaning in her dark message, Lindy entered the circle through the melody of Uhwa's speech. The world was not the one she had been coasting through, not an indifferent place. That realization began to overcome her nausea and fear. No wonder she and Joeab, two outsiders in an uncomprehending world, were drawn to the old women. Wasn't Uhwa the reason the two women weren't worried about him?

To judge from his reaction, Joeab agreed with her. His eyes were closed and he beamed his maximum smile. He was bouncing gently within the cage of the old man's arm. For his part the old man's expression was wary, as if Uhwa had produced a gun. Seelah, frowning, went to Uhwa to steady her, or perhaps to make her sit down. Uhwa shook her off, and turned to her right as she had done while the old man was the only one speaking. The nearest object in that direction was a tall crape myrtle tree, so old that its knotted trunk had no bark and the few blossoms were far up at the top.

Split the air my son Abel, Uhwa said, *overshadow him whose pleading is small and twisted, who began to kick with design from within my body, who turned to his artifices, who drove us from the gentle way. Shape your task with strength my son Abel and whelm his guile. We set you the journey, we are nearer by far, Death has graced us this day. Our invocation is bearing its fruit. He who speaks has no place in the birthing. Pick up your drum-gourd rattle, and drown him who treasures noise, who blocks the way back to life.*

Uhwa was addressing the mauve-crowned tree as if Abel were sitting in it. Cain's name for Abel was longer than Uhwa's—an extended version, a diminutive. Another certainty, though Uhwa hadn't said a word that was like any of Cain's. The name had condensed like rain streaming from a clear sky.

"Your same voice. Been a long time," the old man said. "If you would just look at me I'd feel hopeful right now." He had relaxed enough that Joeab's ruined feet again touched the ground.

"She don't see the outsides of things," Seelah said.

"You're blind," Lindy said involuntarily. "I'm sorry, I should have seen it."

Uhwa was sliding one dusty foot after the other, she was stalking the voice that offended her. *My son Abel you encountered your brother, there is no offense in that. He sensed your journey, he who must be moving, he comes resisting as always, but why, he who was first among new-made men? He, callow acolyte of Absence? the world bloated with the choice he made? he whose kicks brought body burial?*

"They're claiming you can't see," the old man interrupted. His tone again was petulant, like a child's. "It's time you see the insides of me. I was a little fellow. Brother couldn't do anything but sit and sift the dirt. You took my hand and dragged me toward the old grove. The Man is barred, you said, But we're not, you can be the one to help me. Later it came to me why I pulled loose: I didn't want your same life. You thought it was work I was afraid of. But oh, the tasks I ended up doing for you. Here's the one task you can do me. Make me whole in my heart.

"Wait a minute. Separation, you say? You've still got Brother, in your mind he's all that's here. So then which help is it Brother can't accomplish right now, that he could back then? I sent him out of my world, I meant to. And I'm not proud I wanted it. No way you can claim to miss him, when you talk to him all the time. I'm asking, let me go. The whole world was ours, and it was pure. Now it's solid ticks, that believe if they just keep sucking at the dirt they'll hatch out men. They blanket the ocean and haul it barren—the sky won't dislodge them. I'm reconciled to letting them crawl over me, if you stop lighting into me there in your darkness."

Uhwa resumed her chanting as if he hadn't said anything. *Thump your gourd, Abel-my-son, wake him from the dream, the dream*

184

*he alone fills, that crowds out life—men live too long, speak too well,
vomit blessings on themselves, forgiveness for separations they intend.
Your brother, the first among such men—louder now Abel. Sing loose
his girdle of error until it lies untied at his feet.*

Uhwa by now was near. The four of them—Seelah had not followed Uhwa—formed a group in the untended part of the yard,
not ten feet separating them. Uhwa's garments hung gracefully, and
her gestures, in spite of her hands' heavy tremor, had an intensity
that matched her speech. Cain's shadow made a blunt sundial that
pointed toward Lindy. The boy's expression as Uhwa spoke was his
usual look of expectancy. The old man glanced down at Joeab, and
as if the boy's presence finally had weighed it down, the knife arm
fell harmlessly, its biceps deflating under the crinkled skin.

You, Death, attend me, Uhwa intoned. *I see you clearly, I praise
you for favoring us with your presence while he prunes again his sour
logic. You who have heeded my messenger Abel. Death, come forward
into our clearing, regard not him who once called to you unknowing.
Your will has done these deeds, your will undoes them. Unbegotten one,
restore my son, restore every one of those you have sequestered from us.
This I have earned the right to ask.*

"So that's it," Cain said, "death be undone. Hah! Won't it make
a crowd. Only problem is, I'm one of them, soon enough. You can't
have Brother back to hug and coddle, except you get me next to
you."

*Wait, do not retire, do not ebb away! Stay while I quiet this one.
Hear me my first son, if I address you, if I require it of you, if that might
suffice, if Death then grants reprieve to all who are in his keep, if your
brother Abel is whole again? if you ease your will? Who is she that says
to you, "My son," but I your mother who asks this thing of you?*

What if Cain did stop complaining, Lindy wondered. What
would he have gained? Yet Uhwa had made an offer of sorts, or a
preamble to an offer. No forgiveness anywhere, except the peace that

185

would attend the retirement of death until the next round. That much Lindy found understandable, Uhwa distraught for her lost son. But what of the living son? She moved enough to get a better look at Cain. Was she imagining, or was his expression like a heedless boy's, who knows he has frightened his mother? And hadn't his manner of speaking regressed, too? The tension was evaporating. Nothing could ever be settled, and that formed a solution of sorts. Cain was going away, they wouldn't be sitting down to dinner with Cain. He does this every so often, she thought. He has claimed his right to an audience with his mother, and now we all get on with what's left of our lives. But people had to come to their right mind, didn't they, even if they had grieved for a thousand years—especially if they have grieved for a thousand years. She found it impossible not to feel sympathy for Cain. He would be leaving by himself, all the others could stay. What must it have been like to be Cain, the first born to a couple who were already grieving, who had lost a life no child could make up for? What had been Sunshine's grief, that three little girls couldn't cut through it and make her stay?

The old man's voice was strained. "I don't bring harmony. If I do end up in your blind keep, don't count on any spirit songs. Just the same, that would be fine by me."

Oh, Cain, Lindy said to herself. If only you could keep your mouth shut, your mother might hear what you're saying.

The old man continued, speaking rapidly. "My earliest recollection, just about. I knew to respect darkness, but you had been off somewhere ever since dinner, and Daddy hadn't called me in. I was outside, stripping some long thin branches—I broke them off, I was already that strong—and arranging them in an even pile, and enjoying the guilty moonlight. I didn't notice you come back, but then I heard you making sleep sounds, from inside. Only it wasn't like Daddy's rasping. It was a brand new way of saying something—color and length, long up-and-back lines. I went and stood by the opening, but of course the darkness blocked my sight. I went any closer I'd wake you up and then I'd be in trouble. In the dark you were breathing this sparkling new way. I began to make out that it was words, too. 'My son, my son, my lovely, my perfect son.' In the morning I would be able to ask you what wonderful things you and I were doing together in your vision. But now I was wide awake, so I went back to my sticks, balancing them and leaning them together. I was making a better house for us, I was building a tower to your song. So I believed. Then you called to me from the door and I ran to you, you were leaning down, you had a package to show me. My heart twisted—who was that tiny little wrapped-up man? I knew how bad I was to disobey, but he brought you outside. You hadn't been asleep, and he was the reason you figured out how to sing. You raised up a song for Brother. But never one for me."

Joeab began to hum, in his high-pitched little boy's voice. Lindy didn't recognize the tune; it wasn't any of the ones Adhah preferred. He continued for a long minute—it might have been an entire song—then he stopped and looked straight up at Cain. Now, in the silence, he shifted gears. "'Wuh, 'Wuh, 'Wuh." What sounded like grunts became a sort of cheer for Uhwa that ended with Joeab dissolved in laughter. Sweat dripped from his nose, his elbows rested on the old man's encircling arm as if it were a railing. He was laughing helplessly and sputtering Uhwa's name. Uhwa had registered puzzlement at Joeab's humming. His laughter brought forth a shout of sudden pain and a series of exclamations, short bursts, harsh and rhythmic but with none of the gliding purity of before. This was no lyric, it was oaths like an axe striking a tree. It was, Lindy realized, the old man's name, or what stood for the name.

Cain! Cain! Cain! Joeab echoed excitedly. The word was not Cain. Joeab was laughing and pulling himself up, not trying to escape but gaining height to say something.

Brother! Joeab cried, though the word wasn't brother.

Seelah began to lumber toward them and then to run, something Lindy wouldn't have believed possible.

Uhwa yelled, *Do not lift your brother again!*

Brother! Joeab repeated in Uhwa's language. *Come and dance with us, Wuh!*

Lindy didn't recognize it as a blow. Cain only rubbed the knife across Joeab. He didn't draw the knife back, he only wiped it easily across Joeab's midsection, a motion like slitting open a bag of mulch. And raised it toward the vertical, a used-up gesture of completion. Lindy lunged forward, too late. By diving, by ignoring the man, she was able to catch Joeab as he fell. His eyes were open. Blood was everywhere; his arms were slashed, too. She cradled him and turned his body until her thumbs and forefingers found the edges of the main wound and squeezed them closed. For a moment he was Joeab, straining over his shoulder to look at her, then his yearning expression drained away and he was unconscious in her arms. So much blood from such a small boy. She couldn't afford to trace out the wound. She could only try to keep her grip and try not to think about the damage beneath the ridged edges. The odor of Cain was still on Joeab, and little boy sweat, and the sharp copper smell of his blood.

"Help me stand up with him. I can't let go, he'll die right here."

Seelah was already lifting her. Her fingers on Lindy's waist felt like iron, and her tall hummocky body took their weight easily. Uhwa was wavering where Seelah had abandoned her. No trace of Cain.

"Support his legs," Lindy said, when Seelah reached down as if to pick up both of them. "They're pulling down on it. We've got to get him to the hospital." Together they walked with Joeab toward the truck. How were they going to manage, Lindy wondered, since she couldn't let go of him? Thank goodness the tailgate of the truck was down. Thank goodness for shade, he wouldn't be burned by hot metal.

"Here," Lindy said, "brace him. Use your shawl—anything to work around him for a bandage. Then I'll be able to hand him to you. Are you going to want to sit back here, or can you fit up front with him?"

"Adhah," Seelah said. "She's coming." And she was. Adhah strode up with an armload of folded cloth, and set it on the tailgate. Cradled in the stack of fabric were two small stone vessels and a green mason jar filled with a clear liquid, and an ornately embossed scissors that looked to be the original pair.

"Turn him around," Adhah said, gesturing with her head toward Seelah and indicating that she wanted Joeab laid flat. Using the scissors to notch the material, she quickly tore a series of strips. The weave of the fabric was open; fragments of lint flew into the air. Then she opened the glass jar and poured half its contents over Joeab's middle where Lindy's hands held it. "Water," she said to Lindy's quizzical look, and patted away some of the blood. "The balm has to get right down inside."

Wrapping the first layer took all three women working together, and for a moment revealed, inside Joeab's abdominal cavity, pale twisted shapes Lindy couldn't identify. When that was done, and his arms were also bandaged, they laid Joeab on Adhah's shawl. Lindy unbuttoned her blouse, wrapping the tail of it around her finger to clear the blood inside his mouth. His eyes were closed—that might be a good sign. Now Adhah dipped a hand into one container and applied the blackish gelatinous ointment to the bandages. With her thumbs she wedged open the lid of the second jar and shook it until something as viscous and orange as peach preserves flowed over the first application. Powerful herbal smells. She let Lindy smooth and blend the two salves. Finally they wrapped two more rounds of the torn cloth.

"Help me, sister," Seelah said, placing Lindy's hands at her waist and trying to heave herself backward onto the bed of the pick-up. Lindy jumped up into the bed and pulled her up. Seelah crawled forward and leaned against the back of the cab. "Hand him here," she said. Lindy transferred Joeab to her. With Joeab settled across her lap, Seelah reached out and squeezed Lindy's blood-crusted hand. Black and orange oozed over their intertwined fingers.

"They bind together," Seelah said. "The unguents. They meld into a poultice, a concordance for healing."

"Why are you taking him off from here?" Adhah asked from where she stood. But Lindy was already in the cab. She started the truck's engine and began to back and turn. Adhah went to the old woman.

CHAPTER 15

Listen! The voice of your brother's blood
is crying out from the ground.

Genesis 4:10

The street beside the levee led right through the Blackmon Medical Center, low white-brick buildings strung out along both sides of the street. The sign, vertical letters "emergency," directed her to turn at the far end of the complex, past the heart institute.

"Sit still," she yelled to Seelah as she ran for the door. "I'll get someone out here." Inside was like a hotel lobby, high ceiling and gleaming terrazzo floors. People sat inert, some of them collapsed in sleep. To the right she could see glass-walled conference rooms. What looked like the concierge's desk was unattended. An enormously wide hall opened ahead. Where was the emergency room? Lindy ran toward the hallway—and there it was on the left beyond more glass doors. She hurried past a Staff Only Beyond This Point sign, to a busy counter and a collection of curtained cubicles. "Outside! He's terribly wounded!" Her yells echoed in the lobby. Some of the seated people stared at her impassively. Seelah came through the outer door with Joeab. His arms and feet dangled limply. Two attendants appeared with a gurney and immediately laid Joeab on

it, and escaped with him down the corridor. This time a green uniform stopped Lindy at the door. Seelah walked up heavily and they
stood there.

No one had spoken during the transfer. But now a woman in a
peppermint-striped jumper approached Lindy and Seelah. "You're
the grandmother," the uniformed woman said to Seelah. "Follow
me." Her face was kind, but her voice was remote. She walked rapidly toward the receptionist's desk.

"You go sit down," Lindy said, gesturing toward the rows of the
side-by-side chairs in the waiting room. "This is about insurance.
We have to get in touch with Eshana." Seelah turned toward the
entrance to the emergency room, where two straight chairs flanked
two wall-mounted pay telephones. "This place is nearer," she called
across to Lindy once she was sitting. She gestured toward the glass
doors. "They'll be needing me." The two women using the phones
cupped their handsets against the noise.

The receptionist alternated her questions with spells of rapid
keyboarding, without ever looking at Lindy. She took down the
facts as Lindy gave them to her. Joeab Barmore, age nine. Yes,
she—Lindy—had hospitalization; but, no, Joeab was not a depen-
dent. She wished—no, he couldn't be covered. That was not his
grandmother, she was a neighbor. Mother? Eshana Barmore. Lindy
didn't remember the address, and the number? she didn't know the
number, she lied—the call was not going to be from this stranger.
No, the mother didn't know about the accident yet. A little boy
playing with, playing around in the yard. He found a machete,
an old cane knife, and fell on it—the macabre pun only dawned
on Lindy as she spoke. She left the woman and ran outside to the
truck and found her phone in her purse. The battery was dead. She
hurried back to the telephone station, where one of the phones had
come open.

"Eshana, this is Lindy," she said after Eshana's greeting quit.

"It's"—she looked at her watch, and rubbed it against her jeans—"it's eleven-thirty-five. Sunday morning. I'm at Blackmon Medical, downtown. You need to call me at this number." She read off the number. "I'm at the emergency room. This is a pay phone, but I'll be right here. Joeab's here. At the emergency room. He's going to be all—." Cut off. She called again and repeated the number twice more.

Seelah looked up quizzically.

"She's not there. I was talking to her phone. Did Miss Johnson have one?" Seelah looked away. Had she thought the other women were talking to the wall?

Lindy took the other chair. The uniformed woman glared across at her for a few moments, then came past them and into the main part of the hospital. A hard-looking man, red-faced and shirttail out, came up to use a phone. Lindy realized their eyes were following him, in the same absent way she and Seelah had been watched when they came in.

The young doctor was making no pretense of politeness. Lindy had stood beside the nurses' station for several minutes before she got a chance to buttonhole him. Bull-necked and slit-eyed, white-jacketed and stethoscoped, he hadn't responded when Lindy twice asked him how Joeab was doing. On her third try he said, "Too soon."

You wouldn't think it was too soon to tell me, her eyes told him, if you were old enough to have a nine-year-old back there.

"Are you family?" the doctor asked. He was suppressing a pissed-off smile.

"Yes. Family. How would you describe his condition?"

"He's in ICU," the doctor said after a moment.

"They haven't moved him. We've been sitting right here the whole time."

The doctor turned away and picked up a chart. A woman staffer said, "Ma'am, you get to ICU through there."

"What about Joeab," Lindy said to the doctor's hog-round back. The wobble in her voice surprised her.

The nurse answered. "They've called for a surgeon. His little heart is strong."

"No surgeon?" Lindy said to the room. "Who was that guy? He bled so much, Adhah couldn't undo that. He's bound to be afraid."

The doctor had returned and was making take-it-easy motions with his hands.

"You hang around out here," he said. "We take care of back there. That's how it's done. Don't get personal."

Lindy and Seelah had sat for a long time without looking at each other. Earlier, Lindy had shown Seelah what to do with the telephone if it rang, and had gone to the cafeteria for change. She had stopped leaving messages after the third one. "How much time before we see him?" she asked. "It's been almost an hour."

"Hour, time." Seelah made both vowels Lindy's flat *ah*. "Say another one of them."

Lindy sighed. "Too soon to say. Too late. Time running out."

"You make it sound like water, but it doesn't run out, it bucks and bolts. Can a person ride a little word back to where they wish they were? Say another one."

"Two weeks ago. Forty-two years."

"Ugly creatures." Seelah's expression was placid.

"Is Joeab going to get well?" Lindy's question released her tears. She cried as quietly as she could for what seemed an eternity.

"Adhah always brings along her remedies," Seelah said at last. "Generally she's able to take care of whatever it is."

"Adhah's extraordinary, I don't doubt that. But will Joeab come out of this?"

"One way or another. You do right to cry."

Lindy leaned forward and looked across at the telephones, then sat back. "I believe you, Joeab will pull through. Of all things, I can see Cain's point of view. Can you? Uhwa is a treasure—royalty, if you look at it a certain way. But that doesn't excuse the way she talked to Cain."

Seelah pursed her lips.

"Oh, wait, say Cain's name for me. What is the old man's name?" No approximation of what Uhwa had called him made its way to Lindy's tongue.

Seelah's expression was distant.

"What about the son in the crape myrtle tree, the 'my perfect son' son? The dead son?"

"Uhwa's son."

"His name, can you say it for me?"

"We didn't know him."

"I'm going to call him Abel. Cain and Abel."

"Cain, Abel" Seelah said, making Lindy's diphthongs.

"Is there a name for Uhwa's language? I was able to understand basically everything she was saying."

"I make Uhwa's language more useful than I do this one. Everybody used to talk it."

"Why was Cain speaking English?" Lindy asked. Seelah didn't acknowledge the question. "Don't you think there would be a time for a mother and a son to be reconciled? Up to Uhwa, Adhah said, as if it were a small matter. She said she was speaking for both of you."

"Both of us, partly. As far as a matter always being between who's present, why yes. Adhah looks at both sides the same. I see two sides, neither one of them touching."

"Uhwa's voice was made for forgiveness, it's too poetic to speak hate. How much do you think she understands about what happened to Joeab?"

"You see why we'd as soon he didn't show up. Bad follows him."

Lindy knew she couldn't keep after Seelah about Cain, but if she could find the right question, Seelah's politeness might overcome her reticence. How about asking, How many times has he found you? "Was today bad enough to make youall pull up stakes?" What a selfish thing, to want them to stay. She would probably be sending out her resume within weeks. All she wanted to do was sit with the old women and go to bed as soon as the sun went down, or else go out into the world and do some important job perfectly. No, fuck work.

"Whether we stay or go, wherever we stop is the same place to him and Uhwa." Seelah's tone was matter of fact. "Some things no unguent can cure."

"How have youall stood everything?"

"If we were counters, if we collected every detail that fell in our way, it would make old women out of us. Look at Uhwa."

"You and Adhah know exactly what each other is thinking."

Seelah chuckled. "You get to be the same person."

"The ideal marriage."

"It hasn't run out." The stiff plastic chair creaked rhythmically under her weight.

"My daddy died, that's why I was gone for so long. Do you see the dead? I do."

"Oh, terrible, oh sad." Seelah stood and leaned forward with her heavy hands on Lindy's shoulders. The two women remained knee to knee until with a sigh, Seelah resumed her place.

Lindy wiped at her eyes with sticky hands. She was too drained to wash up, and Seelah's voice must not be the one Eshana heard when she called. In her mind she began replaying the scene with Cain. This time she got the knife in both her hands and easily wrestled it away from the sorry old man; then she started over, lunged for the knife and missed and felt the blade enter her heart and from the ground saw Joeab's throat slashed. She found a fallen limb and clubbed the old man to his knees before he could do a thing. She struck him again and he fell forward while Joeab ran to Uhwa. Yet always she waited in disbelief beside the old man, and watched, a hundred times, the casual swipe of his arm. How could a child suffer—what could matter in the whole world of events, compared with Joeab's survival?

She experimented with disbelief—tried to turn Cain into some local farmer, tried to imagine him as a schoolboy seated behind a narrow wooden desk, tried to picture him peeling corn to his chickens or underneath milking a wide stupid cow. She tried giving him a name, since Seelah wouldn't: Verlon, Joe Charles, Edgar. Cain's last name? Ridiculous, always he came up Cain. Every time she came back to the women's house, the old man materialized from no farmyard, from no family except Uhwa's, for no purpose except to plead for his mother's love. Because, crazy as he was, Cain made sense of the old women's stories, and a deluded old man would mean that Joeab was in there alone for no reason.

Where had Cain gone? Why hadn't she formed the question until now? By the time she had looked up from grabbing Joeab he had disappeared. But Cain wasn't any miracle. He couldn't fly, he wasn't Jesus ascending into heaven. Or halfway to heaven—like the one hymn claimed, it hadn't been all that long ago. Anytime she had happened to hear Stone preach, she would bury herself in a hymnbook and read until the twenty minutes had passed. She found a hymn that claimed the waves and winds still heard the voice of Jesus. His absence was recent, was the message, and the singer should feel extra guilt for ignoring that. The sentiment

made her wonder how far Jesus could have gotten by now, floating upward from Jerusalem toward glory at fifty miles an hour.
An absurd reverie—Cain, whatever he was called, was real, and
he had to be not too far away. The clouds at the old women's
yard were dissolved, the air had moved on; but there were bound
to be physical traces of Cain. The police could find him. They
would comb the parish and would pick him up, if she went to
them with the story. Why had she already known that she wasn't
going to do that? Was that the reason it took her so long to start
thinking about Cain on the run? The old women seemed to have
forgotten about Cain as soon as it was over. She looked across at
stolid Seelah and tried to match her expression to Seelah's. What
they did with the silences—no wonder Seelah and Adhah thought
she was insubstantial, she couldn't let go. If I did let Cain go, she
asked herself, if I don't bring in the police, what kind of excuse
would I give to my soul? She examined her grimy hands. Was she
ever and always thinking of herself?

"Could I speak with you?" The woman was standing in front
of Seelah. She was tall like Lindy, and wore a severe suit and a
white blouse buttoned to the neck. The laminated hang tags and
the clipboard marked her as hospital staff. Her face was as closed
as a corpse.

"Certainly." Seelah raised her bulk and shook out her robes.
The smell of unbathed old woman overcame antiseptics and floor
wax and the staff woman's strong perfume. "He's better." Seelah
made it a statement. "We caught it in time, then. Come on, Lindy
dear, she's taking us to Joeab."

"Over where we can talk," the woman said, and took Seelah's
arm firmly. The three of them passed all the same people occupying
the same positions, and took chairs in the far corner of the waiting
room.

"Now. What can you tell me about the accident, you called it?"

"How is he?" Lindy asked. "Are they operating?" She had heard indecipherable public address system blabs that included "doctor."

"He was in your care at the time, this is true?" the woman asked Seelah. "There is a mother I understand? Where is the mother at the present moment?"

"A body can see right away you enjoy gathering stories," Seelah said patiently. "But Joeab needs our attentions."

"That's not possible," the woman said. "Tell me how the accident happened."

"How much internal damage was there?" Lindy asked. "I don't know any anatomy." The woman repeated her question to Seelah.

"You keep saying accident," Seelah said. Lindy reached out and touched Seelah's sleeve. Seelah went right along. "You don't claim he doesn't know what he was doing? He knows, all right. You might say it's an accident that we had something to work with."

The security woman tapped her pen against her lower lip.

"This much. It mightn't of happened." Seelah gave her forward head thrust. "Adhah had him full talked out of it. I have to think he was surprised, in a way. But accident?"

He, him. It was true, Lindy decided, she couldn't bring herself to say Cain's name.

"Are you trying to tell me that a small boy attempted suicide?" The woman stopped scribbling on her notepad. "This woman"— the woman's eyes dwelled on Lindy's ruined blouse—"described it as an accident. But the wound, they tell us, lacks laceration. And the arms—both arms. We will need you to produce the instrument."

"As far as the blade and his arms," Seelah said, as if this were a clinical consultation, "why, the boy wasn't lying down. That doesn't figure one bit. The main thing is we get Joeab better. Lindy, you go out yonder and fetch Adhah. Adhah didn't do yet, all she knows to do."

"Can you tell that he's out of danger?" Lindy asked. "Are you going to keep us out here all day?"

The woman abruptly stood. "You"—again to Lindy—"do not leave, you do not bring anybody. You, at least, seem able to handle plain English. We will need you to give a statement to our people." Lindy watched her out of sight.

"Her people. They can't rouse a surgeon on Sunday morning, but they can muster a battalion of security types."

"Battalion," Seelah said. "Does 'accident' mean something else among these military folks, than what it always means?"

"Come on," Lindy said. "You don't need to meet any more soldiers today. I'll get you home."

The sun was getting low when Lindy arrived at her apartment complex. Hurrying out of the parking lot and into the shaded entrance of her building, she almost ran over Stone Prather. He must have seen her coming and stood up, because he was brushing off the seat of his gray triple-pleat slacks. When she got closer, he blanched and took a couple of awkward steps backward onto the stair. His black knit shirt showed off the newly defined abs he had brought to her dad's wake.

"This is my day for lurking men," Lindy said. "You better not be carrying a knife."

"I told you I come through Ash Run sometimes."

"And if I hadn't showed up right at this minute? You didn't call ahead, did you?"

"I don't have a cell."

"I forgot, you don't want your congregation calling you. Come on up while I wash off Joeab's blood, and I'll tell you what happened between Cain and Eve today. Uhwa is Eve, that Eve, and she lives out past the edge of town. Joeab is going to pull through okay, it looks like. Cain wasn't paying close enough attention to kill him."

She dodged past Stone and ran up the stairs. His Italian loafers sounded behind her. She found the clean-up goop under the bathroom sink and undressed and scrubbed away most of the residue of Adhah's potions. And showered and dressed for dinner, all with the door open so she could yell a summary of sorts: who the old women were, and who Joeab and Eshana were, and how Eshana had put her onto the old women, and what had happened. From the couch Stone answered with monosyllables. In a few minutes she emerged, feeling revived. Stone looked at her noncommitally.

"Do you want to adjust the thermostat?" he asked. "It's freezing in here."

"I did that when I got home last night. Sixty-three degrees puts the mildew back to sleep. Just as well you arrived and made me dress up. I need to look decent for Eshana's sake. Eshana will be at the ICU by now, and with her there, they'll let me in. I'm sure she found Joeab improved. Can we take your car? My truck is a mess. I left a bunch of messages on her answer machine. Let me try one more time, and we'll go."

CHAPTER 16

To get to intensive care, where Eshana's mother spent so many of those final days, you go through the ER. At the far end, alongside the levee. She forces herself not to turn at the parking garage. During the month of therapy, her mother, already too weak to be an outpatient, had been admitted to the fourth floor. Eshana was here seven days a week, and overnight as often as she could persuade Joeab to stay over with neighbors.

The glass door resists hard before it swings aside and she is in the refrigerated cave of the ER waiting room. The same odor, always, the smell she used to think of as ether, but came to know as disinfectants and everything disinfectants can't cover. In the lobby, no Lindy, only hopeless-looking people who stare at her dully. Nobody at the registrar's desk, not surprising for Sunday evening. The pain this time isn't distributed the same way it was when she walked into Detroit Receiving to deliver Joeab. But the ache is connected to the same evil place, to possibility slipping away.

Around the corner at the ER nurse's station two uniformed,

very young women are standing at attention. Both of them are Halle Berry beautiful in their soft green outfits.

"Joeab Barmore? I'm his mother?" Hoping.

"We not—we didn't started our shift yet," one of the young women says. "Irene or Vitrelle, one of them be out in a minute. We trainees."

"A small boy. I'm not certain he's been here. A friend called me, she sounded confused. He may have been in and already out." Would Lindy have taken him to her apartment?

"They don't keep them, usually not. Wait, a little boy? No, I don't believes, not right now." She looks at the other, who is nodding negative agreement. "You try the waiting room?"

"Let's see," the second trainee asks. The two girls are exchanging glances. "How long it been? Didn't they, maybe ICU, it's—."

But she is already running down the dingy hall. How long has he been here? The Chinese-inflected voice on the impossible-to-program old answer machine had said, "Thursday, 2:17 A.M." Along the hall she passes staff, all women, none of them white. Sunday evening, the three-to-midnight shift. Waiting for the elevator, she reads the plaque: "No Children Allowed Above This Level."

An older nurse is seated at the ICU control station on the third floor. She looks up. Her skin glows ebony-blue in the light from the monitor. Her face falls.

"Ms. Barmore? Eshana?"

"Where is he?"

"I'm Nurse Henry. We called you, at least, oh, five, or six times. We put him in a room, for now." Her speech is studied. Each idea is worth a pause, each phrase a breath and a widening of her eyes. Her badge gives her name as Patricia Henry.

"Oh, mercy, darling mother, you been working all day long."

Eshana puts her hand to her polyester blouse, feels the buttons that pull open across her bra, looks down at the too-short pants legs, wide as red stove pipes. Her third Sunday of extra shifts at the chicken place, eight to five. Four more before the Oldsmobile can get a new transmission—she's not taking it on the interstate without one. Every dozen burgers is Atlanta one mile closer. Driven presumably by the training videos Eshana refuses to watch, the chicken shack manager—who looks to be about sixteen—has been asking her, "What do you want to do with your life?" Don't ever use a credit card again, Eshana told her.

"What is his room number?" Thinking, I should have resurrected the Mastercard.

Nurse Henry gestures and stands, and leads the way down the hall. She walks formally with her head held high. Her steps are too quick and dainty. Eshana realizes that the nurse's knees are gone. It's the same walk of pain as her mother's had been.

"Why is he in here?"

"A bad cut. Cross-wise, on his belly. They gave him something to help him sleep."

"How many stitches? Sleep, for a cut? Who brought him in?"

"It is you?" the nurse asks mildly. "You the only Barmore. Eshana's a pretty name."

The telephone had been flashing "full." There weren't that many nuisance phone banks in the world. But who, what mix was it? Cloteile called on weeknights. The primary for governor was months away. Mrs. Thomason about Joeab? Not likely, Mrs. Thomason believed in telling you in person, and telling you at extreme length. The frozen yogurt place—that's where she would take him, Eshana decided. For whatever he wanted, strawberry more than likely, with a paper cup of sprinkles on the side for Joeab to make designs on the table with. An arrangement of pink, of red and white and pink, less of blue and little of green and nothing of violet, except for the three or four tiny purple dots that Joeab would set aside.

Lindy's voice was message one. A greeting, then an exhalation and a long pause, and then one long sentence until Lindy's forty seconds was up. Blackmon, Joeab, an ugly doctor—the hospital telephone number flew out of Eshana's mind in the jumble of words. She rang Mrs. Thomason's number. Had he taken sick? Not a broken arm, not after never being sick or hurt after she finally got to bring him home.

"Hello, this is Eshana. Has something happened to Joeab? I just got a message—"

"He with you. Ain't he? He an angel child today, as usually." Mrs. Thomason's tone was placid. "The finger-painting, those are fishes. You check the backyard?"

"Joeab?" Eshana cupped the receiver and called out, but he never failed to come skipping when the car pulled up. She was scanning the yard through the kitchen door.

"You didn't let him leave. You didn't. We have been over that and over that."

"He needing to go home," Mrs. Thomason said. "Didn't I hear you say you off at noon? Don't tarry, I tells him. Go straight home now. He say 'tarry,' he learning. I watch him across the street till he inside the door. I picked me up a small fever, afraid the baby might catch whatever it's going to be. You shan't forget to send his name tag with him on tomorrow, I hope."

Eshana waited through Lindy's message again and got the hospital number. Three four rings while apprehension blossomed. A bad dog grabbed his face. A rattlesnake, in that wilderness between their house and the old women's place. At ring six she grabbed her purse. Joeab's birthing, and the rest of it, appeared all at once, not like a memory of time, but like a burning house would if everything inside the house was visible too. Doctors aloof as jailkeepers, crisis after crisis. And now Joeab in the hospital again. Frail as he always had been, it was as if those weeks in Detroit Receiving had pumped up his immunity. Never so much as a cold after they released him.

It hadn't been until she approached Blackmon that she thought to ask herself how Lindy was the one who found him. And wait a minute, who was "we"? How did someone know to call Lindy? If Joeab's name tag holder hadn't come open, which it usually did, the phone number sure as hell wasn't Lindy's. The old women. Lindy was already out there. Lindy was part of it.

Nurse Henry is peering around the door, looking back at Eshana, smiling. She guides Eshana in and closes the door firmly behind them. The room feels twenty degrees warmer than the hall.

"He's resting. Sleep is the best medicine."

There lies Joeab in the small, overheated room. Joeab with his eyes closed and looking tiny between the raised railings. There is no pillow on the bed. A sheet covers him to his neck and a stenciled cotton blanket over the sheet, except that his arms are exposed and are held straight by bandages, elastic fabric over gauze from his forearms almost to his shoulders. An IV into each wrist, from plastic bags on a roll-around hanger. A fall, Eshana decides. He fell on something wide and sharp. There is an oxygen clip at his nose, and two more tubes that snake out from under the covers. In one tube, urine, obviously. In the other, a slight flow of pinkish droplets. Oxygen, IV's: except for the second drainage tube, and the fact that his body is covered, it could be the preemy unit at Detroit Receiving. The room is as warm as an incubator.

"Hey, baby." Eshana kisses his forehead. His skin feels cool, normal, not fevered. His eyelids flicker. His breathing is perceptible through the covers. She starts to rub his body, then thinks of the wound and instead reaches for the covers to raise them. Nurse Henry is quick with a restraining arm.

"Honey, we can't. Might disturb the patch." The nurse is gripping Eshana's wrist and squeezing it gently, repeatedly.

"A pain patch?" Remembering her mother.

"A patch, that's a temporary bandage, over his stomach. It's nothing but a patch under there yet. Because they were hurrying, because he'll go back into surgery as soon as we get some more O negative. You heard the news, that eighteen-wheeler ran over that van out on I-49? We're lucky we still had two units of O negative. Some more's on the way from Baton Rouge."

"Did you see him before they put the patch on?"

"Dr. Scroggins, he'll explain to you, everything. The EMTs will beep the doctor when the blood gets close. Us, too."

"Is he at the hospital, Dr. Scroggins?"

The heart monitor, as Eshana looks past Nurse Henry, is suddenly all straight lines. Her heart stops, she points. "No darling dear that's nothing." The nurse speaks quickly for once. "That sorry machine always slipping." She goes to it and makes adjustments. Rows of pulses spring up and race across the screen. Nurse Henry takes the clipboard chart from the foot of the bed, writes something. She glances up.

"There's some paperwork down at admissions. That can wait till in the morning. They put down Boy Barmore?"

"Joeab." Lindy hadn't told them his full name?

"Joab was King David's right hand. The toughest man in the whole Bible, Joab. He chased away the Syrians *and* the Ammonites. Little Joab, now, he puts me in mind of young David, the shepherd boy. 'Withal of a beautiful countenance, and goodly to look at,' First Samuel, chapter sixteen."

"It's J-o-e-a-b, after Momma's oldest brother who helped raise her." The nurse is right. His features in repose are as symmetric as a movie star's.

"They said it was two white women found him. Said one of them was barefooted."

"I knew it, the old women." Old women like coiled rattlesnakes.

"Cefoxitin." The nurse fingers the line from one of the hanging bags. "Number one antibiotic for trauma, by far. Child, you going to need to sit down for a while. We've got to be strong for the baby."

Eshana's hands move over Joeab's bandaged arms without quite touching them.

"You can get the doctor?"

"Most certainly. I'll go call him. His arms're not nearly bad as they look." Nurse Henry adjusts the oxygen, pauses to study Joeab. "His diaphragm's not involved. He's breathing fine. Not much edema."

The sound of a voice in the hall and suddenly Lindy is in the room. She is wearing an elegant long skirt, a knit cotton top, and dangle earrings, as if she were on her way to a fancy reception. Her fingernails are still black-rimmed and her eyes are blazing. She is already talking.

"I sat out there for hours, I only went home to change clothes. I'm sorry, it took me forever to get partly clean, and Stone showed up, he's here." Lindy's speech is preemptive, like expert typing. "Your car is fixed? I hope all those different messages didn't scare you. Seelah came with me. Adhah stayed behind and took Uhwa inside. Adhah's medicines made all the difference, they basically stuck him back together. I couldn't believe how the bleeding stopped. I took Seelah home. I'll go back out there and check on them tomorrow."

"Miss, you can't stay in here," Nurse Henry says at the first break in Lindy's filibustering.

Lindy ignores the nurse and moves past Eshana to Joeab's bedside.

"I'm happy he's—oh my gosh, listen to me. I'm *relieved*, so relieved that Joeab is going to be all right. Isn't he gorgeous?"

"What were you doing out there in the first place? On a Sunday?"

"I thought they would never get around to doing anything. I mean the surgeons, the nurses are always helpful." Lindy smiles at the nurse. "It is a literal marvel he's lying here getting better. Thank goodness for Adhah."

"Did he fall off their porch?" Eshana asks. "He couldn't have cut himself like this, he's not strong enough, even if they did give him a knife to play with. What did he fall on?"

"Ms. Barmore, I'll be up at the desk," Nurse Henry says. "I'll be reaching Dr. Scroggins, and I'll be praying some more for Joeab. Come out there when you free. The blood call should be any minute." The door closes behind her.

"She's nice," Lindy says. "Gosh, it's hot in here. The other nurse told me someone was already in here, said I'd have to send you out—one person at a time, she said. I told her 'sure,' but they don't mind, do they. I cannot believe how amazingly wonderful he looks now, compared to—I didn't want to say before, what I thought when we got him here."

"What did I tell you about those old hags? You haven't told me a single thing. I don't even know how bad it is."

"They are the kindest—it wasn't Seelah or Adhah," Lindy says cheerfully. "Or Uhwa. Well, Uhwa. I guess I might as well say it. Uhwa is Eve. You should hear her talk—it's wonderful, like the best kind of dream. Adam's not around, he's dead. I'm so afraid for them, if people find out. Promise me you won't tell anybody."

"Lindy, you being there, you with your truck, I appreciate that. But you're one reason he kept going back to see those crones."

"I'm so, so, sorry, Eshana. Did you notice, you dislike them so much you won't say their names either? I'm sure I'm saying 'Adhah' and 'Seelah' right. I settled on Babel, and they picked right up on that—but they both shift to Alabaman at the drop of a hat, because of me. I can't call Uhwa Eve, because I already got to know her as Uhwa. It's terrible when you're cut off from somebody's true name. It makes them an imitation of who they are, like a Greek mask over their face. They become the mask. Like the slaves and European names, you know? It's as bad, don't you think, as when you have nothing but the name and you can't find the person that goes with the name. Like my Sunshine? Like your daddy? Like too many Jimmy Davises?"

"And what's this one called?" Eshana asks.

The door is open and the new visitor is looking at Lindy quizzically. A stocky man with apple-red cheeks and a shapeless nose and senatorial half-gray hair. In a tight-across-the-shoulders sports jacket, pleated gabardine pants and pimp loafers, he is as overdressed as Lindy. He clasps his hands together and bows slightly.

"Here you finally are," Lindy says. "Eshana Barmore, Stone Prather. Stone is passing through from Mississippi. Traveling man. A minister of the gospel. Of a sort. What kept you?"

The man purses his lips and semi-bows again.

"My apologies, Ms. Barmore." His voice is fulsome. And to Lindy, "I wish you hadn't just breezed on in. They stopped me at the desk. I had to tell them I'm new in the CPE program. Clinical Pastoral Education." The last he directs to Eshana in the same affronted tone. "They didn't buy it."

"So you're still out at the desk?" Lindy asks. "What did you do, call on the preacher's stalk?" She demonstrates the posture: nodding gravely, her right arm at her side, the hand cupped as if over a large book.

"I wish you had acted out that deal the first time I met you," the man says.

Lindy gives Eshana a significant look. "I told you about Stone. He was my husband awhile back."

The pale room is sparsely furnished, only the bed and the low cabinet beside it and one large chair. No framed pictures, no curtains over the closed blinds. A tiny bathroom, no closet.

Eshana gestures toward the single chair. "Why don't you take it, Reverend. No use for the whole crowd of us to be standing."

The preacher picks up the heavy vinyl chair and sets it nearer the bed. Two gold knuckle-rings adorn the hand he lays on the edge of the mattress. He looks toward Eshana distantly, and then at Joeab, and finally at Lindy. Lindy is tracing her hands in the air over Joeab in an exploratory way. Both of them are at the bed, both of them between Eshana and Joeab.

"Can we cut through the bullshit?" Eshana asks. "Tell me how this happened to Joeab."

"I wish I could tell you his name in Uhwa's language, it might help. Both names—I try to bring them up." Lindy's mouth twists and she spits out several harsh syllables, and stammers the syllables again.

Eshana signals "hold it down."

Lindy looks abashed. "I can't form Uhwa's words, I only know what they mean."

"What who means, Lindy? For God's sake."

"That's it, I can't say either of them's actual name. I kept asking Seelah, but it's like she hates the one and she may not believe the other one's there. It's as if by not saying their names, she's more in control."

"What are you talking about? I don't even know what it is that did this to Joeab. It matters."

"That's what Adhah said, 'I don't know.' She's more worried than Seelah. He's Uhwa's son—well, obviously. He came to ask her, I'm not sure what he wanted except to be left alone. He doesn't live anywhere in particular. Bahbellah—Seelah and Adhah both said it, two weeks ago. You know, Babel. Babel—Nimrod, and the destruction of the tower to heaven? If it even fell. It doesn't say it fell."

"Lindy, was it a machete? What did he run into that was so sharp?" Eshana looks at Joeab to make sure that he isn't hearing them.

"It was more of a skinning knife. They have this five-thousand-year-old medicine—two parts to it, one black and one orange, that once you mix them together you can't wash off either one of them—that closed the wound. Until then it was indescribably awful. Poor sweet Joeab, look at him. I can't help feeling like I should have been able to keep it from happening."

Lindy is fiddling with her fingernails. She begins to discourse to her ex-husband, about Noah's ark, and about the old women in some other boat which obviously is not any boat Eshana has imagined. Everybody bobbing around in their own little boat. All that worry about Joeab falling in the water, and Lindy is running on about Noah's ark.

Where is our boat?, Eshana muses. Where is a proper river to take us away from this place? Not the one outside the hospital. Long before the Army dredged it into a ditch all the way to East Texas instead of spending the money to protect New Orleans, that river brought the slaves up from there. Acheron was already the end of the line; there was a log jam for fifty miles upstream from Ash. Her great-grandmother Rushing had handed down the stories: high ground on the right bank of the river, malaria and "everybody off" on the left bank. A story told also about three sisters sold, one of them named Eshana, and of how some passengers had jumped into that roiling mud rather than be offloaded at Ash. Take people to the edge of the world, some of them were bound to jump. Or get pushed.

Lindy is still running on to the minister, about rain and fish guts and arguments on one of the boats. Eshana jams the fingers of one hand upward into the open palm of the other, the T-for-time-out sign.

"Lindy, go home. I'll call you tomorrow."

"I don't want it to sound like I'm only thinking about myself," Lindy says. "If you could have been with us when we brought Joeab in—I didn't even give you a hug."

She reaches out and embraces Eshana, and keeps talking right above her ear. "It's too much. Your momma, and then my daddy, and now Joeab. That was the very lowest time, when they wouldn't let me into the emergency room with Joeab, and I couldn't be sure he wasn't dying, and nobody with him but strangers. How Daddy managed to drive himself to the emergency room before he passed out in the car, nobody will ever know."

"Wait," Eshana says. She holds Lindy at arms' length. "Your dad has died?"

"Suddenly, we buried him a week ago tomorrow. I never did get to have that talk about Sunshine."

This explains some of it, Eshana thinks.

"Look at this." Lindy holds out her arms. "I scrubbed them raw and I still couldn't get all of Adhah's medicine off." Her hands and forearms are redder than usual, but other than the grime under her fingernails there is no stain on her. "He was hurt so badly. Seelah took him, and Adhah came out carrying the ointments. And some water. And they saved Joeab's life." She rubs her forearms together, a gesture like fending off the cold.

Eshana can't let this pass. "They saved him? No, Lindy, whatever country they came from, they brought death with them."

"They wouldn't hurt a soul."

"They're life quenchers. They don't have to do anything, they only wait, and harm comes calling."

"I'm not defending them, Joeab almost got killed." Lindy sighs deeply. "But Uhwa has suffered. Think how much she's suffered. That doesn't excuse how she goads him, I don't think."

"How many times did I tell you? There's no comfort in being

right about it. Lurking out there at the end of the road like spiders, how many kids have they put in danger?"

"That's not Seelah, she makes him toys and teaches him stories. That's not Adhah. She and Joeab sing together. He started to singing today, so perfectly, that was—."

"You talk about not knowing those witches, not knowing their names. Here's some true names that hardly got used. Thomas, he's my oldest, the first one that didn't live to term. And Larenzo, Junior? He would have been thirteen now if I hadn't miscarried. He was going to be way taller than me, I know that. And Keiran, who lived one hour? I named him after Mama's second oldest brother. Are those women grieving, that they never got a shot at Thomas and Keiran and Larenzo, Jr.?" She realizes her voice is too loud. "Excuse me, Reverend."

The preacher rises as if to shake Eshana's hand. "Prather, Livingstone Prather."

"Excuse me, Reverend Livingstone, because you're wanting to start in on harps and robes and crowns. You preachers all shout eternity, but you keep your Blue Cross paid. Joeab's staying with me. He's not going anywhere near heaven."

The minister pushes against Lindy's back and turns her toward the door. She is shaking her head disconsolately. Her shoulders are slumped more than usual.

"We're going," he says. He turns and puts his hand on the railing near Joeab's head. "Ms. Barmore," he says. His back is to Eshana. "If I could give Joeab the blessing—but we can't give the blessing, we can only accept it. Little Joeab has taken it, it shines in his face. The mother's blessing, the highest and the best."

"Let us bring you something to eat," Lindy says. "One reason I'm—this way, is I'm starving. What do you want us to bring you? We're on our way to the Royce."

Eshana is looking away toward the unseen river, that even at night would be visible from this room if the window blinds were opened. The river that the Army should have reamed toward some useful place, Pittsburgh or Charlotte. She can't bear to look at the others any more, especially the little preacher with his big voice and his canned sermonette. The two stand awkwardly for a little while, then they are gone.

She listens to them hissing each other down the hall. Then she lowers the near railing and hikes herself onto the foot of Joeab's bed and begins to rub his feet and calves through the blanket. This has to be all right, there are no needles in his feet this time. He makes a slight musical sound. In his answer she hears it all: what the night school professor was lecturing about in the European History class, how loudly her armchair creaked with the first abrupt contraction, and, once she was in the delivery room, how quickly Joeab appeared. And how thin the sound is, of a twenty-ounce boy's first cry.

"What were the doctors promising you this time?" she whispers to Joeab. "Did they say they'd make you all better, did they tell you the new needles would deliver you back to me? How long before I can hold you, sweetpie? How long before we dance, dumpling?" They had let her hold Joeab for about five seconds in the delivery room. His crying stopped as soon as she touched him. Joeab's head fit in the palm of her hand, his eyes so transparent she couldn't tell if he would ever see. He gave her a little burp-smile, as if to say he was done with crying; and he meant it. His hands and his feet, when they took him away, were perfect.

The Detroit hospital was like the old women, strangers who couldn't leave Joeab to be Joeab. And now the Acheron doctors. Would there have been a Joeab now, if she had been down here at her mother's, in a town this size, when he was born? Or was it about the doctors at all? She had been married two years—she and Larenzo were both twenty-two—the first time. Thomas. After that she took all the medicines and the condescending advice, and when she got pregnant again it happened exactly the same way. Larenzo, Jr. For Keiran she went to bed and stayed. That helped some, but not enough. She was twenty-seven when Joeab came to her, when Joeab was able to hold on to her for six months, two weeks short of six months. Joeab was perfect to start with, but every time they promised to unhook him some other hospital bacteria grabbed him, or an organ almost quit from all the medicines. Four times they told her to expect him not to make it. Having him at home was wonderful, but it soaked up her time and all of her energy. Always would, all her energy and all her love.

Strong for the baby. It was the separation and the unendurable pain, before he ever got to go home. That's why he wandered. He was looking for the time he had been denied, he was searching for the peaceful place he left too soon. Joeab, slipping away on tiptoes to somewhere he had never been, moving as delicately as you would into a room where a marvelous surprise waited. Joeab, on the verge of retrieving what he'd lost. Joeab smiling confidently, because this next place would probably be the one.

"We'll find it, baby. Together."

She pulls her legs up onto the bed—there is plenty of room below Joeab—and closes her eyes, and watches herself stand at the plate glass. And now in memory Larenzo arrives and stands with her. She and Larenzo are looking through the big window at the rows of incubators like microwaves with sleeves. The two of them, now going back toward her room, Eshana gliding tentatively in her terry cloth slippers, Larenzo keeping close to the wall. Larenzo, not having touched Eshana. Back in her room she is in the bed and he is sitting on the edge of it with his head back as if he is looking for a sign. She can feel how the weight of Larenzo's body pushes down on the bed. His eyes are closed and his head is tilted to one side. And now straight, and again jerking to the side—Joeab has borne him a tic. Larenzo, getting up with his eyes still closed and with his back to Eshana, standing there a long time. And leaving the room, his head still jerking, a dialogue with no questions and no answers.

She opens her eyes, rouses herself, and slides her feet to the floor. She faces Joeab's bed and takes a deep breath, and folds back Joeab's covers. First the blanket carefully, and, very gently, the sheet. And looks, and weeps.

Under the sheet he is naked. His feet are turned in, his toes touching. The catheter, thin as it is, seems too large to fit into his body. The abdominal drain emerges from under the bandage, which is not a bandage but a transparent, loosely taped piece of what looks like plastic wrap. It covers, and reveals, Joeab's torso from his chest to his pelvis. The doctors' incision is what makes it so big. It runs from his rib cage almost to his groin. What for? So they could slide their big fingers inside Joeab? The incision is longer than the wound, although the wound is the whole width of his body. The side-to-side wound is stitched shut with red floss, a relatively few looping whip stitches. Around it there is something dark as tar: the old women's home remedy. But the longer part of the incision has been left open, so that Joeab's insides, orderly and gray, are visible. Eshana has never seen inside anyone. Joeab's body has been opened from side to side, and all the way up and down. That's the word Nurse Henry had used. Cross-wise.

CHAPTER 17

They had reached an armistice on the subject of Cain, and were dealing with their glutenous dinners. Stone toyed with a fist-shaped chicken breast, Lindy forked at her pasta to expose another People's Republic crawfish tail. She had already eaten a dozen of the things; the flavor was plausible, but the consistency was disposable pacifiers. She held this one up for a better look. Ming Dynasty orange-red—did they have prisoners sitting in cells and painting these things? Surely, in the hotel's glory days the Steamboat Dining Room of the Royce Hotel had not been located to the basement. There were almost no other customers—but then it was Sunday night. The lone waiter was leaning against the wall at the far end of the low room, and every time Lindy signaled, he would come forward with a puzzled expression: bring the menus? some water, you mean? and the glasses of house wine you ordered? additional glasses of wine? Certainly, eventually.

Small talk. Curious how it went. You wanted never to see some-one ever again, but then they reappeared, and what the two of you had in common showed up too. For every such category they were failing to agree, which now that Lindy thought about it, was the way their conversations had gone from their first date forward. They had gotten past current relationships. Neither admitted to any worth mentioning. They moved to pastiming about friends, swapping names that the other couldn't remember. And about her work—a thumbnail profile of Bea, a little about the Moulton Foundation, and her dread of arriving back at work. She would not be going in on Monday, not after today's events. Stone told her about his new book, which he was going to call "But a Sojourner Here." While they picked at their food they talked about eating, about the handful of neighborhood fried seafood places they had frequented in New Orleans. The crawfish were doing acrobatics in her stomach. "Why don't we talk about you?" she offered. "Does your new church just love you to pieces?"

"It's a good place. It's plain Goodwin Road Church now, we dropped the denomination tag. It may be the best place in the world for someone like me, divorced and literary and all."

"And all."

"They always oversubscribe the budget." He grinned delightedly. "I get six weeks study leave every summer. That's how I'm able to do the books."

"How many is it then?" A collection of his sermons had been under contract when they split.

"Four so far, not counting the one on country music."

"And your major subject is depression? You're the most energetic person I've ever met. Could anybody in the world believe you're depressed?"

Stone's face, already flushed from the wine, became almost crimson. How was a grown man able to blush? It was a quality Lindy had once been able to find appealing.

"The depression book was a kind of bridge, a memoir really.

Managing the Darkness. It was well enough received, so I spun a couple of variations on loss."

"And what you lost inside your dark soap opera shadow was me?" He seemed as distant from his desperate subject matter as a history professor describing the genocide of the Armenians.

"Well, yes, I wrote about the divorce. And the diagnosis that I'd always been depressed without knowing it. I was hospitalized, you know."

"Hospitalized for what?"

"What did I say?—depression. I was in the Benton asylum for almost a week. It's rough being on the other side of the gate in a place where you've worked."

"Your buddies did that for you. I notice you're pretty cheerful about your darkness." Darkness, and Loss, all those big-word titles that publishers hoped impulse buyers wouldn't be able to resist. Loss, doubt, pain, honor, grief. And Stone swimming in those waters. Except that he was saying his publishers were too tiny to advertise. What pain, to publish in the shadow of the big New York self-help guys and gals. What an honor, to endure the grief of lost sales.

Stone was warming to his safe topic. She didn't bother to nail him, because she was taking in only a little of it. That was all anybody ever got from words, wasn't it, a little bit. Babel, she told herself, isn't when nobody hears what the other is saying. Babel is when you talk to yourself and can't hear what you're saying.

The windows at the top of the outer wall opened at sidewalk level, so that she could have seen the scissoring legs of pedestrians, if there had been any. The windows framed the wheels of passing cars. They came by in groups. Two or three cars would drift past, then a long interval before another tight, slow cluster, accompanied by the thump of speakers. Teenagers, cruising the night in tandem—not quite hooked up, like a first date with you sitting at one end of the sofa and the nervous boy upright in your father's recliner. To Lindy their evasive chat felt less like a date than like some kind of evaluation, as if a real estate appraiser, Stone, was making a slow tour of a property—her—that anybody could see was crawling with active termites. Certainly the scenes that infested her head were more real than the Steamboat Room, and swarmed louder than their conversation.

Joeab's suffering was the pulse of her awareness. There were other pictures, too—the laborers cranking up the backhoe to close the loamy soil over her dad; the recovering addict at the Helping Hand Center who wept with her the whole while she signed over her dad's goods; Seelah, comforting, while they waited at the emergency room. Most of all there was her regret that she had not been able to anticipate Cain. It played now as foreground, now as background, and from all angles and distances. Cain right in front of her, Cain within reach, Cain's face that she hadn't gotten to study up close, while Stone studied her from three feet away. While she and Stone were failing to come up with a single recent movie they had both seen, the restaurant walls were overlaid with a long view of the old women's place—as if she were in a helicopter hovering over the scene. The motley neighborhood behind her, the lake glistening beyond the gardens. Trees everywhere, hulking green spectators to the six of them foreshortened and dragging their stubby shadows in slow motion. A glint of sharp light from the old man—from this height she couldn't make out the knife. And the tall young woman, creeping past the old man as if wishing she were invisible. What was wrong with the woman that she could never change the way things came out? Lindy watched Lindy stand behind the old man, watched her wait for the understanding that would tear her life apart, Uhwa's understanding that now threatened to fade into knowledge.

She was in Cain's face, demanding that he grow up and forget

Uhwa, like she had done with Sunshine. Uhwa was right, of course, Abel's death justified any amount of bitterness. But justification can't be the outcome. Cain was staring at her and blinking. That should have been all the impetus she needed, the way he didn't see her. And the way that when Uhwa spoke, calmness opened like an umbrella in a rain shower. Cain's coarse face morphed to Stone's, and she was back to the depressing certainty that nothing could prevent the suffering of all the Abels who would ever live.

One thing she could do, between Cain's manifestations, was to cradle Joeab in her mind's arms: Joeab fallen, Joeab at the truck, and—if the idiot staff hadn't stopped her—Joeab in his room when she and Seelah first got him to the hospital. Her side of the conversation with Stone materialized around her, while from deeper inside she urged Joeab to hold on, and reassured him that he would be all right. Thinking, he understands a lot more than people recognize who can only see surfaces. Joeab, relaxing in her lap while she ate. Joeab nodding agreement to all of this, Joeab patting her face—his arms healed, the scars barely visible.

While she and Stone rang the changes on their lives, she refined her apology to Eshana. You're exactly right not to care about Cain or Uhwa, and of course you blame it on Adhah and Seelah, and on me, on me. She excused herself to look for a phone. Very modern, there seemed to be no pay phones in the hotel.

At long last the plates were removed—hers swabbed clean, Stone's looking as if he hadn't eaten but had ridden a bicycle through it—and they were left with their fourth glasses of wine and the subject of Cain.

"You covered for the man who stabbed Joeab."

"I did not. I tried to tell Eshana his name. She was too distracted to understand what I was telling her."

"On the way to the hospital you couldn't stop talking about

the old man, and then afterwards too. You never told her how it happened."

"We didn't get around to it." But she had not understood why she was being dodgy, even while it was happening. Was it because Uhwa was Uhwa—a truth too strong to keep describing? She looked down at her hands that were stained with too much knowing. "What is Cain to you and me?" she asked.

The check arrived. While Lindy rummaged in her purse among blood-smeared tissues, Stone slapped several twenties into the plastic-leather folder and took it to the waiter. They walked up the stairs into the deserted night.

"Let's go for a walk," Lindy said.

"If you'll let me jettison this coat."

They deposited his jacket and her purse in his car. Lindy steered Stone by his elbow past the Corinthian columns and stone gingerbread of the hotel's facade. The pavement played out after the aluminum sculpture at the corner of the museum parking lot. She let go of Stone's arm and led the way straight up the steep grass of the levee, and paused at the roadway that ran along the top.

"It's manicured down that way," Stone said when he caught up with her. He indicated a perfunctory park downstream at the riverside, with benches and picnic huts and a stand of magnolias around a small amphitheater. Everything in that direction was brightly lighted by towering light standards which, to judge from their steel hoops, doubled as Christmas trees in season. Upstream a steel drawbridge perched on concrete caissons. No boat or barge or dock relieved the river's tameness. She followed the levee away from the lights.

"I need to see a river up close, and this one will do." They walked under the drawbridge. Overhead the traffic thunk-thunked with self-satisfied vehicles. Stone was keeping pace behind her.

"They made it a Corps of Engineers ditch," he said.

Lindy was trying hard to contain her weeping. Her tears were not only for Joeab. They were for Adhah and Seelah and Uhwah in the water, and for how alone they had been. Past the bridge she began to work her way down the embankment, which was steep enough that you might slide right into the water. There was enough sky-reflected light to show them the path that ran along the water. By breathing deeply and holding in, and by not wiping her eyes, she was keeping herself under control.

Muted smells of mud and of stranded fish, the residual hint of a free summer river, as if planted there by the Acheron Chamber of Commerce. A small white shorebird, startled by their shadows, squealed and dodged over the water. "You want to stay away from the very edge," Stone said. "Moving water will undercut a bank."

She moved quickly, a few feet from the water. They had passed a couple of rock weirs that extended a hundred feet from the bank. The weirs pushed the remnant river farther out, enlisting the river to do the work of maintaining its artificial channel. At the next one she stepped onto the narrow pile and began gingerly to make her way from the shore.

"Lindy, don't," Stone said from behind her. "Please, don't do it."

The gallon-sized rocks under her feet felt solid. As far as she could tell, there was no danger of the wall giving way and throwing her into the water. Where the river was quiet it all but disappeared. At the end of the jetty, when she reached it, the current swirled thick as batter. She could feel the darkness welling up. Why was it she had always pictured floods happening in the daytime? Was that because you can't take a newsreel of a flood at night? Adhah and Seelah and Uhwa, at their river, had the moon. Out here moonlight would have revealed no more than that the water was deep. She imagined water to her waist and more arriving in a vast, calm wash, and lifting her, taking away both warmth and cold, damping the world of sensation.

"Lindy, answer me. It's not as awful as you think. The Bible stuff, these perceptions fall away. These ideas spring from stress. Will you wait?" Stone was stressing the last word or two of every phrase. It was preaching—as if she, a congregation of one, had dropped into the back pew and now refused to come down the aisle.

"Haul on out here, bud. We'll kneel together."

Lindy's tears had stopped, but her chest was tight with separation. The women were never going to mend things with Cain, who was their only close kin. Uhwa would not be reconciled to Abel's death. Seelah could talk about a family bearing up, but when the best you could do was to bear up, your life might as well be over. Was that what Sunshine had felt, she wondered, that you have to swim for the surface even if you end up at the bottom? The two women, sweet as they were, were past acting. And Cain was going away, and she hadn't confronted him. She spread her arms for balance, jumping along the rough rocks, looking down against the light from shore. Flying back.

"Let's go," she said. "I've made up my mind."

"You listened to me. You'll come into the light." His voice had the self-absorbed vibrato.

"Oh, your wonderful little book. Think we can manage the darkness between here and the car?" They retraced their way. "It came from downstream," Lindy said as they walked. "The water was intentional, it came looking for Uhwa."

"Your women have been talking about a flood that moved upstream along here? It works that way. If the women were describing the 1927 flood—water coming from everywhere and nowhere. It rained for two solid years."

"Were you even *in* Joeab's room? Theirs was saltwater, theirs was Noah's flood. Cain saved them with his skiff. He came and rescued them, but he can't save himself from being hated. Did you know the ark was black?"

"Black? Ark? Sure, that's in the book."

"I might have stood it, landing up in a backwater like Ash. What I didn't conceive was how a person who is miles out of the current can still get swept away."

"Were Alda and Cecilia—the women—talking about Eve and Cain and Abel before your dad died? Did they seem to you to be Bible characters before?" They were standing next to Stone's car, outside the Royce Hotel.

"I'll drive," Lindy said. "I know the way to the old women's place, and you don't."

"We need to take you home." Stone was looking down at the pavement. "He doesn't have a car. None of them has a car, right? Where can he go, besides his house? Or he'll end up back at their house meek as a lamb."

She held out her hand. "The keys."

"If you want the sheriff to help you, you have to have a story. What role can you play as long as you claim Eve is behind it all? Listen, I'll still be here tomorrow. We'll take another look at the situation after you've slept."

"Give me the damned keys."

CHAPTER 18

Hear my voice, you wives:
for I have slain a man to my wounding,
and a young man to my hurt.

Genesis 4:23

From within the old women's house, the soft sound of singing. No moonlight, but Lindy could make out shapes in the middle of the yard, shapes that might be dogs.

"Let me have that thing."

Stone handed her the flashlight he had taken from the trunk of his car. It had been his father's, an old-fashioned six-cell one as long and as heavy as a billy club. The beam revealed not dogs but a family of raccoons. The hump-backed alpha coon glanced toward the light. The others continued their examination of the ground. They were gathered where Cain had attacked Joeab, so it had to be Joeab's blood they were licking. Their sideways eyes threw red light, as if his blood inside them was afire. Lindy ran, waving the flashlight and stamping her feet. The animals let themselves be herded away by the packaged brightness, but unhurriedly, with many backward looks. They knew whose territory night was. In the wavering light the signs of the afternoon's events were easy to read. The maroon-brown dried blood pooled and trailed into the crescent-swept dirt.

One of Joeab's shoes lay some way from the blood. Lindy picked it up.

"The sock is inside, they're always sliding down. We'll leave it on the porch until I get back out here." The shadows emphasized the more distant footprints. You didn't have to be an Indian scout to see that the old women had been barefooted, nor to tell what direction Cain had taken. "There he went," she whispered, pointing with the light at the shoe prints. "Around the right side of the house."

"Oh yeah," Stone said. "And he only has twelve hours on us. Can I have a look?" He took the flashlight and studied the patterns. "No shoes—the women?"

"They don't. Turn it off a minute." The renewed darkness reinforced the women's song. "Listen to them. That's not English." It was a close sort of harmony, Seelah's voice pitched below Adhah's warbling soprano. Or maybe they were singing unison and Adhah's voice had broken upward into overtones, the way old people's voices did.

"I can't tell," Stone said. "It sounds like humming." Lindy took Stone's arm and led him to the house. When they stepped onto the porch, the singing stopped.

"It's Lindy." She spoke through the open window into the dark bedroom. "I didn't think you'd still be awake. Since you are, can I tell you about Joeab? Looks like he's going to be fine, I saw him and Eshana at the hospital. I brought someone with me." The long pause before the women answered gave Lindy time to review the reasons she should have come out sooner.

"That's good to hear, child, about the baby," Adhah said through the frayed window screen.

"If you came back later in the day, it would be better." Seelah's voice was breathy, as if she had just waked.

"No, dear," Adhah said. "After all that's happened. And if she brought a friend. Lindy, you and your friend have a seat."

228

Rustling noises from inside, and thumps of feet hitting the floor, and involuntary-sounding groans. After a minute Adhah's shape appeared at the door and guided them to the two chairs, and herself dropped onto the bench against the wall. Her motions seemed to Lindy abrupt, but why wouldn't she be peremptory, rousted out of bed after such a day. Lindy slid her chair backward to be closer to Stone. She wished she could tell him to turn the flashlight on. As it was, Adhah could have been any wide woman in nightclothes.

"They let me see Joeab," she began.

"Wait," Adhah said. "Wait for Seelah. Else you'll have to tell your story two times." There was none of the hushed tone that the women had used the night of the flood story. Seelah arrived and sat heavily beside Adhah without a greeting.

"Oh, excuse me," Lindy said. "This is Stone Prather."

Stone leaned forward in a sort of seated bow, as if they could really see him. His "hello" brought a "we're glad to meet you" from Adhah. An ordinary social call, Lindy thought—here we are, four grown people, average age two thousand, sitting in the dark and talking as if the nearest murderer was a million miles away.

"Stone's over from Mississippi," she said. "Pure coincidence, he's on his way to Lake Charles—he went with me to the hospital. Stone's going with me to look for Caheena. Caheena, is that how you pronounce his name?" And to Stone, "It's all inflection, like Chinese."

"And you didn't say about Joeab," Seelah said. She and Adhah were merged on the backless bench.

"They've got him bandaged and sedated—he needs to sleep till he gets better. Tubes everywhere. I watched his heart monitor, the pulse shapes looked normal. I've got to be optimistic. I could—" could not drive them into town to see Joeab, in a few days. Eshana wouldn't be able to stand that.

"They'll keep him in that fortress a right smart, don't you imagine." Seelah's tone was resigned. "That's soldiers' ways."

"I won't be crossing over to there," Adhah said, still sounding half-asleep. "He'll come see us soon as he's better."

"I wonder, Adhah, before we take off after Caheena, if you would fill Stone in about him?" From her conversation at the emergency room, Seelah certainly wasn't going to. "I couldn't tell much, except that he's Uhwa's son, so he's as many thousands of years old as she is." Stone needed to hear them say it out loud: Uhwa was Eve. Neither of the women answered.

Stone abruptly stood up. "We'd better get started."

"You ain't going to run into that one," Adhah said, "unless he means for you to. Best you go straight home."

"Could it have turned out differently—Adhah's way of talking to him, if she hadn't gone inside and left Seelah and Uhwa?" She realized that she had begun to refer to them in the third person, as if they were exhibit A. "How was he able to find you? You could have been anywhere in the wide world." Without looking, she reached for Stone's wrist. She didn't intend to leave until she got something out of the women.

"You get to where you can't rest," Seelah put in. "And here he comes, sailing under the mountain. His talk is bad enough, without this kind of dust-up."

"He all but killed a little bitty boy," Lindy said. "That's a dust-up?"

"You got a look at him," Adhah said. "A whole lot better for you, if you was to let him run."

"He and Uhwa do have forever," Lindy said, thinking, I don't. She tugged on Stone's arm to let him know she was speaking to him. "And sailing—he's still a fisherman?" She waited, but the women didn't respond. "The whole globe is water. He could work without necessarily talking to a soul, on a big Russian fishing ship or something. A few hundred years is nothing to him. Please tell me if he's the one who killed Abel."

"That's what you call him?" Seelah asked.

The group sat in silence for a while.

"How is Uhwa?"

"Uhwa's strong," Adhah said. "She doesn't exactly sleep."

"I'll keep you posted about Joeab," Lindy said. "And about Cain, whatever we find out. Here, let me give you a hand." But the two women were already on their feet and offering their fragrant good-bye hugs to Lindy.

Lindy pushed Stone through the door after them. "We'll go through this way," she said. "He went around behind the house—we saw his tracks." She waited until the door to Adhah and Seelah's room was pulled to. There was enough light to navigate through the hall, but she took the flashlight and shined it ahead of them. She spotlighted the oval photographic portraits on the wall one after the other. Their patient expressions seemed to be saying, We're sad about Joeab, too. When the beam traced the vessels along the walls, a red squirrel froze at the lip of a basket before it dived out and darted for the torn screen door at the back of the hallway.

"You don't think the house signifies." She was almost whispering. "You've got to admit it smells like a pharaoh is buried somewhere around here."

"Rare, a dogtrot that isn't abandoned." He had never spoken softly in her presence.

"We'll skip the kitchen," she said, thinking of undisturbed rodents. "It looks too much like my office." She shone the light on Uhwa's door and pulled Stone's hand up to press it against the warmth. "Uhwa's room. Eden must have been tropical." That hadn't occurred to her.

"Someone in there is talking," Stone said.

"It's the TV. Too many preachers." She led them to the room

across from Adhah's and Seelah's. Miraculously the door didn't stick. She closed it behind them. "This is the room I haven't been in."

Neither had anyone else, for long enough that the floor was covered with a powdery film. More clutter than Lindy would have expected. An iron bedstead, the bare mattress pocked with small craters—creature burrows. To the left, a dresser, and a large table that barely fit between the dresser and the bed. Six straight chairs like the ones on the porch were stacked pairwise on the table, and six smudge-darkened kerosene lamps: a houseful of chairs and lamps. A long cloth cloaked the mirror above the dresser. A narrow armoire blocked the door to the kitchen. On top of the armoire, two wooden cylinders, hat boxes. Piles of fabric filled one corner beside the armoire, and in the other corner lay a harp—no, a small loom, and portable, to judge from the frayed fabric strap. The room had once been papered. Shards the size of sycamore leaves curled from the walls and lay in drifts at the baseboards. The curtains were little more than threads; only the rolled-down shades kept the world outside. A bedroom that someone had turned into a storage room. Was the furniture the Johnsons'? Did the covered mirror mean that one too many Johnsons died, and they stopped coming in here?

"We can talk," she said in her normal voice. "I bet you there's something in here."

"Even if the floor doesn't give way, they can hear every step we take."

"It's okay, nothing upsets them—they're the most tolerant people I've ever known. What does matter to a person after a thousand years, I wonder? They still sleep together."

"This is transgressive. I feel like a thief."

"You hold the light now, while I look. What are you scared I'll find? Evidence that I'm not as vaporous as those curtains?"

The dresser's left-side drawers were tilted open. The top two were empty. The bottom drawer, when she slid it out and set it on the dresser, held two decrepit books.

"If one of them was a family Bible," Stone said.

She lifted the larger volume, whose cover had been lost. Chunks from the brownish pages stayed behind, and the rest began to break and crumble in her hands. All she could do was to dump the residue back into the drawer, where it lay like the debris from the bottom of a cereal box. The other book was blocky enough, but the spine was a light-hearted green, not Bible-black. She set aside the loose front cover with its intertwined dolphins. The pages felt like fabric. Their edges were serrated, like tiny rodent teeth. The sewn sections separated under her touch, nothing for it but to treat them like so many booklets. Oh, here was a tissue-thin map. Unfolded, it showed the Mediterranean region in surprising detail, from the Black Sea to Gibraltar and from the Baltic to the Sahara. "Let me find the title page. Here it is. *Tales of a Traveler, Illustrated.* Volume one. New-York, with a hyphen. 1846. Harper and Brothers, they're still in business, aren't they? No author's name. What do you think it means?"

"It means you're tearing up old books."

"Listen to this, 'I will whip you over a piece of the most classic ground.'"

"Is that your proof text? You keep saying they don't read."

"They don't read. Wait, here's a picture."

She tugged out a glossy plate and held the illustration under the flashlight. Two boats with triangular sails, close together and both burning. "'Night engagement off the Bosphorus,'" she read. The stiff page broke off and flew from her hand. She swatted at it—all in pieces.

"They certainly must study the illustrations," Stone said. "Constantly."

"They don't claim to be on the run from the Sultan's navy.

Look at this, it's a little quotation. 'When the world was fresh and young, And the great deluge still had left it green.' Oh my goodness, how they put Noah down. Seelah accuses him of knowing most of his family would die in the Flood, including his father—his grandfather was Methuselah. If it hadn't been for Cain and his boat."

"Methuselah. Is that what they'll tell the police?" He turned the flashlight beam toward his feet so that she was all but in the dark.

"Pity the poor police, if they get here." Lindy reached out to add a cluster of pages to the stack on the dresser—and knocked the whole bunch onto the floor. She felt for the armoire and ran her hands over its grimy door. "Shine this way. Damn, it won't open and there's no key." Her skittering fingernails didn't work either.

"How are you coming on your research?"

"Get your ass over here. We're going to do this, now—do you understand? This one more thing to check out." She started digging in the heap of heavy fabrics. The smell was old women and a good bit more, a lot of it fungal. Some of the pieces of material in the baskets were clothing—half of a shapeless sweater, a couple of burlap-y tubes like enormous skirts. Most of them were scraps, including some brightly colored clusters of joined together triangles, rich reds and yellows and intense purples as tightly woven as tapestry, that were like nothing the women wore. "These are their traveling kit, you've got to admit it's been ages since anybody wore this kind of stuff."

"They brought Victorian furniture with them from Chaldea?" He waved the light around the room and let it end up at her corner.

"Thank you graciously. Look here, what else could it be? Look at this clumsy black thing." She held up the cloak and walked toward Stone. "Nobody down here ever wore something this heavy. Smell of it." She pushed it toward his face. "That's not Louisiana mold. Nobody's dressed like this since the Middle Ages, nobody carries all their possessions in burlap sacks."

"Homeless people."

"Okay, I give up on you. Let's go round up Cain."

Behind the house Lindy swept the beam along the double row of the front garden, her garden. In the yellow glare of the flashlight the bean vines were withered, the tomatoes done for. She needn't have worried about being late returning, all the plants were used up anyway. Their shadows moved across the weedy yard like a funeral procession.

"My garden has died without telling me good-bye."

She used the beam to narrate the property— the lake out there where the cypresses started; the unused barn past the right end of her garden; the leggy ligustrum that once shielded the outhouse and now all but swallowed it.

"Believe it or not, that's their garden back there on that side."

"Eve's garden, then?"

"If you look at it that way, I assume Uhwa helped plant it. Adhah and Seelah tend to it, like you would manage a dewberry patch." The remnants of Lindy's field peas rustled dryly as she and Stone pushed through.

"The privy is about to fall over," Lindy said when they came close to it. "They're bound to still use it—they don't talk about such matters."

"I can't imagine the man wouldn't keep on running," Stone said.

"I hate to think of his plan, if he did hide around here. Uhwa's tired, how much more can she take?"

"Keep the light on it," Stone said. He pulled at the privy door and dragged it open. One termite-tracked board snapped and angled like a broken finger. Nothing inside except cobwebs and odors, and the bench with its polished twin openings.

"You grew up in the country," Lindy said. "How many years can you use one pit, before you have to set the house over a new one?"

"Twenty years? It seeps down."

The doors of the low barn were secured by a massive Yale padlock that was corroded with age. Stone tugged at the lock; the hasp held. They circled the barn and the pigpen-smelling compost heap behind it—no openings large enough for a man to crawl through—and continued in the direction of the lake. Lindy led the way.

"What did you expect we'd do, if he had jumped out of the outhouse?"

"Grab him, why not?" Stone sounded unconvinced.

"Daddy's rifle was a twenty-two automatic rifle. He helped me kill a lot of Coke cans when I was little. That's me and weapons."

The tangled thicket was ahead; they followed the path inside. To Lindy the things dangling overhead looked like nothing the women had brought to the house, apart from the giant beans. "No artificial light allowed in here," she said, and turned off the flashlight.

"There is a certain feeling," Stone said. "These people are singular. Do they actually call this Eden?"

"Eden was a place, not a seed catalog."

"You think so? Your old sailor carries a knife. This Eden is here for the retaking." Stone's tone was joking. "Technically, Cain and Abel were born outside—before the expulsion the first couple wouldn't have known how to do it. But where's the fiery sword? And the guardian babies? You know about the sword that was set up to keep them out, and flying cherubs with their crazy sleepless eyes? The cherubs would gladly nab him for us."

"Don't tease me with outrageous stories. I personally don't think Uhwa was ever banished from Eden. Adam was the only one who mattered to Noah. Who *is it* telling us that story?" With every tentative footstep she could feel soft disintegrations under her shoes.

No wonder they didn't worry, they had all anyone could ask for. Litter, for them, was sowing.

Stone stooped and picked up something. Lindy moved to him and spotlighted it—orange-purple, the size of an egg. She stood close enough that her breast pressed against his shoulder, her thigh against his hip. She reached around him and took the fruit from his hand. "It's the wrong color for any apple." She turned it over before their faces. "Choose your gender role. Who gets the first bite?"

"Genesis could have been an actual apple," he said. "Apples originate from—" He stopped in mid-sentence. After a moment he sighed. She relished the feel of his slow, deep breaths, the slight dampness of his shirt. I know better than to do this, she thought, but he'll have to be the first one to move. Why was it you couldn't stop caring for someone even when you hated him? Was it because they had made no children, no new people arriving to see them as individuals? She put away that line of thought and hurled the persimmon, if that's what it was, into the darkness.

"Your turn with the flashlight," she said. "Out of here."

At the lake there were the scuff marks where the skiff had been. "Some kind of small boat was pulled up here," Stone said.

"I moved it down the shoreline, to keep Joeab from getting hurt. We can check if he took it."

In the flashlight beam a trail of disturbed duckweed snaked away among the cypresses. An uncomprehending turtle sprawled at the surface of the tannic water.

"Cain is no amateur, like Noah was," Lindy said. "I'm going to bet he found the boat I hid." And that way she wouldn't have to claw through the brush again.

"You were always the navigator. I'll drive."

CHAPTER 19

And he set a mark upon Cain,
lest any should kill him.

Genesis 4:15

A long the lake four, five, six lake houses so far, between stretches of woods. Each house was set in a neglected lawn that went down to the water, and every house had been dark. None of them was large; some were no more than single-wide trailers. But they were set up for permanent occupancy, it seemed to Lindy, since fishing camps wouldn't have that many vehicles around them. The whole way, once the road had found the lake again, she had slowed at each dwelling while Stone scanned with the long flashlight. They could make out homemade docks beyond the houses, but no boat house for Cain to crawl into. The boats were on trailers, and every one of them with an outboard motor attached. She kept expecting to be hailed from inside one of the houses. Anybody awake at this hour would have been bound to see a couple of suspicious characters cruising their property, likely boat thieves.

"Look at that one," Stone said. "In that yard." Lindy braked to a stop. The grounded boat was V-bottomed. "Lights on in the house," Stone said. "The front door is open." The house was tiny, brick veneer and on a slab rather than raised. Lindy had been so intent on boats that she hadn't noticed the lights. "Wrong boat, but let's ask them," she said.

The lay-out through the screen door was a kitchen-den and a couple of bedrooms to the right. A bald, shirtless man sat at a chrome-legged table near the kitchen door, which was open for whatever breeze might happen. He was leaning forward with his forearms across his belly, his chin almost touching his chest. Stone rapped on the screen, but the man took no notice. Stone knocked again. A woman came to the door of one of the bedrooms. She was barefoot and was wearing shorts over a one-piece swimsuit. Her hair looked like red Spanish moss. She smiled in their direction, but made no move toward the front door.

"Your dog run off?" she asked slowly. "I see that flashlight. Ain't seen nothing that long since my cousin used to take me out for what was supposed to be frog-gigging."

The man had not looked around. He might have been made of wax.

"We're looking for a boat," Lindy said. "A man took it. From the other side of the lake."

Apparently moved by the sound of Lindy's voice, the man reached for the bottle in front of him and added to his half-full glass. "What kind of boat?" the woman asked. "Nobody don't live over there, I've fished every one of them trees." She took a few wavering steps toward them.

"Anything like the one in her yard?" Stone asked Lindy.

"I wish somebody would take that sorry thing," the red-haired woman said. "Pink has left the bass boat in the shop since way last April." She turned and threw a look at the man. "You can't catch nothing from the bank."

"It's really the old man we're looking for," Stone said. "May we come in?"

"Nuh-uhn," the man said loudly. He drained the glass audibly and resumed his wax museum pose.

"Alzheimer's?" the woman asked. "How'd he get the motor started, then? Knobs and dials is the first thing to go." While she was speaking she opened the screen and joined Lindy and Stone, and the mosquitoes, outside. "They will break loose," she said. "Pink's mama, if you was to drive by the home, she's the one with her face flat against the front door glass. Waiting for somebody to buzz in. You're lucky if she hadn't shed her old stained dress, and her teddy and all. Can't blame them, I don't. Why shit, if it was my last juice was sputtering out—."

Pink by now had padded to the door, behind the woman, who hadn't noticed his presence.

"Well, see, he," Lindy began. Her expression to Stone was meant to say, am I supposed to tell this huge drunk about Cain being on the prowl, when I doubt I could make him understand who Johnny Cash is?

"Can't y'all buy your old daddy no decent clothes?" The man's voice was surprisingly thin for someone so bulky. "Look at how you dress—you been to a juke joint? And him wandering the byways looking like a goddamned hobo."

"Pink is sweet as chess pie, ordinarily," the woman said. "Except for nights and weekends."

"You think you saw him?" Stone asked. "Where?"

"How tall is he?" the towering man asked. "Tell me that and I might tell you."

The man pushed the screen door open far enough to grab at the woman's arm. She brushed his hand away.

Stone looked at Lindy.

"Very short," she said. "Very old—very strong. Uncombed hair, bushy eyebrows, sleeveless shirt?"

"You the son," the man said, "why you leave your wife to talk?

She sure as hell ain't his seed." He laughed, a high-pitched coughing laugh. "I won't say runt—meaning him not you, I don't want no trouble. You got your vitamins, he never did."

"We need to find him," Stone said, "you understand—soon. He came by on this road?"

"I never thought nothing about it," the woman said. She was examining her arm. "You scratched me, you uncaring son of a bitch. We was coming back from the flea market over by Hessmer, that's twenty miles—you ever go?, oh they got glass. You see somebody walking the edge of the bar pit, so what? But your daddy is, excuse me, a determined-looking little individual. That's the one, Pink? Halfway between Talley and Echo?"

"Can you give us directions?" Lindy asked. "Never mind, we've got a map." To Stone, "Between Talley and Echo. You remember that, Mr. Navigator."

"I hope you don't find him laying armadillo dead in the road," the woman said.

"When was it you saw him?" Stone asked.

"Today," the man said. "What day was it you let him out?"

"Right after dark," the woman said. "Wasn't it, Pink. Pink was driving, we was arguing."

"Shut up, woman, and get in the house." The man had turned from the screen door and was walking to the table. "Ought to be ashamed, you out there buttering up such as him."

"If I'm this tired of driving shaggy back roads," Lindy said, "how must Cain feel? Forever walking them, and every acre a foreign country?"

"That is, if the old man is walking," Stone said. "Why wouldn't he have holed up at home hours ago?" He noisily refolded the map.

A few miles back they had passed Talley, such as it was, a rotting frame grocery store and the renovated cottage behind it. The terrain was less flat now. At every curve the headlights revealed the bases of huge pine trees below the scraggly hardwoods. To Lindy the sloping ground suggested islands in the river's old delta. There must not be enough of the old-growth trees left to justify logging them.

She was thinking about the Jesus signs. When they had approached the Talley country store, a series of hand-lettered placards were strung out along the road, small and square and wordy, like the long-ago Burma Shave signs her dad could quote. Lindy had caught part of the first one. *Let the righteous smite me, it shall be a kindness.* Psalms something, she didn't get the full citation. The next one was *For he will never pardon my transgressions. Exodus 23.* Sentiments like those, she figured, would be enough to have persuaded Cain to keep walking. No need for them to stop. But Stone, treating it as a game, had insisted. While he took the flashlight toward the old store she got out, leaving the headlights on, and inspected the nearest sign. A highway mowing crew had been by recently. Gray slain weeds piled up on her shoes.

This sign was lettered in the same steady hand as the others. *And hast thou not known the things which are come to pass here in those days? Luke 24:18.* What exactly had brought this on?, she wondered while she proceeded to the next sign. It read, *But I say unto you, It shall be more tolerable for the land of Sodom in the day of Judgment, than it will be for me. Matthew 11:24.* The tolerable thing for me, she said to herself, would be to stop reading some stranger's misery, and maybe kneel in the grass cuttings and find Cain's spoor. But here came Stone across the yard behind his wavering light.

"This place is too creepy even for Cain," Lindy said. "Look at this—'it will be more tolerable for Sodom than for me.'"

"Did you see the Deuteronomy one back there, with the tortured verbs?" Stone asked. "'Cursed shalt I be when I comest in, and cursed shalt I be when I goest out.' Comest and goest are third person—'thou comest.' He's turned the texts around, the man is condemning himself with perverted scripture."

"Good thing for you that whoever put up the signs wasn't home. You would have gotten yourself shot going up to his porch. Or more likely he would ask you to shoot him. No wonder Cain kept going."

That had been ten minutes ago. Tangles of vines and shrubs had taken over from the pine trees—no more uphill, no more ditches. Somewhere to the left, behind the thicket, lay the channelized and leveed river—or maybe not, perhaps the river had already turned away. When they had studied the map, Lindy was surprised to see how the river veered from its southeastward track and swung north, away from the big Mississippi, before merging with some other rivers, whose names she no more recalled now than she could name any of the trashy weeds they were driving past. She was feeling foggy.

A pair of lights approached, moving fast and straddling the center line. Lindy moved her right wheels off the pavement to let the huge dual-axle pick-up pass. Good thing it hadn't arrived at one of the narrow highway bridges. The driver's exhausted-looking face made her think of her trip to the hospital with Joeab and Seelah, which she still couldn't remember. "You ever think, when you're on a two-lane road, how many zombies are headed this way?"

"We don't have to keep on," Stone said. "We can call the police in the morning."

The present desolate stretch felt like all the anxious trips she used to make and wouldn't have to make again. "Do you have a favorite grim road? Mine is that low, muddy country west of Lucedale. Do you remember the high-water mark up around window level, on every house?"

"Highway 84 west of Natchez," Stone said. "And the other

fairly direct way to Acheron is worse, some huge low lake, totally swampy. Over across the river from here."

"The night after we buried Daddy we found his bourbon and drank a good deal more of it than we meant to. I got a notion to go looking for Sunshine. So I turned off, Lubie and Lorie and me, onto the Lucedale road. That is bound to be the road Sunshine and Buddy Millard ran away to Wyoming on. But we didn't get far."

"Sunshine is dead."

"She is not dead."

"Another conversion experience?"

"Some things I already knew. Lubie and Loretta were so loaded they didn't notice we were on our way to the Rocky Mountains. A wreck on the road stopped us."

The road's boring sameness continued. Stone was after her about Sunshine. What made her think Sunshine was alive, wasn't that all settled, where might Sunshine live if she was alive, without some lead what difference did it make? He was answering his own questions, and she was pointing the car into the oncoming waves of sleep. Breathing through her mouth. Was Cain able to sleep and keep walking? Sleep walking, keep and sleep talking? Sunshine just beyond the limit of the headlights, running away not walking. Sunshine holding Cain's hand while they strolled toward the dawn. Sunshine stopping on her motorcycle and offering Cain a ride. That woke her up. "Where is Echo, five miles?" she asked.

"More like ten," Stone said. "Pink and his bride saw someone somewhere along here. He could be another dozen miles by now. Even next to the river, there's bound to be a side road. When we get to it, which fork do we take?"

"He. You called me on Cain's name, and now you won't say it. If Cain isn't along here, we'll turn around in the next intersection without finding Cain, and we'll forget about Cain."

The brambles were gone now, replaced on both sides of the road by thorny palmettos clustered under scrub oaks. Stone was leaning forward and inspecting her face. She flared her eyes to indicate how wide awake she was. "Will it help if I talk to you?" he asked. "I could tell you about the father and son that lived at the Benton facility."

She rolled her eyes and stifled a yawn.

"They shared the identical delusion, heard the same Martian voices telling them that Bill and Hillary Clinton were alien space twins. Otherwise they were what you would call normal-seeming. A matched pair of goofballs."

"You're talking about Adhah and Seelah. Been there, thought that." What were you supposed to do? You wouldn't bring a satchel of DNA test kits to a family reunion. Should she want to stick needles in Uhwa? Would Stone have her exhume Gran's bones and take a scraping?

"Is that him?"

"Where?" Lindy hadn't seen anybody.

"Off to the left. You didn't see the man just inside the gate?"

They were past the driveway, or plant entrance it must be, before she could stop. Stone was looking out the back window. Inside the high chain-link fence were several buildings. The whole place as brightly lighted as a shopping mall. She backed up and pulled into the drive. There was no one in sight. The wide metal gate was partially open—both halves were bent inward, as if someone had used a truck to smash into the property. Corroded Posted No Trespassing plaques hung from the wire, and to one side a large sign on twin posts, some kind of official declaration. "Warning" was the only thing legible, all the fine print was overgrown with green algae. She and Stone got out of the car. Their footsteps sounded large in the gravel.

All the buildings were plain, old-fashioned, and clearly long disused. The only modern element was the brilliant illumination. Purple-green mercury light poured from tall standards identical with the ones at the river park back in town, the poles rearing like concrete hydras above the dissolute buildings. Near the entrance a simple frame house on high brick piers had obviously been an office. Most of its windows were broken. Farther in, a much larger, corrugated metal building stood barnlike, boxy-square and windowless. The baleful chemical light rendered its roof and sides all but black. A jumble of boxes and pieces of equipment lay outside its closed doors.

"If they thought bright light would embarrass vandals," Lindy said.

"The EPA made them put up the sign," Stone said. "Made them install the lights, too."

"What does the expert on environmental law think this awful place used to be?"

"Do you see, way back there at the edge of the light, the big pipe running above the ground? This was a gas pipeline pumping station. The compressors would be in that row of buildings." Four dingy metal buildings stood at right angles to the exposed section of pipeline.

"Lined up that way they look like piglets feeding."

Far past the office a small figure came into sight. Even at that distance Lindy was sure it was Cain. He was stalking resolutely away from the entrance—away from them, though she doubted he had noticed their arrival—and in the direction of a ramshackle wooden framework that showed above tall weeds.

"There he goes, toward the cooling tower," Lindy said, pointing. "He wouldn't hurry if we were a hundred bloodhounds. Oh, he's gone."

"There should be no way out back there," Stone said. "You can call 911."

"Why did you think I was chasing around the hotel trying to call Eshana?"

"Or we could try to tie the gate, and leave him penned up. I have battery cables in my trunk."

"Come on, I know what the first thing I want to ask him is." But all the questions she had intended to rehearse were a jumble.

The bare area ahead of them looked to have been soaked with something like motor oil. Lindy expected their shoes to be ruined, but the surface was solid as asphalt. It smelled like the stuff her grandmother used to spray from an atomizer like a bicycle pump. No worry about insects out here. They followed the figure into shoulder-high weeds full of small stumps, as if the same entity that installed the lights had done the brush removal. Another blighted space opened in front of them, the earth here as barren and crusted as the other, but burned-looking and smelling of bleach. They passed racks of small-bore pipe and scattered oil drums stenciled with "Delphi Pipeline Corp." This area ended at a waste pond that was full to the brim from the recent rains. The old man was kneeling at the edge of the water.

They stood at his back, surrounded by shadows of all lengths from the multiple lamps. Skeletal dead trees stood around the pond. The film that covered the water was pocked by bilious bubbles, new ones still arriving.

"Caheena?" She had to try the name. "I'm Lindy Caton, I was at your mother's house this morning. My friend Stone Prather came with me. We don't intend you any harm."

The old man continued to cup the liquid toward his mouth. The knife in its scabbard protruded from the waist of his trousers.

"You know that stuff is poison."

Without looking around, the man laughed hoarsely.

"See," she said to Stone, "I told you he speaks English. Do you remember me from Uhwa's house?" The question came out too loud. She realized she was mimicking Adhah's solemn mode of address.

The old man pushed himself up and turned, wiping his hands against his stained trousers. Here under the uncanny flood lamps, this was not entirely the face she had remembered. His skin tone seemed jaundiced, but that might be the light. His wrinkles were deeper, his jowls more pronounced. Old people's plastic faces, so hopelessly departed from their youthful shapes that they only took life from motion or mood. Fatigue wiped out their elderly composure, and the old man looked worn out. Cain had lived such an enormous time, and what did he have to show for it? But what did she herself have to show for her years? Eternity—she would waste every day. He seemed to her too forlorn to last until another dawn. Easy to think that Uhwa was too hard on him, and that he was a good son for all that. One thing for sure, he didn't look dangerous.

"Is this about the end of the line for you?" she asked.

The old man cleared his throat. "How did you know I'd have anything for you?" His old man's voice creaked. It had none of the power he had mustered against Uhwa.

"What *do* you have for me?" Lindy asked.

The old man was looking obliquely at Stone. "You count yourself a storyteller."

Stone shrugged. "Well, sir."

"You have the aspect of a spinner. Did you bring a start with you?" The old man was puffing, the same puh-puh Lindy had seen when he was facing down Adhah. So it hadn't been a matter of weariness with talking. Was it a heart condition?

"He knows me," Lindy said to Stone, "or else he wouldn't connect us to what happened."

"He hasn't said anything happened."

"Why don't you just keep out of this." And to Cain, "I brought him, but he knows nothing. I need to tell you, the boy—."

"This light," Cain said. "You should have heard how they sang a story, before anybody knew to substitute for the night."

"I'm Lindy Caton, I'm the one who was at your mother's house today. Start with your name. Say it slowly, a couple of times, we have bad ears for names. Tell us why you came all this way, and I'll tell you about the boy."

"We are willing to help you," Stone said, "but you'll have to hand over the knife. Do you live near the others, the women?"

"Will you just let me talk to him, Stone? I see your side, Caheena. I would have told you at your mother's house. I understand why you feel wronged."

"You can't sing it," the old man said. He extended one hand toward Stone's shoulder and gestured toward the ground with the other. "So tell it flat. Your kind can draw a swerve up through their feet—this is fertile ground for venom—and can call down misdirection, and churn it together." He was panting harder than before. "With a stranger's life. Eddy it around, make it sound heavy, and everybody gathers around. I've seen too many of you."

"You want a first line?" Lindy asked. "Joeab is his name, and he's alive. The boy can sing in Uhwa's language. That's two lines, pick one. Now tell us why you went ahead and hurt him, when all you had to do was walk away."

"I do—well actually, I do that sort of telling," Stone said to the old man. "That's very astute."

"And you've got the gold on your body, to show for it," the old man said. "My mother's door is four hundred thousand paces from the sea. Make a journey of that. And a riddle: crooked paces, but a straight path."

"Don't talk to Stone—this man here. He'll misappropriate it. He doesn't care about people. Not about you, not about me. Not about Joeab. He especially doesn't care about Abel, and he's made a living telling about you and Abel. Shit, I don't have Abel's name."

"A journey from violence and grief led to the sheltering sea," Stone said.

"Backwards, I like it. Now make it Mama and me. Wait, put in that the sea is rounded over."

"Is your house close to your mother's?" Stone asked.

"My steps are down-turned," the old man said. "To walk the world globe is like tracing my finger along an orange—yes, a rough globe. You, teller, are shocked: the world is as round as a drop of spray, and in the sky's account book, as unworthy of notice. Droplet, globule, you find the diverting word. Mama and me could have worked our business out, whatever shape the world proved to be. The other two were always butting in."

"Stone, there's not a word of truth in that. Adhah offered him dinner and a bed to spend the night. And then she went inside, before Uhwa ever said anything. Seelah was pleading with him to study Joeab for the example of forgiveness."

"The escape was blocked by others," Stone said. "Thus the son's choices were—blocked. I understand." He looked around at Lindy.

"Why are you doing this to me?" she asked.

"Doing what? He wants to get it out in the open."

"Disrespecting what I saw, that's what. It's like, 'Bleat on, goat creature.' Joeab could have gotten loose. I was watching. Listen, you, I was watching, and you would have let him go, until Uhwa joined in." But that hadn't been what happened, had it. It had been Joeab's singing that set Uhwa off. Let it ride. Stone didn't need to know that Joeab was the catalyst. Joeab didn't need to be part of the reason.

"For goodness sakes, Lindy, don't rile him up or we'll never get him out of here."

"I held Joeab's life in my hands. You take for granted that he's dead, don't you."

"I'll need the knife now," Stone said. "We're going to help you to get home. Lindy, you take his one arm and I'll get the other one, and we'll walk him to the car. I've got a digital recorder in the car." Stone, in spite of his words, didn't move. During all the palaver, Cain had not looked either of them in the eye.

Lindy could feel steam rising in her. These two talking, man to man, and Stone, Cain's clueless therapist. She took a couple of steps forward, close enough that she could have struck Cain. "Who do you think you are, that you can slash a child and walk away? It's all to do with kinship, kinship is why you didn't stop to notice whether he died. Joeab to you was a piece of pottery you could throw down just to make a point. Stone, I think not even Adhah and Seelah are human in his eyes. There was Adam, but Cain's particular us was Uhwa and him and Abel. Until he made Abel the first them, and the world became us and them. Did you know,"—this to Cain—"that Adhah can undo your worst work? Joeab will get well. Joeab is a human being, and I am too. You little scumbag, we're kin."

"The moon has moved nine points through the archer," the old man said. "Enough of gabble."

"There's no moon tonight," Lindy said. "He can't tell the truth about anything."

The old man laughed, still without having looked directly at them. "Draw out your story, young man, and repeat it in the cities," he said. "Your fame will grow. Do not trouble the old woman my mother. To her say only that I will explain the meaning of roundness."

"It was bound to end up Uhwa," Lindy said, raising her voice. "Because for her it's been Abel, first and forever, and that has cost the world. I'm sorry that she couldn't start with Abel and you equally.

Because then it could have been everybody, from the start, and you could have seen Joeab as your brother. I believed I could help."

"Sir, you will have to give me the knife," Stone said.

"Uhwa's not anywhere around, he's not going to hurt us."

"We can't leave a wanted man."

"Here is what I want." Lindy drew herself to her full height and pointed to her face. "Look up, little man, at where the truth is. I know who you are. I was there, I saw it all. This man with me is nobody. Your tale-spinner believes you're a simple-minded vagrant. Can I hear some one thing that's not a lie?"

Stone put a restraining hand on her stomach. What if she gave in to her fury, and grabbed Stone's arm and wrestled him over to the vomitous pond, and threw him in? And Cain right after him, why not? And if Cain climbed out and attacked her?—it would be easy enough, she wasn't going to run from him. What good would any of that do?

"Turn yourself in," Stone said. "That makes sense."

"Ah, the preacher has become Mister Reasoning Man. And with Cain, the cosmological killer. You guys put your heads together. Reason is the tool that men hone, in between murders."

The old man tilted his chin up so that his eyes were half-closed, such disdain that for an instant Cain might have been as blind as Uhwa. He made as if to leave, and Stone stepped aside and let him pass. At each stride the old man's left leg lifted and splayed so that he seemed always about to change his mind and turn aside. They kept close behind; the three of them might have been out for a stroll. "Sir, that's not the way," Stone intoned in his pulpit voice. "Why don't you get in front," Lindy said. "You can lead him into the sheriff's office." In spite of their slow progress she was wringing with sweat.

The old man's path led them past the four small compressor buildings and alongside the large barnlike building, straight toward the tall fence. "Why does he bother?" Lindy asked, while the old man ranged back and forth, blocked by the tall wire. "What is there for him, back in the outside world? Every time he crosses an interstate—or good lord, stumbles onto a Wal-Mart—it must look like maggots on a bloated carcass. No wonder Adhah and Seelah would rather sit on their porch until the end of time."

Apparently giving up, the old man turned back toward them. Lindy jumped into his path. He turned silently toward the nearest of the compressor buildings. She blocked his way again, but he veered toward the large building. She caught up with him and caged him against the dark rusted wall, sensing his stale breath and for an instant the feel of his bony shoulders, but he slipped underneath her arms and was gone into an open doorway.

"Uhwa is right, you are impossible." Lindy stepped into the building's stored heat and moved a step at a time away from the light. Stone ought to be pleased, the whole thing was degrees of darkness. The big flood began in the dark, and the Ark had been pitch black inside and out, Noah claiming deliverance when he drifted away inside his private dungeon and left everybody to drown under the pale stars. Where else would you follow Cain but into obscurity?

From behind her the big flashlight flared. Stone played the light around the interior. This was primarily a warehouse. Ranks of tall shelves ran out from the walls. A whole inventory had been crammed into the shelves: motors and pumps, coils of conduit, all sizes of electrical boxes and switches, fittings large and small; two at least of everything Lindy could imagine the operation would ever have needed. Toward the far end of the building a fraction of the stores were strewn, abandoned she supposed by the same thieves who broke open the main gate. Above the ranges of shelves a platform like a mezzanine was piled with spare sheet metal, large half-built boxes, and duct work—some of the tubes large enough to walk through—and enough corrugated flats, it looked like, to make another building. The longest wooden ladder in creation leaned upward into the gloom. Underneath the platform was a shop area with lathes and drill presses, and a diorama of abandoned work: piles of curled metal shavings and stubs of pipe like spilled cigars. Against the wall a dozen lockers with peeling name tags and curled pin-ups, and a counter with a French drip coffeepot on a cob-webbed gas burner. And Cain, who had the doors open to a cabinet near the lockers. In the flashlight's beam the old man's skin tone was olive. His workout had invigorated him; he looked less feeble. And this time he didn't look away, but glared at them. His pale eyes were startling at close range. The whites were yellowed and scarred, but the irises were starbursts, blue-green and ringed by violet. She studied his eyes and looked away. His history is strong in his eyes, Lindy told herself, and it's not our history, we're like dogs to him. Wouldn't a dog struggle if you held its muzzle and forced it to face you? Her determination to link up faded in the otherness of his stare. Cain's gaze could make a person sick.

"You're not any uncle of mine. I'm turning you in."

She moved toward Stone for a united front. Her back pushed against a shelf that, top-heavy, swayed. A brass fitting clanged onto the floor and bounded against the wooden ladder. The ladder be-gan a scraping descent toward them and fell away into the darkness. A crash at the back of the platform, a loud snap, and that part of the platform shuddered and collapsed forward. She grabbed Stone's arm. They dived for shelter, but it was shelter that was coming down, sheet metal raining off the edge with the sound of whining thunder.

As quickly as it had begun, the commotion subsided. Lindy lay still for a moment in the darkness. One knee was hurting, a scrape. A timber creaked, a hint of what was still overhead. She retrieved the flashlight where it made a long teardrop of yellow on the floor, handed it to Stone, and they ducked together through the angled space under the collapsed platform. "You okay?" she asked when they were in the clear, at the open center of the building. "No problem. Want to share the rest of your plan with me?"

"I'm going back and look for the twentieth century."

"I'll buy your ticket. Listen to that."

A faint thumping was coming from within the jumble of fallen sheet metal that, in the light that came through the gap in the big doors, looked like a giant's house of cards. The ominous wooden groanings had stopped.

"The old man," Stone said.

"That's him. I hope he's pinned. I hope he's hurt bad." Her words shocked her. That he might be in awful pain, might be dying, were untenable possibilities. The source of the old man's drumming was a fallen sheet metal box taller than Lindy. It was apparently open at the top—and certainly at the bottom, since the old man had not been crushed. Overhead more rectangles and cylinders looked ready to slide down the slanted platform. The box was tapered toward the top, a potential chute for a nasty piece of metal that was poised to fall. Behind that piece an even bigger cylinder leaned toward them.

"Are you all right in there?" Stone asked. The drumming continued. Lindy put her hand against the box. The vibrations were strongest at chest height, which meant that Cain was standing. She reached for the top edge of the box and felt an electric pain in her palm.

"Oh man, that stings." She wiped her hand on her skirt. What was a little more blood on this day?

The sounds from the box stopped.

"Sir, that's good," Stone said. "You need to not touch anything."

"Why doesn't that biggest one push the boxy thing off?"

"It will."

"Let's stand over there and consider that." They moved away from the threat. By now the flashlight was through; Stone shook it, but the bulb only flickered. Lindy felt a weight like the whole building settle on her. "We can't do anything for him, can we?"

"You've done quite a lot for him already."

"Let's talk about our options," she said. What could happen, what all might happen to Cain? If things slid off spontaneously and he was killed or mortally hurt? If he struggled and things fell? If things tumbled and he was okay—if he got loose? Cain might not die. Or he might starve to death out here. If he and the sheet metal stayed put, the sheet metal won.

"There's only one option," Stone said. "They come out here and claim him." From his cage Cain shouted wordlessly. "Listen to that," Lindy said. "People like him, crazy people who have a weapon and don't know how to back down. They'll shoot him."

"Some things that happen are just accidents," Stone said. "Hooking up with you, for example."

"Or like how you turned out a fool," she said. They were facing each other in the light from the big front door.

"It's a long way to town."

"You go. I'll wait here." She watched Stone walk away, watched him pause at the front of the building and signal. The scalded ground outside looked inviting, but she was already turning toward Cain's cage.

"You are back?" the old man asked of her footsteps. "I have more for your hearing. Send it first of all to my mother. But you retain the use—pass on to the tribe of tellers, what little you may comprehend." The building was quiet, though overhead everything was precarious, the same danger to the confined old man, and now to her. "Good enough. You remain. Transmit what I say, by way of your girl."

If he thought Stone was there, fine. He had Stone pegged, a thief of tales.

"Have her say to my mother, 'It is your choice that my legs are breaking with resentment,' and to her servants say that their comfort corrupts. Say that they have drawn her too far from the sea and worse, half the globe away. Instruct your messenger to stay away from explaining; a story must be transmitted precisely. But hurry to them." He paused. "They know that I refuse to submit my body to the ground."

You are not beyond giving in to fatigue, Lindy said to herself, and neither am I. She eased herself onto the concrete floor. She resisted the urge to lie down, sitting was enough for now. With her dad she had waited when she might have gone to sit with him. She had left Eshana sitting with Joeab. Sunshine had left her in favor of the wide motorcycle seat. Whether Stone waited at the car or went looking for the authorities, or if he simply took off, as he had done before—she would stay with Cain for a while.

"Listen with precision." The old man's disembodied voice resonated. "Shape it well. Send to them that I am netted, that all depths are closed to me. Tell what I have learned this day from being hounded and trapped. School the girl, tell her not to be put off when they do not answer. A truth may be useful without being understood, indeed without being believed. Next say this. The least baitfish has value, because it exists at the surface. The minnow darts along, creation contained, whereas I in my mind have entered the very ground and am swimming through and up, until I shall breathe again at an innocent and sunlit sea. Look to the minnow for proof that seeking will not find. They will know I speak of the boy."

"School me, chump. As if I hadn't heard your story four times."

"Shut her up," the old man said evenly. "I depend on you to

describe a baitling boy. Paint for them one whose hair by its smell carried the clean sun, whose heels were not slaves of the ground, whose singing was weak but accurate. Draw out the beauty of it, how he has been exalted by his contact with me, how my touch does not destroy but defines. Later, you may let your audience believe it is your own vision. For now, make the women ponder their shame."

Even if Uhwa and the others were suddenly to be impressed by his bullshit, did he expect they would send help? He described a boy, but it had to be more Abel than Joeab. A fresh new memory, a remastered memory of the day Sunshine left. Linderella sat facing a corner formed by two large boards. She was throwing small handfuls of damp sand behind her, so as not to lose the progress she had made. A tunnel almost as deep as her elbows—did the sand reach down all the way, forever? Sunshine's voice, a tone of explaining something. But the puzzle of the wet sand was too important. Linderella wasn't going to look up and risk being made to stop digging.

A loud tympanic thump came from Cain's enclosure, and scratching sounds. Lindy scrambled to stand—no reason to die in this particular place—and the old man crawled out, and stood up and limped away.

"How did you do that, you devious—?" Was she supposed to think he could have gotten out of his trap whenever he forced himself to kneel? Or was the opening too small for him to have noticed until he fell?

"Wait a minute! Stone! He's escaped!" It wasn't a matter of catching him but as always, a matter of what to do with him. They crossed the pumping station yard together, the old man mumbling under his breath rhythmically. It was some kind of cadence, keeping time with his walking, and the words weren't English. Lindy followed, close enough almost to touch him. She wanted him back in his cage, though caged, he deserved to be free. Neutralized was what she wanted. Stone was nowhere in sight. They reached the waste pond, the old man intent on achieving the distant corner of the compound. Stone had been wrong—back there the fence lay flat, like the aborted watermelon vines in her garden.

"You sorry little monster, are you the best God could do in the first-born department?" She was yelling practically into his ear. They were at the edge of the lighted area. Beyond the broken fence would be palmettos and poison ivy and diamondbacks, and eventually the river, and she wasn't going in there. Cain's knife was all but dislodged from his waistband. She grabbed it, and the sheath. She had the knife in her hand, opportunity, and the chance to shout, "I'm going to kill you." But she could only wave the sheathed knife and turn away.

Lindy could hear the music while she was still fifty feet from the car. She climbed in, the knife hidden by a fold of her skirt. The voice rose to a shout at the end of each line, the guitar walking along companionably like a faithful dog. "All my crying will be over. I won't have to cry no more." "The Reverend Blind Gary Davis," Stone yelled as he turned the key and the engine caught. "Nobody like him for sincerity." "I'm gonna sit down on the banks of the river," the singer declaimed. "And I won't be back no more."

CHAPTER 20

Lindy asked him right away, as soon as they reached the parking lot. "Come on up."

"It's too late," Stone said.

That wouldn't do. She wasn't ready to be alone.

"That's my point," she said. "We need a drink, and we're fixing to have a drink, and the bar at the Holidome closes before midnight."

"I have an eight-thirty appointment. I want to be working out by six."

"At the river, you seemed concerned. You said, 'I'll take you home,' and now we're home."

"Home, that's good, you're coming down."

"It's as simple as this: I'm not going up there by myself. I will not let you run out on me. Bring your toothbrush, you've been talking hard." She stood by while Stone silently opened the trunk and retrieved his kit. His movements were jerky, like a boy who was being hauled in from play.

"Wait, hit the unlock again." Cain's knife. Concealing the knife hadn't been difficult. After she told him that Cain had escaped and was headed for the river, Stone had not looked in her direction the whole way home. The long drive back had been spent in the company of Stone's bluesmen, while Stone's talk—who the singer was, how important this one couplet was, and how he meant to twist its meaning to fit through the keyhole of his mind—obscured every song. With Stone in the driver's seat, the blues was nothing but dead men talking.

She retrieved the knife and sheath from the floor of the car.

"Where did he drop his knife?" Stone asked. "I would have thought you might hand it back to him. Didn't you think he would need it?"

"The man is a degenerate. Hurry up, I need to pee."

Upstairs, her apartment was freezing cold. This was better, this was more like it. She went to the kitchen cabinet. Such negligence: the only whiskey was Bushmill's, and probably not enough for both of them if she had a double double.

"You want a beer?"

"Leave the refrigerator door open, please, for the heat."

She turned the thermostat down another degree and brought the drinks. Stone was studying himself in the mirror over the buffet.

"I'm not fit to sit down."

"I'm proposing you take a shower. You need to shake the dust of Acheron from your sandals."

"Ah man, these pants are totaled. Four hundred dollars."

"Do you want breakfast?" She knew there were no eggs, no bread or butter, no juice or milk or cold cereal. "Grits and grape jam? How do you feel about raw okra?"

"Damn, these are Martin Margiela."

"I'll bring your suitcase. No, really, get in there. The towels are in the cabinet."

261

Along with his bag Lindy brought back Stone's big wallet of vintage CDs—why not? She slid a random four into her changer, set the mode to shuffle, and spun up the volume. Inside the steamy bathroom Stone's head was visible behind the crimson blob that represented the sun—through the only clear part of the shower curtain, which otherwise was a jungle of dark-green tree ferns, yellow-green reeds, incongruous pink peonies, and a colony of cactus-like green lumps. The tiny leopard at the bottom, Lindy had decided, was not attacking the tiny solid-black human figure but was jumping up to be petted. She hung her long terrycloth robe—for Stone—over her summer robe, set her whiskey glass on the counter beside his beer, and quickly undressed. It was like entering a rain forest.

"Whoa!" Stone backed up beneath the shower head, as if the stinging water would exorcize her.

"Trade. Quick, let me get my hair wet."

Climbing into the shower might be insane, but Lindy claimed the right as a token of what they had just been through, a nod to the lost past. Sharing the shower—including the ratcheted-up hot water—had been a routine in their courtship days, Stone going first because he craved the water more and in any event would stay until it ran out, Lindy arriving later and directing traffic. The downflood of warmth didn't feel routine. It reminded her how needy she was feeling. They jockeyed for position in a fog of steam, and heavy chords from the living room. A sharp word or two, then monosyllables and taps on shoulders. Stone, up close and naked, looked diminished. Compared with Harold's height and breadth—all of Stone's working out couldn't change that. Looking him over, the prideful triceps and haunches, she couldn't help thinking of a numbered butcher's diagram: chuck, round, flank, rib, plate, shank. His tan line was being overtaken by the heat, the hot water writing over some of the evidence of his devotion to his body. His buffed-out pecs under the familiar chest hair; his back as he turned, smoother, swathed in new flesh. Between his shoulder blades, the new pair of muscles like incipient wings—how many hours in what position had those cost him? What would you ask the butcher for, tenderloin of Stone?

Stone hadn't ogled men, not that she had ever picked up on. His eyes had always narrowed at lean, athletic women—utility grade, not prime. Compact, blonde, stacked young women: juvenile Lorries and Lubies. They swapped places again, awkwardly sliding past each other while he handed her the shampoo. His look said he hadn't changed his mind. Who in the world are you?, his look said. In spite of her wanting to feed his shower habit by hurrying when she had the jet—knowing he couldn't stand to be in the cooler edge-spray—and even though his reddened skin looked healthier than the old Stone's, their bodies were squabbling. Maximum hot water had been one thing they agreed about. What ten harmonies did it take for two people to end up together? A bad outcome couldn't change people's tastes. Unless there were children, of course, children grounded the spark.

Steam clashed with the bathroom's air conditioning, the whole ceiling was dripping. The door was open; would the vapor run out before it drenched the whole apartment? Now that she had elbowed through to rinse, there was no head room. She was bent forward. Stone hadn't seen these full, pendulant breasts, not even before she took up running. Her race to slimness, how much of it could she trace to sex slipping away? All of it.

They were facing each other, her hair shampoo-stringy, Stone's bald spot waterlogged and unripe. He was hogging the water, his body was uniformly red. If you were a lobster, she said to herself, Bud you'd be ready for the table. His semi-excited state, did that represent heat absorbed from the shower? Another question for herself, What about HIV? Was it true—something she had half-heard on the radio?—that you couldn't get it from oral sex? Yes, she decided, you can't. Of its own will the soap bar jumped from her hand and slid to the drain between Stone's feet. She knelt and grasped the soap and placed it at the corner of the tub, and reached around his hips with her left hand—long arms were better for certain things—and guided him into her mouth with her right hand. Water sluiced down his belly and over her face; cold drops from the saturated ceiling spattered onto her back and her butt. Stone wasn't resisting. Whatever he was thinking, his body was cooperating.

Neither of them said a word on the way to the bed. A fresh beer and the last ounces of the Irish whiskey, and now they had lain without speaking through four or five tracks—disconnected, varied, the blues didn't seem to take any one form—from the stereo's personal choices. The sound had moved the bedroom to another continent. No, not another continent—no matter what Cain might say, you couldn't swim into a continent—but toward another dimension. Not another dimension, there were too many of those already, but another medium, not air not water not solid anything, a continuum of lined old faces giving her advice she wouldn't store and couldn't refuse. She wasn't having to swim, either. The swimming was being done for her.

It was Stone's turn to comment on their situation, at least to reveal why he had moved to bed so willingly, but he was intent on the music. He was, she supposed, engaged in research—like the visitors to those Mississippi Delta roadhouses with the banners that said Sponsored by the National Endowment for the Humanities. In the slow wash of happy laments her mind was doing what the natives did, the dirty bop. On the other hand, Stone might be asleep. How was she supposed to tell in the weak green light of the clock? A sublime instrumental track had taken over from the shouters. Time to check.

"Is the variety of it what jarred you into my bed?"

"I just thought of a new chapter theme, 'When Words Are Not Enough.'"

"You expected that thing to slide off and decapitate him."

"What are you raving about?"

She began rubbing Stone's thighs and calves. In the shower she had deliberately not brought him all the way, in hopes that he would remain aroused, but while she got the comforter from the closet he had subsided. The massage could be Plan B.

"He assumed it was you, not me there outside his cage. He kept telling you to teach me word for word what he said. People used to be able to remember any quantity of words. Let me try one. He said to tell Uhwa, to tell all three of them, that his touch ennobled Joeab. No, he said 'exalted.' He called Joeab 'the baitling boy.'"

"We'll get back to the old man in the morning."

"No we won't. Cain is a blowhard, forget about Cain."

"He slashed the boy."

"He won't be back for a thousand years."

Her hands were guided by her memory of his favorite place, the small of his back, and of her favorites the little extra knobs of bone at the front of his hips, that he had said were caused by playing kid football without pads. She found the knobs, all but masked by muscle—nobody had muscles there. The tendons on the outside of his knees had become tubes of muscle. She despised the new sheathing, the way it hid his real body.

"So when he got away," she said, "and you were sitting parked there, I knew you preferred letting the warehouse kill him to having to deal with the police. You would have killed him, that's what it amounts to."

"You don't believe that." He was completely motionless. Stone, the formerly wild one; Lindy, forever the initiator.

"I drew the knife back," she said. "And I yelled at him that I was going to kill him. I didn't want him to get away like that, but when he was in the box I didn't want him penned up. In, out, neither way works. He jarred loose a memory of me and Sunshine. My sandbox was huge. My hands were all gritty, I remember wanting to dig my way out of our backyard."

"I haven't seen the oldest woman, but the man and the other two are close enough to regular death. All you had to do in the first place was leave him alone. What was that about, chasing an old man all over hell."

"I'm psychotic, you said it."

"A preliminary diagnosis. They won't put you away for stupidity."

"Stupidity for Dummies—you're the man, write it. They'll give you the Pulitzer Prize for Out to Lunch."

Nobody was close to sleep now, and Stone wasn't hiding the fact that he was excited. His arousal, she knew, was not because of the pleasure her rubbing gave him, but the arguing—not the subject or the fact of arguing, but the meaning that such exchanges always lent to their being together. She pulled him toward her. He was completely ready, but he held back from full contact. Now he rolled away, with much rearranging of the covers.

"You had the knife," Stone said in the direction of the wall. "He moves at one mile an hour. You finally wanted him to pay for the boy."

"I repented."

"He would kill again. That's not the only knife in the world."

"I'll admit, a life sentence for Cain has an odd ring to it," she said. "Do you think that murder is always the answer? It's over with. You call anybody—anybody—and I'll take your weight room ass down."

"Slut. You and whose mother?"

She breathed on the back of his neck. He slid closer to her, into a perfect spoon. A clue, a cue—she lay back and rolled him on top,

guided him into her, and he was again the fierce Stone, as self-occu-
pied as in the early days, when she had felt that she didn't personally
have any business in the room with him, except her own business.
More of a workout now—but two could play at that. Up and down
were the same, both of them moving each other around. His favorite, her legs over his shoulders. No kissing, from the first there had
been almost no kissing. Swimming, rolling: this blues track was so
thick. Not easy to concentrate on your reality when somebody was
treating your crotch like the fulcrum of a gluts machine and yelling
what might be instructions if you could hear them over your own
voice.

Silence, exhaustion. The job had gotten done. One language,
indeed. People all speak the same language, she decided, until they
get out of bed.

"I had myself tested," she said. "I called for the appointment the
day the divorce papers came."

"A reasonable move."

"It wasn't easy to do, Ash is a small place. The test was negative." The negative HIV result had made her more sympathetic
with Stone, his apparent deprivation in the years leading up to their
split. Or was deprivation implied? Maybe it was all right, maybe
one time wasn't enough when the current of the music was washing
away the act. She would never remember any of these songs, which
was the way the singers meant it to be. They weren't offering a picture album or an essay, but blood, saliva, pulse, digestion.

"Would you push the syringe?" she asked. They lay parallel but
not touching, like washed-up survivors of a shipwreck. "Have you
injected me? You're not HIV positive?"

"No—yes. Not positive."

"Thank you for that, unless you're lying. It wouldn't be a death
sentence, not in the same way it was."

"It's exactly like a death sentence now," Stone said. "Before the

267

good medicines, it was death, but now, no matter how long a person holds out, no matter how much hope, the sentence stands. I've been driving up to Parchman to visit a man, Larry Wireck. I know that doesn't figure, but I go. He's been on death row for fourteen years, and he's been to AIDS and back. I don't ask him if he brought it with him or found it inside. No expense would be too great—they bring a specialist up from Jackson to mix special cocktails for Larry."

"And you want him to die."

"I want him to be in shape to die."

"You never caught it? That naked guy at the hotel in New Orleans, there was zero probability he was clean."

They were silent for a while—and here Stone went again, out of nowhere, another of his old habits. He was on her, another quick mile with Lindy as the treadmill. What had set him off? Who was he imagining? What did she care, when it was beginning to get good? Good, on balance, certainly not bad. For all his sexual athleticism, you could be yourself the whole time with Stone—a person didn't always like having a horse rolling on them. Lindy moved on top anyway.

"Are you on the—?" Stone asked between maneuvers.

"The pill? Why would I be?"

"Woman, you endanger yourself and others."

"I *like* apples. Do you know how to do withdrawal?"

They were separated, Stone's mess having rendered the sheet between them a no man's land. Lindy was thinking about the soft plum in Uhwa's garden, its big seed. The tree that bore it had to be a female, didn't it? Because the female carries the fruit. All the male trees in the world couldn't band together and produce one plum, much less another tree. So why did they call the male stuff seed? That was Medieval at best—nothing would grow from sperm. Her body, warm and swollen, was not dirt, not a passive garden patch. So much injustice from men believing that theirs was the main job of transmitting life. Uhwa didn't seem to mention Adam, that's how essential she must think he was. She probably didn't understand that Adam had any role in the whole thing. Had Uhwa ever wanted to stop the magic, of children appearing? Cain—there were two sides to whether Cain should have lived. When Uhwa saw what he was like, she wanted another chance, was that it? And then Abel dead. So much grief, Uhwa living on the love of a shadow. But she, Lindy, almost all her life, with a daddy who had done it for love of Sunshine. What had he really thought when Lindy arrived? Was she the baby daughter he hoped for? Topwater girl. A six-foot minnow that didn't hold enough of the world to make anybody marvel.

"Do you suppose I could call Eshana? I know she's awake."

"You didn't use to be so cold-natured." Stone had the covers pulled up over his face.

"I hope she doesn't blame me."

Someone was in the room. A child was in the room, except that it wasn't her bedroom. A little boy was standing beside her bed, except that she was at the level of his almost-white eyes without feeling her weight on the bed. His intense loneliness threatened to make her explode. It was Cain, little bitty Cain—but how could she hurt from within his small body, unless from within her own little-boy body? Because she too was Cain, that was how. Hers the round baby-fat cheeks and spiky fine hair, hers the dainty week-old beard and the deep awareness that the last time anyone cared about her had been forever ago. This was wrong, this was ridiculous. She was awake now and little boy Lindy was dissolving inside her.

It had felt like a short dream. Nothing was left of it except the dream-certainty that now Uhwa would be able to come and live with her. A brief dream for true—no extra light bordered the curtains. Stone was not in the bed. It didn't take her long to verify that he was already gone from the apartment. The music was still playing, a spare organ accompaniment under a man's voice. She couldn't say whether she had heard it earlier, but it wasn't any blues. Had Stone left his stash? No, his case was gone. He meant this one. The accompaniment had fallen away, and the voice alone was spelling out grief. It was about a flood. "If again the seas are silent, in any still alive, it will be those who give up their island to survive."

"You're not talking to me," she said to the singer. "Because it's a new day for me." She would go to work for a few minutes, get in and out, gather her paper mail before Mollie got there. She would talk to herself as much as she wanted to. How was that different from singing along, and wasn't there always music somewhere? Thumb the thermostat up to a civilized value. No shower, only a quick rinse of the essentials; hair brushed, shorts, tank top, sandals. Half past five in the morning, there was no time to waste.

Outside, light sky and heavy air, the aura of tire leavings and asphalt. Where was the dawn scent of a hundred awakening flowers? Of course. Any blossom that chose August in Acheron to get fragrant would emit its life away. The weight of Cain's knife in her purse felt comfortable.

CHAPTER 21

Everything musty was grooving inside the Moulton building. The old varnish was slightly sticky under Lindy's hand as she felt for the light switch. Not varnish, but shellac; they made shellac from the lac beetle—an office so old that it was coated with beetle crap, and smelled like it. Or was she hyper-smelling, since she didn't remember smelling the walls before? Half of a person's brain was supposed to be for smelling. Could an identifying smell be misfiled and retrieved in place of another one, like garbled trivia? Who did the fourth president after Benjamin Harrison smell like, anyway? Whatever, she was energized. Mollie prided herself on getting to the office at seven o'clock, which left a lot of time with not much to do except to gather the mail and take it, and make a list at breakfast. Her sandals clattered on the pine floors as she moved around, Cain's finagling voice in her head. Cain fleeing, Cain a solid figure in the world. Make another list at breakfast, questions for Uhwa. A stack of journals, they'd go into a book bag. Book bag, purse—Cain's knife in her purse. What to do with it? Put it with the other contraband in Bea's office. Hide it good.

There was, somewhere, a ring of keys that she had never used. Bound to be one of them. But Bea's door wasn't locked. Inside Bea's office for the first time—what an amalgam of odors. The Object stood in the corner where Moses in a Yankee uniform had been. Where was Moses? She sniffed Cain's knife in its sheath. No odor but old fish. She could put it at the back of the shelves, but she had to be aware of the possibility that she could damage something. She didn't want ever to damage anything again. She lifted the tops of urns and peered down. It had to be a place where Bea wouldn't even hear it when she moved whatever the container was. She noticed again the clean band of wood where the Object's neck fit into its torso. That had to mean the Object could be taken apart, the head removed. But the head didn't want to come off. She wrestled with the figure, wishing it were Stone she were choking. There! The smell of ancient death filled the office. She turned the Decapitated Object toward the light. Something black and dessicated, a lump at the bottom of the opening, death's physical presence. Was the opening deep enough to accommodate the knife? Drop it in there, right on top of the shriveled heart. It barely cleared. And still be able to put the head back on? Yes, after several attempts—but only because the middle of the head was hollow. Good-bye, Cain, wherever you are.

She was left feeling surprisingly spent. Cain's knife, like Cain in a way, was buried, but not gone. As a child she had thought Sunshine vanished meant Sunshine dematerialized, though she had no such word. She had thought Gran's body went immediately to earth, that the process of burial itself acted to erase everything, even the biggest bones. She knew better, but she never thought to reconsider, because it was important for the dead to vacate. Otherwise how could the living carry on? The new craze for prying changed that—the discovery of the *Titanic* on the bottom of the sea, then at almost the same time, the space shuttle *Challenger* falling off the coast of Florida, brought home a new truth. Disappeared could not mean disintegrated. Vanished meant recoverable, for hardware and for bodies. Then, ten years later, TWA flight 800 exploding over Long Island Sound, and the Navy divers chasing death right down to the floor of the ocean to harvest almost every one of the bodies. Gone but not gone. No wonder nobody was prepared for the one case where vanished meant what it said: the people inside the World Trade Center towers.

What had prompted all this ghoulish thinking? Was it the smell from inside the Object, which itself was as lost to its owners, and as substantial, as a vessel sunk to the bottom of the ocean? The upshot was Sunshine. Sunshine, dead or alive, was out there, and Lindy was going to find her soon. How many days to get to Colorado, and then to Wyoming? Or should she plan to rent a car in Denver? Did compassionate leave count against vacation? Why was she still holding the Object in her arms?

The added smell was Bea's perfume, and it was getting stronger in spite of Lindy's not having heard anything.

"You had to come back." Bea spoke from the door.

"Oh, yes. I'm sorry it took so long. Did you ever have to empty out a house?" Bea surely had not. Bea's family filled houses up, their houses functioning like those tombs in New Orleans where every few years the cemetery employee came around with a baker's push rod and shoved the current bones to the back of the crypt. "How was your trip?" Thinking, the knife is safe. But I'm in her office. She hasn't sat down in here for years, her desk is chest high with primitive paintings. But it is her office, and I am standing here with my arm around the neck of this ugly mother with its head on crooked.

"So you felt as if your business was not finished here?"

273

"I saw a carved bird in a shop in Mobile that looked like that one." She pointed with her free hand while Bea stared at her. The wooden bird, sitting right on the face of an oil painting, was rather elegant. "Only it was bigger. Indonesian, right?"

"What's that horrible smell?" Mollie said, Mollie at the door, Mollie edging past Bea into Bea's office, Mollie cutting off Lindy's exit. "You didn't let the Terminix man in? I never let him come until I'm ready to go home. I get headaches. Oh God, I don't know why I put up with this place." Mollie and Bea were staring at each other. Bea was patting her foot. What inner tune could it be?

Mollie began to relate to Bea a story she had heard at breakfast. A sad case, told by a medical resident—the resident was smoking a cigarette right in the cafe, the little bitch. A resident who worked at Blackmon and smoked, and had to leave the hospital to find a place where people were too polite to tell her to stub it. You couldn't yell at her, she had worked ICU Lord knows how many shifts. The poor child never had a chance, he was too hurt even to be heli-lifted to Shreveport. The same thing had happened to a family on Mollie's street, except that time, it was a little boy that ran through a glass patio door. It was only his leg, but it was an artery; the neighbor was never going to get over it, how could she? This one the resident was talking about—Mollie, absently waving away the idea of smoke—was a little black boy, they said he was cut half in two, practically. A dozen pints of blood, whatever, they were short, it arrived late: some rare type of blood, you know their blood is different. While Mollie talked Lindy's cornucopia of odors began to converge. Old man Cain while he held Joeab; the whole reeking hospital; the herbs Seelah was washing while Joeab played at the back steps with his dried okras. The smells faded into their images: vision stays with you. The Object's head was at a slight angle. Its neck was too long but its head was firmly in place. She released her grip and made for the door. Hard as she curled her toes down, her sandals still flopped against the pine floor.

Mollie took three quick steps and adroitly caught the tilting Object before it reached the floor. Neither she nor Bea acknowledged the footsteps that might have been receding rifle shots, or the slam of the outer door. "Bea, that's human hair on that thing. The little neighbor boy, you wouldn't think a leg. That pitiful woman. Death follows her around, doesn't it."

CHAPTER 22

Lindy had no trouble finding the church—Eshana's mother's church, she assumed, since Eshana had always made it clear that she didn't have a church. If the brick streets preserved the blood-red run-off from the Rocky Mountains, then the soft-brown bricks of Cabot Memorial contained the muddy river itself. A perfect miniature chapel built from the river bottom. There was no parking lot and no one else was approaching the church. Three days had elapsed since Mollie brought the news of Joeab's death, time spent locating boxes and packing tape and calling utility companies, and hauling home the personal items from her office—brazenly, during office hours, Mollie silently watching as she came and went—and dismantling her apartment. No Bea sightings, no way to know within several thousand miles where Bea might be on a given day. Moonlighting firemen had brought their van and carried everything to the self-storage unit. She was acquiring self-storage units. She had all she needed: clothes and credit cards and a good truck, and a new road atlas from K-Mart. The rest could sit in Ash.

Her phones had not rung once, no word from Stone. This morning she had mailed her resignation to Harold, copies to the rest of the board. A sudden personal problem, a family matter; impossible to give prior notice. She had scouted the roads to Colorado. The tips of the Rockies would be in front of her windshield before the letters were delivered.

Who, she asked herself, would inspect a church for three minutes before going in? Someone who no longer had confidence in what she was seeing. Skulking, that was the word.

Better to be here early, since this would be her only chance to see Eshana. A deep-voiced man had answered her first telephone call to Eshana's house a few hours after Mollie's news. He left her hanging on for a long time and returned with, She can't come to the phone. A hesitant follow-up, Could Lindy come out, could she help in any way? He would see. A long silence, then, She don't need you. His tone made it clear that there was no point in calling back. But she called twice more that day; the next day three times; yesterday while the movers were there, once only, shamefully. All the voices were anonymous, but the coldness escalated. The name Lindy was known at Eshana's house. The voices had been enough to make her afraid to go out there. This morning she had made one last try, before hitting the road, and had reached someone who was giving directions to the church.

Every feature inside the little church seemed to retain the mark of the hands—slave or free?—that made them. An inscribed dedicatory pane in each simple frosted window. Pews of heart pine, first-growth pews. A perfectly maintained museum of a church. Bright, glossy paint set apart the rear of the sanctuary. There Lindy found a serving window and behind it two elderly women fussing about in a small kitchen. The women wore white dresses like whole-body aprons. She leaned down and spoke through the opening.

"I'm Lindy Caton, I'm a friend of Eshana's. So wrenching about

Joeab. Is there visitation before the service?" They wouldn't have visitation at the funeral home immediately before a funeral at the church.

"The dismissal dinner going to be at the senior pastor's house, after the graveside," one of the women said. "Pilgrim Rest."

"I understand the wake was last night," the other woman said.

Both women were wiping now. Surely the two were sisters. Neither was more than five feet tall.

"Would you take coffee?" one of them asked.

"We have punch," the other added.

"Coffee, thanks, I guess," Lindy said.

The coffee sister filled a thimble-ish foam cup from a large urn and handed it through, the strongest coffee Lindy had tasted in a long time. Hardly any aroma, though—the dust of packing had set off her allergies and all but deleted her sense of smell. The small scale of everything back here added to her sense that she was the one grotesque element. How could she, knowing what she knew, go around gawking at architecture and judging people's appearances and the quality of their coffee? She sipped self-consciously while the two women busied themselves in the kitchen, and people arrived and went directly to pews. Lindy decided not to try to ignite conversation with the women. I'm Lindy Caton, did I tell you I'm currently a non-person among the perfectly nice citizens of Ash Run, Louisiana? Hello, I'm Lindy Caton, Joeab might be alive today if I weren't a coward. Would you dear ladies like me to introduce you to Eve?

Gawking and skulking could get to be a way of life. What else did she have to do—what else would she ever have to do? This might be the first time in her life when she was looking forward to time on her hands. Blood in her mind, time on her hands.

More people were gathering. Nothing for it but to take a seat and wait for Eshana to arrive. Even in her best blue suit and her

darkest panty hose Lindy felt negligent among all these black funeral suits, on formal men and women who put dressing for death
high in their budgets. Grotesque and negligent. A slender young
man slid in next to her on the pew and cut his eyes toward her
shyly. Or was he all that young, in spite of his unlined face? The
fabric of his suit, the mandatory black, was worn to a sheen; the
lining bulged through one shoulder seam. Many of the mourners
were very old, eighty looked to be a popular number. Was this the
decline of the mainline church and the rise of the suburban mega-
church? Or were these early arrivals friends of Eshana's mother? The
church gradually filled. There were a number of white people, but
no familiar faces. An obviously make-do choir took its place, half a
dozen middle-aged women and one teenaged boy.

A side door opened suddenly, directly from the street, and a
small crowd of mourners came in. No, it was a band of preachers.
Lindy counted seven of them—undeniably preachers, their various
self-designed regalia marked them. After them professional-looking
young men in perfectly cut black suits began to bring in masses of
flowers, sprays and smaller baskets, until the front of the sanctuary
was filled. The elegant young men went out through the bright
doorway. When they reappeared, two of them were rolling a child-
sized bier and four carried a small casket. The casket was crafted
of exotic wood and gleaming brass, a work of art. The young men
closed ranks while two of them made adjustments. Then Joeab was
visible, propped up on a large satin pillow, and the young men
had shut the brightness away behind themselves and were gone.
Lindy craned forward. Joeab's black suit fit him perfectly. From this
distance his face was transformed. There was none of the almost-
maturity she had seen at the hospital. That had been pain. Now
he might have been five years old; he looked ready to start the last
four years of his life over. They had not been able to give him back
his smile.

No one stirred, no one stood. No line formed to view Joeab. Was there a chance that they had all already told him good-bye, that she had missed it and they planned to just close him away, a couple of hours from now when all the preachers were through spouting?

Still no Eshana. But Joeab had displaced Eshana, it wasn't really Eshana she had come to see. That had been pride, that had been not wanting to admit—every shameful thing. She was here to speak to Joeab. She was here to touch Joeab. A funeral ceremony was for people who needed words. Touching a person you loved for the last time was for people who couldn't live unless they were allowed to do that. Best done at the funeral home with no one watching. Regrets, even then. In spite of herself she had settled for stroking her father, her awkward arm across his chest and her wet cheek against his lapel. Was no one going to embrace Joeab one last time? Could Joeab slide away into the darkness like this?

A plain-looking woman in an electric blue suit was the host minister, to judge from her officious moving around. The other clergy—none of them was dressed in black—had settled themselves onto the benches on either side of the pulpit. A couple of them looked slick enough to have their own TV outlets.

Lindy glanced around—she couldn't help herself—for television cameras. Of course there were none. This funeral would not be transmitted into Uhwa's bedroom. No camera was aimed at Lindy while she formed the resolve to make her way to the front of the church under the eyes of a hundred strangers and a parcel of preachers, to present a last kiss to a royal boy. She rose and excused herself to the young man in the tattered suit, edged past him to the center aisle, and moved resolutely toward Joeab. She was three rows from the front when the side door was thrown open, and a cloud of women escorted Eshana in. Lindy fled back to her seat.

All the women with Eshana were weeping. Not Eshana. Two of

them had their arms around her, as if she might collapse. In spite of that she moved as gracefully as always. Eshana looked good, apart from looking dead. The whole group guided her toward Joeab. On the rostrum the preachers were exchanging theatrical asides and chuckling confidently, except for the one who, to judge from the way his suit swallowed his wizened body, could be a hundred years old. The crowd of women dissolved, leaving Eshana standing at the front pew. A woman reached up and helped her to sit, a woman whose head was as strikingly well-formed as Eshana's. This had to be Cloteile, the sister. Lindy hadn't noticed her, nor the two alike-looking young men beside her who must be her sons.

The couple sitting directly in front of Lindy were crooked with age. The husband had been humming the whole time since they sat down, his low intermittent tone somewhere between beating a bass drum and clearing his throat. As if generated from that ground, a hymn now grew from within the congregation. Everybody sang but nobody stood, not even the jumped-up choir. The host minister was still working the crowd. Lindy started to reach for a hymnal, but what for? The young man sitting next to her mouthed the words silently, or was he only repeating the same syllable? The old wife's thin soprano flapped all around the melody, but in full voice the old husband sang a strong, harmonious bass. Lindy considered the possibility that his persistence in singing—the very vibrations in his chest—might be all that reminded his irregular old heart to beat.

The hymn ended. The woman minister with the neon blue suit, now in the pulpit, began to introduce the visiting preachers. All of them represented churches Eshana's mother had attended. Seven churches, including this one. Lindy mentally divided the mourners by seven, or should she multiply by seven? Either way, it was time to settle in. She would not go to the graveside service uninvited, so saying good-bye to Joeab, and to Eshana if that were possible, would have to happen here. Cemeteries, a person could come back to. Joeab in the ground, her daddy too—who would be left to move around? People who couldn't abide what had happened, people who had merely survived, that's who. That would be Eshana, and she herself. And Cain, moving over the ground or scuttling for the sea. Only an ocean would be deep enough to float his forgetting. Sunshine was out there, and she had damn well better be navigating. Sunshine had no right to a comfortable place underground. Uhwa and Seelah and Adhah? Their job was to sit still. By fully surviving, they reset the axis the world turned about.

Dead but not gone. Alive but not present. Bob Caton waiting, Joeab waiting; Eshana on the front pew, forced to wait a while more. Lindy, seated in the back row of her own life. Sunshine, dead or alive. Cain moving over the ground while Uhwa, the stabilizer, rocked in her heated room. How would she explain to her that Joeab was dead? Cain had struck out on his every at-bat in the Abel Is Dead contest. Well, she didn't have to hurry out there. She didn't have to go out there at all, she could wait until she had something positive to report, something positive about herself—was it possible? There wasn't any hurry now. Joeab would be here at Acheron. Her daddy was settling in at the Bluff Springs cemetery. He was saving her place, the last narrow slot between himself and the fence. What about Sunshine, found? There would be cremation, no service would be held.

She told herself that she would pry open Joeab's casket, if it came to that.

Sunshine alive or dead. Sunshine could not be more disappeared than a plane crashed at sea was. Lindy, a search party of one. She would start by tracking down the Alice Caton McNite whose obituary Loretta had found. Castle Peak, Colorado, however, where Alice Caton had lived, seemed not to be a town but a mountain—two mountains in different parts of the state. Castle Peak must be a subdivision, or a dozen of them. She had already studied the maps for ways to get to Denver without using interstates, because there had been no interstates when Sunshine and Buddy roared away on his bike. They had to have gone through Denver. After 98 from Mobile it had to be highway 80 as far as Dallas. She could pick up 80 an hour or two north of Ash, then skip north to another old east-west US highway, 82. Paris, Sherman—from Wichita Falls she would follow their trail for a long while on 287. Somehow evade Amarillo and I-40, cross the dipper end of Oklahoma. At Lamar she would get a better map of Colorado, one with more of the right-angled plains roads. Maybe she would try asking around in Castle Rock, just south of Denver. Another option for getting started was Louisiana 1, upstream along the river and away from the place she and Stone had found Cain. That might feel better, her escaping inland while Cain skimmed away downstream.

She would have thought they would let the oldest guest minister go next, but here was preacher number two, smiling in anticipation of his own eloquence. His knee-length midnight blue tunic could have been divided between a couple of Marine officers. He was drawing anticipatory Amen's and a few left-over That's Right's. The old man in front of her had been adding unobtrusive Uh-Huh's to his humming. Weren't any of them going to describe Joeab's life? Nuh-uhn, she wanted to say, We already know what your hang-ups are. Tell us what mattered to Joeab. Tell us what it meant to be Joeab.

Why had she been picturing herself speeding along alone in the truck, and not with Joeab? Why hadn't it been Joeab who came into her dream the night he died, rather than little boy Cain-Lindy? Lindy-Cain—she would not come back until she learned to accept the presence of others within herself. Looking at Joeab, she imagined her return. Pure eighty-mile-an-hour interstate, first to the turn-off to Pilgrim's Rest and Joeab, and then, fast, to the Bluff

Springs graveyard, to the new grass in front of the black marble single headstone that she had not seen because it took a month for the blank to arrive from Indiana. She would be driving far over the speed limit in hopes that the wildflowers, dozens of varieties gathered on the way out of the mountains, would be almost fresh when she began to lay them over her dad. And they would be, wilted but fresh enough. Dying, after all, was the lesson flowers taught. One stem at a time, she would arrange them. Side by side, the careful killed flowers. One stem at a time, until the settling grave was almost level again.

Bored with the sermonizing, she held her eyes open for longer than she ever had, staring at Joeab until her eyes were burning. This was the way to memorize Joeab. This was the most you could do, this had to be enough. Continuous sight became unbearable, so she closed her eyes and watched as the scene re-formed in front of her eyelids. Everywhere dark had been was brightness, a negative of what had reached her retinas. The casket lining had disappeared, its bright satin worn away by too much seeing. Joeab's face and his little suit floated and glowed. Glowed and floated, soft blue and pale green, new colors all around.

She opened her eyes and waited while the redundant scene faded and the arbitrary world outside her head resumed its control. Had the old women ever walked across a high mountain valley? They started out clinging to the shore; they talked about needing the coastal warmth. Where all had the women been? They spoke of hating the cold, so they must have experienced the north. Boats, they knew about boats. What about a long walk to India, like Alexander had done? What about a nice island, Hainan, or Rhodes? What about Ethiopia and Morocco and the rest of Africa? What about South Africa—had the arrival of the Dutch chased them away? All of it preparation for Acheron, Louisiana.

Ash was a long way from the Gulf. Obviously, the other two

women had settled Uhwa far inland so that no ordinary flood, no storm surge nor tsunami, could reach them. Far enough from the coast that when the Antarctic ice shelf sweated and tumbled, the aroused water would not take them. They had to be in Ash because Uhwa was too weak to swim again. Lindy could bring back to them news of regions they had never seen. Regions she had never seen herself—the realization brought her up short. She had been born practically at the Gulf of Mexico, real water, not some muddy river; had been across the Atlantic, but not the interior West. Trouble seemed to arrive when she got too far away from water. So then Colorado and Wyoming, maybe Montana—to Saskatchewan, if Sunshine had wandered that far. These were not going to be any picnics. She would make it to Colorado and find out, and hold on, far from the sea, for as long as it took.

The failure of Adhah's unguents, that was going to make it harder to tell them. Or would it?, she wondered. Nothing challenged Seelah and Adhah. You do what you can. That's the measure of how long you need to travel the world—until you don't care so deeply about what you see. That's when she would come back, when she had covered enough territory that she could see her own life in the distance.

Preacher number three claimed the pulpit and started in. He was unconsciously fanning himself with his red soft-cover Bible. Hardly anyone was answering him. Lindy was free to seek Sunshine in her mind. It was a valley and the valley was huge—and high, the chilly draft blowing into the truck told her that, because of course it was summertime. The land was sere. Dark sage and clumped brown grass and flowers like jets of flame spread out for miles over the saucer that was the valley. She hadn't expected this; dryness didn't seem fair. Here and there desert-varnished boulders stood as big as upended cars, boulders far too large to have been carried by the river that wiggled and jumped beside the gravel road. There had to be a river—and there had to be a road, or she couldn't be driving on it. No structures anywhere, in particular no magnificent aspen-log houses, so this wasn't a magazine memory. No distant SUV raising a whirlwind of dust, which told her she hadn't traveled this road on television. A movie, then? A hundred movies? How could there be any place in the world that you didn't remember, when borrowed locations were always flooding in? Was that Sunshine's mountain ahead? No, it wasn't. What she had taken for a line of peaks was distant clouds like moon rock. Bringing herself back into registry wasn't going to be as easy as climbing one mountain. But the feeling had to be recoverable, the feeling she had when Uhwa spoke—the beauty of Uhwa's own language that equated with the beauty of living. At the front of the room an over-dressed, long-winded man was pleasing himself before a grieving crowd. Why did the congregation put up with these intervals? Why weren't they always breaking into song?

The river grew smaller in her mind as she followed it up the valley. The truck would be rattling now, she would be slowing abruptly to ease over rocks that would take out the transmission of a sedan. This terrain was the whole reason she had gotten a truck. Patience, she could make it. Yes, now the road played out in a level patch that might have been a campground. The grass was high and un-disturbed, no tent had flattened it recently. She would need to walk from here, in among the tall conifers that enclosed the river, which had become little more than a brook. Could something like this be the headwaters of a killer lowland river? The conifers became a tunnel, and a rocky trail wove next to the stream. Good thing she could imagine the expensive hiking boots and the name brand canteen. The light shifted and faded, so that the little stream became a dimpled avenue, a pewter streak pointing perhaps to Sunshine. Flowers, secure in the shade and splashed by a hundred tiny wa-terfalls—minuscule white flowers, ten thousand of them wouldn't cover one grave. Fragile bugs flew past her uphill; dragonflies rested on dragonfly fingertips. Steepness on both sides, hundreds of feet to the treeless ridge lines—an almost canyon. Lindy's fingers were tingling. How near was the hidden mountain?

This much nature was making her alert. The sun came out above the canyon, and the simple stained-glass windows of the church woke up and glittered. Doubled sight was pleasant. Maybe the tingling was not Sunshine's presence, real and far off, but was the anticipation of touching Joeab one last time. This was not negative sight with skewed colors. It was a vision in positive color.

The piano was introducing another sad, sweet song. The choir members were rising, one after the other. For the first time in her life Lindy wished, really wished that she could sing. She would go away, and whether she heard Sunshine's version directly or took it from a high plains breeze, she would come back singing midsummer light and a perfect peak behind a dry ridge.

EPILOGUE: CAIN'S VERSION

I have tied the wheel, the boat sails itself. The turquoise shallows lend false vitality to the dead coral. I could not resist this excursion, northward to confirm that the margin of the peninsula is sinking. And now away to the south, a straight course for the Antilles channel on a convenient northwest breeze.

Land's end is a low populated cay, the terminus of a close-set group of islands. It has been directly visible for some while. Before that it was apparent from below the horizon, by the usual trick of the light. What I had thought was a further distortion, a concrescence far taller than the shimmering island, has solidified into a mass whiter than what passes under my keel. No such tall feature stood at land's end when I was inbound to our mother's house. We shall comprehend it soon enough; another eighteenth part of the sun's arc and we will pass near. Time enough to examine, to understand, and to jettison more of this boat that I liberated four nights ago.

I had no choice but to find transport. While I was away someone removed my own trim boat that I had beached in front of a large residence. An anchorage was within sight, a forest of masts. This smooth ketch that I took is all metal and manufactured roundness, its displacement ninefold what a man needs to reach his destination. But it was the cleanest-appearing of the ones that could survive the open sea. Only when my good right foot splintered the cover did I find the cavern of excess below decks. To my dismay there were six chambers piled with bedding, with a hundred cabinets and drawers and innumerable lockers crammed with goods as if for a bazaar. I have thought to make it seaworthy by means of dismemberment.

At dawn today I consumed the last of the fish which, along with a change of clothing, I borrowed from a thronging warehouse at the shore. Odd, to have found that strain so far from Madagascar. The fish were lost: flaccid, their eyes sunken. I found ample hooks among the rods with their spider-web lines; rectifying the harness of this palace has not kept me too busy to rig a streamer for better fare.

Let me add something that recommended this boat. Its stern is stepped, so that I am able to eliminate directly into the sea without calling on the slops bucket.

The masts are far overbuilt, as if speed were all. Raising a sufficiency of sail left me tired—although to be sure, I ate only water and grass tops while I paced the ground to Mother's and back. There was not time to involve the deck spools and their drivers; I may yet break free the mechanisms and sink them. The boat's engines are many and various. One of them provided fire to lanterns throughout the boat, so that I continued my simplifications during these past nights. Easy to master, all of it, a matter of matching a few keys from the bundle I found, and of touching the likely seeming tabs.

My studies with keys and buttons set off a remarkable din. At its height a voice began calling to me—not one of the alarms like bird cries that accompanied my trials, nor any of the puppet voices within the amusement boxes. This voice was directed to me: a repeated cry of numbers and names that sounded from a small box above the helm. For an instant I thought the engines were begging to stay. I immediately strangled the voice by ripping out the box.

The principal engine, without which I doubt the landsmen could leave the wharf, is an insult and cannot remain. The rear boom will serve nicely to hoist it out and evict it to the ocean bottom, once I loose it from its stays. This is my first direct encounter with such machines, but I knew already that they render their masters blind. One dark night on the inbound voyage the running lights of a motorized fisher as large as a modest ship overtook me to port and almost immediately disappeared into the bow wave of a vast low hulk, one of those that plow against the currents like icebergs gone mad. The larger ship did not even shudder. I heard the cries of the crew. Sailors would not have died.

After I chose this boat and was under way, I slept after my fashion until I reached the depths of the embayment—I heard them call it Mexico. When I was rested to a degree, I began the job of hauling up and ejecting. First went the charts. Without unrolling them, I knew what they must be. From the same cabinet I dispatched what was obviously a sextant, its function and name having come to me by hearsay. I did not realize how much labor it would need to cast out all such sailor's crutches. This one, the small flat, metal-and-glass box that now rests in my lap, is the last I will handle. I find its contents intriguing.

All manner of cushions and pillows and sleeping covers went overboard, and armloads of wiping cloths—I kept a few such. Paper, rolled and flat, and bound between boards both stiff and flexible; an uncanny hoarding of bottled liquids, kept in bins built for the purpose; pans and pots and racks, and an arsenal of utensils. The fishing apparatus except, as I said, hooks and a good length of the heaviest line. From the bulkheads of one of the two large chambers I unbolted and flung away elaborately scribed firearms of questionable utility. Mounted alongside the guns were knives more refined than the thick awkward specimens from the cooking room. I have kept one of the better ones against the day I am able to replace my lost knife. Near the main engine I found black boxes more dense than steel and capable of emitting sparks if touched carelessly—as indeed are many of the sheathed metal strands that everywhere come and go. It was all I could do to convey the smaller of them to the sea. Much easier were the hundreds of their kin, small spark-filled cylinders. From an icy long box like a grave I hauled away cubes and slabs, the frozen flesh of unknown animals. Of desiccate supplies I dumped great masses, enough to feed for a year, four of the lummoxes I have seen riding vessels like this one.

Make the dry stores and the meats my offering to the sea creatures.

The largest sleeping chamber reeked of a hundred types of dead flowers. I took from it, besides bedding and fabrics and cushions, repeated armloads of gossamer garments, along with shoes made for no foot I have seen, and stacks of flat likenesses under glass. Also, intricately decorated boxes that I recognized as clocks, whose type did not fit the mood of the boat, and which in no case could function at sea. I know something of clocks. Men who cannot determine the posture of the heavens, require them. From the same bedchamber I carried away in the slops bucket, quantities of jewelry, and soft bottles and small vials—these were the principal source of the odors. I should better have ignored that most tomblike of the chambers. The quantity of removables was numerous, the weight was trivial; but by then I was besides myself. Moreover, it was there I discovered, concealed under the very floors, duplicates of many items I had with so much effort heaved overboard. The same is true underneath all the quarters. I have decided not to go below again.

The clearing out began for efficiency and grew into a statement against the land-dwellers, until it became frenzy. It was as if eviscerating this thing should stand for cleaning the whole foul world. Yet I cannot make a true boat of this object. When I have crossed to the Skeleton Coast, I will scuttle it.·

I have understood the box I hold, why it is illuminated, what it holds.

Meanwhile this edible tidbit, a souvenir of the rations, chews easily enough now that I have broken through its covering of metal leaf. It tastes of oats and honey. Practice for the day when I return to eating grain, this time grown by others? Have no doubt of it. You would know this, if you could retain knowledge. The sinking land is not the only signal. If I feel myself being poisoned by the diet I have made since I first found the sea? Who with eyes could look past the silent sigh? The sea is breathing its last.

Sooner than I, however, Mother and her women will be accepting the garbage offerings of strangers. Their garden will wither in the general malaise, if the sea does not somehow claim them first. Though they cannot evade their future, yet they might have listened to me and made themselves ready. They attend to nothing but their daylight duties. Their choice to live away from the shore denies them manifest signs. Her mouth!—she has lost many of her teeth. That much I could have prevented.

Distracted by the general diminishment that this boat embodies, I might supply your words, Abel, as well as mine. I might have you say to me, *Brother, I was there. I saw how our mother looked,* you might say. *I watched her, and you with her.* Thus for your speech if I chose to supply it, if I did not hew to truth.

You were not there.

Your pardon while I prepare to divest this flat illustrated box, and its wires. Its secret? It is one of the navigation devices. A navigation device—do not fret at what you cannot understand. I am provoked enough by what I see within this one small box, without you starting in. Let me try to bring it to your level. They—those your peers who eat experience and shit forgetfulness—make for themselves devices such as this tablet, that to my discredit I have studied so thoroughly. The boat was riddled with such, even in the sleeping quarters. One set, with surfaces like large windows, could be made to fill with scenes and with false likenesses of figures. I removed some of them. Others I smashed where they crouched, along with a similar group which on command produced varying glyphs and brightly colored lines.

This one I have reserved—the one I hold—is the most insidious. Its representations shift when my finger in the least touches the surface. It brings up maps—and more than maps. I would hold nothing against a map, if I were a half-wit. Do not take that personally. Let me explain more gently, that I would have nothing against maps if I had never lived a life. No purpose would be served if I described what causes the transient maps to appear, or in what ways they confirm the geography I have assembled in my mind by means of travel and by listening, by summing and culling what others uncomprehending say.

If you had lived, eventually you would have sought for tablets, whether painted sheets or chimera that fade when wires are severed. As it is, to explain could weaken me: narration harbors threats that rear up in the telling. You always required too much explaining. Listen to me, Abel! Do you remember how, after I would tell you—a dozen times—how to return to a certain high pasture we had found, I at last would have to guide you there? A map would have released me to productive work, if I could have made you see by it. If you had lived at all.

There, the map panel overboard! See how it glides, see it already reaching the bottom. The ocean's kiss will rot it.

Let me tell you what went down with the panel, aside from the tracings that obviously functioned as the charts do. Every tenth touch, as I found out, brought up an embellished map in colors arbitrary. Turn the box until Western Africa is to the right, and the land mass hereabouts edges the left. The middle part, then, is the Atlantic. In between, most amazingly, a series of discs in orange and red, each a carbuncle on the represented ocean. I toyed with the device long enough to see the blobs move westward. The pattern, therefore, is one I long ago surmised: a procession of storms, spun off the African desert and marching this way! Thus warned, I will not rethread the island debris that slowed my inward passage, but will continue straightway across the shipping lanes to the southern land mass, which I will skirt coastwise, far down. I allow a month and a quarter, more perhaps, I have sailed none of those waters. A simple crossing on the southernmost trades, while great cyclones torment this coast.

Timing is all.

I begin to make out details of the apparition at land's end. It is squarish, like a detached cliff, and marked by multiple strata as if limestone. It is not a cliff, its striations are too regular. It is something they built.

Boats suitable for a man could be had at Walvis Bay on the south coast of Africa, the last time I passed that way. Or at Diaz Point— let the westerlies decide. Though by then I might be recruited to superfluity. Such a crossing, such speed with such safety: I may become addicted to wallowing. A jest, my brother, a jest. Nonetheless, in this large boat I might submit to the antipodal wind that some speak of, that blows around the globe without encountering land, and thereby might move forever without seeing any of them.

The tides shift only once daily along here, and their range is so slight that the least wind contends as an equal. Make nothing of it. Did you think, when I spoke of the ocean's imminent death, that

I meant the tides would pass away also? There is no sign in it—my home sea sloshed as weakly when I first waded into it. Long after the oceans are senile, storms will track, and the tides' dead repetitions will everywhere lick at the moribund land. The outcome that the heavens, and the oceans, and the purblind ground could not together accomplish, a veneer of humanity has set in motion.

I register your complaint, Brother. You will ask, when I speak of the ocean sighing, *What about my weeping, from under the sea?* In this dying place I receive a better truth. You are not lurking, that was my wishing for home. You never once wept, that was only my yearning for Mother. You never saw the sea, nor yet felt its brine draw at your skin.

You are not here.

How comes it that I have been talking to Abel—as if to Abel? I am speaking aloud, this is true; speech is natural. And yes, he has lived within me. But I never debated him in this fashion. It is of a piece: choosing this miscast boat, exhausting myself to strip it; giving attention to material objects. And telling it all to a fool of my own invention. I have been more bothered than I would admit, by Mother's intransigence. The burden always is mine, of carrying the old way, of remembering what we have been—of defining Mother, and of creating Abel. It is time I brought myself to my senses.

The white mass all but looms. Ah, it resolves itself. Little wonder that it did not come into registry. I have been staring at the stern of an immense ship. What I saw as layers of stone are the recesses of its multiplied decks, which are piled preposterously high onto a wide but inadequate hull—such top-heaviness, even allowing for the artificial depth of the anchorage. It might, I grant, cross a calm sea when empty. Populated, it will find occasion to capsize. Any one of the wild, circulating winds now moving out from Africa could be the executor. My course is true, I will pass almost within reach of the tethered behemoth. There, from its port side, a gangway slants into the low structures of the island. The effect is of a horse mating with a turtle. And I called this ketch grotesque.

Was the ship brought to evacuate the island? The Spaniards, I know, sailed west and returned east, no more mastering the season of storms than they did their equipment or themselves. The Portuguese as well, and many others, followed unto the present day. An archipelago such as this one would have yielded many captives. Would the masters take account of the coming cyclones, and bring a great ship? No. Who would trouble to move slaves from point to point, when life is no longer scarce enough to merit a good price?

From close by, every element confirms the features the stern suggested. It is as if they were denying the ocean's very presence. Not everything that floats is of the sea. A raft may be slow to wet through—consider the floored barn that left the women adrift. Or a bloated corpse may persist while the sharks are busy elsewhere. This tower, also. Such projects begin with exclusion and incorporate death.

I am brought alongside. I am passing under the overhang of the hull. High above me a mob crowds the railings and raises a great racket. I should not have encouraged them by looking up. They are waving their arms as if I were an acquaintance, and many of them shout incoherent greetings. Bright loops are spinning to the surface. Flowers are drifting away in the breeze. I am surrounded by blossoms, necklaces are pelleting the boat. Why would they offer their possessions? Because they have no occupation, must they also abandon intelligence? Their noise puts me in mind of a fool of the women's, the boy the Spaniards took. One of the women said I would know him, because he would be the one singing. No doubt. He would have chosen to join in the general commotion, even if silence meant liberty. Slavery has become redundant.

I wish Mother could be alone when I locate her again. It is always the same with the other two, I find them with an imbecile.

I knew when the recent boy approached me at Mother's hut, that he would not survive, and that they would take pleasure in trying to save him. The boy should not have been with me while I spoke with Mother; but he ran to me, he took my hand and tried to lead me inside, all the while repeating his nonsense syllables—his name among them, I suppose. I might have dispatched him before I called to her, but I had thought that holding the boy was a way to gain her attention. True, she came out to me, all unknowing of his presence, as it developed. Yet the slightness of his existence dominated our discussion. His absent mind called down the concentration of all who were present. They will find a new pet. Meanwhile I have been sold out by another defective.

I am feeling more at ease, in spite of myself. A brisk pace, the land is absent though the sun is not yet low. Blue all down to the horizon, blue depths around and beneath me. How can sapphire be compounded from such clarity, except through a kinship with the sky? Both are fully transparent, yet both are tinted, so that the surface becomes a fiction. A man may not fly, yet a thousand fathoms gives him wings.

At last, a chance to reflect. Silently I excuse myself for having thought I was speaking to Abel. Who did I take to be my listener, before I was grabbed by the need to address him? My mother, of course, always; but she wrecked that beyond reasoning. My conversation with her is staved, I must take it to dry dock. Abel seemed for a while to move into that gap. Now I speak—silently—to neither of them.

So much hung on the meeting at Mother's house, and nothing came of it. What should have brought closeness brought instead—Abel? Who was Abel? Who, or what, is the Abel I today banished? If I am to flip from my fingers the last drops of him—of it—I must understand how two such different persons as he and I sprang up in one household. Animals breed true, but an animal has no duty to itself and thereby cannot fail its type. A man may fail and know he has failed. Mother cannot get enough of claiming that I delivered pain from within her body—I, within her body. Likewise Abel, within her body. I accept that, although it has caused me more pain than ever I did her. A dam demands a sire; a wife, a husband. It follows, does it, that Abel and I share equally all the qualities of Eve and Adam? We are twins? So much for the pathway of logic. No, a man is himself, and no one else. There will be semblances, right enough. One parent suffices for that. My wife hid her will to dominate until the cancer at the last freed her tongue, yet she readily passed to her son the cold brutal resolve that was latent. He was none of me. A son can be a mother's son, or he may be a father's son. He will not be both.

Like a crop in an uncultivated field, all such reasoning is overgrown by enough fallacies to defeat a thousand truths. It is just as well, for I have grown tired of teaching—of wishing to teach Mother, of failing to teach Abel, of shaping my thoughts for no fit listener. Yet I must harvest a determination.

The newborn, must he resemble the true parent when that parent was a newborn? It is not even a proposition, since newborns have no traits of their own. What resemblance then has the child, to which version of the ever-changing parent? This much I know: there sat Adam, past all utility; and here arose incompetent Abel. If ever proof was needed that the woman can carry other than herself, I offer Abel.

I then *may* be my mother Eve's son. And I *am* nothing of my father Adam, though in memory I make our faces and our bodies like enough. There stands a proposition with one outcome. I am Eve's son. But wait. Why then are we estranged? Because we are alike? No, to prove that we are like requires more subtlety than I can marshal. My arguments have faulted her for not reasoning to conclusions, but in the end her very assumptions out-argued me. I am stuck. Consistency can only be found in simplicity, and simplicity—like silence—does not exist. It is the same conundrum that drove me frantic with the ground and its unreliability, its tares, and its sports. I have no brother, this is certain. I am no man's son. When I again meet my mother, she will tell me if I am hers, and she will welcome me.

Why should a man keep silence about such matters?

Hold on, what is this that discolors the sea? The late sun is not to blame, its slanting rays merely emphasize the near depths. While I have been lost in philosophizing, a cloud of near-opacity has surrounded the boat. The boat sails through not blue, but yellow-green. And what are these objects that swirl and swim and dodge my wake? They are nothing alive, though the particles swim and bob. These are not glass eels, they are translucent paper. Others, though they resemble small jellyfish, are species of bladders. There rise knots of cloth and cotton, and shards of vegetable matter—but terrestrial, they are no kind of kelp. There, just passing, are the heads of chickens; and there—and there again—entrails. And everywhere human waste beyond description. I am cruising schools of offal. If I am flying, my wings push against urine.

Why should this circumstance please me? And it does please me. I ask a riddle, but one so simple that any doomed, damaged boy might guess it. A simple riddle worth speaking aloud. Why should I restrain my voice? For whom should I keep silence?

Why withhold the answer? Here it is: I am become a rare explorer. I have discovered the future of the ocean.

I drop the sail. The heavy boat slows quickly and stops. Or rather it seems to stop, while the current bears it along, the same current that carries the bilge, the current that will carry me at the same speed, so that I preserve the choice to reclaim the boat by way of its low stern. Now I dive.

What can I relate, of what I encountered? Deep down, impossibly far down—you have no basis to doubt my stamina—I met the margin of the flotsam and came into the clarity of the sea. Below me was the sweet darkness that harbors the large-eyed night creatures, and all above me was foulness. But the depths are no longer the sea. There is no sea here, nor is there pure water anywhere.

Let me add—although there is none who deserves to be told—something of my purpose in entering the foulness. One morning, before ever Abel came to disrupt us, Mama went to the grove nearest the garden. Unseen I followed, and watched from behind a tree while she disposed into the ground those remnants, the tissue that might have become a man. What she was doing—that she had nurtured and borne what she laid into the ground—I only understood much later, when I saw my wife's son born. Thus much for the memory of Abel. I took with me, and left below in the ruined depths, what might have been Abel. Abel, a miscarriage of memory. There was precious little to discard, of the thing I carried down, and like Mama I will not speak it again. I bring you, however, this word. Nothing remains of the oceans but filth and memory. They are only names. There are no natural divisions to the world: no sea, nor ground, nor sky, nor beyond sky. There is only the spilled blood of idiots.